A Known
Evil

Aidan Conway was born in Birmingham and has been living in Italy since 2001. He has been a bookseller, a proofreader, a language consultant, as well as a freelance teacher, translator, and editor for the United Nations FAO. He is currently an assistant university lecturer in Rome, where he lives with his family. *A Known Evil* is his first novel.

🐦 @ConwayRome

A Known
Evil

AIDAN CONWAY

KILLER
READS

A division of HarperCollins*Publishers*
www.harpercollins.co.uk

KillerReads
an imprint of HarperCollins*Publishers* Ltd
1 London Bridge Street
London SE1 9GF

www.harpercollins.co.uk

This paperback edition 2018

1

First published in Great Britain in ebook format by HarperCollins*Publishers* 2018

A catalogue record for this book
is available from the British Library

ISBN: 978-0-00-828117-5

Set in Minion by Palimpsest Book Production Limited, Falkirk, Stirlingshire

Printed and bound in the UK by CPI Group (UK) Ltd, Croydon CR0 4YY

For Graziella

PART I

One

They'd found the body in the entrance to their block of flats where, sometimes, bleary-eyed, they would avoid treading on the dog shit some neighbour couldn't care less about cleaning up – teenagers on the way to school at eight in the morning. They'd been the first to leave the building, apparently, although it was now known the victim didn't live in the same complex. Paola Gentili, mother of three, a cleaner, on her way to work. Multiple blows to the cranium. No sign of sexual assault. No attempt to appropriate money or valuables. No sign of a struggle.

So, it seemed she had been taken completely unawares. Better for her. Husband had been informed. Distraught. Had given them the few preliminary details they required without the need for any formal interview. That would have to wait until they got the go-ahead from the presiding magistrate. But the guy seemed clean enough going by the checks the new 'privatized' IT system had given them in record time. What social media access she had was regular and only moderately used. Meanwhile, they'd started looking into the other stuff. No particular leads. No affairs. No money issues. No links to known families in the organized sector. Worked in a ministry in the centre of the city. No unexplained calls. Just waiting now on the forensics guys to come up with something more concrete to work with.

Inspector Michael Rossi had only just driven through the gates in the Alfa Romeo. He had known immediately that something big was coming by the urgency of Carrara's steps as he'd emerged from the baroque archway leading from the Questura's offices to the car park. If Rossi had bothered to switch his phone on before it would have got him out of bed, what? Twenty minutes earlier? But that wouldn't have saved anyone's life. Now, the debris of takeaway espressos and sugar sachets violated the bare desk space separating them in his office. Their own cleaner had just been in, chatty as ever, oblivious as yet to the news.

"Other than that," said Carrara, "we're totally in the dark on this one. But it does look like there's a possible pattern emerging."

"You've been busy," said Rossi.

The second such killing in as many weeks. The modus operandi and the victim profile bore distinct similarities but no one had dared yet to use the term. Serial? Was it possible? In Rome?

Detective Inspector Luigi Carrara. Five years Rossi's junior, several years under his belt in anti-mafia, undercover, eco-crime, narcotics, now on the Rome Serious Crime Squad. Recently married, he had the air of one of those men who never seem to have overdone anything in their lives: hardly a wrinkle, haircut every month, bright, fluid in his movements. Just the man Rossi needed on a Monday morning like this one.

"How similar?" said Rossi, still struggling to form what he considered decent sentences, though his mind was already whirring into action. "The weapon, for instance?"

"Blunt instrument. Iron bar or hammer, probably."

"Who's on the scene?"

"A few boys from the local station. They got the magistrate there sharpish though. Hopefully they'll have disturbed as little as possible. She was carrying ID, so we got to work with that straight off, once the news came in on the police channel."

"Press know?"

"Not officially. But they will."

"Silvestre?"

"Out of town, I think."

"Good. Let's go," said Rossi grabbing his battered North Face from the coat stand, feeling more vigorous and even a little bit up for it. "I want to see this one for myself."

Two

The press had got their picture. As usual, in the confusion between traffic police, municipal police, carabinieri, and the state police, someone had left the poor woman's feet sticking out from under the blood-soaked tarp, like the witch in *The Wizard of Oz*. A final ignominy to grace some of the seedier papers' inside spreads. They had only partially succeeded in keeping the crowds back and sealing off the street, but the citizenry was beginning to grow impatient. Close off a road in Rome and the already mad traffic goes berserk with all those narrow cobbled streets peppered with potholes, the ancient city walls' archways forming designer bottle-necks, not to mention the one-way systems and the curse of double parking. It didn't take much to tip the balance. So, the quicker you got everything back to normal the better for everyone.

"Remember, it all starts with good forensics guys," said Rossi ambling onto the crime scene. The "guys" in white gave him minimal glances of assent from under their cagoule-like hoods while snapping and sampling and moving in to examine the body in greater detail. Rossi was the most senior officer on the scene and he and they knew it. He turned to Carrara, who was flicking through his mobile for news.

"Got anything more on her old man, officially or unofficially?"

"Still in shock, but according to the 'reports' he's clean. No apparent motives. Family man. Besides, he was still in bed. His own bed. And alone. Shift-worker apparently. And no strange cash movements, no dodgy mates we know of. Nothing, as yet."

"No links with the Colombo case? Anything in common? Friends, work, family, schools, anything?"

Carrara shook his head.

"Nothing. Just similar methods, married woman but different workplace."

"And the kids?" said Rossi, finally allowing a dark sliver of the human reality to sink in.

"With their grandparents. We've got counselling on to that too."

Rossi tried to put it to the back of his mind. Remain objective. He was a policeman. This was his job. Find the evidence. Find the killer. Stop the murders. Limit the murders. More than this he couldn't do, and God knows that was what it was all about. But it didn't get any easier. So much for an experience-hardened cop.

He glimpsed that one of the white-hooded moon-men, as if in contemplative genuflection next to the victim, had changed rhythm and was getting to his feet.

"What is it?" said Rossi, sensing its importance.

"Paper, sir. Note or list by the looks of it. Nailed to the sternum."

"Not shopping, I trust."

Blood-soaked but legible and left visible enough inside her blouse to be discovered quickly, it was in block capitals and written in English.

LOOK INTO THE BLACK HOLE FOR WHAT YOU WANT.

Was he growing in confidence? Already? Toying with them maybe? Now I do, now I don't. Work it out. Want another clue? You'll have to wait. And there's only one way you're going to get it.

13

Special delivery. They might be able to find what model of printer or machine had been used, the make of paper, but more than that? It was hardly going to narrow the field. There'd be no prints.

Rossi looked at Carrara. "Any good at riddles, Gigi? Or are you still more of a sudoku man?"

"Looks like your area, Mick," replied Carrara. "A late Christmas present."

Rossi looked up to where the magistrate Cannavaro was skirting around the crime scene.

"And how would you say our magistrate's doing?" said Rossi. "Ready to refer all this to the professionals now?"

Three

Yana Shulyayev slipped her long, lean body into the steaming bath. She wasn't going to move a muscle for anyone now. It had been a busy one. The pensioners in the morning then the children. Then off to the accountant to sort out more interminable paperwork, not to mention trying to get across the city during a transport strike. And the cold was like something she had never experienced in Italy. So, she'd ended up walking, in the wrong shoes, most of the way and after a day spent on her feet, dancing and stretching and standing in queues, she was exhausted.

The phone rang. Shit! She'd left it in her coat! No. She wasn't answering. She was out! They could call back. And if it was important? The accountant needing yet more papers before the office closed? She couldn't afford to risk it, not with the threat of repatriation always being dangled in front of her. She hauled herself out and skipped wetly into the hall. It had stopped. Shit again. She checked the missed calls. Might have known. She thrust the mobile back into the coat pocket and swore again, and again for good measure, in Russian. It was Michael.

But she wasn't in the mood to listen to his story. Not yet. Not today. Sometimes she liked to hear his accounts: his frustrations, his occasional victories, his funny anecdotes about the absurdities of the Italian police and legal system. The screw-ups with evidence, the Public Prosecutors in search of glory sending them, the cops, on wild-goose chases because they wanted to nail such-and-such for whatever reason, real or imagined. If only it was like in Britain, he'd say, instead of all these judges and magistrates and officials getting in the way. Over there, a crime's reported, cops go to establish the facts, they evaluate the likelihood of an offence having been committed, they investigate, they make an arrest, interrogate, then they charge a suspect, and he goes to court. She'd heard it so many times that it had become a mantra.

He also liked to remind her how it wasn't like in the films, but for her it seemed pretty close, at least in terms of its frequent effects on their relationship. "You should get a cat," she'd tell him. "It won't give a shit what time you get home, you won't wake it up, and you won't need to take it out anywhere."

As she lay in the bath, the phone gave a last vain trill but this time she didn't stir. She was somewhere else now. Somewhere where no one could reach her. She negotiated a little more hot water with her toe and heard a message coming in. That would be him. So he'd be on the case and when he was on a case she didn't exist. So, cancelling tonight, no doubt. She tried to re-establish the pleasant world she had slipped into before the call. But try as she might, against her will, she was drawn away from where she'd been, where nothing else mattered except the warm water and dreams.

She'd heard about the murder at work. Terrible business but the police had no idea what or who was behind it. The girls in the gym were sure it was the work of an immigrant. A rapist probably. Never an Italian. Italy was going through another deeply unpleasant period and especially Rome. Politicians were playing the race card and the feeling was spreading, or being spread, that crime was on the rise and the only culprits were the foreigners. Every day on the TV news there would be a hit-and-run, a robbery, a mugging and the usual nationality tag stuck onto the suspect.

She'd felt so awkward about the whole thing that she'd practically agreed with them. After all, they didn't even think of her as an outsider anymore, and not just because she was their boss. But sometimes even she felt happier laying the blame at the door of some generalized alien monster. The Romanians, the Serbs, the Ukrainians, the North Africans. The fucking Italians! But she always kept the last one on the list to herself. *Now, where was I?* she thought, manoeuvring herself back into her own world, the safest one she knew. Then she began to turn over the possibilities available to her without necessarily ruling out the option of a quiet night in. Or even a night out, without Michael.

In the warm water, her hand strayed down along her body. She felt the firm abdominal muscles her students aspired to and which some envied too. Though the deep beach tan was gone, many Italian summers had left her skin an almost permanent honey colour. Her fingers then felt and found the faint line of the scar. Yes, it was still there but hidden to all but the most prying of eyes, the most forensic or curious of observers as her bikini line was old style. No drastic depilation for her. She wondered if Michael was one of those observers, if his cop's curiosity had noted it. He had never mentioned it, had never asked and she had not divulged the secret. To what extent it might be considered a secret was debatable too. That she had had a child when still effectively only a child herself was a part of her personal life but had very little to do with Yana the person, her personality.

She didn't feel anything like regret, even though, at times like this – perhaps because of the killings, like in wartime – some instinct in her was pricked, some part of her conscience maybe. Elena had a good life, went to a good school and had been lucky in so many ways. Her effective mother, Yana's youngest aunt, in Kiev, had been only too willing to take on the responsibility having lost the chance of starting a family of her own after Chernobyl. She had survived cancer but been left infertile and

Yana's tragedy had become her treasure. The letters came regularly from both of them, in Russian and in Ukrainian, and she was glad that she had learned both tongues so well. She would need them in the future, she was sure. Yana's visits, though rare, were something they all looked forward to, living as they did like a happy family, something Yana had never had.

One day, perhaps, she would tell Michael too but, in the beginning, she had not even thought of burdening him with the news. He had done enough for her and even if she had known in her heart that it would never have driven him away – the idea that she might have been seeking some insurance policy for both her and her daughter's futures – she had chosen to conceal it. She provided for Elena, working hard, and sending all she could to give her the best start in life. Besides, at that time, even before she had met Michael, it was already a matter that had been closed. Back then, Yana's own life, in contrast, had spiralled out of control as her stubborn-willed plans had foundered on realities nothing could have prepared her for. She shuddered despite the warm water enveloping her whole body. The memories of being imprisoned against her will and forced into virtual slavery would never leave her but that was long over now. Gone. She had moved on become successful and free. She was never going back.

Four

He had been surprised, at first, at Maroni's eagerness to let him head up the investigation, bemused even, but, all in all, happy enough. Once the scene-of-crime magistrate, Cannavaro, had established the facts, he hadn't delayed in assigning investigative duties to Maroni and the RSCS – when someone's had their head smashed in there's clearly a case to answer. Cannavaro was old school at heart and despite some memorable forays on a few cases, he tended to keep his nose out of investigative affairs. Maroni had given Rossi some spiel first about how he himself was far too tied up with any number of other investigations that seemed infinitely more intricate and sensitive. But there were other reasons. There were always other reasons.

"So, I'm giving this one to you, Rossi, and the Colombo job. I've had to move Silvestre off, for operational reasons."

"'Operational reasons'?" said Rossi.

"Yes, operational," Maroni replied then glancing up at the unmoved Rossi and sensing his perennial need for detail added, "for ClearTech. They need secondments from all divisions. First I knew about it, and Silvestre's name went forward."

"Ah," said Rossi. "So that's all going ahead as planned."

"It's a miraculous system, Rossi. Saves us time, manpower, resources, you name it."

"But it's privatizing investigations."

"It's just a holding, Rossi, within the Interior Ministry. It's not for profit. It makes perfect sense. Let the eggheads get on with it, I say. They're just crunching the numbers anyway."

Centralized Liaison Electronic Analysis and Reports. CLEAR. Being in English, of course, gave it a little something extra, didn't it? That was the system, and though he'd dozed through the seminars this much at least he had remembered. But he knew what he thought it meant. Another layer of management bureaucracy and cut-price solutions to complex and important problems, making someone else a buck along the line. Not to mention the rest. The other reasons.

"Anyway, be a more straightforward job for you," Maroni went on. "What do you think? Given your recent record, that is."

Record, thought Rossi. *Nice euphemism.*

"Well, I'd better get down to work, hadn't I?"

It was just after midnight when Rossi left the Questura, deciding to leave the car and walk. It would help him to think, he told himself. He pulled his collar up against the bitterly chill wind now blowing from the North and his footsteps beat their rhythm on the cobblestones as he turned over the day's findings.

The initial autopsy and forensics had revealed nothing particularly noteworthy other than the confirmation that the murder weapon had been heavy, probably a large hammer, and that several blows had been delivered to the victim's head by a male of around 5'10". The nail had punctured the victim's left atrium, although cardiac failure due to trauma and blood loss had likely already occurred. There were no DNA traces to follow up on as yet, except to exclude those of family members and pets. There were no closed-circuit cameras in the area and no reliable witnesses, only the usual freaks who had been plaguing the understaffed switchboard with hoax calls.

Rossi had put available officers on door-to-door enquiries, to see if any of the early-bird shopkeepers might have seen passers-by acting suspiciously. But the area was largely residential and it had soon become clear that there was little hope of any useful leads emerging. Given the apparent absence of any sentimental motive, he doubted the killer was going to be the type to give himself away easily. He would have followed at a safe distance, hooded, probably, in easily disposable clothes. He would have made sure he was alone, knowing that, in winter, balconies were not frequented except for quick or furtive cigarettes. Then he would have struck and dragged the poor woman through the open gate and into the doorway, where he finished his work. She wouldn't have even had time to scream.

There would have been blood on his hands, and he'd have had to wash, perhaps at one of the fountains that so usefully and civilly featured on Roman street corners. Check fountains for DNA? A long shot and it had rained too since then. So, until something else came in, they had only the note to go on and any similarities between this case and the last one. He'd got Bianco looking into the work side of things but, again, there was no office gossip to go on, no particular career jealousies, no career. Just a regular working lady. So, they would have to be lucky or wait and see if he would strike again.

His thoughts turned for a moment to Maroni. He annoyed Rossi, it was true, but he wasn't a bad man, certainly not the worst, and to his credit he hadn't given him anymore bullshit than was necessary when they'd met. As it was nothing to do with anything organized, nothing to do with narcos or vice rackets, Maroni and his superiors probably thought it would keep Rossi out of their hair. Not that they were all involved but somebody always knew somebody who got the nod from someone else and all the filth trickled down. Favours were owed and the people that had got to where they now were, often with minimal effort, were always put there at a price. Then those same favours got called in, sooner or later, by those who had granted them, and someone would be picking up the phone and giving it, "what the fuck's your man doing down there? Do you know who he's messing with. Does he know? Get him off our backs or there'll be hell to pay!"

So many times he had got close to the big boys, the guys who never got their hands dirty, *i mandanti*. The shadowy figures behind the scenes, "those who sent" others to do their bidding but who, blood-sucking vampires that they were, never emerged into the daylight. He rolled the word around in his head as he walked. Then there was the note: LOOK INTO THE BLACK HOLE. He had been thinking in Italian but he sometimes did his best thinking in English. Now it was looking like he might have to.

Of course, the reasons for transferring him or relieving him of his duties were always dressed up as something quite innocuous or easily explained away. There was the ubiquitous issue of stress, brought up as a kind of panacea for all their concerns. "You need a break. We're giving you a week to get yourself together." Or they felt his cover was weak. They'd had tip-offs suggesting it would be safer to try a change of tack. Or they needed his expertise to crack a stubborn cold case. Either that or they'd feed him red herrings for as long as was necessary for their own man to cover his tracks or evaporate completely. That was an exact science in Italy, not taught at Police Academy but which was widely and well-practised. *Depistaggio*. Sending you off the trail, off-piste, if you like, if skiing was your thing, which, for Rossi, it wasn't.

And then there was disciplinary action. Some character would come in spouting accusations about foul play, being roughed up. There'd be talk about his having flouted the usual procedures or taken a bribe. Hard to prove, hard to disprove. Mud sticks, doesn't it? And he'd be "encouraged" to take the easy way out, though, of course, everyone knew he was innocent. Exemplary officer. Blah, blah, blah.

Still, despite all that, the way it was going and the way it looked so far, at least, for now, he felt he'd have a pretty free hand. Be thankful for small mercies? The public were shocked, afraid even. They hadn't stopped talking about this one and the Colombo killing in the bars over their cappuccinos and morning *cornetti*. It even seemed to be supplanting the political chatter, giving them a break from all the election talk, the stunning emergence of the Movement for People's Democracy, the MPD, which was rocking the establishment, maybe even to the foundations.

This was not one of the drugs-war killings that sometimes stunned the seedier parts of the city. Neither was it any vendetta. The feeling was growing that he – and a he it surely was – could well strike again. The press would love it, and Rossi knew he'd be shoved into the public eye, under pressure, and then it would all come to a head and that's when he'd be expected to deliver the goods. Hah! Rossi laughed to himself. Of course, that's why he was being gifted the case. Sure, if he got his man, great! And there'd be slaps on the back all round and everyone basking in his reflected glory. But if he didn't, it was his fault. Tough shit, Michael. That's what the people pay you for. You're on your own. Bye, bye. *Ciao, bello, ciao!*

He crossed Via Labicana and came to Via Tasso. It would bring him to San Giovanni Square avoiding the busier roads. On his right, the shining tramlines led away towards the Colosseum and the Roman Forum. This, though, was a humble, anonymous street that saw little of the usual tourist crowds. Yet, it was somewhere he would often stop to reflect, for it was here, during the Nazi occupation, that the Gestapo had set up its headquarters and its interrogation centre. In this very building the Bosch had had its torture chambers and, within those walls, many patriots had given their lives for what they believed in: a better, free Italy, without dictatorship, without hatred and division. *Could that be the black hole?* he wondered, with a spurt of unexpected enthusiasm. The black-shirted fascists who'd aided the Nazis in their massacres and whose modern-day heirs were getting a new lease of life of late? Their graffiti seemed to greet him on every other white-washed wall these days. *Forza Nuova. Italia per gli Italiani.* Italy for the Italians. And they'd never really let go, had they? Indeed, that was their very motto, that the flame still burned.

But it could be anything. And nothing. A distraction to tease them with while the killer got his sick kicks. Or perhaps it was a financial reference, but again he reminded himself the victim had no apparent links with the banks or big institutions. She was a cleaner, even though the ministry where she worked was the Treasury. But how many Romans worked in ministries? Thousands. He could put someone on to it in the morning, just in case, but he didn't place much store in it as a real lead. Tomorrow they would have to get to work on the note.

He put a hand to his jacket pocket. It was nearly one o'clock and in the sudden quiet of the side street he realized his phone was buzzing. He had forgotten to turn the ringtone back on and had accumulated a message and four unanswered calls.

WHY DO YOU NEVER ANSWER YOUR F******G PHONE?
GONE TO BED. GOODNIGHT.

One too many asterisks there, he noted. It wasn't signed. No need. There were no kisses. It was Yana.

Five

"C'mon," said Rossi, glancing at his watch as they strolled back to the car. "Talk about a wasted day but I reckon we've still got time to get over to the Colombo scene before dark and run some office checks before we go to the mortuary. Let's see what Silvestre failed to pick up on there."

The best part of a day spent trawling through past cases and suspects vaguely fitting a broad possible profile had produced nothing of note and had succeeded only in giving Rossi a thumping headache and more lower-back pain.

"Have you got the case notes?"

"There," said Carrara as he opened the driver's door and jerked his head to indicate a thin folder on the back seat.

Rossi got in and turned to look at the meagre offering.

"Been busy has he then, Silvestre? Lazy sod. Have to do that one from scratch, won't we?"

"It's actually off the Colombo," said Rossi, leafing again through the scant inherited offering. A modest car park by a school on Via Grotta Perfetta. Road of the perfect cave. This certainly had given it a twist of the grotesque too. But in Rome, sordid murder locations were soon enough forgotten when the media coverage dried up. They were rubbed out by the eraser of the daily city grind and few victims got epitaphs. Serial or no serial. Carrara turned left off the Via Cristoforo Colombo's zipping dual carriageway, driving slowly then until Rossi had picked out the turning.

"Tucked away, isn't it? Easy to miss, wouldn't you say?"

A sloping slip road led up to the smallish car park, which, in turn, gave onto grass and play areas that formed part of the long extension of the Caffarella Valley Park, a precious green lung in the midst of south-east Rome. It was empty and unremarkable. Broken glass, cigarette packets, and in the corner where the vehicle and the body had been found, the usual discarded tissues, wet wipes, and prophylactic paraphernalia could be seen.

"A lovers' lane then," Rossi concluded. "Not much lighting at night. Ideal for trysts." He shuffled through the scene-of-crime photos showing the victim sprawled next to the front wheel on the passenger's side. Blood was smeared across the bonnet.

"Do we have the car still?"

"Dunno," said Carrara.

"Well, it's clear enough she was outside the vehicle when he hit her, isn't it? And no lovers? Nothing?"

Carrara checked the notes.

"Luzi's statement says he was training for a marathon – and he does actually run marathons – while she was at a yoga class."

"Any phone calls? Any calls to men?"

"The care worker looking after Anna Luzi's mother – lives, lived with them – got a call from her but her phone wasn't found at the scene. Could be important, if someone didn't want it to be found."

Rossi let out a sigh.

"We'll have to get onto the telephone company to get transcripts. Can you do that? All her calls. We'll have to check everything. Or does that have to go through ClearTech too? Was there an address book, by chance? I know no one uses them anymore but …"

Carrara shook his head. "Not as far as I know."

"OK," said Rossi.

"Shall I pencil in another chat with Mr Luzi?"

"Yes, you could pay him a visit," said Rossi. "And check his movements again. See if you can find a witness for that running story. A flower seller, a petrol-pump attendant or something. And see if his wife really went to the yoga class, what time it was, and what time he went running and for how long. See if he wears one of those armband thingies, for measuring his calorific output. They all have them, don't they?"

"You think he might have done it?"

"Why not? Husbands kill wives. How many times have we seen it?"

"He just doesn't seem the type. Very Christian and all. You know he's treasurer of The Speranza Foundation?"

"Perfect cover."

"Sure you don't want to come?"

Rossi shook his head.

"Where shall I drop you?"

"The bloody Questura," said Rossi, "may as well keep working through the case files. See what comes up."

Six

An array of stacked leaflets and promotional material for The Speranza Foundation – bringing hope to the hopeless and light where darkness rules – were the most striking feature of Luzi's fourth floor executive's office in Italian State Railways. Carrara had gone back to the beginning and, so far, could find nothing suggesting obvious foul play on the part of the slim, fit blue-suited man he now had before him. His sportsman's physique did little to hide that he was now a shell of a man. Dark rings were scored under his eyes. In his vacant, defeated face Carrara detected some shadow of the departed – the confident manager Luzi had once been, just like the others shuttling between high-power meetings, phones glued to their ears, dispatching secretaries with alpha-male authority. That was all gone. He still went through the motions, which was enough, for the time being, at least, but bereavement by vicious unexplained murder had left him in the darkest of places.

Carrara had put his sympathies to one side and was looking for any sign of guilt in that void Luzi now occupied. Perhaps it was still the effects of shock or some ingrained sense of duty and propriety, but he answered all Carrara's questions with remarkable steadiness. Not once did his emotions overcome him. Carrara could only conclude that it had to be a defence mechanism. He had to be postponing the reaction, only deferring collapse. Luzi couldn't come up with any hard, fast witness for his own 20k run that evening, he was able to provide the name of the gym where his wife had been, as every week, from 8 p.m. to 9 p.m. for her class.

"I would normally go for my run around 8.30 p.m. and finish about 10 p.m., depending how long it was. It's late but it's a quieter time for traffic. She would usually meet up with a friend after her class and we'd see each other at home before going to bed. I'd have my training meal and watch TV or deal with correspondence for the foundation until she returned. Except, that night, well, she didn't, did she?"

Carrara had seen other men break down at points like this. Luzi's mouth twitched slightly, at the corner. Nothing more.

Carrara's impression was that they had been as happily married as any other young middle-aged couple could have been. No affairs on her part – though he did admit to having had what he called "an infatuation" with a colleague, which was long over. "I did my time for that," he tried to joke, "and we'd been back on track, for years. We had a good balance, with our own interests and jobs. And then. Just like that. Gone. You never expect it. You can't plan for it."

"Do you know why she might have been there?" Carrara asked. Luzi shook his head but glanced downwards for a fraction of a second before resetting his attention on Carrara.

"Perhaps just to make a phone call, to check on her mother – she's got Alzheimer's. She always pulled over to call – never at the wheel. Or maybe just to think; she did that sometimes. She said she liked the peace. Dealing with her mother was hard and she bore the brunt of most of it. She's in a home now."

"Might there have been some other reason?" Carrara asked, sensing in his reaction the slightest sign of a crack in his composure.

"Well, the engine had started playing up of late," he began, too calm for Carrara's liking.

"But given the manner of her attire?" Carrara probed, recalling from the scene-of-crime photos the short skirt, the suspenders, and high heels which, while not vulgar, at least suggested a possible erotic agenda.

"Well, I can't believe there was any other reason, if that's what you're saying?" Luzi said, as if, in his innocence, only then realizing what Carrara was now driving at. "Is that what you're saying?" his voice finally breaking into something resembling real anger. "That she was having an affair? In a car park?"

So he was human, after all, Carrara thought. He had infringed on the sacred memory of his wife and the reaction was, if not textbook in an innocent man, at least more reassuring.

"We have to stop the murders, Dottor Luzi," he replied. "I have to ask you these questions if we are to have any chance of doing that."

Carrara looked again at the ordinary, proper man before him. He hadn't flinched in holding his gaze, but... But... *Was there still something*?

"Oh, by the way," Carrara continued, changing pace like a bowler to see if Luzi would deal with the delivery, "do you record your running route, Dottor Luzi, on your phone, with GPS?"

"No," Luzi replied, his tone still hard. "I'm kind of old-fashioned on that score."

He raised his left arm. "Just my wristwatch and then later I sometimes measure the route on a maps app on the PC."

Carrara nodded and made a note. Well they could track that down anyway, if they had to, or check whether he'd left the phone at home, he thought, noticing then that it was his own mobile now that was buzzing.

"Excuse me," he said. "This could be important … yes. Carrara."

It was Rossi and it *was* important. He had struck again.

Seven

With the third victim, the killer was set to acquire a nickname. The headlines in the following day's *Messenger* would proclaim that 'The Carpenter', due to his apparent preference for a hammer and nails, had indeed killed again. They would not be publishing anything about the notes, however, for though there were now two to consider, Rossi had asked his contacts not to reveal that particular detail. Not yet. In return, he had promised to keep them informed and to give them what he could. He needed the press on his side and still had some people he hoped he could consider friends, though who was a friend in a murder investigation was anybody's guess. There was meat on the menu and it was not going to be easy persuading hardened carnivores to pass up a meal.

"And I thought we might have finished for the day," said Carrara who had cut short his informal chat with Luzi to pick up Rossi. He was motoring towards the scene while Rossi, a sheaf of papers in one hand, had an ear cocked to the radio as the excited officer who'd been first on the scene recounted what he had found. The victim had been ambushed in an underground car park on the Via Tuscolana. Her face had been beaten to a pulp, so they'd have to wait for a positive ID, especially as they had no personal effects to go on, no keys, no handbag, no ring. Nothing.

"OK, OK," said Rossi. "We'll be there in five."

When they arrived, only the preliminaries were already underway. No forensics yet. No magistrate had arrived, so had likely already been informed and had thus delegated the investigation directly to the RSCS in line with the usual but not exclusive practice.

"Is it too much to ask that they not touch anything?" said Rossi, running an irritated hand through his hair and giving a protracted sigh.

"Parking problems, sir," said a hassled-looking traffic cop. "We're getting all sorts of earache from them that've got their wheels in the car park and those that want to get theirs in. There's the match later, you know?"

Rossi turned his eyes heavenwards.

"There's a murder in their backyard and they want to see the match?"

The officer looked down at his own shoes then sneaked a glimpse at his watch. Him too.

"Let's just hope they haven't destroyed key evidence this time. Hasn't anybody learned from Perugia?"

It had been late afternoon or early evening as far as the young female pathologist, whom Rossi had never seen before, was prepared to venture. *Like the health service*, thought Rossi. *Never get the same doctor twice. Was a bit of continuity out of the question too?* The excited officer he had spoken to over the phone was now filling him in but in person. Once again, there had been no one else around. A suburban area without CCTV.

"Personally, I dislike the ever brasher intrusions of Big Brother into daily life," Rossi lamented, "but in cases like this we could have used it." No. This wasn't London where your every move was filmed. There was still something that resembled freedom here, strange as it was to hear himself saying it. Yes. Here you could quite easily get away with murder.

By the time forensics had arrived, it was plain to see they had an identical situation. A woman, head smashed in, and now another note for them to ponder. The same enthusiastic-looking officer had handed it to Rossi in an evidence bag. *He'll be studying law in his spare time*, thought Rossi. *God help us if he becomes a magistrate.* The note read: THE DARK MATTER.

"An answer to our riddle, then?" proffered Rossi.

"Could be," Carrara replied, "but I wouldn't count on it being that simple. Would you?"

Rossi stared at the note and then looked up and took Carrara by the arm.

"See those trails of blood, mixed in with the oil stains? Assuming nobody else has moved the body, what does it say?"

"She wasn't killed there."

"Maybe finished off, yes, but moved. Get them to work out which car she might have been in without compromising the integrity of the crime scene. If there's a print, a footprint, or a fingerprint, I want it. Have we got the lights up and the ultra-violet? Who's doing that? Who's shadowing the forensics?" Rossi clapped his hands together to get the attention of a cluster of dozier-looking uniforms. "And run checks on all the cars within a twenty-five metre radius. Any warm engines, for example. Has anyone got on to the vehicles yet?" he shouted above Carrara's head to everyone and no one in particular.

Eight

Rossi threw into the boot the remaining profiles of perverts, murderers, and violent stalkers released from prison in the last ten years, as well as those of similarly inclined suspects still walking the streets. Another day of paperwork, computer-screens, and head-scratching. And now this. The workload was doubling every 24 hours. And they were getting no nearer an answer. It was like a blank crossword staring back at him. After knocking the lads into shape on the crime scene he'd managed to carve out enough time to keep a planned appointment at the hospital of legal medicine to see what they could get on the second, more detailed autopsy on Paola Gentili. Nothing particularly useful had come out of the trip except the discovery that she'd had the beginnings of a particularly aggressive cancer in her right lung. And she didn't even smoke.

"Bitch of a life," said Rossi as they left the building to be greeted by a blast of the now customary wintery air. Carrara was musing in his own world. The place had that effect on you. Leaving its confines wasn't like leaving any normal hospital where you had that feeling of relief that you weren't in there yourself mixed with lingering concern for the person who was. Here was different. This coldly modern, austere, imposing building concealed within its walls real-life horror stories and tragedies in equal measure. And then there was the final ignominy of being carved up by experience-hardened doctors-cum-butchers to see how you had been dispatched from this mortal coil. A necessary evil, Rossi managed to convince himself, if they were going to stop this beast. Yet another necessary evil.

They decided to leave the car and take a stroll past the Verano cemetery. They ventured across the tramlines gleaming like blades that carved up the piazza and on which the number three passed then swept away into the dank concrete tube of the railway tunnel leading to San Lorenzo. 'Red' San Lorenzo, as it was known. Historically, solidly working-class and the cradle of Rome's Communist and Anarchist communities, it was now becoming like another sort of Trastevere, a nascent mini Covent Garden with bistros, boutiques and wine bars sprouting on every corner.

But Rossi wanted to think, and he thought best when he had eaten, but not in the police canteen or the other cop haunts within walking distance of the Questura, and away, too, from the usual press-frequented places in the centre.

"Formula One?"

"Sounds good to me," replied Carrara appearing to perk up. Many's the time Rossi had put everyday concerns aside there, as a child, with both his parents, and back in his Roman high-school days. All that before the Erasmus experience. Before, for better or for worse, everything had changed in his love life and in the professional direction he would finally choose to take in life.

The pizzeria's busy evening was almost coming to a close. Waiters dawdled with the look of men counting the minutes until they could knock off. But it was open. They took a table with a view of the street and ordered stuffed, fried pumpkin flowers as starters and half-litre tankards of Moretti.

"So here we are again," said Rossi. "We're talking serial, or spree?" he proffered without raising his eyes from the plate.

"Looks that way," Carrara replied, busy with his own.

"And Rome's never had a serial killer."

"Not like this."

"And he's leaving notes. In English."

"He could be English. Or American."

"He could be anyone, a freak, full stop. And the psychologist's report? Are they building a profile?"

"Too early to say."

Rossi looked up, knife and fork gripped. "What? We need a few more dead women first and then there'll be something to go on? Is that what you're saying?"

"I'm saying that it's not that helpful. It's the usual kind of thing. Nothing that really narrows the circle. Woman-hater. Egocentric. Low self-esteem. Absence of sexual relations. Abuse victim himself, possibly. Certainly above-average intelligence, though. Won't let himself get caught, but leaves clues and likes playing games."

"But he's killing ordinary women, not prostitutes or foreigners. He's not going for marginalized targets, outsiders. It goes against type."

"True."

"And now he's giving us the answers?"

The waiter passed, and Rossi added two more beers to their pizza order.

"Right," said Rossi. "Inside a black hole there's dark matter. But what does that tell us?"

Carrara gave a shrug.

"Of course, there's always time," said Rossi, appearing to drift off with his thoughts.

"Time?" Carrara replied. "Time for what?"

"The black hole, Gigi. Bends time, doesn't it? Einstein's theory."

"O-kay." His friend was trying to keep up with him.

"It takes us back. Outside of time, even."

"Meaning?"

Two pizzas as big as cartwheels sustained by a white-shirted waiter's arms were flying across the restaurant high above the heads of the engrossed diners.

"*Capricciosa*?" the waiter boomed making some nearby foreign tourists start from their chairs.

"For me, said Rossi."

"And Margherita?"

Carrara raised a hand in distracted acknowledgement.

"Meaning, I don't know," said Rossi. "But it could be significant."

"And in the meantime? Every woman in Rome needs to stay at home. We bring in Sharia law? Or they'd all better get themselves a gun, or what?" said Carrara.

Rossi was already carving into his tomato base, spread with slices of cured ham, artichoke hearts, black olives, and all topped off with halves of boiled egg. A meal for lunch- and dinner-skippers; a policeman's meal. He reached for his beer. It was icy-sharp, clean, and lightly hoppy. Already he was feeling it and the food's anaesthetising, calming effect on his stomach and, as a consequence, on his mind. As he lowered the glass, making more room on the cluttered table-for-two, his eyes were drawn to that portion of the menu where the names of the dishes were translated into something resembling English for the convenience of tourists. They usually got it right, to be fair, but sometimes the renderings were comical. One word, which should perhaps have been platter, had become instead plater.

"Or maybe not all women," said Rossi.

Carrara lowered his fork.

"Do you know something I don't?"

Rossi took another large draught.

"And if, say, it wasn't matter but mater?"

"As in 'mother', in Latin? You think he's killing mothers?"

"I don't know. Or it could be symbolic. The Mother Church even. Sancta Mater Ecclesia. Our Holy Mother the Church.

Remember your catechism? Might need to check if they were practising Catholics."

Rossi's phone, for once occupying prime table space, began to vibrate.

"You'd better answer that," said Carrara.

Nine

It wasn't the phone call they had both feared and even in some way almost willed, yet it afforded them some relief. They needed time to think. But they also needed evidence and the killer was giving little away, aside from the sick notes. Sick notes. Rossi dwelt on the irony as he ate. Maybe there was something in that. For being excused, from games, from school. A sick note for life. *I don't belong to you and your moral order and here's my little note that says why.* He remembered how such boys had often been treated with open contempt by some teachers, at least at the school he'd attended in England for those few years. Pilloried and humiliated in the gymnasium and the changing room for their perceived weakness, cowardice, their lack of male vigour. Could they grow up to wreak such terrible revenge on society? Ridiculed outsiders wielding their new-found power and enjoying it. Repeating it. Needing it.

It was someone with a very big axe to grind. Someone hard done by and conscious of it, not like those wretched creatures who strangled and knifed but could never articulate the reason why. Maybe they never even knew themselves. They didn't have the mental apparatus, the support system, to process their feelings and frustrations or even put a name to them. But kill they did. Often without warning or without apparent motive.

He shared some of his thoughts with Carrara as they both leant back, satisfied and contemplating dessert. There were also factors that pointed towards a clean skin, someone with no record of violence, at least in Italy. The foreigner theory couldn't be discounted, though Rossi winced at such politically populist apportioning of blame. Or even the smouldering suggestion of an Islamic plot. Was it someone who hadn't killed before? They had as yet unearthed no particular similarities with unsolved crimes. There was no clear motive. Unless this killer had been long-incubated, a slow burner, and had chosen a propitious moment to hatch from his dark cocoon.

"Look, we're not fucking magicians, Michael," Carrara concluded, tipsy now and a little the worse for wear from tiredness. Rossi glanced up from his plate.

"Kid been keeping you up?" he enquired. "Or is it the enforced abstinence?"

Carrara returned a forced smile.

They both opted for crème caramel, and Rossi asked for the *limoncello*, telling the waiter not to bring coffee until he asked for it. He wanted time, time to savour and time to think. Carrara declined the liqueur.

"You can leave the bottle," said Rossi. The gruff waiter shot him a look askance, his hopes of an early finish dwindling.

"We definitely won't be getting a smile out of Mr Happy tonight," concluded Rossi.

They split the bill, *alla Romana*, each paying an equal share irrespective of what they had consumed, and decided to walk a little and drop in at a bar on their way home. They stopped at a news stand with international papers for Rossi to pick up *Le Monde* and *El País*. He liked to keep abreast of European events, finding their coverage superior to that of many of the Italian papers, obsessed as they were with internecine politics and endless wrangling and the labyrinthine complexities of one financial scandal on the heels of another.

A bill-sticker smothered in a hat and scarf was slathering election posters onto the wall next to the tunnel. *Here we go again*, thought Rossi. It was one constant election campaign. Governments forming, falling, then getting into bed together (literally and figuratively) in bizarre, mutually convenient coalitions. The brush-wielder slapped on more of the acrid adhesive and a rancid, hypocritical ghoul now loomed over the street. He held a pen in one hand, ostensibly symbolizing bureaucratic ability, *saper fare*, and, perhaps for the many less well-educated voters, simply his ability to read and write. His other hand was positioned on his knee, the wedding ring to the fore. Family man, and good for his word.

It repulsed Rossi, all the public money sliding down into the abyss of corruption, interests, and rampant, unashamed nepotism. Yet, it did now seem that they were living in more interesting times. No one had really believed that the MPD would actually start to threaten the big boys, but they had. They'd harnessed the Internet, seeing its potential earlier than anyone else, and had begun raking in huge consensus among the young, the underpaid, the unemployed, and students who saw no future. Now a power block was ominously taking shape, threatening the sclerotic party system and its cynical and systematic carving up of the country's resources.

They took the tunnel back towards Piazza Vittorio and the Esquiline hill, one of Rome's seven. Though dirty and ill-kempt, it was a characterful area and one that Rossi knew and liked, partly, if not only, for its preponderance of Indian restaurants and readily available supplies of oriental spices in the Bangladeshi mini-markets. Many of the other shops had become Chinese-owned, alleged fronts for money laundering, among other things. The older residents lamented the decline continually. Yet, it was a real melting pot, something of a bazaar and, despite some well-publicized concerns about racial tension, everyone seemed to get on with their own business and mingle on the busy streets quite peaceably.

At the steps leading down to the Metro, Rossi bid Carrara goodnight then set off to take a walk around the square. He knew its history, that it had been built following Italy's unification and, as such, was typical of the northern Italian style. The echoey arcades with their rows of columns and arches afforded shelter from the inclement weather in the Piedmont, be it snow or rain, whereas here they served more as welcome shade for the searing Roman summers. It was under these same arches, too, that his courtship with Yana had begun, in another winter. They had played childish games of hide-and-seek behind the columns and then, arm-in-arm, had performed a comical three-legged walk she taught him, all the way back to her old shared apartment near Porta Maggiore.

She had worked hard after that, getting her MBA, setting up the business with Marta and, when the profits began coming in, finally making a down payment on a place of her own which she was now well on the way to paying off. A small but well-proportioned flat with a mezzanine split-level of her own design, it was where Rossi was now heading, specifically to the calm oasis of her bedroom.

The call in the restaurant had been from her. He'd gone outside to take it where it was marginally quieter, and they had talked. She had been more relaxed and interested to hear about the case. They'd both had tough days and amidst the mutual expressions of solidarity, Rossi had persuaded her to let him come over later. He had his own key but never entered without prior arrangement. Yana had her rules and had her reasons and he respected that. They were together, an item, maybe, but there were limits and lines drawn in the sand, even if he felt sometimes that the tides of their two lives changed and shifted the sands so much as to render such confines meaningless. Periodically, they disappeared completely only to then reappear, perhaps, in the cold light of day, or when he had overstepped the limits of reasonableness. That said, the bond, though unusual, was strong.

She would be asleep now. So, he would let himself in, as quietly as he could, slip off his shoes and maybe, no, definitely, help himself to another cold beer. He would watch a little TV with his feet up, perhaps glance at his papers then climb the wooden steps, placing his feet where he knew he wouldn't cause the boards to creak before finally sliding in beside her. He'd test the water to see if she wanted to satisfy his more primal nocturnal needs, knowing she'd probably just shove him away. But tomorrow, if she was not working early, they could make up for lost time.

A shivering street-worker in black leather boots and a short fake-fur jacket peeled herself slowly off the corner where she had been trying her best to recline.

"Hello, darling. Looking for fun?" she said through gritted teeth.

Rossi stopped. Was she a mind reader? He smiled, and declined, adding a polite but sincere warning concerning the concomitant risks of being out at night, a woman, and alone. Not all the girls had pimps here, he knew. They wanted, quite rightly, to be free agents but it could be a double-edged sword, especially at times like this.

As a matter of course, he put a hand to his jacket pocket to check his phone. A missed call from Carrara. He rang back. He must have just got off the Metro, he thought. His heart was beating faster now. Not another victim. Not so soon.

"Gigi?"

"Yes, we've got news, Mick. ID on the third victim."

"Anything interesting?"

"Very. She was Maria Marini. A lawyer, 35, single mother, separated and ..." Carrara paused.

"And what?" said Rossi

"You're going to like this. Her father's a judge. Guido Marini, anti-mafia, Palermo pool, in semi-retirement but put a lot of people inside for a long time."

"Has he been informed?"

"Informed? He identified the body. And we got a handbag with ID inside picked up by the Tiber. They ran some checks and it seems the lady had missed a regular dinner appointment with her father and wasn't answering her phone. Out of character and all that. He called the police around 10 p.m. then came straight over."

Rossi was thinking at full tilt. So, Maroni had kept that to himself until now.

"Are you there, Mick?"

"Yeah. What have you got on her personal life?"

"Like I said, her father told us she was separated, got a kid too."

"And the ex?"

"Looks clean enough but not exactly in a state of shock. Took it rather philosophically, shall we say. He's in Milan for work. Travels a lot. He's been informed and is heading to Rome 'as soon as he can'."

Rossi had turned on his heel and was heading towards the square.

"Gigi, send a car to Piazza Vittorio, Fassi's ice-cream place," he said then shoved his phone into his pocket.

The girl was still propping up the wall like an eroticized flying buttress.

"C'mon on, hun," she said. "You know you want to. We'll have a ball!"

"No, thanks, love. Back on duty myself, I'm afraid."

Ten

When Rossi awoke it took him a while to realize where he was and that he was alone. He listened for familiar sounds and, hearing none, threw back the covers. The heating was on, but the flat was still a bit on the chilly side. There was some coffee still left in the machine. It was more warm than cold. Drinkable. By the kitchen clock it was nine. So, Yana had performed all her morning duties without even waking him or perhaps without even trying to wake him. At least she hadn't come around with the Hoover.

He had finally let himself in at, what was it? Four or five? He tried to reconstruct the night's events. Yes, after they'd persuaded the judge to let them check out his daughter's flat. It had been a hassle with that guy, and Rossi remembered his own exasperated words: "Anything could help, you must understand that, sir. So, if you'll just give me the keys we'll get it over and done with tonight." It had been, as always, sobering, with the judge standing sentinel-like as he and Carrara and the officers had gone through bins, opened cupboards, drawers, the fridge, in the search of any indicator that might point to a motive other than sheer, random, insane violence. As he checked levels in liquor bottles, read personal notes and, ever the foodie, squeezed and sniffed groceries for freshness, Rossi could feel the judge's disdain as though by these very actions his daughter were being violated for a second time. "Nothing much to go on here," Rossi had concluded with the standard phrase. "We'll come back tomorrow to tie up any loose ends, if you don't mind."

He had slept late. She must have given herself the early shift after all. Or changed it. He couldn't detect any sign of emotion, neither anger nor indifference, in the otherwise empty flat and, scratching his head, he wondered whether she had let him sleep out of pity or a simple desire not to have to exchange strained pleasantries with him. Maybe she hadn't felt she had the energy to confront him head-on. Maybe he didn't either. *Was that a bad sign*? *Time would tell*, he concluded and splashed some milk into a saucepan then sat down to mull over more of the events of the previous night.

Of course, once the powers-that-be had learned of the possible judicial connection they had all become very interested. So, it had been a torrid night of claim and counter claim and a back and forth of theories about "reprisals" and "warnings" and "clear threats to the institutions" – the judiciary, the government, and so forth. Rossi, however, had resolutely maintained his line that it was pure coincidence. The modus operandi, the signature, were all consistent with the previous killings. Apart from the handbag having been subtracted from the crime scene – probably a self-conscious act of arrogant defiance – it bore all the key traits of the first murder.

They'd learned then that the girl's father had been pulling all the strings at his disposition and had even wanted to take over the case and put his own men on the job. Rossi gave a dry little laugh to himself. How quickly things moved when tragedy touched the lives of the luminaries. Yes. When sometimes there wasn't even money to put petrol in a squad car, along came one of the Establishment and they were sending up helicopters and cancelling leave right, left, and centre.

To his credit, Maroni had held his own, for the sake of the

force, ostensibly. Possibly. He'd had to leave the opera midway through and was faintly comical in his evening garb. It was only the Rome opera though. Not as if he'd been to La Scala or San Carlo. He had, nonetheless, insisted on leaving the investigation in Rossi's hands now that he had begun. "Rossi has my full confidence and the full confidence of my superiors," he'd rather grandly announced at one point, which had tickled Rossi not a little. They had agreed to keep all and sundry informed of subsequent developments, should anything have arisen which might indicate a mafia or other organized backdrop. A press conference was to be arranged, in part, to placate an anxious business community now that the murders were becoming news, international news, and in part to keep a lid on the possible motives. The Home Secretary had even phoned from the ski-resort where he was contributing to the nation's economic welfare by giving a significant boost to consumer spending, albeit with taxpayers' money, and racking up a quantity of sexual misdemeanours sufficient to keep priests busy with confessions and journalists replete with favours paid for by their silence.

They had concluded matters in the very late early hours with Rossi agreeing to meet with the judge again the following day, which was, as Rossi now noted, today. Maroni wanted him to probe a little more into the woman's private life and business affairs but also to keep her father at a manageable distance. "We don't want a bloody judge sniffing around," Maroni had hissed, "and following our every move, Rossi, so work on him. Soft soap him. You're good at that, aren't you?"

He tried to remember the time they had set for the meeting. His morning mind was fuzzier than usual and then he remembered how he had needed two or three visits to the bottom drawer, that of the filing cabinet, where the emergency supply of whiskey was located. That and extra nightcaps to wind down on the way back over to Yana's. Not to mention the third of a bottle of Limoncello, and the beers. It was all mounting up to something approaching unjustified excess. Carrara would know. He went to look for his phone. God only knew where that was.

The front door clicked. Rossi turned to see Yana standing there.

"Well," she said, "are you going to tell me what's going on, or what?"

"Shouldn't you be at work?" said Rossi.

"I felt guilty or something," she replied, dropping her bag into the corner and pulling off her scarf. "And if we don't talk now I don't think we're ever going to talk, are we? Besides what is it they say about never letting the sun go down on an argument?"

"Even if it was only in the form of a text?"

"You got the message though? I was expecting you at a respectable hour."

"Am I forgiven?"

She threw her coat across the chair and walked over to him.

"Well, it's winter and I didn't fancy my chances of seeing you before dark tonight. Having a boyfriend in your line of work, one has to live for the moment, shall we say. You got drunk, didn't you, last night?"

"We had a late one," said Rossi. "There was all sorts of 'shit going down', as our American friends say."

She went closer and sniffed around, testing him and still showing something of the disdain for him which was part and parcel of their sometimes tempestuous love affair.

"Well you brush up reasonably well, Inspector fucking Rossi. What time's your first appointment?"

"Now, it's funny you should mention that," said Rossi, "but I can't find my phone. Going to give me a hand?" But before Yana was able to do the time-honoured call-the-lost-mobile-routine, somebody had got there first. "It's buzzing," he said, throwing cushions hither and thither as he tried to home in on the vibrations.

"Got it," said Yana sliding a hand down the side of the settee. It was Carrara.

49

"Just reminding you not to forget that you've got an appointment with the judge at his place. All right?"

"What makes you think I would have forgotten?" said Rossi, knowing his gravelly tones were giving him away. But Yana, who had pulled the curtains in the lounge, had already begun to unzip her top and was shaking her head, mouthing "no, no, no."

"Look," said Rossi as Yana came closer now and put her arms around his waist. "Give him a call, will you?" he said. "Tell him that some lab reports have come through and that I'll be over as soon as I can. It's not like he'll be going to work today, is it? The man's got a funeral to organize."

Eleven

"Rome is Afraid." That would be the headline for tomorrow's paper. That would get copies moving and, to his delight, ad-space had already been filling up fast. Giorgio Torrini, editor-in-chief of the *Roman Post*, was not quite rubbing his hands but had the look of someone who has just bagged a sizeable win on the horses or the lottery. Until now, the public had been taking more interest in the apparently drug-related killings spilling out of the usual run-down and deprived ghetto territories and into the "civilized" centre, sometimes in broad daylight. Yet people didn't really feel threatened. Just like with the dodgy heroin-killing junkies, or the ex-husbands losing their jobs then losing the plot and massacring entire families; all that was still going on but it didn't make people afraid. But now The Carpenter had made sure they were. More cautious husbands weren't letting wives go out on their own. The city was becoming a virtual ghost town after dark. Taxis were doing a roaring trade.

Torrini had his best man on the story and he was dictating what line to take now that Marini had been identified.

"Nobody cares about Mafia," he was saying. "Unless they start planting bombs outside the Stadio Olimpico, in St Peter's Square, or in pizzerias, it's water off a duck's back. They've heard it all before."

"So we stick with the serial-killer line?"

"Rome is Afraid," he repeated, holding up hands which grasped the extremities of an imaginary banner headline.

"And tourism? Isn't it going to hit tourism? All this negative publicity."

"Tourism?" spluttered Torrini. "Tourism? They always bounce back. They can drop their prices. Probably boost tourism once it all dies down," he added, "and I mean, how long is it going to last? A couple of weeks, a month or two? By Easter it'll all be forgotten. Mark my words. It'll be history. More history for Rome. More guided tours. 'This is where The Carpenter killed his first victim.' Blah, blah, blah."

Senior reporter Dario Iannelli was taking notes. So far, he had only written "mad heartless fucker". Dario knew a good story and had the knack of finding them but what he wanted was the scoop that went right to the top and could let him get at the real criminals. Serial killers were one offs, sad fucked-up losers, true enough. But the others, those who were selling the country down the river for thirty pieces of silver? They were the real nasty pieces of work. It was them he wanted to nail.

But he was also beginning to feel that there might be something more to this story. Rome didn't do serial killers. It wasn't in its nature. But he couldn't prove anything, not yet. So, for now he would have to go along with the official line. Fear sells papers. Fear is good. Tell the Romans to be afraid. But he was searching; he was on the lookout for any and every clue, the slightest slip that might let that crucial something come his way.

"So, you get your arse down to the press conference, right, and get a good question in, on mike, and on camera, if possible, so stand up or something?" Dario nodded.

"I want everyone to hear the *Roman Post* is covering this story. Fuck the nationals. We're on the ground here. This is our big one."

Dario made another careful note: "egomaniac arsehole. Fuckwit".

"Let's milk it. Oh, and try and get something on his methods."

"Meaning, sir?"

"His methods!" blurted Torrini, popping out suddenly from the comfort zone of his ego-bubble. "What he does!"

"He kills them, sir," said Iannelli, scenting a prime piss-taking opportunity.

The editor's face contorted in a sign of near total non-comprehension before he finally put two and two together.

Never been quick on the uptake, have you? thought Dario. Romans often weren't.

"I mean, does he cut their fingers off! Does he carve shit into their skin or something? I don't know!" He leaned over the desk at a more intimate distance. "Does he fuck them, or what? We've got none of that yet. Is there something they're not telling us?"

"Ah," said Iannelli, "those methods. I'll see what I can find, sir. Do my damnedest. Try and get something out of Rossi."

But for now he knew he would still be keeping his word. Rossi was about as close as anyone could be to being his friend, but he might need to cash in a favour from him, perhaps sooner rather than later.

Twelve

The Metro brought him to a very convenient distance from the judge's apartment on a side street just off the broad busy thoroughfare of the Via Tiburtina. He crossed the bridge over the railway junction with its spaghetti tangle of lines spewing out of the immense Brutalist concrete station. In the distance he could see the Roman hills, the Castelli, each of which had once been the sight of a castle, with its lord and servants and feudal power structure. To Rossi they served as a reminder of feudalism's ever-present role in Italian affairs. King-like figures still dwelt in the shadows, subjects still curried favour, assassins took their king's shillings, and heretics and rebels, if they were foolish enough to expose themselves, had to face the consequences of their treason.

The hills looked near enough to touch, their variegated mossy colours vivid and sharp. *Beautiful*, thought Rossi, beginning to drift, but then, like a surgeon, truncating the reverie. There was work to do and yet, as he turned his gaze back to the streets, he reflected that it might be a sign of further rain or even snow, given the cold snap, and he couldn't help but feel its metaphorical weight. Most of the multi-storey buildings here had shot up after the war, gobbling with grey the once-green space that had skirted the old Rome. Still, despite their functional, un-classical facades they often concealed large, sprawling apartments with dark, bourgeois, chestnut and mahogany-rich interiors. He flashed his ID at the pair of plain-clothes officers idling outside the building. The judge's place was no exception. The brass fittings and elegant stairwell were graffiti-free and there was a well-maintained porter's cabin at the entrance. The names on the intercoms were neatly printed or in dark, fluid italics. There were doctors, engineers, architects and lawyers all with their names clearly prefixed with their respective titles. *Dottore, Ingegnere, Architetto, Avvocato.*

The door opened to reveal a tall, still quite athletic man somewhere in his mid-sixties. He was wearing a suede, blouson-style leather jacket, the type favoured by men of his age, not necessarily only bourgeois types, but all those conscious of, and still proud of, their own masculinity and vigour. He seemed to have either recently arrived or to be about to leave. His handshake was firm and decisive, his face haggard and grey.

He showed Rossi in with a gentle sweep of his hand but moved about the flat with the hesitant uncertainty of one not used to living in a place. In fact, there were few or any indications that he might be the habitual resident. The blinds were still closed, there was no lingering aroma of cooking or morning coffee, no radio or television on. There were no newspapers, either read or unread. There was only a single book, on the corner of the far end of the long baroque-looking table at which he invited Rossi to take a seat opposite him.

They sat for some moments in silence before the judge seemed to remember his manners.

"Can I offer you something to drink, Inspector? Coffee, a glass, perhaps, of mineral water?"

Rossi was on his third or fourth coffee already and opted for the water. The judge returned with an ornate, miniature silver tray on which were balanced two delicate glasses. He looked around in vain for coasters.

"I'm really not sure where anything is in this house," he

explained. "It was my mother's and then, when I divorced, well. Still on good terms though," he added with scant conviction. "And now with the boy needing to be looked after, it's all so, so up in the air."

He trailed off in his explanation making it all quite clear to Rossi.

Already floundering, he thought. *And now all this.*

The judge left the tray on the table between them and then, clearing his throat, began what appeared destined to be a speech of sorts.

"I feel," he began, "about last night, that I owe you and your fellow officers something of an apology. I was really quite," he began to search for the exact word, then as if contenting himself with a cliché, concluded, "not myself."

"Think nothing of it," said Rossi. "It is quite understandable, really, isn't it?"

Silence reigned for a few moments as the two men reprised their different parts in the previous night's drama.

It wasn't exactly changing the subject but Rossi thought he had better begin to at least get the ball rolling with a more predictable question.

"Was Maria seeing someone?"

The judge gave a shrug of sorts.

"I believe there was someone," he said. "But it was all very casual, as far as I knew."

"Did she mention a name?"

He shook his head.

"We didn't have that kind of relationship," he said. "She would always go to her mother for advice about boys. But that was a long time ago."

"Was she in trouble in any way? Did your daughter ever mention having enemies?" Rossi asked.

"Only mine," he replied. "As far as I can possibly know. She was a very independent woman. Keeping on top of her home life and her work. I can't imagine she had much time to make enemies. If that's what you mean."

"I mean," said Rossi, "was she perhaps involved with any investigations, in her line of work. She was a lawyer, was she not?"

"Yes," he nodded. "She always wanted to go her own way in the world. Not mine. Always did the opposite." He almost gave a little laugh as he seemed to remember something. "I wanted her to take up ballet. I knew certain people at La Scala. But she wanted to do martial arts! Of course, I was misguided. Besides, she was always going to be much too tall to be a dancer. Still, that was her way."

"Admirable, wouldn't you say?"

"You could say that."

There was a loaded pause before Rossi continued. A clock was ticking somewhere.

"She had a part-time position with a studio. I didn't ask her very much. She spoke of regular work: family-law cases, small property affairs. Nothing remarkable. And then," he added, with what appeared to be a melancholy emphasis, "she had her voluntary work."

"For whom?" Rossi enquired, interested now.

"Whomsoever required it. She was good like that. Very generous. Willing to give of herself. Always off travelling to this place or that place."

"So you don't feel that someone could have wanted to murder your daughter because she was creating problems, getting in the way of anything?"

The judge was looking across the table at Rossi. In his lined and fissured face, Rossi could see some other preoccupation, something other than the investigation.

"I believe you are English, aren't you?" he said suddenly.

"You could say that," Rossi replied.

"How do I say my daughter has died, is dead? What is the word for *la morte*?"

It didn't seem quite the moment for language lessons, but Rossi felt a certain duty.

"My daughter is dead. She was killed. She was murdered."

"Oh," said the judge. "I see." He looked up, suddenly, in an almost sprightly manner. "Do you ski, Inspector? You know, I am a member of the Alpine Club of Italy. We had planned a week together, in the Dolomites. We go most years."

"I am sorry," said Rossi, a little confused, not sure what question, if any, he was answering. "I have never learned."

"But you could learn!" he countered. "It's never too late!"

Rossi smiled and shook his head.

"No, it's not for me, really."

But the judge had already drifted elsewhere with his thoughts.

"And do you think they will come for me, Inspector?"

Rossi looked across the table at the judge. He appeared, for all the world, like someone who had simply enquired as to whether or not it would be a fine day tomorrow.

"No, I don't believe so, sir. I really don't believe it is a question of them."

The judge was looking straight at him now, his gaze stony, his mouth pursed tight, as though holding back an avalanche of emotions or profound knowledge.

"I want you to know," Rossi continued, "that I feel sure your daughter was the victim of a killer who chooses his victims according only to his own deranged criteria and not because of who you are or who your daughter was. And besides, his methods," he began again, before feeling an irresistible pressure to lower his gaze, "are not consistent with the type of murder you perhaps fear. I am sure the killer doesn't even know who you are. Just as he didn't care who the first two victims were, and who the next will be, if we don't stop him first."

"Yes," the judge nodded. "Yes. He must be apprehended. At all costs," he added, seeming to have re-conquered some of his old fight and *voglia di vivere*, the will to live. It would have made it

58

all so much more perversely understandable. A mafia-pool judge and the worst possible revenge – that of taking a loved one. It was, instead, a senseless killing. A random folly, like being struck by lightning on a family picnic.

"You know," he began again, "she always refused the protection she would have been entitled to. She maintained she could look after herself pretty well. She refused to live like a prisoner in her own life."

"She was very brave," said Rossi.

"Yes, she was. But it would have saved her."

Rossi reached for the glass and took a sip.

Feeling that it was time to bring things to a close, he asked if he might use the bathroom. He splashed his face and, on coming back into the dining room, his incorrigible reader's curiosity led him to turn over the book lying flat on the corner of the table.

"Ah," he said, "Buzzati."

The book was *The Seven Messengers*, one of his favourites. Its title story told of a prince who, on leaving his father's kingdom to discover what lies beyond the confines of the realm, takes with him seven riders to relay news between the old world and the new one he is to discover. As time passes, however, the narrator realizes the growing futility of his system as the future relentlessly and inexorably eclipses the past.

"You can have it if you like," said the judge. "It was for my daughter. I had been putting aside the whole series for her as they came out with the newspaper. She loves, loved to read."

Although he knew he had a copy of the book on a shelf somewhere in his flat, Rossi accepted it then handed the judge his card, should he need to get in touch.

"There was just one more thing," said Rossi. "I was wondering whether I could ask you if you have a picture of your daughter, sir, one I can use for the investigation."

"A picture? A photograph? Yes, of course, one moment." And he slipped out and into an adjoining room. He returned carrying a large album into which, over the years, many extra pictures had been accommodated, so much so that when he opened it some spilled onto the table. For a moment the judge seemed to be lost in some bitter-sweet melancholy of reminiscence as he searched for a recent image.

"No. She seems to be just a little young in these," he said, "her hair's quite different. Now, let me find something more up to date," he said, almost jumping up and leaving Rossi alone again. There was one photo which Rossi felt could, nonetheless, be of some use to him and he slipped it into his jacket pocket.

"Here's what I was after," the judge exclaimed on returning, then, as if dampening his own temporary enthusiasm, he placed the image in front of Rossi.

"Thank you," said Rossi, with due reverence.

As he left, descending the staircase, after a moment's thought he was able to recall, almost by heart, the closing lines of the Buzzati story. He repeated the words to himself, like a seasoned priest reciting the requiem: *Tomorrow, new hope will drive me on towards those unexplored mountains shrouded in the shadows of the night. Once more, I will break camp while Domenico disappears over the horizon in the opposite direction, carrying with him my now quite useless message to the far, far distant city.*

Thirteen

"I did think about waking him up," she said, "in case he was going to be late for something important, but then I just thought, sod him. And then I felt bad about it and went back."

Yana was leaning on the reception desk of the Wellness Health and Fitness Complex. She was wearing wedge-like training shoes, ultramarine Lycra leggings and a tracksuit top. Her blonde hair was pulled into a high ponytail. Sporty and sexy. Get the clients in. Give the housewives and harassed professionals something to aspire to but without being too far out of their league. She knew what worked.

"Would have served him right," said Marta, staring into a small mirror balanced on the counter and applying yet another layer of mascara. Her eyes had taken on the appearance of two very beautiful tropical spiders. Always experimenting, there was nothing she couldn't tell you about beauty and treatments. Yana looked after the business and the fitness side but Marta had the X-factor, without a doubt. She closed her little box. "What do you think? Never know who might walk in that door, do you? Could be George Clooney, with his mates, couldn't it?"

"And Fabio?" said Yana, not so very mock-scandalized.

"Always good to have a spare, darling. Never know when you might need another."

Yana laughed and dealt her friend and partner a playful push.

"Your Michael," said Marta, "he doesn't, you know, when he's 'working late'?" and she gave a knowing wink.

"Noo!" said Yana, in fake outrage at the scandalous suggestion. "He's too busy with his books."

"Oh! Him and his books!"

"Uh huh," said Yana, scanning the appointments for the day. "Novels, poetry, theology even."

"Theology! He wanna be a priest or something? Watch him, darling. Hey, you might be left on the shelf, if you follow."

A year in the seminary. How often she had wondered about that, at first – Michael's lost vocation in the Church. But then it just became kind of normal, like all the things that take up their place in a relationship and perhaps to outsiders seem strange or puzzling. Like ornaments around a living room. She wouldn't mention that to Marta, though. Not a secret, just personal.

He had often tried to explain to her his desire to do some good, his love of thought and philosophy, and the disappointments that had pushed him towards a life of reflection and sacrifice. Then he had woken up, as it were, and decided to take a more practical approach. Grab life by the scruff of the neck as he used to say. He thought he had been running away from the world, so he decided to come back and face it. But there was a part of him that was perhaps still monastic, withdrawn, thoughtful. Suppose it helped, at times, she concluded, trying again to make sense of it all and how she'd got to where she was and everything she'd had to leave behind. And she had secrets, too, mind, but they really were under lock and key. In a safe, with a combination for good measure, so to speak.

"On your feet, girl," said Marta, rousing Yana from her temporary dreamy state as the door to the health centre opened. A tall, athletic, Mediterranean male, maybe mid-forties, ambled towards the desk. "Here he comes now, your real Mr Right, or maybe your future bit on the side."

"Perhaps either of you young ladies could be of assistance," he said and deposited a holdall of some considerable weight on the polished parquet floor, the heavy tools clinking inside as he did so.

Fourteen

Despite his initial certainty and strenuous defence of his own interpretation of events, something was nagging at the back of Rossi's mind. He had called the office to let Carrara know he had sorted things out with the judge. He had then had lunch in an anonymous eatery near Tiburtina station and frequented by locals, just to see what the vibe was like. They were talking about the murders in hushed tones, studying the papers, speculating. A couple of Romanian workmen walked in and drew a few dirty looks from the barman and some of the older patrons. Potential scapegoats. It couldn't be the work of an Italian, after all.

Rossi had then decided to take a couple of hours off before the press conference, to think things through. He would take the Metro to Flaminia from where he could then have a stroll through Villa Borghese. It was one of Rome's most beautiful parks, bequeathed to the people in perpetuity by public-minded aristocrats from a bygone age. As he was passing under the archway at its entrance, he noted a pickpockets' graveyard behind one of the ventilation shafts of the Metro system; it was a sorry corner where you might find the detritus of drug users' paraphernalia and, as often as not, abandoned purses, handbags, and wallets, picked clean of all valuables by the thieves that plagued the more touristic stretches of Rome's transport system.

Sometimes there were even coins, Polish zloty, or roubles: useless as they could neither be spent nor exchanged locally and would only risk incriminating any self-respecting pickpocket. So, most thieves were after ready cash or maybe credit cards and, almost as a matter of course, would jettison any ID, which would, sometimes, get returned to its rightful owners. He'd even witnessed bizarre scenes of freshly fleeced individuals getting their wallets thrown back through the closing doors of a tube train about to depart; a little lighter for cash but at least freeing the owner of the trauma of having to drag themselves through the Italian bureaucracy.

The judge had left him feeling slightly perplexed. He was evidently a cold individual, and likely still in a state of shock. The two factors had combined to render his replies somewhat enigmatic but as yet Rossi hadn't been able to put his finger on what it was that was bothering him. He was also thinking about Marini's handbag and why the killer might have taken it. It had been cleaned out but by an opportunist third party, or even the killer himself. Had he decided to make a little bonus while he was at it? Had he needed cash? For drugs, possibly. But then why hadn't he left it at the scene? Maybe fearing prints, and they had been able to get some, but they could have been from any passer-by who had taken a hopeful peek.

There was also the possibility that he had been disturbed, had heard someone approaching, and taken it with him as he made his escape. Like a wild animal slinking off with its kill so it can be studied, savoured, enjoyed in peace, away from the nagging attention of jackals and hyenas. Or had he been looking for something? Even the calmest person, in the least stressful of situations, can sometimes feel like they are losing their mind while trying to find a house key at the bottom of a bag chock-full of items, and in poor light, too, not to mention the risk of being seen. Was it all beginning to add up to something more complex? But what could he have been looking for? And why? He stopped by the ornamental lake and took out his phone to call Carrara.

"Gigi?"

"Yes, boss."

"Put the press conference back to six or seven. Something's come up. I think the judge might have been on to something all along."

"What do you mean? Mafia?" Carrara's voice betrayed ill-concealed incredulity.

"Something," said Rossi. "Something that doesn't quite fit. It could just be a feeling, but we need more on the girl first. Have you found anything?"

"Nothing special. It's just as you said. Wrong place at the wrong time. He must have studied her movements to ascertain whether or not she was a mother, if that's still the motive, but other than that ..."

"OK," said Rossi, "check out what exactly she did in her voluntary work. See if you can find out about her clients. Try to discover a bit about them and why she was helping them."

"Will do," said Carrara. "Is that all?"

Rossi thought for a moment.

"Go back to her flat, too, and seal it off if it hasn't been done already. And while you're there see if you can find a phone, a computer, files, clients' lists that might be sensitive. See if anything's missing."

"And her ex?" said Carrara.

"Is he in Rome yet?"

"On his way apparently."

"See if he knows anything about her activities, her private life. I'll be at the office in half an hour."

Fifteen

One more stroke with the whetstone and the blade was gleaming, sharp as a razor's edge. He held it up and admired its glint in the street light filtering through the window into the rented apartment. He often sat in the dark at this time of the evening, looking down, watching, while safe in the knowledge he could not be seen. It had always been a favourite game – being the voyeur, the watcher. They, meanwhile, walked along the street, oblivious, as he imagined which of them might put up a fight, who would crumple into so much dust under the blows. Sometimes all it took was a single swing. Other times they had to be pummelled. That was messy. But he liked it like that too, if there was time, and time was of the essence.

He thrust the knife deep into the chopping board at the centre of the table, spearing the official communication that lay there, the three letters that spelled out his now particular form of mortality. The knife was for show, for fear, not for killing. Not yet. He took up the gun then, removed the magazine, and jerked the slide, ejecting the compact round from the chamber. Then he wiped the hammer; not to clean it, but ritually, as if he were a mother drying a small child, dabbing and caressing it before lapping it in its sacking. What did mother say? A good workman cleans his tools. A bad workman blames his tools. So, he was doing well. The holy trinity of hammer, blade, and bullet. And yes, the plan was established, the traps were being set, and the chase was on. But there were so many clues to reveal and so many more had to die before he could have his finale. These had been but the opening lines in the first scene of the first act of the tragedy. Or was it a comedy? Tragedy. Comedy. Tragedy. Comedy. He thought it was both. He really couldn't quite decide.

It certainly made him laugh out loud to see how the hoi polloi now were running scared. The bars, too, were suddenly so much emptier once darkness fell, the proprietors fretting over lost revenues, cursing the killer who had made their neighbourhood a no-go-zone. Then there were the furtive looks on the frightened faces when a foreign workman threw down his bag and hefted out a hammer as he set to mending the city's roads and broken paving stones. He knew what they were thinking now. Was one of them the Luzi killer or the Marini killer? Did he pick them up in his van, violate them, smash their skulls then dump the bodies?

He had heard the talk himself, irony of ironies, as he sipped his morning coffee and pretended to pore over the latest local gossip in the *Roman Post*. Perhaps he would start killing some of them too – the *stranieri*, the foreigners clogging up the country like the saturated fat in a sick man's veins. Perhaps he would start slaughtering the fat men themselves, the ones he watched askance as they suckled like oversized infants at the dry, consoling teat of the sports pages in these self-same bars. Or maybe the pensioners and half cripples who fed their fistfuls of small change into the fruit machines from dawn until dusk in hopes of sudden ecstasy.

The letter stared back at him, pierced by the upright blade – night's sundial casting its dead meridian. It complicated things? Or made everything much simpler? An existential question then – which was his stock in trade. To be or not to be. Life and death. Smell the flowers? Crush them while you can. But he would lead them a merry dance and oh how he would laugh. Laugh at them all. Them all.

Sixteen

Beware of Carrara bearing gifts, thought Rossi as the door to his office was opened by a jab of his colleague's foot. He was balancing takeaway coffees on a stack of files and had the spritely demeanour of a cop on the verge of cornering his man.

"Cat that got the cream?" quipped Rossi from a semi-horizontal position in his office chair. Carrara gave a wryish smile and set the mini plastic cups down where there was an islet of desk space. Yet more caffeine to fuel the sluggish afternoon. "Let's have it then."

"Well, first up, she was working for one of the top guys in the MPD. Luca Spinelli. Legal consultancy, voluntary, by the way."

"So she was working for a political party," said Rossi. "Not the crime of the century, is it?"

"No, but they were also having an affair. And he's married."

"So, what? She was a single woman, pretty, good luck to her." But Carrara hadn't finished.

"And she broke it off, much to the disappointment of afore-mentioned high-ranking MPD lover."

He reached into a file and pulled out a sheaf of printed papers.

"Exhibit A: e-mails from one pissed-off politician, or should I say anti-politician, citizen. What do they call themselves?"

Rossi, graduating to an upright, seated position reached out to take Carrara's first fruits. He scanned the pages. The content was a disturbing mix of insane affection, lust, suicidal reverie, and some degree of menace.

"Enough for a motive? Is that what you're saying?"

"Enough to merit digging deeper, wouldn't you say? And the method's the same as Gentili and Luzi. He could be our man."

"Where did you get these?" Rossi asked.

"The ex. Her ex-husband. He arrived last night, and I went over for a chat. I asked if there was anything I might need to know regarding Maria and he told me straight out about the affair. Seems she'd been trying to get things back on track. That was the initial reason she ended the relationship with Spinelli. But there were some furtive phone calls and stuff and the ex starts smelling a rat, gets a bit nosy and decides to print off her private e-mails – he just happens to be an IT security consultant – in case he might need proof for divorce proceedings and so on. Not too bothered otherwise, it seems. He confronts her, thinks she's not playing a straight bat, but she plays the whole thing down; says your man's all bark and no bite. But hubby's not having any of it and they break off again and, well, the rest is history."

"Did she go back to Spinelli?"

"Seems not, but she did continue working for the party. She was helping them with libel cases. You know how the bigs have been trying to cripple them in the courts, scare them off with huge damages actions. She might have been able to use her father's contacts to some extent, but we don't know that for sure."

"And the ex is going to get custody, of the kid? You do remember, don't you, she had a son? Do you think he wants it?"

"I doubt it. He mentioned something about his work commitments 'not being negotiable' and the kid's grandparents being 'the easiest solution' for everyone."

"Nice guy."

Carrara gave a shrug.

"Haven't you noticed how many kids get brought up by their grandparents in Rome?"

"Has Maroni got any of this then?" said Rossi.

"It's not his case," said Carrara. *Ever the idealist*, thought Rossi.

"It's always Maroni's case, especially when he needs it. But does he know what you've got?"

"Came straight to you, Mick," said Carrara, "but listen, there's more."

"Go on."

"Well, the forensics, for one. They've got some DNA from her clothing and in the car and if they match with the other crime scenes we might be onto something. We could try Spinelli."

Rossi let out a sigh.

"Are you telling me that this Spinelli guy has faked himself as a serial killer as a perfect cover, or actually became a serial killer, murdered one or two innocent women just so he can bump off his ex-lover? Sounds a bit off the wall, don't you think?"

"Unless," countered Carrara, "he heard about the note on the second victim, got a tip-off or something about it being a possible serial killer. Then he hatched himself a plan."

Rossi was swinging in short, rapid, pensive arcs in his chair.

"Iannelli knows. I told him to keep it to himself, in return for tasty morsels, obviously. But it's way off the mark."

"But we're still going to have to give this to Maroni, right?" said Carrara, "and then the public prosecutor might want to make a move. Impatient for an arrest and the like. You know they want to be informed."

Rossi felt it was Carrara who was piling the pressure on now. *Time to release the valve*, he thought.

"I think we'd better make a little visit to Mr Spinelli first, don't you? Just for a chat. As someone who knew the victim, he has valuable information to offer. No need to make it official. No lawyers. Routine enquiries. Can we hold off until tomorrow?"

"Possibly," said a guarded Carrara realizing he'd have to put the champagne moment on hold.

"Any of the guys go with you to the ex?"

"Just Bianco, and he's onside, I'm pretty sure."

"Well tell him to keep it under his proverbial. And the press conference? We'll have to put it back to eight o'clock now. They're going to hate us but it might give us time to see what this crazed lover has got to say for himself."

Carrara made a note.

"We can say we're still waiting on some forensics. I'll have a word with Loretta in the lab. She'll cover up if we need her to."

"Good," said Rossi. "What's his name and where can we find him?"

There was a knock at the door.

"Come in," said Rossi.

"Call from Chief Superintendent Maroni, sir," said a uniformed female officer whose name he couldn't remember but whose smile always brightened his day. "Says it is of the utmost urgency."

But Rossi had already got to his feet and was gesturing to Carrara to do likewise.

"Tell him I'm not here. I'm out. No, at the dentist. Terrible toothache. Can't even speak. Face out here," he said miming a mild deformity of the cheek area. "He can call me on my mobile," he said, grinning now while grabbing his coat and giving Carrara the definitive signal to move out. "And I won't be answering that in a hurry," he added, sotto voce, as they headed for the car.

Seventeen

Early forties, exuding a twitchy, impatient enthusiasm and an earnest if weary expression, Luca Spinelli was the new face of Italian politics. They had agreed to meet at his office where it was clear that he'd been both working and living since the break-up with Maria and the subsequent collapse of his own marriage.

"I've made a pretty good job of losing it all, don't you think?" he said as he faced Rossi and Carrara across his desk. "A marriage, the woman I loved. Still have my work though," he said with a liberal dose of acid irony.

"And we won't be keeping you from it for long, I'm sure," Rossi reassured him. "Just a few questions but it would be helpful if you could tell us anything you think may have aroused your suspicion in recent weeks."

"With pleasure, Inspector," he replied maintaining the same satirical tone.

Rossi passed the sheaf of e-mails across the desk. "You can, I presume, confirm that you wrote these? In particular, the last one, written in the early hours of the day on which Maria was later killed."

Spinelli's expression went from shock and embarrassment through to apparent incredulity.

"How did you get these?"

As Rossi explained, Spinelli went back to leafing through them, reliving the strange, voyeuristic dislocation that comes from seeing your own words already become a form of history. He stopped and held out one of the sheets.

"I didn't write this," he said. "I couldn't have written this. I mean it's not possible. It's not me. It can't be me." He began to read out some of the more incriminating sentences: "'If I can't be with you then you can't live either, you are coming with me, then we will always be together, I won't let you get away with this so easy, if I can't have you no one can … I'll do myself in or both of us …'"

"It's your e-mail account," said Rossi, "and we can pretty quickly ascertain if it came from your own computer, in which case, if it did, it makes things, shall we say, at best, awkward for you."

"So you're saying that I did it, that I'm a suspect?"

"I am saying that circumstantial evidence could implicate you as a possible suspect at this point in the investigation – for the murder of Maria Marini and those of both Paola Gentili and Anna Luzi. Unless perhaps you can explain why you wrote it."

"Or who wrote it," he added. "Who, Inspector."

Spinelli's tone had turned combative, and he now had something of the cornered look in his eyes, a look Rossi had seen many times before.

"Does anyone else have access to your account?"

"No."

"So you are the sole user."

"That would appear to be the case."

"And you aren't in the habit of letting other people write e-mails for you. A secretary, an aid. Maria herself, maybe? She was helping you, I believe."

"Oh, yes," said Spinelli, "and I often give people the keys to my flat too and say 'walk right in, go on, help yourself'."

Rossi gave a partially muted sigh.

"So, when you say 'who' wrote it, what do you mean exactly?"

"Well," began Spinelli, "call me an MPD conspiracy theorist, by all means, but has the thought not occurred to you that they might have hacked it, Inspector?"

Rossi never liked the way the final inspector was tagged on like a sardonic Post-it note, but he'd grown used to it. Comes with the job, he mused internally, nobody likes a cop, unless they need one, and then they're never there, are they? Ha, ha. Come to think of it, he didn't even like being called inspector when it wasn't used ironically and would happily have deployed his first name but then it just wasn't done, was it? Hi, I'm Michael and I'm here to help you. Like fuck you are. You're here to bang me up as quick as you can and get yourself another stripe. Back to work.

"And you think there might be a reason for that."

"To frame me, of course!" Spinelli exploded.

"But do you have reason to suspect that someone is trying to frame you, Dr Spinelli?"

Spinelli fumbled in his jacket pockets then wrenched open a desk drawer before locating his cigarettes. He lit up and smoke-whooshed a reply.

"Her ex, for starters. Or maybe just the whole political establishment," he added with a mock-ironic flourish, standing up and beginning to pace the small office, making it look, at least to Rossi's eyes, as if it were turning into a cell. He stopped at the window and turned around. Rossi could see he was shaping up for a confession of sorts. But which? There were those that revealed all, those that left out the awkward or shameful particulars, and those made up to take the rap for someone else.

"Look, Inspector," he began with greater, if rather more, mannered sincerity, "I wrote a few things, in the heat of the moment, which I shouldn't have. You see, I'd already been drinking, rather a lot as it happens, and since the break-up, well it had just got worse and worse." He made a hand gesture towards the street. "I've been spending most of my evenings in the piano bar round the corner from here. I get something to eat and try to switch off a bit, and then I come back, sleep on the sofa and then I dust myself down and start work again in the morning. The glamorous world of politics." He stubbed out the half-smoked cigarette and sat back down again. He paused to collect his thoughts, joining his hands and holding the fingertips just under his nose, as though gently drawing up through his nostrils some delicate perfume they exuded.

"That day, the day Maria was killed," he went on, "I woke up and my mind was almost a complete blank. I was still wearing my clothes and my head was pounding. At first, I thought I must have been hitting it harder than usual and perhaps, perhaps, when I had come back the night before I logged on and just started writing that stuff, but it wasn't me. It was someone else; I was out of my mind; I didn't feel that way. I didn't want to kill anyone."

Rossi looked him in the eye.

"Did you kill her? Perhaps while, as you say, you were out of your mind? Had you gone drinking again that afternoon?"

"No."

"Did you follow her, stalk her?"

"Stalk? No. Look, I went to her place once or twice when I was drunk, on other occasions, to talk, but that's as far as it went. Just me leaning on the bell until the madness passed."

"Did you want to kill her?"

"No, of course not!"

"Did you ever fantasize about killing her, for revenge, for going back to Volpini, for screwing up your marriage?"

"Do you really want me to answer that question?"

"Yes, Dr Spinelli, I do."

"Sometimes," he said, "the thought might have occurred, in my mind, in my wildest moments, in my worst moments, but I would never, ever have done it. Haven't you ever thought about revenge, Inspector?"

Oh, yes, thought Rossi. How he had thought about revenge, planned it even, down to the last detail. The hit, the getaway. The cleanest, most perfect of crimes only a cop could commit.

"Yes," said Rossi, snapping back from the reverie, "probably, but as far as I know, I have never as yet put it in writing."

"And neither have I."

A good firm answer. Rossi liked that. It meant he was on the right lines. It might mean less work, too, and he wanted Maroni off his back about this guy. He was clean. Screwed-up but clean. And besides, there was no material link. No weapon. No witness. No DNA.

But Rossi sensed Carrara was uneasy. He would be concerned that his squeezing of Spinelli was going too far emotively. Carrara was Mr Logic. It was what he did and he did it well, and Rossi knew he was itching to put his oar in. He gestured to his colleague, ceding the floor to him.

"I was just wondering," began Carrara, "do you think I could take a quick look at the computer, Dr Spinelli?" he asked, glancing askance at Rossi and, like seasoned team players, getting his immediate tacit assent. "I think we might be better off just checking a few things here and now."

"Feel free," he said and machine-gunned his password into the keyboard.

"That's not written anywhere, is it?"

"No. Memorized and difficult to crack. Numbers, letters and symbols and case-sensitive."

Rossi was more than glad of Carrara's serious nerd tendencies when it came to computers; it meant he could save precious time and dispense with tedium. He was clicking around now on Spinelli's e-mail, opening strange windows he'd never seen before and seemed to have already located something of interest.

"I note," he said, sounding very much the doctor rather than the policeman, "that you've been checking your sent items a lot."

"I honestly don't remember," Spinelli replied.

"On the night before the murder you checked some recent e-mails you sent to Maria. Why would you do that?"

"And why would I do that?" asked Spinelli his tone a blend of puzzlement and returning mild contempt. "I was drunk and emotional. I couldn't give a damn what I'd written about the night before. I might have been hitting all the wrong keys. There's any number of explanations."

"Well," said Carrara gauging from Spinelli's reaction that there was no damning sign of guilt, "I don't know for sure, and we may need a linguistics report on this, but could it be that someone, someone else, really was in your account and was trying to, shall we say, discover your style, see how you write, and then," he looked up at a frowning Spinelli, "write as if he, or she, were you?"

Rossi, intrigued now, was eager to combine forces.

"Doctor Spinelli, are you sure you came home alone that night?"

"I told you. I was very drunk. I remember next to nothing after 9 or 10 o'clock. I blacked out and woke up with a headache from hell."

"Do you think anyone could have seen you, as you were coming home or leaving the bar?"

"The barman, maybe. There was a girl, actually; I remember that."

"And did you drink with anyone? Did anyone buy you drinks?"

"Maybe, yes, usually, but I couldn't say who. Some people know who I am and we often get talking but, really, it's all a blur. There was the concert, people coming and going."

Rossi turned to Carrara.

"Luigi, why don't you take this man for a quiet drink in his usual bar and see if you can find a witness who saw him leave and with whom. Then get him down to the lab, if that's all right with you," he said, turning his attention back to Spinelli who now had his arms crossed tightly across his crumpled, white-shirted chest, "and run a blood test and a urine test."

"A blood test?" spurted Spinelli.

"For what?" said Carrara.

"Anything," said Rossi, "but sedatives mainly, fast-acting ones, although I do get the sneaking feeling we could be talking Rohypnol here."

"The date-rape drug?" said Spinelli, shifting in his chair.

"Got it in one," said Rossi. "And if it was, we should still be able to pick up any traces. Judging by your symptoms, the blackout, the after-effects, I'd say you got a spiked drink. Maybe someone taking a shot at you, or a poor-taste wind-up. I don't know. Whether or not they then came back here with you or slipped in while you were distracted is more difficult to prove."

Rossi turned to Carrara.

"And see what prints you can get off the PC, the door. We can always run them through the databases and see what comes up."

Spinelli seemed more relaxed; like he'd been through the mill, yes, but to some extent relieved. The look of an innocent man who has found someone to believe him?

"Time to cut down on the sauce, perhaps?" Rossi ventured, more than a little pleased with himself, and then remembering what Spinelli was going through, added, "I'm very sorry about Maria. We're going to do everything in our power."

"Thank you, Inspector," said Spinelli.

As Rossi headed for the door, leaving Spinelli in Carrara's capable hands, a thought occurred to him. He turned towards the now ex-suspect, as far as he was concerned.

"Do you think there could have been other reasons why they, or whoever it was, wanted to kill Maria? Did she have anything in her possession, did anything go missing that you might be aware of?"

"She had a laptop, of course, disks, memory sticks with a lot of our data on. You know, the court cases, the legal actions against us. The work we were doing on constitutional reform. The prison reform. You didn't find anything, presumably."

"Nothing. Her bag was ransacked and subtracted from the scene."

"Well, our new lawyer is going to have some work to do. But not to worry. Starting from scratch is what we're good at. Or perhaps I should say climbing the mountain. Yes, mountaineers. That's what we are. Well-prepared, with clear objectives, and a tough lot."

Not Kremlin mountaineers, I hope, Rossi thought but decided to save it for himself. You can't expect everyone to be into Mandelstam, he conceded, but the comparisons being drawn between Stalinist control freakery and the power structures within the movement were maybe not so far off the mark.

"Like Sisyphus?" he said, compromising.

"Maybe," said Spinelli, "or maybe that's how you see things, but I like to think we're actually getting somewhere, Inspector, that it's not all quite so futile. And I think we've got a lot of people in high places more than a little scared. You see, solving Italy's problems is not difficult, despite what they say. What's difficult is getting the privileged to give up their cosy little arrangements. They cost us billions, the Church too, with all its privileges. But when the people begin to understand, we'll put our plan into practice. We'll remove the Church from every part of civic society. No more secret banking. The Lateran Treaties guaranteeing the cosy coexistence of the Vatican within the Italian state and all their fascist inheritance will be torn up."

"But the treaties are part of the constitution," cut in Carrara.

"Exactly," he said, his eyes burning red now, from grief, anger, and exhaustion, "and when there's enough support we'll change the constitution and Italy will be a real Republic. Not this hobbled pseudo-democracy taking orders from the cardinals, multinationals, and old-money fascists. Then we'll be free. And Maria will be a hero. She won't have died in vain."

"Well," said Rossi, enjoying the speech and the little game that had sprung up between them, "just remember, that when you do get near the top of this mountain you're climbing it's merciless, it's lonely, progress is painfully slow, and you'll need to carry all your own oxygen."

"The oxygen of the truth, Inspector, or just the plain old stuff that keeps you breathing?"

"Oh," said Rossi, "I'd say you'd do well to have them both, and in abundance."

Eighteen

"I tried not to," said Bianco to Rossi, who had just slipped back into the office to be greeted by a grim, conspiratorial silence. "He was, shall we say, insistent. Very insistent."

Maroni had been going berserk. In Rossi's absence, the whole team had incurred his wrath and, homing in on the weakest link, Maroni had managed to squeeze at least some information out of Bianco.

"He's got a lot of people on his back," Rossi countered, having grasped where it was all leading and beginning to soliloquize.

"Oh, and he said he wants to see you 'physically in person,'" Bianco added, "about Spinelli but before the press conference."

"And they'll be pushing for an arrest," a newly bored Rossi continued, slumping into a vacant chair, "just to keep things quiet and to keep the hacks happy. Give the dogs a bone. Then he'll go to trial and he'll probably be convicted, on circumstantial evidence. Then there'll be an appeal and after about four years they'll all realize what idiots the judge and, of course, the police had been the first time round and he'll be out again, and the news, the talk shows, and the afternoon trash TV will be talking of nothing else. Sound familiar?" Bianco just hung his head.

"No? Well, I'll tell you. It's called what often passes for Italian justice!"

"He threatened me with a transfer. Well, not exactly threatened, but you knew what he was getting at."

Rossi nodded. He knew both Maroni's methods and that it was always only a matter of time before he would have things moving in the direction he wanted. But while Rossi had time on his side and was still ahead, he could at least try to make hay.

"C'mon then. What did you give him?"

"I told him about the e-mails but," he said, slipping back into his usual chatty tone, "but the funny thing is that he asked me if there were any."

"He asked you if there were any e-mails?"

"Yes, he said there'd been an anonymous tip-off and he needed to know if it could be trusted. Said it could be life or death."

Rossi dismissed Bianco, who seemed at least relieved to have got the whole thing off his chest. Then he sat down, took up a pencil and began to run through the possibilities. He took a deep breath.

Scenario one: Maria Marini's killer had given the tip-off about the e-mails to throw them off the scent. So either he had known about the e-mail correspondence or he knocked them out himself, if the Rohypnol theory held up. Which meant he'd wanted to get Maria out of the way, leave the MPD with a serious PR headache, and have Spinelli and his party fighting for their political survival.

But if somebody just happens to tip-off the police, didn't that actually presuppose that Spinelli was likely innocent and being framed? How could anyone have innocently come by the information. A casual comment from Maria's ex? A worried friend? But it would still be way too shaky in a court of law.

Scenario two: Volpini, Marini's ex. After all, he was the aggrieved party *in primis*, the cuckold. The e-mails had given him the perfect opportunity to lay the blame at his love rival's door. But from what Carrara had told him he didn't seem jealous enough, at least emotively. And if it emerged that Spinelli really had been drugged? Could Volpini have organized that little caper too? Again, unlikely, as Spinelli would have recognized him. And he was in Milan, unless he had hired help to get the drugs into Spinelli, gain access to his apartment and then write an incriminating final e-mail. But that was real professional stuff, way too far off the scale.

Third scenario, thought Rossi, his pencil blunting fast. *What if it was all a ruse by Spinelli, first to set himself up in order to later get himself off the hook?* It would work like this, Rossi said to his junior detective alter ego: *make sure the e-mails get found via an anonymous tip-off and it looks like it's game over. There's a strong sentimental motive, circumstantial evidence to support it, no cast-iron alibi, and no witnesses to his going to sleep early rather than to the usual bar. Sooner or later the investigators would check his e-mails, but Spinelli goes belt and braces and points the finger at himself with his own poison pen. Then the Rohypnol theory kicks in and throws enough doubt into the equation to theoretically save him.*

What if we cops hadn't come up with it? Well, that would be Spinelli's ace in his sleeve, his alibi. He could have given himself a dose of the stuff, holding off but planning at the last minute to say "hey, look guys, I felt terrible the other night, what if I was drugged and while I was zonked out on the floor someone got into my computer and set me up?" And maybe he'd even left the bar with some MPD groupie, saluting all and sundry to make sure it looked like he hadn't left alone, thus furnishing a nice suspect for the cops to run around after. It was a real gambler's option but it would leave sufficient doubt for him to get away with it and leave the case wide open.

Rossi's head was spinning. It was feeling more and more like science fiction. But he also knew that before the facts could become the facts they could be anywhere and could be anything. Reality wasn't like a film, a book; the plot was unwritten or unwritable. People were being murdered and the chances were that it was by someone they knew. It was a question of probability. The difficulty lay in unravelling the human messes of love, hate, politics, revenge, and ambition, not necessarily in that order, and the technical and logistical framework within which they operated – put simply, space and time. That, and establishing how far someone was prepared and able to go in order to remove another human being from the face of the earth. So what was at stake?

His gut instinct was telling him Spinelli was clean, but experience now suggested that he was up against a formidable array of possibilities and a formidable confederacy of deviants, as well, probably, as some dunces, in his own camp. There was a slew of circumstantial evidence, there was political expediency and the constant, pressing need to get a quick conviction. The tip-off story stunk, too, and combined with the urgency trickling down the chain of command via Maroni, despite himself, he feared history might be repeating itself, that this might be another political case dressed up as common crime. Even if you did never step in the same river twice it was still a river, you still got your feet wet.

So much for the straightforward murder enquiry. So much for keeping Rossi on a case that had nothing to do with the powers-that-be. In substantive terms, Maroni knew no more than he did himself. But Maroni also had to jump when "they" said jump and jump bloody high.

No. The more he mulled it over, and the more he processed what had happened in the space of what, three or four days, or two weeks counting the Colombo killing, the more he began to think that something, some mechanism might have snapped into action. Apart from having a killer on the loose, he was going to be coming up against darker forces than he had expected to be facing. His mobile phone rang again. That would be him.

Nineteen

The atmosphere in the conference room where the journalists were gathered was verging on the festive. Working for state-funded newspapers and TV, if you were on a good contract, was a junket and the lifestyle was easy to get used to. Everyone knew everyone, some better than others, of course. And some – how many? – had got to where they now were by dint not only of their wordsmithery but also in varying degrees thanks to the intimacy of their acquaintances, although the gender balance was, *stile Italiano*, rather more skewed in the predictable direction. Others may have not slept their way to success and though bed-hopping was about par for this course, there were other variations that could be registered on your scorecard too.

The Grand Hotel, being central and within walking distance of Termini station and the underground, had been chosen both to accommodate the revellers and to cater for the expected stampede of local, national, and even foreign correspondents. It provided the necessary space for national TV crews and their entourages as well as for the usual mike-toting local hacks from the galaxy of more or less obscure cable stations.

There was a palpable sense of expectation. All murder enquiries brought out the feeding frenzy instinct and this one was no different. It guaranteed weeks of copy for the crime correspondents, what with the endless speculation, the tawdry spectacle of interviews with victims' families and neighbours and the footage of the crime scene. Then, like some second stage in a feared and now all too real malady, there would be the morbid pilgrimages to murder locations that sometimes ensued when a killing was perpetrated within the community, or, even better, within a family. The apparent randomness and viciousness of these recent crimes had aroused a particularly grim interest and the hacks were fishing now for more juicy details.

Iannelli had arrived early and secured himself a place in the front row. He'd always taken the hard way, fully aware that his choices would condemn him to pursue the slow build, the long haul, yet he didn't have to avoid anyone and his name rarely featured in the gossip over drinks. All the usual faces were there and he'd been careful enough to press the flesh and backslap his way around the room, devoting a few moments of special attention to Luca Iovine of *The Facet*, already pencilled in as his future employer.

But he'd been here since five, and he wasn't the only one beginning to think that if they put back the scheduled start-time again, the jovial atmosphere might turn rather more sour as first aperitifs and then dinner appointments got interfered with and grumbling stomachs and editors' demands began to have undesired effects on tired brains. There was little worse than a projected early finish transforming itself into a protracted all-nighter. One downside to the job then.

There were signs of movement, however, coming from the temporary wings set up to give the conference room its heightened air of police-like institutional drabness. TV crews had just switched on their lights before a row of suited men, some in plain clothes and others in uniform, filed out and took their positions on the podium. They moved at a pontifical pace and with what seemed to be an equally apparent disdain for what constituted urgency in the non-police world. Despite their indifference to the long wait to which the waiting media men and women had been subjected, it was clear that they would not be hanging around either. And if the press wasn't ready, it was their problem. Iannelli scanned the faces, but there was no sign of Rossi.

"I will be brief," said Chief Superintendent Maroni, head of the Rome Serious Crime Squad, at the centre of the seven-man line-up which included the city prefect and two of the three magistrates so far involved. "I think most of you know who I am by now and, well, there have been," he continued, briefly looking down at his notes, "certain developments regarding the recent murders of the two women in Rome and the earlier murder near the Via Cristoforo Colombo, and it is with some cautious optimism that I can say we are pleased," he said turning briefly to survey his colleagues before recommencing, "to be able to confirm that these developments are 'significant'." As he raised his head, there was a wild paroxysm of flash photography and a forest of phone and pen-clutching hands shot up hoping to spear a question-asking opportunity.

At the back of the conference room, Michael Rossi entered through a side door and took up a position where there was still a little space. He had a shaken, ruffled appearance, but despite his still simmering anger he was also quite resigned for he knew exactly what was coming next.

He knew because before leaving the Questura he had already accepted yet another slice of his fate. Nonetheless, he was glad at least to have had some time with Spinelli. It had been crucial. As such, he had taken the call from Maroni, deciding to swallow the toad sooner rather than later. Incandescent, his superior had summoned him to a private room where in no uncertain terms he'd dressed Rossi down, ordered him to steer clear of making any trouble, and told him exactly how things were going to be played out later before the press. Then, true to form, Maroni had half-excused himself for his barbarity before sending Rossi away with instructions to "be late for the conference because you're so fucking busy chasing killers that you can't remember your own name."

"My officers and I would like to thank in particular Inspectors Michael Rossi and Luigi Carrara and their team of investigators, who have been working flat out on this case and have not been able to join us, as yet."

"Well here I am," proffered Rossi, like a madman taunting his other self and anyone else who might hear him, but all eyes were on Maroni.

"My officers and I have been able to reconstruct a significant series of events leading up to the murder of Maria Marini, the details of which will emerge in due course but suffice to say the information we have so far been able to gather has been judged sufficient by the public prosecutor for us to move in the direction of making an arrest in this case with a view to bringing charges."

More hopeful arms were thrust into the air to the accompaniment of rabid camera flashing and clicking but all to no avail as Maroni continued what was turning out to be nothing more than a statement.

"I will not be taking any questions now as there is, as I am sure you can all imagine, much work still to do. If there are any further developments this evening, we will endeavour to inform you forthwith. Thank you and good evening."

And with that they filed out as indifferently as they had when they arrived.

Rossi, moving towards the centre of the melee, had caught Iannelli's eye. The two men exchanged a glance, the import of which they both understood.

"Fancy Arabic?" said Rossi to the journalist now sitting beside him in his car. "We can talk there, it's off the beaten track, don't worry."

"Suits me fine."

Twenty

They found parking easily enough on Via Merulana and walked up the slight incline of the broad flagged pavement in the direction of the Basilica. In January, with Christmas done and dusted, the area saw little human activity and, with the pall of fear over the city, tonight it felt deserted. In winter, from this spot, if you could ignore for a moment the hypnotizing fairy-tale gold mosaics and baroque facade of Santa Maria Maggiore which greeted you, it was possible to see in the distance the sister basilica of San Giovanni by looking over your shoulder down the dead-straight boulevard. When spring came the plane trees would burst into life making the same long road between the two basilicas richly forest-like and mercifully cool, dappling the fierce sun held at bay overhead. But now, in the dark, all was bare and skeletal against the ashen sky.

They slipped into the warmth of Shwarma Station and ordered liberally from the dazzling array of Syrian and North African specialities at much saner prices than some of the more *di moda* kebab joints where conservative Romans went to be cosmopolitan. Stuffed vine leaves, falafel, couscous, hummus, and kebabs. There was no alcohol but they could wait. They took a table under the TV at the back of the room. There were the usual diners:

expatriate Arabs, students, nostalgic types relishing the simplicity of paper table cloths and ordinary people and just a little edge. This was a meeting place, too, for the Islamic community and in the coming and going of Moroccans, Egyptians, Arabs, and Libyans there were, for sure, some less than legitimate characters caught up in the mix. For a good five minutes they ate in silence until they had seen off the first wave of their hunger.

"So, what's new, Dario?"

"Depends what you mean? You mean the local shenanigans or the murder mystery?"

"All right," said Rossi, "if you could give me some firm leads on either score, I'd be buying you dinner next time as well as today, but I'll take whatever's going."

"Well, as far as my theories on the immigration rackets are concerned, I can't get much unless you can secure me those wire taps on a few key individuals."

Rossi shook his head.

"You know that's impossible. No judge will give me the time of day if it's anyone near the top of the tree with connections to high-ranking individuals. They'll laugh me out of town. And for me to take the law into my own hands on this one, well that would be signing my own, I won't say death warrant, but it could be close."

Iannelli had the air of the mad scientist on the verge of the big discovery but thwarted by factors beyond his control. Rossi could almost imagine him screaming at the unbelievers "The fools!"

"I know I'm onto something big there, Michael, big and transversal. Do you follow? Everyone could be involved. Left, right, centre, Church, the co-ops and charities, even ex-terrorists. That's the word I'm getting. We just need those taps and we could do something. Somebody would have to listen then."

Rossi was intrigued but he knew that in these matters the system moved at a speed and in a manner comparable to that of plate tectonics in the earth's crust: vast strategic interests that bordered one another yet only clashed decisively in certain key moments and when perhaps you least expected it. But nothing was likely to move until someone wanted it to move. It had to be at the bidding of some deus ex machina, but not a general saviour, rather some saviour of yet higher interests. Russian dolls. Stories within stories. Yes. *The Arabian Nights*.

"And the murders?" Rossi enquired. "What's out, Dario? I mean, the notes, the suspect? This prick-teasing at the press conference. What's the word on that?"

It was Iannelli's turn now to shake his head.

"Nothing from me, Michael, I'm holding fire, but sooner or later somebody's always going to let something slip. You know that."

"And tip-offs?"

"Nothing."

"But d'you know who they're going to arrest or not?"

"Well, I do have a sneaking suspicion it might be someone close to Ms Marini, if that's what you mean."

"Obviously, but who?"

"Look," said Iannelli, wiping his fingers on a napkin, "I know about the MPD link but until there's an arrest we won't be going with it. 'Police are close to an arrest in The Carpenter case', if you like. Something like that. But you clearly know how close, don't you? Though you don't look exactly tickled by it."

Rossi rolled an olive across his plate with his fork.

"What do you want out of this, Dario? The same as me? To get a killer off the street? Or to have a high-profile show trial that can run for God knows how long? Or do you think there's more here than meets the eye? Do you want it to be more than the sum of its parts? Is that where you think this is going?"

"Michael, isn't it always more than the sum of its parts when there's politics in play?"

"So you think Spinelli is involved?"

"In some way, yes. He has to be."

"But guilty?"

"That remains to be seen. You're the policeman here, aren't you?"

"But no smoke without fire. Is that what you're saying?"

"Look," said Iannelli, "if a high-profile politician's lover is brutally murdered close to the most crucial parliamentary elections in recent Italian history, there has to be something going on. It has to be more than coincidence. And added to that, she just happens to be a judge's daughter, a mafia-pool judge's daughter. Well, what do you think? What does your instinct tell you?"

"I don't think he did it."

"Why not?"

"I have my reasons. It's partly gut-feeling but it just doesn't fit."

"So why are you here talking to me?"

"Because I need your help."

"And do you think I want to help you?"

"I think we have a common goal here, Dario."

"Go on."

"I think we both want to see something finally change, for the better, in this godforsaken country. In this godforsaken political establishment."

"And this is how it's going to change? Chit-chatting over kebabs?"

"They want Spinelli to go down, Dario! They've practically taken the investigation out of my hands, so something has changed here, for sure."

"Who wants him to go down?"

"Well," said Rossi, "I was hoping you might tell me that."

"All right," said Iannelli, throwing his crumpled napkin onto the empty plate and sitting back to deliver his peroration. "Nothing happens by chance. Think Pasolini. Think Pecorelli.

Think Dalla Chiesa. Go right back to Enrico Mattei. All killed because they got too close to the truth, too close to nailing the corrupt politicians, too close to getting the Yanks and their petrodollars out of our economy and off our backs."

"So it's a conspiracy," said Rossi, "and the puppet masters pull the strings we can't even see to cut, never mind get to the guys themselves?"

"Except maybe the game just changed."

"The MPD?" said Rossi.

"The MPD."

"OK," said Rossi. "So how are the old guard going to win their public back now that there's a clean act in town? Copy the new guys?"

"Ignore them, bad mouth them, discredit them, get their media friends to tell the public they're being conned. It's all PR."

"Set them up as murderers, liars, deceivers?"

"Why not? And then tell everyone the state is under attack. But better still, actually insert a few extremists of your own design first. It's that much easier to predict the notoriously unpredictable course of political history if you are actually writing that same history as you go along, don't you think?"

"So the Movement's already been infiltrated, clearly, as a matter of course?"

"Every party is infiltrated and as long as no one in the ranks steps too far out of line then they're free to go on peddling the usual platitudes, feathering their nests, and faking very visible and audible arguments so everyone thinks democracy is in rude good health. Except it's all been wearing a little thin recently, hasn't it?"

"Hence the MPD being on the verge of an historic, totally game-changing victory – if they are to be believed, that is. We've all become so cynical, haven't we?"

"Yes, but they will be stepping out of line. They're really going to shake the tree. And that's when the sleepers'll have to wake up and start doing their thing."

"What about the plans for the Lateran Treaties?"

"What plans?"

"According to Spinelli, the MPD want to put it to a referendum, change the constitution. Marini was working with him on it at the time."

"That's a game changer. That's big. Those treaties have guaranteed the special relationship between Italy and the Vatican since the days of Mussolini. We're talking a lot of reciprocal privileges and a lot of money above all."

"And I didn't tell you, right?"

Iannelli paused for a moment.

"You know there's this theory that Blair was, allegedly, a long-term CIA plant. Picked up at Oxford, set on his way and then, with the help of a pliant media establishment, when Bush and company needed a friend, he was already nicely positioned. Long-term planning. You know there's a photo of him, from his Oxford days, Tony the lad, having a laugh, one of us.

"But what you don't see is that the photo's been cropped-down. What you don't see is that he's giving the wanker sign to the camera. And it never got out. No one ever made it public. And that is power."

Iannelli laughed then continued.

"And everyone's having a go at Russia and China, but here it's more subtle, worse in some ways because so many people just don't realize they're being lied to constantly, systematically, assiduously."

Rossi had heard it all before. It all seemed so plausible, so right, so ecstatically, beautifully and liberatingly spot on but what he needed were facts. Physical, tangible, incontrovertible facts. This was the day job and it brought out the rational-atheist in him, the sceptic who couldn't be doing with the wacky stuff from the other side.

"So you see a narrative here?" he asked.

"I see the powers-that-be, Michael. Give them whatever name you want."

"I just want to know who's killing the women, Dario. They're wives and mothers and I think there could be a message there too, apart from the notes. This mother thing. Sancta Mater Ecclesia."

"And what if he's not this mother-hating serial killer?" Iannelli said, sitting up a little to confront his friend. "What if it's all just a front, a disguise, a way of filling the front pages and removing the thorns in the sides of the interested parties? The TV's going bonkers over all this, at least the private channels. If that's the case, it's not like you're trying to catch a maniac. It's like trying to catch the whole damn system."

"The system!"

"Yeah! The system! Do you still think the Red Brigades were fighting for a Marxist takeover? They could have been hand in glove with the real powers-that-be when they needed a result."

It was getting out of hand. There was always something else behind everything that occurred, some darker cause, some more sinister objective, some hidden hand going right back to the kidnapping and murder of the prime minister Aldo Moro, in 1978, in broad daylight, in the capital city.

Someone had ratcheted up the volume on the TV screen above their heads to hear the latest on a rolling 24-hour news channel. From the pictures they could see that a hastily convened news conference at the Questura was in progress and that an announcement had been made.

"A man has been arrested in connection with the deaths of Paola Gentili and Maria Marini. Police say they are questioning Luca Spinelli, a prominent figure within the MPD and for whom Marini had been working as a legal adviser. Neither representatives of Mr Spinelli nor his wife were available for comment this evening."

Rossi leapt to his feet.

"Right! So the little game's up and running!" he said.

"The MPD murdering adulterer," added Iannelli. "That's why

they delayed it. They wanted it to coincide with the news and all those families sitting down together watching after dinner. Goggle-eyed. Sucking it all in. A crime of passion, of course. Hey, it might win the MPD some votes from the Neanderthals."

"If they can read," said Rossi, stuffing a stray, hummus-smeared falafel into his mouth. "Have to go. Can you get a cab?"

"Sure but it was just getting interesting!"

"Sorry. Thanks for the info and all that."

"Think nothing of it but …"

"Don't worry. I'll keep you in the loop."

"But watch yourself, I was going to say," said Iannelli, to nobody now, for Rossi had gone.

Twenty-One

Rossi headed back to the office hoping to find at least Carrara still there. Maroni wanted them to press ahead with Spinelli. Rossi wouldn't exactly be permanently off the case because, as far as Maroni was concerned, the case was already as good as closed. Just the washing-up to do, although he had at least rung Rossi later to thank him. But from here on in, the public prosecutor would be preparing the case. The Luzi and Gentili murders remained unsolved, however, and Rossi and Carrara were to continue the investigation but Maroni was having none of the serial killer theory. Unrelated. Coincidence. Whatever. And that was that.

From what Rossi had been able to gauge out on the streets and in the bars and restaurants, public opinion was divided between those who saw Spinelli either as the dark architect of all the murders, or just that of his lover, or the MPD patsy being stitched up good and proper. It could go any way. What Rossi did have was the blood test. He hoped Carrara would be able to shed some light on who, if anyone, might have been with Spinelli on the night of the murder. He tried his phone. Engaged. The wife probably. Perhaps tonight he would get to touch base with Yana. He thought for a second about giving her a ring. Later, he decided. She'd be tired after her shift. His phone rang. It was Carrara.

"Gigi."

"Mick, you heard then?"

"Yep. On the TV. Where are you?"

"I'm here," said Carrara. "Maroni told me to take some leave, but I convinced him I had some unfinished business to be getting on with, and besides we're still theoretically working on the other two cases, aren't we? Are you coming over?"

"I'm on my way."

"Have you eaten?"

"Lebanese," Rossi replied.

"*Bastardo.*"

"I'm guessing you haven't then. I'll pick you up some pizza."

The Inquiry Room was semi-deserted although the desks were replete with the innumerable files, papers, and the assorted trappings of the enquiry. Behind them on the wall was the collage of the victims' movements, crime-scene-photos, and hypothesized spider diagrams. Without the hubbub of activity of detectives and uniforms together working flat out on the case the space felt like some school room visited on a weekend, their handiwork a forgotten project, an unfinished epic. It was as if the enthusiasm and buzz that had characterized the place over the previous couple of days had been chloroformed into a sudden forced sleep.

"The Marie Celeste," said Carrara.

"Nothing to be done," Rossi countered. Spoilt for choice, he took a seat at random. "So, what now? Have the tests come through?"

"Maybe tomorrow."

"So late?"

"That was early, according to the geek."

"And your friend?"

"Had to work on other priority tasks. Geek's orders."

"I get it. It's total then, the shutdown?"

"Looks like it."

"Well, there really is 'nothing to be done', tonight, as far as I can see."

"And if the test comes out positive?"

"It means the guy had Rohypnol in his bloodstream on the night of the malicious e-mail and in the early hours of the day on which Marini was murdered. They can suppress it anyway. And what am I going to do? Report it to the police?" Rossi laughed with cynical abandon.

"Go to the papers."

"Yeah, and following a geological timescale the truth may one day emerge, when everyone is dead, retired, forgotten, or all three. You know the way things work here, Gigi: the truth, the news, reality itself; it's a pantomime."

Rossi took a seat and put his feet up.

"And yet we keep on going," reflected a more pensive than usual Carrara. "Even though it seems the state, the state as we perceive it, as it should be, the one we grew up believing in, sometimes doesn't even seem to exist."

"It's precisely because we believe in it, Gigi," said Rossi. "It's like Schweitzer and the Historical Jesus."

"It is?"

"Yeah. You know who Schweitzer was?"

"Um. Heard of him."

Rossi had relaxed a little and was settling in to his teaching persona. It was perhaps his lost vocation.

"Well, around the turn of the last century you had this situation where scholars were sitting down and looking at the sacred scriptures and saying, hang on, this isn't history; it's actually much closer to a fairy tale, a myth – it doesn't add up. Is Jesus anymore real than, say, Hercules? Is our faith no more deeply founded in reality than that of the ancient Greeks and Romans? Anyway, belief was thrown into crisis. So, theologians and archaeologists and whole swathes of the academic community decided that, as they had the means and the methodology to try to find the proof of whether Jesus existed or not, they should set about the task."

Carrara, too, was now enjoying the professorial diversion.

"And they found it, the proof?"

"No. Well, what they found, shall we say, pointed decidedly in the 'Jesus as we know him probably didn't ever exist' direction. Maybe there were two or three Jesus-like characters who got blended together into an idea of Jesus, a sort of composite. Anyway, one after another, theologian after theologian, Schweitzer among them, set off on their quests only to be thwarted when they came up against the inevitable brick wall, a black hole, a dead end. Gaps in the story, a lack of evidence, inconsistencies."

"And that was that?"

"Well, Schweitzer, who was a doctor, hung up his theologian's hat and spent the rest of his days in Africa as a missionary, helping the poor, the oppressed and the sick, building hospitals and living the gospel rather than trying to prove it."

"So, the moral of the story is?"

"The moral of this story is that even if 'He' didn't exist, even if we can't prove that 'He' walked this same earth and performed the miracles we attribute to 'Him', it's the message that lives. And the same could be said to go for the state. It's the message that drives you on, the idea, the principle, if you like. Even if you look around and you can only see shadows, even if you run into brick walls, up blind alleys, dead ends. You've got to live the gospel."

Carrara leant back and let out a whoosh of a sigh.

"That's pretty deep, Mick, for eleven o'clock in the evening. Correct me if I'm wrong but did I hear you mention at some point the quest for the historical bottle of Jameson's Whiskey? It does exist, doesn't it?"

"That will be the bottom drawer, I do believe."

Rossi had poured a first generous glass for each of them when his desk phone rang. They let it ring out as they took their first sips. Then it rang again.

"I suppose I'd better answer that," said Rossi, getting up to cover the ten or so paces to his desk. Carrara nodded slowly and sagely, savouring the gleaming gold liquid. He had his feet on a chair and, to an observer, could have appeared to be ruminating some finer point of their discussion.

"Inspector Michael Rossi?"

"Speaking."

"This is St John's Hospital."

"Yes," said Rossi, anticipating more unwelcome procedural boredom. "How can I help?"

"Could you confirm your relationship with Ms Yana Shulyayev."

"My 'relationship'?"

"Yes, your relationship, Inspector Rossi. Please, try not to be too alarmed but this evening Ms Shulyayev was admitted to hospital and documents in her possession indicated you as next of kin along with her daughter, whom we have not been able to reach."

Rossi almost let the glass slip from his hand then attempted to steady himself against the desk, his thoughts now rapid, confused.

"Her daughter! Can you tell me what has happened?"

"Ms Shulyayev is in a stable but critical condition, Inspector. She was violently assaulted near her home. She has serious cranial and vertebral trauma. But it would be better if you came to the hospital where we can explain. Inspector Rossi? Inspector Rossi?"

But Rossi wasn't listening now. He was back firmly on his feet and surging through the Incident Room.

"Come on! It's Yana! He's tried to kill Yana!"

As the car screeched away from the Questura, the two friends and colleagues had snapped into character and like seasoned performers taking the stage or players confronting the maelstrom of a hostile stadium they plunged back into the cold Roman night.

Twenty-Two

When Rossi and Carrara burst through the doors there was an added hive of activity to complement the usual chaos that epitomized the busy central Roman hospital. Black-uniformed carabinieri dominated the scene and some of Maroni's closer plain-clothes RSCS confidantes were there too and involved in tense exchanges with exponents of the rival law enforcement organizations. A quick calculation told him the local police must have been first on the case, a possible explanation for his not being informed by them but rather by the hospital authorities. At least he hoped that was the reason.

Cut to the chase, thought Rossi, and bypassing the scrum, he headed to the information desk where a white-coated nurse was fielding enquiries at cruising speed and with undisguised indifference. Rossi placed his badge on the desk in front of her.

"Inspector Michael Rossi, next of kin of Yana Shulyayev, admitted this evening. I want to know what's going on!"

His tone was terse enough to jolt the nurse-receptionist into giving him her sudden full attention.

"One moment, please, Inspector." She turned to pick up a phone into which she uttered three magic words.

"Inspector Rossi. Yes."

At the rear of the front office a door then opened and a male colleague appeared and, in a business-class tone, asked Rossi to follow him.

"Gigi," Rossi hissed over the heads of the mob, "wait here, and keep your eyes and ears open for anything and everything."

His heart was pounding now. The clinical disturbed him. He wanted some emotion, some sign, but knew that this was how it had to be. The white-smocked orderly glanced at a clipboard and stroked his unshaven chin, then with a hirsute outstretched arm, showed Rossi into an office where a silver-haired doctor sat behind a spartan grey metal desk. The door closed. Rossi, on the second invitation, took a seat. He was beside himself: *why couldn't he see her immediately*? What seemed like a hundred questions were ready to leave his lips while in his head there were another hundred *what ifs* and *whys* and *hows* and *when or if would he see her again*? Other, sane voices were telling him she was alive. She was critical but stable. But until he knew where she was, until he could see her, touch her, he was hostage to his own guilt and the terror of losing everything he had.

"Inspector Rossi," he began, "I am Professor Renzi, the consultant on intensive care." Then, exhaling, as if trying to expel at least a part of the accumulated years of procedural ennui, he scanned the papers in front of him. He looked then at Rossi. "As you will know, Yana was admitted this evening after being attacked and receiving serious head injuries as a result of a series of blows delivered to the skull, neck, and forearms. She has fractures to the radius and ulna of her," he looked again at the papers, "left arm, which would seem, in part, to have mitigated the force of at least one of the blows." He paused and dwelled again on the paperwork before him before closing the Manila folder. "I do not, at this juncture, believe that her life is in immediate danger but she was unconscious at the time she was admitted and we now have to wait and see when she will regain consciousness. In some cases, coma can be induced, pharmacologically, to limit the risk of damage, to the vertebra and such like. In this case we hope also that the possible damage to her brain has been minimal."

Rossi allowed himself to release a degree of the tension his terror was putting him through. It was as if the doctor's matter-of-fact reassurance allowed him to make a half-turn on some impossible-to-define scale, the limits of which he could not know.

"We also measured photosensitive response to which there was a positive reaction. Her irises are not permanently dilated. We work on a scale from 1–15, the lowest number being a very slim chance of survival while the highest represents a normal person, like you or I. Values in this case would appear to be nearer to the upper range."

"Can I see her?" said Rossi. "I want to see her."

"Of course, but we do intend to operate at the earliest possible opportunity, if the scans currently being carried out reveal any bleeds which could compromise her recovery."

She was alive then. She would live. He would accept anything so long as she lived.

"And by head injuries, you said head injuries. What exactly do you mean?"

"In layman's terms, a fractured skull and severe trauma to the vertebrae but, I should add, Inspector, that given the very violent nature of the assault, Yana is somewhat lucky to be alive."

There was a pause as both men, for differing reasons, couldn't but begin to reflect on how they had become real players in the drama being lived out in their city. Rossi was as certain as he could be that the killer had attacked Yana because of him. This could be no coincidence, not in a city of five million souls. But the why and the how had passed into a distant second place for now.

"And what are her chances of recovery?" said Rossi, fearing the very words as he feared only death itself and knowing that her survival could be temporary, a cruel trick of fate, raising his hopes first before dashing them, perhaps to the sadistic satisfaction of her would-be killer.

"Time, Inspector. The only definite answer I can give you is that time will tell. The earlier she begins to react the better. But that is statistical. We base our knowledge on the statistics and the literature. It is not an exact science and in the area of neurology, quite frankly, we still know very little. I see she is very fit, a strong lady, and relatively young. All points in her favour, which could speed a possible recovery. But as I say, it is a matter of time and patience."

The consultant stood up and walked to the door. As he opened it, holding it and turning slightly then beckoning to Rossi to accompany him, the lapels of his white coat flexed slightly to reveal a fine-quality tweed jacket. Rossi had already noted the immaculately fastened tie and in that instant the additional detail of the jacket had, for some reason, produced a reassuring, soothing effect on him. It was epiphanic, chiming perhaps with some echo, maybe of that same style his own father had preferred but which he himself, so far in his life, had largely eschewed. So far. The doctor was waiting. Rossi pushed back his chair. Childlike, vulnerable, a shell of himself, he followed.

Making his way on foot in a near-aimless, meandering fashion in the approximate direction of his flat, the image of Yana in that cold, technical, and yet scrupulously safe environment was a stubborn paradox he couldn't erase from his mind's eye. The plastic tubes, the pulse monitor around her finger like the ring he had not yet seen fit to give her, the strange hotel that was a hospital room. All vied for his attention and conspired to mock the ease with which he was now walking and breathing and going about his own life on earth. But it felt like half a life, less than half a life if it were to be without her. Where was she now? Suspended between this world and the other? Or nowhere? Or was she fully there but trapped as if behind some screen or in a vault the key to which was lost, or broken, or had never even been cut? He sank down on his haunches to gather himself, a dizziness and a coldness sweeping over him. Passers-by looked but walked on. With an effort he got back on his feet and took a drink from a nearby fountain.

He'd left the hospital on the consultant's advice that he "get some rest", like in the films, and with Maroni's "orders" that he take indefinite leave still ringing in his ears. He hadn't even had the strength to put the more obvious questions to him about why he hadn't been informed sooner, this story out of the blue about a daughter, whether there had been any leads on the assailant, any witnesses. He had acquiesced and now, clearly in shock, he was wandering across a Piazza San Giovanni peopled by only a few stubborn, coated couples perched on the pocked marble benches, or an unfortunate figure or two sheltering in the lee of the towering white basilica's facade. A screech of brakes and a voluble litany of swear words jolted him to his senses as a taxi froze inches short of catapulting him over the square's bronze statue of Saint Francis and into the public gardens behind.

"Aoooh! *Ma ke katza sta' a fffa! Crre-tiiinoo!*"

A stunned Rossi, feeling more lucid again thanks to the outburst, put his hands on the bonnet as if about to push the vehicle back up the hill and glared through the windscreen. His stare must have been manic for the taxi driver was instantly silenced. Rossi reached into his jacket and produced his badge, stood up, opened a door and then got into the back of the stationary cab. He proceeded to dictate an address to the now cowed and obsequious recipient of his cold rage, telling him to put his foot down, unless of course he wanted to end up a squeegee merchant in his next professional incarnation. He was in pieces, he felt alien and out of his own mind but he was getting back on track. He was going to Yana's place and before anyone else got there first.

Twenty-Three

One thing was being a cop and rifling through people's most intimate possessions and another thing was doing the same with the person you shared a bed with. Where to begin? The flat was in order, as usual, not least because he hadn't seen much of it in the last few days. The phone was flashing with an incoming message. He managed to navigate the menu's commands and listen, but it was in Russian. A woman's voice. Or was it a girl? Could be anyone. He sat down in the kitchen and looked around. What was he searching for? The secrets she had kept from him? Well, why didn't she tell him she had a daughter and what bearing, if any, might it have had on the attack? He had an idea where she kept her most intimate, private things but had no stomach to start rummaging through her memories, a part of her soul. Not now. Not like this. But if it produced a lead? Something to bring this maniac at least into range?

He stood up, walked the few paces to the drinks cabinet and pulled out the first part of the answer to his questions and with it half-filled the closest thing to a whiskey glass he could find. Adding a splash of water straight from the tap, he sank into the sofa and drank it down in two quick draughts. Good. Better. The taste was irrelevant, the effect almost instantaneous, but it had to battle hard with the demons the night had now unleashed. He went back and filled the glass again. Other demons now surfaced. He felt them gathering like wraiths from the past.

The murky world from which he had helped her to escape was part of a previous life about which he knew many things but not everything. For her sake, he had put aside numerous questions he could have asked, not wanting her to have to revisit memories perhaps best left forgotten. But now he felt they were looming again like the shadows cast by things he needed to know more about. Like betrayals forgiven but not forgotten, they were gnawing at the fabric of his innermost thoughts.

Or could it, as he had first thought, all be directed against him? Unless that was his own selfish ego getting the upper hand when he should have been thinking about her and only her. He picked up a framed photo from one of the shelves. The two of them on holiday, in a bright, alien light, both slim, smiling, relaxed. It was only from a few years before but how much younger they looked. Yes, time passed, it fled. He remembered the consultant's words. *Time will tell.* But was the past now catching up with him? Somebody he had put away? In his position, it was always on the cards, no matter what you did. People soon got out and, in Italy, if they ever went inside, they were out even quicker.

He began opening drawers and cupboards. Some were locked. The others were filled with the usual bundles of paperwork one was, by law, forced to accumulate. In the bedroom there were little chests of drawers with jewellery and nick-knacks, a stopped watch, a sea-shell from a place he couldn't quite remember. In the wardrobe he delved deep into hampers of rolled up stockings and underwear. Another time, he might have lingered over the slick fabrics, the lightly grazing gauzes and lace trims, but now he searched. There were boxes inside boxes, medicines, a travel hair-dryer, and a shoebox closed with a length of yellow ribbon. He undid it and lifted the lid. Letters, perhaps a hundred letters, folded and tied into bundles and all in Russian. Get them all translated? And maybe they'd tell him nothing.

But there could still be some useful information that had never come to light when Yana had escaped from the hell she'd been living all those years ago. But, now, as then, he wanted to protect her and that had been the price to pay. Maybe he had allowed love to get in the way of procedure, sacrificing for Yana's sake the freedom and even the lives of other unknown girls. Perhaps some poor soul chained to a radiator in a dank Roman cellar, living as a sex-slave, or others being shipped across the continent still believing their dreams of becoming dancers or actresses were going to come true.

Rossi knew he had saved many and he had rightly been praised for doing so but the snakehead had evaded him. He knew Yana might have been able to tell them more but he'd held back, to spare her. He'd also been boxing shadows because someone higher in the chain of command was in it up to his neck and the mafias always got their cut too. Or they ran arms and drugs operations on the same guaranteed routes. The silk-road, they called it, because it was so profitable and so smoothly run. Then there were the officials pocketing bribes and turning blind eyes first to the trafficking from Eastern Europe and then from the Middle East and Africa.

Rossi closed the box. He was shaking, sweating, his mind was racing out of control. It must have been the post-trauma stress catching up with him and which the alcohol had set free. He shoved back the drawer as if trying to cauterize the source of his mania. This grand theorizing over plots and conspiracies was clouding his judgement, making him cynical, yet his instinct was telling him that the plot had thickened. His father had always said to look out for instinct and then to nurture it. It was some-thing like inspiration, he used to say, not a thing to be forced. But you also had to let negativity and frustration run their course until you got to the end of what seemed a dark and endless tunnel. Then, even before you saw the light, you might begin to feel a little difference in the air, a freshness, a breath.

He sat down on the crisply made bed. Thinking of plots and Iannelli's theories had set him thinking, too, about the other side of the case and that Spinelli now had to be in the clear. If the attacker was still on the loose it seemed the only plausible conclusion to reach. And then there were the lab tests on the Rohypnol theory. He'd have to get in touch with Carrara. A dart of panic struck again as he realized he'd clean forgotten about his colleague. He reached for his phone then stopped. He was off the case! He didn't have to radio in and, despite the force of his hardwired habits, he allowed himself, obliged himself, to stop.

He'd take the night off. A night off from himself. He could stay here, send out for a takeaway. Or maybe it was better to go out and be with people and for a fraction of a second his mind tricked him into thinking of calling Yana. He finished the whiskey and walked back through the flat to the lounge. He flicked on the TV. The usual rubbish. He ploughed through the channels in search of something if not decent, watchable, but it was even later than he'd thought. Hospitals could devour time as much as police work. So, too late for takeaway. Unlike London and New York, Rome was, perhaps sensibly, a city that slept.

He went into the kitchen and opened the fridge, his stomach giving tentative indications of need though he had no mental appetite. There was an end of salami, some olives, a jar of gherkins, a couple of pieces of cheese. He opened up cupboards. A half bottle of Montepulciano. Not the best but it would help to get it down. Then, as if he and everything he touched weighed heavier than concrete, he put a pot of water on the stove and fried a little garlic in olive oil. He switched on the 24-hour news channel for company and while the pasta was cooking he snacked on salami and drank the smooth, rich wine. When the pasta was done, he tossed it into the frying pan and added a generous dose of dried chilli and a grating of pecorino cheese. *Pasta agl'oglio*, al Rossi.

He topped up his glass and plonked himself onto the couch for a TV dinner. On RAI 5 a documentary was about to begin. Rory Gallagher. He was almost too exhausted now to worry. Still it was only with an effort of will that he allowed himself to actually rest and after a bout of mental wrestling and yet more replaying of what had happened, what he could have done to avoid it, what he was going to do next, and the life that lay ahead of him, he allowed himself the one simple mercy of not thinking anymore about anything. He turned the volume up as high as he could as Rory's Telecaster blues kicked in. Well, like a bad penny you've … turned up again. But for Rossi the penny was yet to drop.

Twenty-Four

True to form, Carrara had been hoovering up info and following leads with the natural diligence for which Rossi valued him so highly, his sweeper, his very own Franco Baresi. Rossi himself had woken up a little late but feeling the better for a few hours of decent sleep. He had slept on the couch until waking with a start at 3 a.m., decamping then to the bedroom. His head was not giving him any particular trouble and he took a bracing hot and cold shower then tidied himself up as best he could. He would soon make the short trip to the hospital, and getting his thoughts in order in that respect was the more difficult undertaking.

When he phoned, Carrara, ever courteous, had first enquired about Yana before moving on to the case. Again, there were no witnesses. Yana, it seemed, had her reflexes and self-defence skills to thank, managing to deflect the blows sufficiently to save her life until something unknown caused her assailant to flee. But Carrara had kept the most interesting news till last.

"Another note?" said Rossi.

"Found at the Marini scene. It was under a car some distance from the body. Possibly dropped in the confusion, if it was a rushed job, which is what it seems to have been. It was picked up after we'd left the garage."

"Could be a fake, a hoaxer."

"It looks consistent with the other notes."

"Have you seen it?"

"Maroni's got it. I managed to extract the info out of one of my lads on his team. Seems he wanted to keep it to himself."

"And?" said Rossi.

"And what?"

"What does it say?"

Carrara cleared his throat.

"English, again."

Then, as if reading from his notes,

"'Damn you rotters! I'll be the last!'"

"That's it?"

"That's it."

Rossi turned the phrase over in his mind, scanning for clues. The last. A shoemaker's last, a sort of anvil? Something to do with the hammer, the murder weapon. A trade perhaps? And the rotters? Putrefaction? Decay? He was looking for a way in but he also knew he was rushing at it, like a novice, and he didn't want to fall for the any-port-in-a-storm solution. Besides, a note always had to be taken with a pinch of salt.

"How's work going on the psychological profile?" Rossi asked.

"Fairly standard fare, Mick."

No. He'd get on to that himself later. After the hospital. After he'd decided what to do about the other issue.

"Mick, are you there?"

Carrara's voice from far-off jolted Rossi back to attention.

"Thinking, Gigi. Just thinking."

Rossi could tell from the tone that there was more.

"Is there anything else, Gigi?" he enquired, steeling himself for a blow of probably medium to high intensity.

"Ah, yes. The tests. The Rohypnol."

"Go on. Don't tell me it's negative."

"Worse, actually."

114

"How worse?"

"Disappeared worse."

"Disappeared!"

"The sample's gone walkabout. No-one knows where. A 'bureaucratic mix-up', apparently. Could be days, could be weeks as things have been farmed out to private labs here there and everywhere."

Rossi let out a deep sigh. He knew it! They were scuppering the investigation at every turn now, or at least stalling it, just to keep Spinelli in. It wasn't the first time that key evidence had been tampered with or "accidentally contaminated" or had vanished from the face of the earth.

"Sorry to be the bearer of bad tidings and all that," said Carrara, as crestfallen as Rossi to see the inexorable unravelling of what they had considered a tight operation. Their operation.

"We're going to need extra help on this one, Gigi," said Rossi. "The odds are stacking up against us. Have you got any ideas?"

"An early lunch?" Carrara replied.

Rossi glanced at his watch. There was time to see Yana in the morning and go through some more case files.

"Where?"

"At Rosario's."

"Can I bring a friend?" Rossi enquired.

"If you can find one."

Rossi almost laughed for the first time in he didn't know how long.

"I'll start looking," he said. "After all, I've got nothing else to do, have I?"

"That's the spirit," said Carrara. "Chin up. *Corraggio*, eh?"

Courage, thought Rossi, steeling himself now as his journey to the hospital neared. He was going to need it and in spades.

He checked his watch. 2.20 p.m. Crowds spewed out of the Metro stop and onto the pavement, colliding with one another as they got lungfuls of relatively fresh air and tried to get their bearings having found themselves suddenly face-to-face with one of the wonders of the ancient world. That and a cacophonous din of the Roman traffic zipping up and down along the Foro Imperiali, with single-decker buses jockeying for position as the homeward-wending locals tried to secure a seat in the customary scrum around the doors. The traffic police had taken over where the lights had for some reason gone haywire and Fulvio Mirante, carabiniere on security detail, tried his best to marshal the sheep-like hordes of tourists out of harm's way and towards safety as yet another contingent headed in the opposite direction down into the station. A few more signs in English might have made things easier, he reflected, as the tourists stumbled along the labyrinthine passageways or battled with the ticket machines and the pickpockets loitering and also keen to get in on the act.

He made a quick call on his radio. "Group of thieves heading down your way. Head 'em off at the pass, will you?" They were professionals, kids, no more than ten or eleven and trained by their Fagin-like guardians to gather maximum returns on this most profitable stretch of the tourist trail. The Colosseum metro stop was a must for anyone on a sightseeing trip and arriving on their first or second days, their wallets were bulging as their eyes gorged on the wonders to behold. The wise tucked their valuables in money belts inside zipped hideaways, but there were always enough with the devil-may-care attitude of the naive to keep it a happy hunting ground. Fulvio checked his watch. It had been a hard shift and he had been busy already dealing with a dispute between some tourists and travelling salesmen over the price of a selfie-stick that had ended up with their coming to blows.

The crowd ebbed and flowed as he kept his eyes peeled and his radio at the ready. His brief was to maintain a presence, for what it was worth, given the growing fears regarding the security situation. It puts people's minds at rest, they said, to see a uniform. It's psychological. So he was here to make people feel better, rather than putting his detective skills to work on finding this killer. That was all on hold, for now, though. Despite his having eased through the preliminary tests and examinations, his superior had passed on the news that the next stage was temporarily – he hoped – on ice. Cuts, redeployment, jargon, you name it. So promotion was going to have to wait for now. His wife had been philosophical, consoling, as always. Your time will come, Fulvio. Every dog has its day. You'll be running the place before too long. He smiled to himself as tourists gorged on overpriced takeaway pizza and he wondered what he might have for his own now rather late lunch.

Another sightseer bearing a large, poorly folded street map resembling some sort of oversized origami and wearing shades and a baseball cap was weaving his way towards him through the crowd. What did they say? Ask a policeman if you get lost. Well, here he was, the detective-quality tourist guide. "Yes sir," he began, professional as ever, as the tall stranger neared, seemingly engrossed now in the map, before looking up, pulling out a gun complete with silencer and blowing a hole through the historic centre. Then, as Fulvio crumpled to the ground, his assailant stood over him and followed up with two more shots to the chest to finish the job.

Twenty-Five

There had been no change in Yana's condition. Neither better nor worse. He talked to her, trying to steer clear of the case but it was difficult now she was such an intrinsic part of it, of his world. At least they had posted a 24-hour armed guard on the door. He wondered again about her daughter and why she had never told him. He tried, with the aid of hindsight, to piece together parts of the puzzle, but it didn't make things any clearer. Would the girl show up? Interpol had put out an appeal for her to come forward. They had nothing to go on other than a name – Anya – and an old address, presumably that of her adoptive parents, yet it had all drawn a blank so far. Progress was slow, in such cases, even with good information. Yana's mother and stepfather, not possessing even a telephone, had not been reached. Rossi knew, however, that since Yana had left, they had consigned her fate to destiny and the intercession of the icons her mother venerated in their home deep in the wooded Ukrainian wilderness. At least that was the picture Yana had always painted for him.

Lunch with Carrara, though excellent, had been a muted affair. Everything was on hold and they were both letting the frustration get to them. They agreed to keep each other informed of any developments, but neither could see how they were going to make a breach. They went over it again. There were no witnesses, no murder weapon found, no reliable forensic matches with known criminals, and only the most circumstantial of motives attached to suspects, at least in the case of Marini. But they agreed that the attack on Yana had to be a clear message for Rossi. It could have been anyone, considering all the people he'd put away, but ploughing through the records to jog a memory would be another all-nighter, another coffee-fuelled slog that might then come to naught.

After lunch, Rossi had done some essential shopping partly to stop himself from mulling over the case, despite being on leave, before then driving back to the hospital for afternoon visiting hours. The traffic had been insane, again, and he had heard even more sirens than usual coming from all directions and converging on somewhere near the centre and a helicopter circling too. Instinct had kicked in. For once, though, he had decided to let it pass. I'm off duty, he had told himself. I've got enough on my plate.

The doctors had suggested he might profitably read to Yana, so he had done that too. It was something to pass the time for him but, as far as he could see, it had no discernible effect on her. He had stopped, put the book down and closed his eyes for a few minutes.

He woke with a start. He must have dropped off. He looked up, it was getting gloomy outside, competing with the gloom he was nurturing inside, but which was turning more and more to anger. He sat there for a few moments in silence as her bed-bound form dissolved into the invading darkness. He reached out to turn on a light. If only it were so easy. Then, after kissing her dry, motion-less lips, he took his leave once more.

Then, on what he told himself was a whim, but which owed more to his not really knowing what to do with himself, he decided to drop in at the office. He slipped in through a secondary entrance to keep contact to a minimum but still encountered a familiar if not welcome face.

"And what brings you here, Rossi?"

It was Silvestre, loitering with intent.

"Thought you'd been seconded to ClearTech," Rossi replied.

"Oh, just tying up some loose ends. Traffic violations and the like."

"Me too," replied Rossi. "Funny that, isn't it?"

Satisfied with the opacity of his retort he left Silvestre scratching his scrawny chin and none the wiser before climbing the couple of flights of steps to the Incident Room and his office. What he wanted was to lift some old case files without anyone in either Silvestre's or Maroni's area knowing about it. As he pushed through the swing doors at the far end of the room he then wished he hadn't bothered.

What the hell was going on? Everyone who was anyone was on a war footing and swearing blue murder. What was he doing here? So he must have heard. He hadn't? They'd shot a carabinieri near the Colosseum. Who? No idea. *Un pazzo*. A madman. Melted into the crowds. Point-blank, in the face too, and no apparent motive. Only had to go and shoot a guy who's got a wife and kids too, just for good measure. *Bastardo*. When they got him he was going to pay. They'd rip him apart.

Rossi felt numb, tired, and confused. One thing he was sure of was that he was relieved not to have to add this to his to-do list. Shouldn't he have been feeling what they were feeling? A colleague gunned down on the street in cold blood. But none of it was registering. He managed to ghost through to his office and pick up what he'd been looking for. He slipped away by a back exit, unseen this time, and headed to Yana's. After an uninspired attempt at dining, he set about trying to finish his investigations into her affairs then spent the rest of the evening revisiting the villains of his past. They were legion and it was no pleasant trip down memory lane.

After some hours, feeling jaded and none the wiser, he threw the last file onto the pile. He left the flat to stretch his legs and pick up essential groceries, the bare bones. When he returned, he made himself a cup of tea and watched the first news of the evening. Halfway through, when the merry-go-round of political name-calling and faked animosity had become intolerable, he switched it off. He began stalking the flat to and fro, plotting his revenge, fantasizing what he would do when he finally faced the scum who had tried to kill Yana. It was then that he noticed the newspapers he had bought just a couple of days before. They had been folded neatly – presumably by Yana or her cleaner – and placed under the coffee table. He hadn't even opened them.

Hungry for a change of scene and perspective he started with *Le Monde* but found it heavy going and cast it aside before switching to *El País*. He scanned the sports pages, the culture section, then politics and world news. More of the same. Crime, deceit, and degeneracy. There was a short article about Rome's serial killer. It seemed like old news now. He was just about to toss it to one side when another small article in a column of the crime news section caught his eye.

No arrests yet in Bueu murder case.

It was the unusual name that first aroused his curiosity. As he read, however, he realized that it wasn't an unfamiliar word but rather a remote, otherwise anonymous coastal town in Galicia, in the north-west of Spain. A woman, a mother of two, had been murdered there almost a month previously. It bore the hallmarks of a botched burglary, probably by a drug addict. No longer news for Spanish readers familiar with the case, the article unspooled its key details in reverse. It was only as he neared the end of the piece that it revealed to him that the case had aroused interest also due to the victim's having lived for many years prior to her death under an assumed name. The article gave that name, which, to Rossi, meant nothing, and then gave her real name, age, and other particulars. Incredulous, at first, his eyes read and re-read the stark reality of the printed letters. He put the paper down. It was reading these last details that now allowed him to confirm beyond any doubt that it was his own past that was hurtling back like a train to haunt him. He felt his blood run cold.

Twenty-Six

"Troubles come not as single spies but in battalions." Rossi sat in the dim light of a reading lamp, *The Complete Works of Shakespeare* open on his knee. He couldn't even contemplate trying to sleep and had reached for the volume to divert his thoughts from his own helplessness and to perhaps find some small crumbs of comfort. He felt more alone than perhaps he had ever felt. The discovery had left him reeling. He'd done some Internet research and found more details of this new conundrum in the local Spanish papers. He had then tried to get some sleep but had woken as if it were daytime already, yet it was only four in the morning. The worst time of the night to be alone. He thought of a Szymborska poem. Yes, she had known exactly what that bleakness meant.

Unless for some bizarre coincidence, Rosa Garcia, the woman murdered in Spain, had been his first real adult love. Adult love? He'd been in his early twenties, independent, with his own ideas clear in his mind, free to choose, but adult? Perhaps not. Anyway, the love had been passionate and troubled, almost consuming him. And in the end it was he who had abandoned it. He had made the hard choice and with time had moved on and forgotten. He had chosen to live his own life, despite her protests, her emotional blackmail, her begging him to give her time, time, always time. For it had not been a simple affair of the heart but rather a complex play between him, her, and another. And now? Bury it? Definitively? Now there could be no going back. There was no going back. There never had been. But this ending was worse than tragedy.

She must, he supposed, have shaken off her toxic attachment to "him" and got free of her own demons and then found some happiness and built a family with someone else. That, at least, was a glimmer of joy. She must have passed some years in relative peace. That, at least, he hoped but the more he thought about it the more he wanted confirmation. He needed to put his mind at ease. He needed to know that his abandoning her, his breaking the circle then, had been right not only for him but for her too. As for the other, for *him*, he could never ever have envisaged any other plausible future but complete and utter perdition.

He opened a French window and stepped out onto the balcony. Not a soul. In another hour or so the first commercial vehicles would begin to appear, unloading their goods in the comforting light of the street lamps. The cold was penetrating again and the clear sky seemed to have sucked any heat that there was far out into space. He thought then of Yana, across the city, and wondered if she was thinking of him. He felt himself being pulled in three different directions: to Yana, to his own past, and to the case. Yes, the case. He had to get back on it if he wanted to keep his sanity. So much for just doing the washing-up. He decided to try to get some sleep. He would need it. He closed the window and lowered the shutters against an unwelcome dawn. Somewhere out there their killer would be getting ready, waiting to strike again.

PART II

Twenty-Seven

Late again. Cinzia Borghetti pulled the door closed behind her and, fumbling for her keys, dropped them as the lift she had been hoping to catch, departed towards the top floor. More lost minutes. Why life had to be like this she didn't know. She pressed the button. Nothing. She took the stairs down and stepped out through the main door and on to the street.

The morning was chill but she liked it that way. She loosened her blouse a little, opened another button to feel the cold air on her neck and chest. It was liberating, refreshing after the pressure and the stress of the flat. A teenage daughter and a teenage husband, she said to herself. She didn't know which was worse sometimes and if there was ever a morning without an argument it would be a miracle. Why Giulia had to dress like that she did not know. She was rebelling, had to be different, but it hadn't been like that in her day. Back then she'd had to fight tooth and nail to be like the other girls: first, just to wear jeans, and then to go out late, and stay out late, all the time with her father practically calling her a common whore. The protective type, they said. Too much though and too oppressive and her own mother passive and subjugated until the day he died. They had been different times, to say the least. And now Giulia wanted to cover up, dress all in black. What was she? A goth or something?

Work was a release from all that. The salary was important but if she had been paid half she probably would still have done it. She had her friends there, shared interests, her own desk and computer. Freedom – in a word. There was no way she was going to spend the best years of her life dusting and cleaning and cooking and killing the time till the family came home. She cooked when she enjoyed it. The cleaner did the donkey work and she dedicated herself to the more creative side of things.

She passed one of her favourite shops. Closing down sale. Everything must go. She stopped. Not another one. Was this economic crisis ever going to stop? But it wasn't going to spoil her day. The sun was just beginning to illuminate the clouds behind the church. A few bright rays lit up her breath, billowing now before her as she turned into the alleyway to take the short cut for the station. She glanced at her watch. OK. It was quiet she thought, only her, but then from the car park at the other end of the narrow, fenced lane, a figure approached – head down, a council worker, she presumed. The sun was gone, the cold felt less friendly now. She looked up and saw what she and every woman in the city most feared. A hammer hung from his hand. And yes, he had his work to do.

Leaving a hospital could only really mean something when you knew you weren't destined to return any time in the near future, Rossi reflected. Thus, he wasn't leaving at all; he was simply stretching an invisible chord that tied him to it, like Yana herself was rigged up to the machines and tubes, manacled by the unseen forces of … of … what? Destiny? Chance? Science? The morning visit. The afternoon visit. The evening visit. This was the routine that kept him busy and focused now that he was "temporarily relieved of his duties". He stopped. *Where was he*? He'd got himself lost again.

"Nurse."

"Yes?"

"Excuse me. The way out?"

In the fresh air, once he'd left behind the dressing-gowned, catheter-accoutred gaggle of smokers clogging the entrance, he took up his train of thought once more. Could science and medicine bring her out from where she was? He had always been thankful for progress and its contribution to the welfare of humankind. That nature should not always be allowed to take its course alleviated much suffering and saved many lives. But now? If she remained in this way should nature then be allowed to run its natural course, or was he bound to honour the bond, thus making them slaves to that same science?

The consultant could give him little news either way. They had reduced the sedation necessary to minimize damage to the brain and now it was a question of waiting to see if the body would "respond", "wake up" in the popular, misguided (so he'd been told) language often bandied about as clinical terminology. Forensic reports from the scene of Yana's attempted murder had brought little of significance. They had checked her clothes, too, for fibres or organics, but working as she did in a health and fitness centre, she'd picked up hairs of varying lengths and almost all probably female. A DNA check on the database was out of the question at this stage and Maroni had told him so. Cost, time, and nothing hard and fast to go on. They would need more and given that Maroni had already ordered him off investigations until he was in a better state, his pressing was not doing him any favours.

But Spain, too, was nagging at Rossi. The police were looking for her husband of some fifteen years. Rossi had cross-checked everything with the Interpol reports punctually brought to his attention, discovering that he had disappeared around the time of the murder and, in the absence of any other clear motive, had assumed prime suspect status. At a police level, Rossi knew it was nothing to do with him now but he wanted to know. Perhaps he could go there and feel a bit more useful. He was still off the case, whatever the case now was, and on compassionate leave but he was tearing himself up about the rights and wrongs of it all. What if there was a change in Yana's condition? And the notes, and Spinelli in custody awaiting trial for a murder Rossi was now sure he hadn't committed. But he couldn't be kicking around the house, walking the streets, not with so many questions unanswered. He'd speak to Maroni again. Best thing to do. And he might just be able to get him to have a change of mind. He was only another cop after all.

Twenty-Eight

Well, things were definitely looking up. Dario Iannelli got to his feet as Iovine introduced him to the rest of the editorial board of *The Facet*. The call had come out of the blue the morning after the press conference. Could he start tomorrow? He'd resigned his post at the *Roman Post* on the spot and in the ensuing bust-up with Torrini they had almost come to blows. Technically, he was still serving out his notice but in a temporary, unofficial capacity, *The Facet* was now already his home and it felt good. The meeting and greeting was a pleasant formality as he already knew all but a handful of the gathered journalists. They were preparing to stream their editorial meeting, as was now customary, quite unlike the other dailies, and Pietro, the technician, was making a few adjustments to the cameras and equipment.

How refreshing it was to be here. His long-held but besieged idealism had received a welcome shot in the arm and he was buzzing now with enthusiasm. No more humiliating foul-mouthed ranting from Torrini, but instead, serious, ethical, hard-working team journalists. How liberating it was not to have to kow-tow to the interests of the lobbies and the parties or be their mouthpiece when they wanted their side of the story told their way. How rewarding to know conscientious work would bring its just rewards. It was the only paper that was doing anything like real investigative journalism, and while they didn't have much money, at least they weren't living off state handouts. And if the MPD got their way, no one would be getting freebies anymore. They were going to put an end to the state-sponsored media; they'd have to sink or swim on their ability to sell copy and advertising and not on their ability to disguise what the politicos were really up to behind the scenes.

Sure, there were voices of dissent about freedom of information, about pluralism and the inordinate power of the tycoons and their media empires. *Live by the word or die by the word*, thought Iannelli to himself. It was time to tell things as they were. That was the only way things could change in this godforsaken country. But the old guard here wouldn't go down without a fight. Oh no. There was too much meat left on the bone.

Piero gave the thumbs up to Iovine. The first issue on the agenda was to be their take on the ongoing immigration crisis in Lampedusa, the tiny rock of an island flung into the southern Mediterranean, nearer to Africa than to Italy, and which had become one of the main gateways into Italy and Europe for so many hopefuls. Many of these same hopefuls found themselves languishing in a bureaucratic limbo, neither prisoners nor free, awaiting either a cruel repatriation or, if they were "lucky", a dubious liberty in which they would have to fend for themselves as best they could in a country without any formally structured immigration and integration policy.

"Before we go live with the stream, I need somebody to get down there and see what on earth's going on," said an energetic and smiling Luca Iovine leaning forward in his editor's chair. "We've got some copy from Pippo on the ground but I'd like to get another angle, from outside, as it were. Seems there's rumours circulating about ill-treatment and funds going astray and there could be a mutiny in the offing by all accounts."

Iannelli shot up a hand.

"Yes, Dario?"

"I'll go," he said. "I've got a few leads there myself I'd like to follow up."

"Such as?"

"Like you said, funds being diverted, human rights issues, people in high places, that sort of thing."

Iovine looked around the table.

"Any objections to sending Dario?" There was a general murmur of consent.

"Dario it is then. Let's just have a little confab after the meet, OK? A contact has come my way too. I've got a number for you. A pissed-off ex cop, apparently, who's retired to his ancestral home. Could be nothing but there's no smoke without fire, right?"

Iannelli nodded his assent and gave a yet more satisfied smile. *Could things get any better?*

"OK," Iovine continued, "on a not unrelated issue there's the Episcopal conference later today and Cardinal whatsisname, the one with the mega apartment in Campo de Fiori, is addressing the Faith and Freedom annual meeting. It says here," he went on, picking up a crumpled Holy See press release, "he'll be holding forth on ethics and morality, the immigrant crisis, and our old friend euthanasia. Anybody fancy it?"

The response was not immediately enthusiastic as Iovine cast his eye over his staff. There was a general checking of phones, some overly avid note taking and general avoidance of eye contact. A tweet from someone's unsilenced phone broke the tension accompanied by a mumbled "Oh, fuck" at the far end of the room from where a hand then shot up.

"Yes, Rino. Fancy it?"

"I think we might need to adjourn, boss. Says here there's been another one."

Twenty-Nine

"Look, Rossi," said a besieged-looking Maroni from behind his folder-strewn desk, "I am unbelievably up to my eyes in shit. Can it wait?"

"Given the circumstances, I think it's important, sir."

"Well, I suppose you've heard all the details already, haven't you?"

Rossi nodded. He'd got a tip-off from Bianco and had dropped in uninvited at the scene. It was all too familiar, and her body had been dumped behind a fence next to an alleyway in the Cinecittà area of the city.

"We think it's probably murder," continued Maroni. "But it could be manslaughter, a domestic, you know."

Clutching at straws now, said Rossi to himself. *Look at the facts, for God's sake.* But he would play along for now.

"Woman?" said Rossi.

"Yes."

"Mother?"

"Don't know that yet, but married, yes."

"Face smashed in with a blunt instrument, probably a hammer?"

"Something like that, yes, Rossi. Something like that. No

apparent motive, nothing we can really go on and no bleeding witnesses. Not a thing. Look."

He slid some case notes across the table. Cinzia Borghetti, 48. Council employee. Rossi ran his eyes over the repeat scenario. He could sense now even Maroni was shaken. Vulnerable then? But if this was serial killing, why so close together? The cooling-off period was surely too brief. *Better tell him what I came here for.*

"Look, sir," said Rossi, sliding the briefing back across the desk as though operating a slide on a mixing console. I know you want me to stay on leave. I don't agree, however, and I want to get stuck into this case as much as you do, regardless of whether Yana was targeted by the same killer or not.

"I told you, Rossi," Maroni replied, "and it's not me telling you this – it's procedure. Give it up, at least for now."

Rossi sat in silence for a few moments.

"All right," he said then. "If that's how it has to be, fine. But there's something else. Now, I know the timing might seem off but I need to go away for a day, possibly two. To Spain. Does that fit into procedure?"

"To Spain?"

"Yes, sir."

"But what on earth for?"

"Personal matters."

"Personal matters? Now? With that girl of yours in a coma?" Maroni blurted.

"There's nothing I can do about it, and there's nothing I can do here either. The doctors even suggested I have a break. It can help in these situations. Besides, it's not exactly a holiday. More like a funeral."

"Ah," said Maroni, "I didn't realize, Rossi. Er, my sympathies."

"Thank you, sir."

Rossi's superior had a distinctly harried air and was staring at a point on the far edge of his desk, as if willing something to appear. Rossi shifted in his chair. He had initially declined

Maroni's offer to be seated as time was against him and he knew he still had numerous things to see to before taking the 14.45 flight to Santiago de Compostela.

Maroni lifted his gaze for a moment. "It's getting depressingly predictable, wouldn't you say?"

"Yes, sir. I'm afraid it is."

"Anyway," said Maroni, "we're dealing with it, like with the other three, and Yana, of course. We soldier on. We have to, don't we? I've got some good lads on it, you'll be glad to know."

Rossi raised a questioning eyebrow that didn't go unmissed as Maroni's chubby fingers fiddled with a chain of paper clips.

"Beautiful city, I hear, San Compostela," he declared.

"Yes, I should like to make the full pilgrimage one day."

"Yes, I believe it's very 'in', the pilgrimage thing."

"Oh, is it?" replied Rossi, sensing an opening now in Maroni's more chatty approach. He seemed to have lowered his guard, as if he might want to connect with him.

"Can't say I've ever really been into what's *in*, sir. I just do what I'm into."

Maroni furrowed his brow further, disgruntled at having been even partially exposed as a mere follower of trends. Roman trends. The most predictable.

"Well, good luck, Rossi and look, if you do think of anything while your thoughts are elsewhere, you will let me know?"

"You mean you're not so sure now, about Spinelli?"

Maroni clasped his hands in front of his face, prayer-like.

"Maybe we should talk. When you get back. When there's more time. Nothing official, you know."

Rossi held him in his gaze as if awaiting further confirmation. Maroni was looking anywhere but at him, as if tracking the vague peregrinations around the office of an entrapped fly.

"And now with this shooting at the Colosseum the pressure is getting to be, well, I won't say unbearable, but it's coming from every sainted direction."

Maroni gave a furtive glance towards Rossi, whose expression had softened enough for Maroni to feel he could continue.

"There's a lot of pressure on me, Rossi, I don't need to tell you, and that comes all the way from the top. And as much as they might say they want results, they also demand scapegoats when it suits and you fit the bill for some. It's politics, Rossi. It's not about long-term results, it's about quick fixes, and short memories, placating the media and suchlike. But give me a few days and I can get things back the way they were. I know these cases are hellish, and there's no guarantee of success but I personally think you are among the best we've got. Let me see if I can make some other concessions and then we can find a way round any formalities if needs be. After all, it's compassionate leave, isn't it? It can't last forever."

Get back on the case? So he needs me now, thought Rossi. *He must be in trouble.*

Rossi waited a moment longer. Maroni was waiting too. Their eyes locked.

"Go to Spain, Rossi. Do what you have to do. I'll see what I can do this end and then when you're back we can talk again."

"Very well, sir," replied Rossi. "Very well."

Rossi skipped down the stairs to his office on the second floor. Urgency had given him energy, even with the new burdens he now knew he would have to carry with him, perhaps always. He had to print his boarding pass and add a suitcase to the booking. He was forgoing travelling light so as to be able to stock up on wines and delicacies should the opportunity present itself. He was at least entitled to that. Having fumbled through his bag and diary for the necessary codes of access, but without success, he logged on to his personal e-mail to look up the missing booking code. Among the several reasons why Rossi disliked electronic mail was that he always felt some important or tedious communication was waiting there, slyly lurking to catch him out. It was a feeling that could sometimes leave him in a constant state of mild but oppressive anxiety.

Among the spam near the top of his inbox there was, however, something sufficiently out of the ordinary to engage his interest. "For Rossi," it read "I know who it is." Phone calls from crazies, legion during a murder enquiry, rarely got through to him but e-mails from freaks were even less common. Of course, nowadays, your address could fall into anyone's hands; nevertheless, despite his considerable scepticism, and knowing time was against him, he clicked. Anonymous. Might have known. From a Xerox machine. Traceable, yes, but they'd have taken all the necessary precautions. He'd get Carrara onto that anyway. His field. The message itself was short and to the point.

I know who it is. Meet in Basilica San Giovanni, Saturday. 10.00. Alone. Bring phone.

A mobile number followed. Get Carrara onto that, too, though it would only be some SIM card of convenience registered to a hill farmer in deepest Peru. "Well, something to look forward to when I get back," said Rossi to no one in particular but without holding out much in the way of real hope. "Haven't been inside San Giovanni for ages," he mused as he grabbed the phone.

"Gigi, got something for you to check out. Should be in your inbox," said Rossi pressing send and feeling very hi-tech and with it, "now. And I'll be in Rome a day earlier than expected. Yes," Rossi continued, "it's very interesting. Maroni wants us back. Kind of." He permitted himself a little satisfied smile as his colleague celebrated by sending a string of Maroni-directed expletives down the line. "Oh and Gigi, can I ask you to take a look in on Yana, while I'm not here. I'm going to pop over again if I can today before I leave. I'd appreciate it."

With some considerable irritation, he concluded his flight preparations, double-checked he hadn't fouled it all up and then stuffed the pass into his jacket pocket where the two photos from the judge still were. He'd forgotten all about that. *Might have to give that back*, he thought. Or maybe not. He checked his watch. A detour to Via Tiburtina? Was it doable? He could always board with his warrant card if it went down to the wire. He left the office and the building and got into a waiting cab.

"Tiburtina then San Giovanni. Quick as you can."

Rossi jumped out of the taxi and jogged over to the newsagent's stand. It was the one nearest to the judge's apartment. A snazzily dressed middle-aged man was hunched over the papers and magazines. Out of the corner of his eye, Rossi saw beyond the news stand that a silver Audi had stopped suddenly in the traffic. The glass was tinted, and he watched as the driver's window lowered a couple of inches. A lens maybe? The car sped away into the traffic.

"Excuse me, sir. Police," said Rossi, holding up his badge. "Routine enquiries. Have you ever seen this person?" At which he produced one of the two photos on loan from the judge. He studied the picture for a moment and then made a theatrical gesture as if to say *was the pope Catholic*?

"*Il Professore!*"

"A judge, actually, I believe," said Rossi. "Did he by any chance buy a book from you recently? I was hoping to get him a present for his birthday. We're old friends and I didn't want to get him something he's already read. That one there by chance?" said Rossi, indicating the Buzzati volume on the shelf behind him.

The man turned, scratched his head for a second, and raised his finger.

"The very one," he said.

"And do you remember when?"

"Oh, yes. A couple of days ago, if I remember rightly. Yes. The day before yesterday it was."

"Thank you," said Rossi.

Thirty

As the cardinal's black Lancia swung him through the gates of the Vatican City, the Swiss Guards' salutes were tri-colourful blurs that didn't even register for him. He had his head buried deep in his papers. A busy afternoon of appointments lay ahead after lunch. Meetings, visits from foreign counterparts, discussions on key policy documents: immigration, poverty, the family, sexual abuse, the Vatican "bank" (his quotation marks), for it wasn't a bank but an "institute for sacred works" – the ISW. He was, however, regardless of his intrinsic pedantry, in an excellent mood. If he had been walking, he would have had a definite spring in his purple-stockinged step, even with his seventy and more years. And not just because of the sunshine taking the edge off the unseasonably cold weather they'd been enduring. No. He could already imagine the end of this long working day before it had really begun and the joy that was in store for him. His favourite 'boy' was back in town and was, he had been told, bringing a companion.

Boy. The correct term would perhaps have been a compound noun: rent-boy. It was a term he had heard but not a term he, His Excellency, would ever have seen fit to employ, not least because there was and never had been any pecuniary or peccable exchange involved. For him they simply afforded company; intimate, compliant company, yes, although he was aware that other of his "colleagues" made more questionable demands. The boys came and went by arrangement. An exchange born of mutual necessity. They were, he was assured, by his trusted and grateful intermediaries (business men of substance and standing much needed and much appreciated by the Church) not boys in the strict sense but young men. Yet, for a man – and man he was, in spite of his princely status and calling – at his stage of life, that distinction was neither particularly apparent nor in any sense an impediment to his gratification.

The cardinal's distracted thoughts returned again to the crisp lines of text in the speech he was to deliver, his pen poised and ready to refine it. The Church played its part, was playing its part, in alleviating the crisis, the drama of migration. The boys and men and women and children who saw in Europe their only chance of a better life were at the mercy of the worst exploitative elements within society. The Mafia. (*Would he use the "m" word?*) Criminal elements. (Safer.) The boys in his care, however, were fortunate and were thriving. They were not at the mercy of the gangmasters, harvesting tomatoes under a merciless sun for 14 hours a day and living, if living it could be called, in tin shacks and lacking the most basic of necessities. The Church had plucked these souls from the jaws of the leviathan and would guide them into education and towards betterment and opportunity and prosperity. Or words to that effect. One had to be so careful. Don't want to come across as some unreconstructed communist or self-righteous aid agency, or, God forbid, like the UN! When were their scandals going to come out?

Then there were the works to be assigned. His trusted intermediaries, gentlemen of the Church, could be relied upon to provide the means by which important building works could be carried out. There was an abundance of talk about liquidity and availability. In fact, availability was liquidity and vice versa.

Willingness. Duty. Their liquidity guaranteed the health and vigour of the Church in these tempestuous times. Without this helping hand, who could be counted on to erect the structures and to guide the organizations which allowed the gospel to be lived out in full? This was the reality. The "poor" Church they harped on about in some of the more radical (communist) sectors was a negation of earthly reality. Making the Church poor would serve only to open the floodgates and who would step in when Saint Peter's barque had been dashed to mere matchwood on the rocks? The communists, the liberals, the relativists; in a word, the barbarians! This destiny could not be allowed to pass. And it would be his legacy to see that it did not.

The importance of his legacy was not lost on him, for he was the last of his line, so he would leave this to his beloved Church. Too many priests in that family, they'd said, and now no immediate kin to speak of. His thoughts turned to the frail older cousins who had stayed in the village withering into senility like so many olive trees. He would have a papal-embossed 'card' posted to them every Christmas and Easter but his life was conducted *entro le mura*, within the secure walls of the Vatican, the all-embracing, solid, impenetrable fortress of God's Church.

He had been the youngest and despite his parents' injunctions had insisted on taking this path. He had always been drawn to the liturgy, the ritual, the majesty of the Church and, as he had quickly learned, to its power. Now, as always on his few forays extra muralis, he yearned to return to his creature comforts. To the silence and the solemnity. To the invulnerability. Not so very long ago the Holy Father had ruled this city as its monarch, the bishop of Rome. Faced with annihilation, they had compromised and the Church's earthly kingdom now was reduced to these few square kilometres and the treaties underwriting its existence. But the kingdom of the mind and of the spirit was far-reaching. There the great game could still be played, power exerted, majesty displayed.

But he knew also that fissures were appearing in that fortress, hairline cracks, at first, but which would require speedy action if they were not to widen. God's house, like any house, required timely maintenance and skilled hands if it were to stand. The enemy was at the gates and could, given the chance, bring everything crashing to the ground. But act the Church would, as it always had, down the centuries, down the millennia. Always. *Semper et in aeternum.* And if the methods had to be questionable it was because the enemy was yet more perfidious. And in this case, as a Prince of the Church, he felt he had to concur with the words of his fellow Sicilian, man of letters, and secular Prince, Tomasi di Lampedusa: "*Meglio un male sperimentato che un bene ignoto*". Better a known evil than an unknown good.

Thirty-One

As Rossi hurried along the now-familiar twisting route towards Yana's ward he stopped. Someone had called his name.

"Michael!"

"Yes?"

He turned to see the familiar face of Marta, Yana's colleague from the Wellness centre.

"How are you?" he said, kissing her then on both cheeks.

"Fine thanks, just been looking in on Yana. No change, I'm afraid, but there's still time isn't there?"

Her huge, dark eyes were glassy with undisguised emotion.

"There is time," said Rossi, "there's always time."

"Well I hope you catch that son of a bitch soon!" she said. "You are going to get him, aren't you? Sooner or later."

"Yes," replied Rossi, "sooner would be better."

He looked at his watch.

"Look, Marta, I'm catching a plane in about an hour."

"No problem, beautiful. Off you go. You'll get him you see. Was it you who was going to come and take a statement?"

"Statement?" said Rossi, hesitating. "What statement?"

"The statement the policeman that came to the gym said I had to make. He wanted to know if Yana had any problems, with

144

money, affairs, that kind of thing. I told him it wasn't part of her character. Very proper girl and all that. Sensible. Sensitive. You know she was already shook up by that client we had the day it happened. Told her to go home early, I did. I think now if she'd stayed maybe she'd have been all right, but—"

"Excuse me, Marta," said Rossi cutting her short, "but what client?"

"The one who came to the gym that afternoon."

"And nobody came to get the facts from you?"

"Well, I was wondering whether I should go down the Questura myself, but I thought they mustn't have needed it in the end."

"Go on," said Rossi. "The client."

"Oh, well, charming he was, at first, but creepy with it, now I think of it. He tried it on with her. Yana was on massage with Giulia being off. Only said he wanted an 'appy ending when he knew bloody well it's therapeutic massage only. Go somewhere else if you want that kinda thing, I said."

"And you could give a description?"

"Oh yeah. They'll have his photo, too, on the CCTV. Get down there smartish though before security go over them tapes."

Rossi whipped out his phone.

"Gigi, me again," said Rossi, "get yourself or one of the boys down to the Wellness Fitness and Beauty and get the CCTV tapes. We might have a lead. And see what Maroni's crowd have managed to put together while we were away. I think it's time for some old-fashioned police work. Yes," he added, "like starting with the last person to see the victim, maybe, and taking their statements. Oh, and keep your eyes peeled. I think we might have some 'friends' interested in us. Audi. Silver."

He snapped his phone shut.

"Everything all right?" said a now worried-looking Marta. "You're not in any trouble, are you?"

Thirty-Two

Rossi put down his Italian paper feeling less informed than he had felt before he started reading it. Yes, it told him what people, mainly in politics, were supposedly doing and saying, but it didn't tell him why and what the consequences might be. As for the outside world, it got pretty short shrift. It was the old story: a merry-go-round of spin, non-news and sensationalist skewing of reality and it left him feeling perplexed and unsatisfied. Beneath him, the sea was giving way to the coast of Spain. Soon they would be crossing the arid, central wastes with their high sierras topped with blobs of virgin snow. Remote, very remote, almost desert areas as good as cut off from the big urban centres and their sophistication. It could, he thought, be a good place to spend some time.

He turned away from the window and picked up again where he had left off, replaying in his mind his own story and that of Rosa Martinez Garcia from when he had been a young man in search both of adventure and of himself all those years ago. How blithely he had redirected the path of his life back then. Yet, he remembered how, when he had arrived there that first day, he had almost wanted to abandon the whole idea. He knew no one; the city was an electrifying turmoil into which he couldn't imagine anyone willingly throwing themselves. The language, too, was a mystifying babble, despite his best efforts to study it before going. But then he had made friends with other students in the same situation in the temporary hostel accommodation and they'd hunted down somewhere better to live. Then Rosa had arrived on the scene and, soon after, Giuseppe.

She and Giuseppe had been an item. Giuseppe had already been a part of that world, having made numerous visits to Spain, ostensibly for educational purposes, although Rossi was subsequently able to confirm that he had entered the underworld of heroin dealing and other illicit affairs. Giuseppe had met Rosa on one such visit but by the time Rossi got to Spain, cracks had appeared in the relationship and a few months later they had already split up. That was when she had come to live with Rossi in the house in Valencia's Lonja area, via a chance encounter with one of his friends. They had all got off to a great start and before he knew it they had become close, then intimate, and finally, lovers.

But step by step, inch by inch, Giuseppe had reappeared and wheedled his way back into her life, partly by means of his proximity to the drugs scene. At first Rossi had tolerated his presence, thinking in the naive way of the young and open-minded that they simply wished to remain friends. He soon realized, however, that this was not the real reason and even if she had still been attracted to Giuseppe her continued attachment was more closely tied up with her psychological dependence on him and his ready supply of stimulants and downers, which she needed to get through the day. But her need became insatiable and the remedies more drastic.

She had hidden it from Rossi, and had hidden it well, but her mood changes and moments of unpredictability had already raised some suspicions. Then one day when paying her a surprise visit after afternoon classes had been cancelled he had learned the bleak truth of her enslavement. He had pushed open her door to find her sprawled naked on the floor amidst the paraphernalia of silver foil and heroin bags with a grinning Giuseppe, equally, if not more, stoned, slumped in the corner. From then on it became a brutal tug of war. He confronted her, and she flipped as her denial became total. She started using openly then, and Giuseppe was soon staying nights, finally moving in under the pretence of temporary economic hardship, as "a friend". She began to distance herself more and more from the rest of the house, arguments ensued over rent and communal space and the odd couple finally departed under a cloud leaving only their debts behind. Rosa had continued to declare her love for him, justifying her connection to Giuseppe as an irrelevance, something she had no control over, but that he had to overlook, for her sake, if he loved

her.

Then there was the never-resolved issue of the two-bit dealer, known only to Rossi from his furtive activity around the lecture rooms and his subsequent disappearance culminating in the discovery of his mutilated corpse. Rumours abounded and not a few centred on Giuseppe, his supposed role in the affair, and the part played by much bigger fish; rumours which, though never substantiated, persisted. So, as the end of his stay approached, Rossi had broken it to Rosa that their story could have no future and then, unknown to her, had contacted her family, telling them everything he knew. Within a day, her father and brother had arrived to take her, kicking and screaming and swearing vengeance, back to their hometown to get clean. Giuseppe had been outmanoeuvred, while Rossi himself had arranged his own exit from the scene and that was the last he had seen of them all.

It had been hard. He had liked Spain and had considered settling there, but circumstances meant that it wasn't to be. He had gone back to Rome, completed his degree and tried to rebuild his life. He had lost his mother and father in quick succession – his father in an industrial accident and his mother not long after of grief. Being an only child, though well-adjusted and gregarious, he had slid into an existential crisis. It was then when he had been at a very low ebb and had even contemplated trying to find Rosa again that a chance encounter with a priest had perhaps saved him. He enrolled in the seminary and commenced studying to be a priest, his idea being to become a missionary and see the world. The memories of Rosa soon faded and the positive elements of a new life began to coalesce around him but he had soon realized that the contemplative life was not for him, as his discoveries of the inner workings of the Church clashed with his idea of what it should represent.

That had been some twenty years before. He had left the seminary, travelled briefly, and then as the *Tangentopoli* scandal rocked the whole political establishment, he had seen that his true vocation lay in upholding the law in a country where the law was in danger of being swept aside. He had risen through the ranks and, despite quickly earning a reputation for idiosyncrasy and difficulty, they had needed his skills and he had got results. When the special divisions of the police and carabinieri and the financial police were brought together to form the Rome Serious Crime Squad, his had been among the first names on the list. He himself had brought in Carrara, seeing his courage, determination and honesty as qualities rarely found in one man. Now, as a man approaching the foothills of early middle-age, he was going back to close the story. *Per farci una croce sopra*. To plant a cross on it all. To bury the past for good.

Rossi shoved the pages back into his shoulder bag. They were coming in to land.

From the airport he took a taxi, then a local bus which brought him to the town. How quickly and easily he had sailed through security. The Schengen agreement meant he didn't even have to show his passport. *Have to do this more often*, he thought. *Get away from it all*. From the bus in the watery light he was able to see beyond the modern outlying suburbs and motorway the unmistakeable Spanish Gothic steeple of Santiago de Compostela. Not this time, but next time he would stop for a proper holiday with Yana.

He had phoned ahead and was met at his destination by a police officer who gave a cursory check of his credentials before wishing him well on his mission. Rossi made it clear that it was a personal matter but emphasized that should anything useful emerge he would be more than happy to help.

"*Muy bien*," said the Civil Guard, nodding, as if with some surprise. "*Muy bien.*" Rossi couldn't help but notice a certain ambivalence in this type of "very well". It was as if he had perhaps said too much and as such had given away his motives, thus weakening himself in the other's eyes. Or maybe not. Maybe it was nothing at all. He produced the map he had printed for himself and followed the route traced in red pen and as he did so went over some of the information he had so far obtained. Trusted contacts at Interpol had furnished him with a good deal of the information he needed and in record time. Giuseppe had been convicted of various drug offences and exploiting prostitution, and although the implication was that there was much more and much worse, no police authority had ever been able to pin anything else on him. The suggestion was that he could boast of protection in high places with his old world Roman connections. He may well already have been capable, too, of exploiting his knowledge of other criminal secrets to effect necessary and timely blackmail. When he had been caught it was thanks to a tip-off but without testimony they'd had very little to go on. It was to be assumed that the tip-off had been from Rosa who had disappeared from circulation at around the same time although her whereabouts were known to the police.

Rosa had initially got herself clean of drugs thanks to the efforts of her family only to be sucked back another time into Giuseppe's world when he had again tracked her down. What then ensued had been a long and protracted purgatory for Rosa until she had managed to find the will and the courage to leave and disappear for good. Interpol had put Rossi in touch with Rosa's sister, Laura, who was able to confirm beyond any doubt that it really was Rosa who had been murdered. Laura now lived in the same town on the Galician coast where she had moved when Rosa had finally broken her cover and managed to get a covert message to Laura telling her of her new life and asking her to come and live with her.

According to Rossi's contacts, they had lost all trace of her until she then reappeared as a murder victim all these years later. What had happened in the intervening period was still unclear. Rosa's husband, having gone missing, remained the prime suspect. Among the working hypotheses was that she may have once again become entangled with Giuseppe although there was no evidence to suggest she had been taking drugs. There may have been a jealousy motive, her husband could even have discovered something, perhaps an affair, but as yet there was no proof either way. All they knew was that the revenge – if revenge it had been – had been vicious beyond belief.

Rossi stopped and looked up to check the name of the street. He walked on until he found the number then rang the bell of the smallish house, one of a row of single-storey, villa-like dwellings set back from the road and facing the pines and yellowy, scrub-covered hill overlooking the sea. The door was opened by a slim, dark-haired woman, around forty, he thought, wearing close-fitting jeans and only a loose, long V-neck jumper.

"*Sí?*"

"*Soy* Rossi."

"*Soy* Laura. *Venga*," she replied and, standing aside, gestured to the inspector to enter.

While she prepared coffee in silence, Rossi sat in the lounge. There was a small wooden table, a sofa, and easy chairs and in a far corner the dining area. She placed the tray between them and sank into the sofa opposite him but didn't drink herself.

"So, what is it that you want from me?"

She had curled her legs under her and flicked a strand of hair out of her eyes. The likeness was there, that was for sure, but she was harder, tougher by far than her sister had ever been.

"I wanted," began Rossi, "to know what happened to Rosa during these past years, from someone who was close to her."

"You could have tried to reach her before."

Rossi hesitated.

"I didn't know where to look. Besides, you must remember, it was over between us and …"

"And it is still 'over'. Very over, now. Isn't it?" she replied fixing him with an intense, rock-steady gaze.

"I didn't expect it to end this way," Rossi countered. "I don't think anyone ever imagines it will, do they? And I suppose I felt guilty, too. As if it was, in some sense, maybe partly my fault."

Laura was scrutinizing him. She reached behind a cushion for a handbag and rummaged for cigarettes contained therein. She took one, automatically offering one to Rossi. He didn't think twice, despite not having smoked for years.

"Do you know, Mr Rossi," she said, "I think the best thing you could do would be to get on the first plane back to your little Italy and forget you ever met Rosa. What good can it do anyone, you being here? I'm sorry if you don't like what I say but there is no point. We know who killed her. They may find him, they may not, but Rosa is gone and a family is in pieces. God knows if Emilio will return but I fear for the worst. Rosa was his life."

She almost spat the last word at him. The inspector in Rossi began to sense something, his instinct again was picking up signals but what? He would have to gain time.

"So she was happy, at least. That's good to know."

She almost sneered then as she couldn't help but reply.

"I said she was his life."

"So there were problems."

"Can't stop being the cop, now can you, Mr Rossi?"

She leant over and tapped ash into a half-full ashtray.

"And I suppose you think it will help to ask questions about Rosa's private life. Ask in the town," she said with a fluid hand gesture to the window, "they'll give you the answers you want. We women here don't have good reputations – fishermen's wives get lonely, don't they? And Emilio was a fisherman too, after all."

She drew hard on her cigarette.

"Look, she had an ordinary life; a bit shit, a bit of fun now and then, like the rest of us, and a family, and now she's dead. What else is there to say?"

"And nobody saw anything, heard nothing? No one? You have no information that could help catch her killer?"

"I've said what there is to say – to them, to you, to anyone."

She stubbed out her cigarette.

"Well, I think I had better go," said Rossi rising from his chair. He reached inside his jacket and brought out an envelope. "It's for the family and the children. Can I leave it with you?" he said and placed it on the table. "It's just some words and a small gift. I'll show myself out."

Rossi closed the door behind him and turned left then began to descend the steps that led towards the seafront. It would soon be getting dark. A bracing walk was what he needed first off and then some proper food. Real seafood and a good drink. He was flogging a dead horse there for sure but he had tried. *At least he had tried, so may as well make the best of it, Michael*, he said to himself, then back to Rome and their little rendezvous in the cathedral. Along the street there wasn't a soul to be seen, so when he heard footsteps behind him he turned. It was Laura. She stopped.

"There is more," she said, and then in English, "are you hungry?"

They sat on a bench on the seafront watching the majestic breakers rolling in to make their thunderous conclusions. The *empanadas* had been delicious, and she'd made them herself, she informed him, forcing yet another one on him. She lit up a cigarette, Rossi declining this time, and then she began to speak.

"Emiliano was caught up in something, like many people here. The other business here."

"The smuggling?"

"If you like, yes. He had let things get out of hand and I think he was in some trouble, with the Colombians, taking too many liberties, I don't know, but they are ruthless. Rosa didn't know anything. She thought it all came from the fishing and a bit of contraband with the boats, but the fishing here has been in crisis for a long time. He was gambling too. You know, the life you lead here, hand to mouth, uncertainty, the weather, it's not an easy one and, like I said, the nights are long, the winter's grim and everyone – everyone – has their vice, don't they? And like everyone who's fished here, he knew – he knows," she corrected herself, "the ways in, the ways out, the hiding places in the coves, the caves. It's just like it was in the old days. Except what comes in now is the fucking white powder and if you're lucky, or unscrupulous, or both, you can get rich. Overnight. If. And don't forget the police. Don't think they're not in on it too. So, when Rosa was killed, it suited everyone to have a big mystery, what with her false identity and her past, and then putting the blame on her stalker was a masterstroke. Keep the heavies from Madrid from sticking their noses in. Emiliano must have panicked and thought he was next. Maybe they came for him and decided Rosa would do. A warning to everyone not to mess with the big boys from Medellin."

Rossi's thoughts turned to the landscapes he'd seen as the coach had brought him down the stunning Galician coast – the knife-like promontories, the fjord-like *rios* shaped and gouged by millennia of Atlantic barrage and relentless surge, the jagged fingers of coast reaching out westward into the cold grey sea. Yet, despite its glowering hostility it was fearfully beautiful. He turned to Laura.

"So what brought you here?" he asked.

"My sister. She had got in touch with us after all those years and I was on my own again. So she asked me to come and help her out with the family, start afresh somewhere different. I said yes. Why not? She promised me she was clean and told me how she'd left that good-for-nothing and found a new identity, by herself, no police involved. She never trusted them. She'd met an Argentinian girl who'd decided to leave everything and go back home and get married to some high-flyer politician and she let Rosa have her old national insurance number and driving licence. They even looked the same, and so she was able to begin a new life and wound up here. At the world's edge. That was, what? Ten years ago now."

"And were you happy? To see her again?"

"Happy? Of course! She was still my big sis. She had changed, though. She was quieter, and she was a mother with a mother's worries, and all that, you know? That gravitas. Not that I'd know, but you see what I mean. And you, do you have any kids, Mr Rossi?"

Rossi shook his head.

"Not as yet," he said, "as far as I know," and for the first time since he'd seen her, something like a real smile crept across Laura's lips raising the corners of her mouth.

"But you are not alone," she said, stating yet questioning at the same time.

"No," said Rossi, "alone, no," aware now that the easy conversation looked like it was heading for what would be its first awkward impasse.

A pulse of something like guilt went through him as he reminded himself to contact Carrara for any developments from the hospital, bringing with it other thoughts of his imminent return to Rome and then the even heavier concerns tied to the case and its Gordian immensity. They were getting nowhere, and women were being murdered, randomly, it seemed, and yet, and yet. There was the other issue of the judge, his doubts about the book story, and the strange inconsistencies that had surfaced. And Marta and her story about the weirdo no one had deemed worthy to get down in a statement.

The waves were crashing in now with even greater intensity.

"Looks like there's a real storm coming," said Laura pulling her jacket around her as if to ward off something that might at any time emerge from the riotous foam. "So we'd better be going our own ways, I suppose," she went on.

Rossi didn't reply but was all too aware of his own responsibilities and of the choices beginning to make themselves known to him. He had no intention of telling Laura the exact nature of the situation he found himself in; it would be something like a cheap shot, ungallant in the extreme. So, he began concocting the well-worn standard reply to soften the impact of the implicit rebuff to what had been the implicit invitation.

"Yes, and my boss wants a full report in the morning, on anything that might be of interest, to Interpol."

"And what would interest Interpol, in your opinion, Inspector?"

It was the first time she had used his professional title and he didn't quite know what to make of it.

"You think I am going to drop Rosa's husband in it? Is that it?" said Rossi.

"They know anyway. I told you. You'd be lucky to find one of the cops round here who isn't getting a kickback or who hasn't got his hands tied."

"It's a small world, then. I thought I was the only one who was kicking against the pricks. I mean, of course, in the biblical sense; not that they aren't pricks either, some of them," he added.

"So you're the good apple in the barrel, are you?"

"Not the worst, I'd like to think."

"You're too modest, if you ask me."

Rossi smiled.

"And that was the compliment you always fish for, wasn't it?" she continued.

"If you say so."

Judiciously, by Rossi's standards, he'd set his phone to vibrate and a call was coming in. Deus ex machina. He excused himself and walked towards the water's edge. It was Carrara.

"About those tapes, Mick, at the Wellness. Well, there's only been a break in, hasn't there? And guess what's gone missing?"

"Christ! All of them?"

"No. Just the one pertaining to the day in question. Very professional job indeed, by all accounts. No one even noticed until they went to look for it. Replaced it with an identical blank one."

"And the security guard? What's his story?"

"Swears blind he doesn't know anything. He takes the tapes out, puts them on the shelf and every seven days goes over them again. I reckon he pervs over them, by the state they were in but he swears he didn't spot anything out of the ordinary."

"So we don't know when it was taken?"

"No."

Rossi was thinking.

"Look, Gigi, the way things are going, I'm not sure we can even do this, talk on the phone anymore, I mean, do you follow? Listen, call me at this number from a call box in about ten minutes. Hang on."

Rossi pulled a pen from his inside pocket and gestured to Laura to give him her phone number, which, to her credit, she duly did.

"Are you ready?"

Rossi reeled off the numbers using an improvised code. "The year we met, the last digit of your … etc." It would at least give them time to talk without being spied on. Unless Laura's line was already tapped but that was a chance he'd have to take.

"It looks like I'm going to need your phone," said Rossi as soon as he had hung up. "Would you mind? It's actually very urgent."

"Feel free," she shrugged with neither enthusiasm nor reluctance. "I suppose it's a matter of life or death, isn't it, Inspector?"

Through the deepening twilight, Rossi made his way back to the station where the bus had left him earlier in the afternoon. He had been able to give Carrara clear instructions to meet him at the airport that evening and to keep his movements as discreet as possible. He didn't want anyone in on this except themselves and he had very clear ideas about how they were going to go about the whole operation.

There was no scheduled bus for two hours, so he had no option but to take a taxi. At least they were less expensive than in Rome and the driver seemed honest and polite, too, which was possible but not a given in the Eternal City. Once at the airport, he did the rounds of the airlines and with a bit of professional persuasion was able to change his ticket at minimal cost and then settle down with a paper and a coffee to wait for the call.

It had all been so fast and not at all as he had expected but then fantasy and reality rarely did bear any relation. What was imagined always became something else, quite new, quite different, though not always a disappointment. He was pleased, at least, to have tried to close that particular chapter of his life that had so unexpectedly re-opened. His policeman's mind, however, was not comfortable with the versions of the facts he had received. For now he would leave them, as if in a mental ante-chamber, as he turned his conscious thoughts back to the more immediate realities of the case in hand.

All this cloak-and-dagger stuff, all this murder in the cathedral. It could only be a ridiculous hoax and he knew that falling for it would be if not a criminal then certainly a costly waste of his time. Yet he also had a hunch they might be onto something.

The tape going missing, the botched attempt to murder Yana, the botched attempt to get at him. Perhaps it all suggested that the events were not random that there was a thread that he could pick up. And perhaps now there was a thread that someone wanted him to pick up. But why? And was it the one he was looking for?

For a while, he people-watched. The cabin crews crossed and re-crossed each in their own distinctive livery. The more up-market airlines had a commensurate advantage in terms both of their elegance and arrogance. A knot of American tourists plonked themselves down opposite him. Academics, by their conversation, perhaps on a conference or maybe friends from the same college. If academics could be friends. Publish or perish, that was the motto. And it was all pretty damn cut-throat and bitchy as far as he could gather. But there were always some good sorts, just like anywhere else, and for a moment he remembered with some fondness his old professors at the IAUR. He'd been asked several times to go back and give a speech or even teach a course on criminology, but he'd always declined. But maybe it wasn't too late for him to go into academia. He was, after all, always learning. It could be a damn sight of an easier life too.

Thirty-Three

"And what if we find another one tonight?"

Salvatore knocked back his mid-morning coffee, *corretto*, laced with a shot of brandy, ostensibly against the chill but more to calm nerves shot to pieces like a mangled fishing net in need of constant repair. His brother was beside him. His face, too, showed the strain of having to work against hostile nature and even more hostile human realities.

"They deserve a Christian burial. A decent burial. It's the least we can give them."

"And the boats. Do you think they'll come tonight? The weather's to be fine, the forecast says."

"Better for them. It's when it's rough it puts us in more of a fix, so it does."

Then, in silence, they surveyed the sea before them. Despite its beauty and its familiarity, for them it was now a vast graveyard. Who knew how many souls had perished there. The ones that never made it on the hulks of rusting junk laughingly called boats that left behind them the dwindling lights of Libya for the promise of Lampedusa's shores only to sink without trace and with all hands. And then, on dark nights, it befell men like them to haul in their nets believing the unexpected weight to be their good fortune only to find the curse of a bloated corpse staring back at them. It was down to these men and the rest of the hopelessly overstretched local community to give them decent burials while in Rome the politicians hummed and hawed and plotted how best to exploit events to their own advantage.

And then there were the boats in difficulty, drifting with neither fuel nor fresh water, their occupants pleading for help. But there was the law – the new government law, not the age-old law of the sea – which said anyone aiding illegal clandestine immigration could be considered an accessory to that same criminal illegal act. So, the desperate and hungry were criminalized and those who sought to provide humanitarian assistance risked the same fate.

But the boats that were not "spotted" by the radar, the ones that slipped through the security cordons to be met by intermediaries? The boats with hundreds of hopefuls, each of whom had coughed up three, four, five thousand euros, thus plunging themselves or their families deep into debt. Families who would wait and wait for news before finally having to let go, surrendering to their worst fears. Do the math, as the Americans said. There was money to be made whether they got through or not.

And there was yet more cash to be squeezed from the survivors as they were corralled and cajoled into what often amounted to forced labour, living and working as virtual slaves without rights, without papers, and thus without an identity, at the mercy of their masters on the tomato plantations of the South, or the street corners, or in the illegal bordellos of Palermo, Rome, or Milan. Think about that when you're making your pasta, thought Iannelli as he battled with his own inconsistencies, for he too had surrendered more than once to temptation – the promise and the comfort of firm, smooth bodies on lonely nights in the city. So, he was a hypocrite, a part of the system? Or only an end user, as they might say in mitigation? As everyone could say.

He was sitting at the next table, browsing a newspaper, but

listening, straining sometimes to pick up the finer points of the fishermen's conversation through their dialect. He'd managed to get a direct flight to save time, but for the return journey, his plan was to take the ferry to the mainland and hire a car to make the journey over land back to Catania. He wanted to get a feel for the place, to get a bit more of Sicily under his skin. Every now and again his eye would stray towards the TV screen over the bar. It was set to one of the commercial channels, one of the channels owned by the northern magnate whose stranglehold over Italian politics remained unrivalled. How the small screen could be filled with these near biblical images of a tiny island overrun with desperate, dark-skinned foreigners at their lowest ebb. Coming soon to your towns and villages. Anytime now. But it was an ill wind that didn't blow anyone any good.

"Oh, Danilo!" the two fishermen exclaimed as a slim young man in faded jeans and a baggy sweater made his way through the tables to join them.

As the new arrival shifted chairs into a more agreeable arrangement, Iannelli sensed his opportunity.

"Lovely day," he said catching the newcomer's eye. The quick reply was presaged by a good-natured smile.

"Yes, it is. On holiday?"

"More work than pleasure." He reached out a hand. "Dario Iannelli. I'm a journalist."

"Ah," said the older of the two fishermen, with more than a hint of cynicism. Iannelli was unperturbed. He was getting his story and that was that.

"I want to know what's really happening here. Not just what they dish out on the TV."

"Cristian," said the youngest member of the triumvirate. "And allow me to present Salvatore and Francesco."

"Perhaps you would like to join us," said Cristian. "A friend of mine is coming. It could be perfect for you to see what we are doing here."

Cristian signalled then with a wave to a tall man who had arrived at the entrance. He looked no more than nineteen or twenty, yet seemed confident and determined.

"This is Jibril. He's an interpreter. We work together to sort out what problems we can. There are many but we try."

Iannelli introduced himself. The young man's eyes narrowed.

"There are many lies being written about us and what happens here."

"I know," said Iannelli, "and that's why I am here. To discover the truth."

"We are trapped here," said Jibril, "with nothing to do and with little or no communication. We want only to be free. That is why we left Africa, to be free and now we find ourselves prisoners. We want to work, to have a future. We don't want charity."

Iannelli nodded his agreement. He came across immediately as determined, proud, and highly intelligent. Iannelli reached into his jacket pocket and produced cards for everyone then turned to Jibril.

"This is my number. Maybe I can interview you here before you leave the island, about the conditions, how you are treated."

Cristian reached out to put a gentle restraining hand on Jibril before then addressing Iannelli.

"But perhaps you would like to come and help us," he said. "We always need help." He looked at his watch. "We will be serving lunch in a couple of hours and we're a little short-staffed. We work without funding and without middle men. It's all just the natural goodwill of the Sicilian people, the Lampedusan people. Then, after, maybe we can all talk. *Con calma*. No rush. Once you have lived a little bit of what happens here, on your skin, as we say."

"Yes," said Iannelli, "I would love to."

Salvatore was smiling now.

"And how are your sea legs, *Dottore*? Perhaps a little run out in the boat afterwards? You don't get seasick, do you?"

"And now, tell us all about you, Dario," said Cristian. "What's the news from Rome? We've been hearing terrible things about that city of yours …"

Thirty-Four

The day was splendid. The morning air tingled and the rising sun was casting long shadows and sparkling on the cars criss-crossing the piazza while it tried in vain to warm the white stone of the basilica. The huge statues of the twelve apostles with their long beards and flowing robes ranged along its uppermost heights seemed to be swirling with iron purpose and divine certainty. Rossi, too, felt fresh and vigorous. Despite his doubts regarding the veracity of the strange rendezvous they were about to put to the test, he felt anything could be possible today. In short, in one way or another, he sensed a breakthrough was coming from some direction and it raised his spirits about Yana's chances too.

Yet the beauty of the scene, his upbeat demeanour, and the solid dependability of his colleague, Carrara, belied the terror that women across the city still felt, as if it crawled on their skin, every night after darkness fell. Going about their daily business bore no relation to their fearful and furtive nocturnal movements, if they even dared now to go out at night. The vicious slaying of a policeman in broad daylight, not half a mile away, had further compounded fears that criminals now operated with impunity, as if they were taunting the forces of law and order.

"Have we picked the wrong morning?" said Carrara indicating

the streams of black and white clad female converging now on the basilica from all directions.

"Could be a big saint's day. Or a beatification or canonization mass," Rossi mused.

The sheer volume of nuns was overwhelming and, judging by their variegated ethnicities, they must have come from all corners of the globe.

"Maybe Saint Teresa of Avila? Saint Clare possibly?" he proffered.

Carrara, however, was intent again on his phone. As he checked, Rossi scanned the area. A silver Audi had pulled up at a vantage point by the Scala Santa and a figure seemed to be skulking behind it, talking theatrically on a phone to disguise his looking in their direction.

They were to wait inside the church until a message gave them further instructions.

"I'll be next to the confessionals," said Rossi, "and you take a vantage point wherever you can. Perhaps near the papal altar."

Inside, too, the place was humming. There were nuns with video cameras, nuns taking selfies of themselves and each other, nuns praying, and a very considerable number lined up waiting to offload their sins. Rossi took a seat next to the row of dark wooden confessionals, each about the size of a seaside bathing booth, and which ran down the side of the northern transept. He knew it was the northern transept as Christian churches are always oriented East-West, something to do with facing Jerusalem, if he remembered rightly. He was explaining the fact to a not very interested Carrara as they checked that they had decent signals before he took up his position within sight of Rossi but not so near as to arouse suspicion.

It was like being ten years old again, Rossi reflected. Waiting. Waiting back then to get the dreaded thing out of the way for another month. It had always been such a relief, that absolution, as he would fly out of the side door of the spooky-quiet church on a Saturday afternoon, like a free bird. Still, the state of grace was always short-lived, perhaps not even as long as it took him to get home as before too long there would inevitably be a swear, an exchange of boots or fists, an impure thought.

From the signs hung on the confessionals he could see that absolution could be granted in English, French, Italian, and German today. He gazed up at the grand altar and its lavish baroque excess. Here only the Pope himself, who was first and foremost Rome's Bishop, could say mass. Rossi revisited what history of the place he could remember. The magnificent mosaic floor, the cloisters' inlaid barley-sugar-twist columns. He gave a little laugh to himself. Once, right here, the authorities of the day had even put a corpse on trial then thrown it into the Tiber.

Should he pray? he wondered. He needed something, if it was forthcoming. *But what if the answer was no? Would he have to live out his purgatory or would mercy descend like a dove from on high? Had he the right to ask for it? Did he even believe anything anymore?* His reveries were interrupted by the message he'd been thinking would never actually come.

"Are you ready to hear my confession?"

Thirty-Five

"So," said Rossi, "this had better be good."

He was kneeling inside the confessional and addressing the copper-coloured grill obscuring his interlocutor's face. "Or do you want me to say how long it's been?"

He was speed-texting a message to Carrara.

Get between here and the door. Not too close.

"I think somebody's gone and left their phone on?" said a softish female voice. *Shit, must have picked up the interference in an earpiece*, thought Rossi. *A wire probably*.

"Just turning it off. Ready. I'm all yours now."

"Well," the voice began, "as I said, I may be able to point you in the right direction, regarding the murder of the girl in the car park."

"I believe you said you know," Rossi interjected.

"I would know who it was," came the reply, "if I saw him again. You see I was there. But the point is that I wasn't there, if you follow."

"Doing something you shouldn't have been doing?"

"Something like that, yes."

"And just how do you think you can help us by hiding in a confessional and saying you were somewhere and saw someone, but you weren't actually there?"

"Well, I got a good look at his face. I was passing the garage, shortly after the murder, as I later learned, and happened to have a very close encounter with him. At least I believe it was him. He was leaving the garage in a hurry and had blood on his hands and clothes. We bumped right into each other, Inspector. I can tell you his height, his weight, the colour of his eyes and hair. I could probably tell you what kind of aftershave he wears. I have put together a full description but I cannot be implicated in this case in any way. As I said, I was not in the vicinity on the night in question but feel duty bound to tell you what I know, as a citizen, and as a woman."

"Was there anything else? Any distinguishing features?"

"He wore a ring on his right hand bearing an ornate letter. Almost certainly a letter G, or possibly a C. I took the trouble to write down everything I know. I will leave it here."

Rossi pondered for a moment.

"So why the need for the meeting, if I may ask? Do you enjoy this kind of thing? And why only now?"

"As a courtesy to you, Inspector." There was a slight pause. "I know that you, too, are now personally involved."

"I am always personally involved," Rossi shot back, "when a citizen is murdered, whoever that may be. We take an oath, remember."

He waited for some acknowledgement but from beyond the screen there was now only silence. Rossi kicked open the door and span round to open the priest's side of the confessional. Empty. He grabbed the promised envelope from the kneeler and looking round saw Carrara running towards him, with some difficulty, through the swarms of faithful. He was raising his hands in the air in a sign of southern Italian exasperation and then started mouthing some desperate kind of instruction. Rossi heaved his way through to meet his colleague halfway.

"See where she went?" asked Rossi.

"Yeah, for about five seconds, then I lost her."

"What kind of cop are you?"

"She was dressed as a nun, for God's sake!"

The two of them looked around. Rossi was rubbing his chin.

"Was she a big nun or a small nun?" he enquired.

"Above-average?"

"Ah."

"We could try and close all the doors."

Rossi raised his eyebrows at Carrara as if he, of all people, should have known better.

"You mean *after* the sister has bolted? Can't. It's extra-territorial. San Giovanni in Laterano. Don't you remember Spinelli and the Lateran Treaties? This is one of the remnants of the Pope's temporal power."

Carrara let out an expletive much to the dismay of a passing group of tourists.

"When you're here," Rossi continued, "you've as good as left the country. The Pope's the boss, not us."

"So that's why she chose here."

Rossi raised his arms in a sign of frustration and annoyance, clasping his hands then behind his neck where the strain was bringing on a headache of grand proportions. The leader of a passing tourist group had frozen in front of him. He was staring at Rossi but more specifically at his now very clearly visible shoulder holster and its black Beretta automatic.

"He's got a gun!" he said to a tiny, dark-skinned priest who had been ambling along and inspecting the mosaic work. He, too, stopped. Rossi brought his arms down slowly, realizing his error.

"It's OK, Father," said Rossi. "I'm a policeman," at which he produced his badge. The priest glanced at his particulars.

"Not here you aren't," the priest replied. "I think you should both leave."

Carrara was still kicking himself for having let her get away.

"Come on, Gigi. It's not the end of the world," said Rossi. "And I think we've got something very interesting to go on anyway, without the girl."

"Can I have a look?" Carrara enquired, flicking back to his usual optimist self and indicating the slim brown envelope flapping in Rossi's left hand.

"Oh, yes," Rossi replied, "by all means. But I was actually referring to something else."

"Something else?"

"Yes. Theology. Catholic doctrine. Do you believe, Gigi, in the resurrection of the body?"

Carrara looked at Rossi with now undisguised incredulity and very visible concern.

"Do I believe in what?"

Thirty-Six

Rossi's trip to the hospital had followed the by now predictable routine. A chat with the consultant, a one-way chat with Yana, another chapter of the current book, and then some moments of silence in quiet reflection holding her hand until he bid her farewell. He went to take up his coat draped over a chair. He thought it looked as limp and useless as he himself felt.

Apart from the obvious worries, it had also struck him that he had no real legal right to be there. As a non-married partner, he had fewer legally enshrined rights than her biological family, even if they had already as good as given her up for dead before the accident. It was only down to the goodwill and common sense of medical staff that people such as he could come and go as they pleased to see a loved one. He probably had more legal justification to see her as a police officer coming to question her as a witness.

Carrara was waiting and leaning with his back to the Alfa. As Rossi crossed the final lane between the zig-zagging traffic he noticed, on the far side of the piazza now and half-obscured by a clump of overhanging pine trees, the silver Audi and the same figure leaning on the roof, this time, perhaps, with a telephoto lens, though he couldn't be sure. *Company?* he wondered to himself. Then feeling a buzz of tension kicking in, he got into the passenger seat.

"Looks like somebody's onto us, Gigi. Any thoughts?"

"Shall I?"

"Why not."

Carrara gave a glance in the rear-view, eased out of the parking area and, after checking the coast was clear, rammed his foot to the floor. They were speeding in the direction of Piazza Vittorio when Rossi had another idea.

"Do a U-turn and take the tramlines," he said, "quick, against the traffic."

"You sure?" Carrara replied.

"You'll be fine," Rossi assured him, "get in front of that one and you'll have a clear run to Santa Croce," he said, indicating a number eight just turning the corner at Manzoni and heading back to San Giovanni. Carrara handbrake turned as more astounded tourists began immortalizing the excitement with whatever technology they had to hand. The driver of the Audi had been fast and onto them, but with the traffic against him, had been forced into effecting a clunky three-point turn. It gave Carrara the vital seconds he needed to put some real distance between them. As they approached the piazza again, Carrara swerved off the road and penetrated the tree-lined central lane reserved for taxis and electric trams. Rossi was checking the mirror.

"Faster!" he urged.

They'd made time and behind them the number eight was also advancing, while in front the coast was clear for what seemed like two or three hundred metres, as far as the blind corner at the Basilica of The Holy Cross in Jerusalem.

"There's one up ahead too!" Carrara blurted.

"Keep going!"

"It's going full whack! We're going to hit it if we don't move."

The tram driver was now clanging his bell with near hysterical insistence.

173

"Wait," said Rossi checking again in the mirror. "Wait. Now!" he said and as the driver in the approaching tram braked, sending it to a screeching halt, Carrara threw the steering wheel right, slipping in front of the following tram with what could only have been feet to spare.

"Go, go, go!" screamed Rossi, at which they leapt forward as the two trams ground to a halt obstructing both carriages like a cork in a bottle.

"That's what I call a road block," said Rossi.

"And that's what you call a clear run?" said Carrara, wiping beads of sweat from his brow despite the cold.

"Clear for Rome," Rossi replied. "And anyway, who said public transport never comes when you need it?"

Thirty-Seven

Just about a mile across the city as the crow flies, in the Campidoglio Palace, Achille Basso, Mayor of Rome, was back at work. He was not a happy man, despite the unseasonable tan gained from two weeks lounging in the Caribbean sun, free of charge, thanks to a "gift" from a company the name of which he now couldn't recall. Things were not looking great. The serial killer drama, even if not the least of his worries, had been thrown into perspective by the mounting realization that his incompetence and unsuitability for the job were being exposed on every front. He had been elected on a populist ticket promising to sort out the gypsy camps and the Eastern European "immigrant problem" left behind by his wishy-washy liberal predecessor. However, now the real bread-and-butter issues affecting the citizens were coming to the fore.

With mayoral elections looming again, he was short on both money and bargaining chips. He had packed the council with his own supporters, dishing out five-figure consultancies left, right and centre for lawyers, communications "experts" and journalists. For the less demanding but equally deserving plebeian followers, he had conjured a slew of jobs in the refuse collection department, among others. They all counted. Every salary kept a family and could guarantee two, three, four or more votes. But there were many mouths to feed and the miracle-working couldn't go on ad infinitum.

In return for favours, friendship, and financial assistance in the shape of weighty brown envelopes, he had also been steering public tenders for all manner of social services and infrastructure in the direction of rather insalubrious figures and their charitable organizations. To name but a few of the potential gold mines there were the pressing issues of social housing, the rising flood of sub-Saharan and North African immigrants into the city, and the old favourite of clans and gangsters: waste disposal.

It had been difficult for him to say no. These suave-suited individuals who came looking for him in the corridors of power or who sent their emissaries with mouth-watering incentives were, almost to a man, either ex-companions in the very same neo-fascist gangs he had been an active part of, or other former criminals active in rival right-wing paramilitary groups. With the passing of the years, many of the once fiercely contested ideological differences had also been laid to one side as the so-called 'red cooperatives' manned with former exponents of their own armed struggles, and not wishing to be left out, also came currying favour. They, too, bore generous gifts quite often sealed in envelopes or rolled up in rubber bands.

The problem was that certain irregularities regarding the transparency of tenders and recruitment procedures had been seized on by zealous elements within the financial police. Then the investigating magistrates had begun giving the order to tap phones. You could bribe and bribe and bribe but only up to a point. Sooner or later a hard-headed idealist would come along to call time on the party. Or it could be orders from on high, very high. Had a deity on Mount Olympus decided it was time to sweep all the mortals away? Had it been decreed that enough was enough and the moment was ripe for a clear-out?

Looking at the assortment of papers and documents, e-mails

and balance sheets, letters and reports, Basso felt like a sixth-former a few days before the exams who's realized it's all rather too late. And the prospect of having to deal with it was sending him into a state of nervous apoplexy. He snatched up his desk phone.

"Micchè? *Achille.* Listen, I need a massage, stressed off my tits here. Yeah, total fucking nightmare. You can? OK. When? Usual place? Is she free? Please! C'mon! Do me a favour! OK. OK. You're a fucking lifesaver. *Ciao, ciao, ciao.*"

At least that was in the bag, he thought to himself, replacing the phone with an addict's modicum of renewed tranquillity. *Now, where was I? Oh yes.* He picked up the phone again.

"Roberto, get your arse down here now. Yeah. 'Course it's important."

Roberto had been on his team from the early days, when both were bootboys in the "ex" fascist collective he had subsequently "reformed". The problem was that Roberto had his head fixed firmly in the bootboy days. A loose cannon if ever there was. They all wore suits and ties now, giving them a minimal veneer of un-photogenic credibility. But while you could take a man out of his neo-Nazi birthing ground, it was somewhat harder to take the neo-Nazi out of the man.

Roberto hammered on the door, entered and launched into a full Roman salute.

"*Presente!*"

"Stop it, Roberto. Stop it."

"At ease?"

"At ease and be normal, for fuck's sake. I need normal fucking people today, OK? Now, sit down."

"OK, boss. Whatever you say."

"Right. How's the accounts? What have we got to play with?"

"We've got a couple o' mill. Depending on expenditure in the coming few months."

"OK. We're gonna be needing that, so ringfence it, right?"

"Ringfence it?"

"It means make sure it's there when we come looking for it. So, don't go splashing out on 4x4s for any of those whore consultants working in your office, or the wife, or anybody else's wife, for that matter. That's public money, see, but we're gonna use it to grease the campaign wheels in the spring when we have to make a good impression. We can put up some slides and swings in the shittier parts of town and tell 'em we're on the ground and listening to their concerns and all that bollocks and fill in some holes in the fucking road while we're at it."

"OK, boss. And the severe weather provision?"

"What severe weather provision?"

"There's talk of this cold snap getting worse, ice on the roads and all that. Part of the budget is, er, ringfensht, for emergencies, flooding and the like."

"Ringfenced!"

"Yeah, what I said. Put aside like."

"So."

"Well we might need salt, boss. Shitloads of salt. And the machines to spread it. They been onto me this morning, the local police and traffic monkeys. They want 'assurances'."

"We'll cross that bridge when we come to it. And anyway, this is Rome, in case you'd forgotten, so I don't think we're heading for the second fucking ice-age just yet, do you? Now, get your head around this. Look."

He shoved an open folder under Roberto's nose.

"Crime figures. Perception of crime. Safety index, blah fucking blah, blah, blah, blah. And this one. Voting intentions, faith in your mayor, trustworthiness ratings. You can see where it's going and it ain't going nowhere good, Robbie. The big dailies and the media are playing up the crime thing, massively, and it's putting me in a distinctly bad light."

"Blame it on the immigrants and the liberal lefties inviting 'em all in."

The mayor gave out a sigh and sank back in his chair.

"On a national level we can do that. It pushes people to the right, towards us, we know that, but I was elected here on a crime reduction ticket and it looks like I haven't done a fat fucking fuck about it."

There was a pause before Roberto replied.

"Well, we haven't, have we? We knew it was bullshit 'bout crime going through the roof when you were elected, but this is real crime now, innit?"

"It wasn't bullshit Robbie, it was marketing. It was electioneering PR. But the point is we're in the real shit here, and what are we gonna do about it? I take it you do want a job in six months' time? What are people scared of?"

"Muslims. We could catch an Islamist terrorist suspect or two. Or get the papers to say this killer's a Muslim."

"Do we have any suspects?"

"We can find some, can't we? There's enough of 'em."

"Could start a race war. Remember what happened after the election?"

"Oh yeah. The whole 'bash the immigrant' thing got a bit out of control, didn't it? Them Bangladeshis getting their shops trashed. Kind of backfired, didn't it?"

The mayor was chewing on his pen.

"The Anarchists?" said Basso. "We could get a letter bomb sent to me, or you."

"Not sure we'd get too much sympathy at the moment, boss."

"You're not helping me, Robbie."

Their two brains played the equivalent of tennis knock-ups without a net for a few moments until the lesser talent piped up.

"The Olympics. We could make a bid for the next Olympics!"

The mayor interrupted his chewing.

"Let's just use a bit more realism, shall we? Stick to playgrounds and holes in the road."

"'Playgrounds and holes in the road.'"

"Can you think of anything better?"

"Erm. No. Not really."

"Get on it then and get the press office onto it too. God knows there's enough of them."

"More than Obama's got."

"Spare me the details, Robbie. And one of them's your fuckwit niece. No offence. But emphasize the positive."

"As good as done, boss."

"Thank you, Robbie," the mayor said lowering his gaze to study yet another page of even more depressing statistics. Roberto's considerable mass remained glued to the chair. The mayor looked up, "Robbie, I said you can go now."

Thirty-Eight

"So, you do like surprises, Gigi, or don't you?" said Rossi smiling now as he pressed the button on the intercom.

"Are you sure you're all right?" a newly worried Carrara enquired. "And don't you think it would have been better to ring first?"

"And give him the chance to say he's out? He'll understand. Besides, I think we're expected."

The intercom crackled into life.

"Yes?"

"Judge Marini? It's Rossi, Inspector Rossi. I'd like to speak to if you don't mind."

Rossi and Carrara sat opposite the judge. The air was heavy, the same clock ticked somewhere and Rossi noted that the table had been dusted and polished. In the low sunlight that penetrated the windows there were the visible trails of a cloth. The judge was about to perform the usual pleasantries until Rossi cut him short.

"Where is Maria, sir?"

"Maria?"

"I know she isn't dead, sir. Please save me and yourself the time. We have murders piling up in this city and I haven't got time for sick criminal games."

The judge gave him a glare and a growl worthy of the theatre.

"I don't know what you're saying, Inspector."

"Well, in that case, I'm sure you won't mind if I take a look around the flat," Rossi replied, getting to his feet. From the flat's dark interior behind the judge there was the sound of a door and then a voice as an above-average height, athletic female figure emerged to occupy one half of the doorframe with her elegant silhouette.

"That won't be necessary, Inspector. I am Maria Marini."

She was dressed in black leggings, ankle boots, and a ribbed woollen sweater emphasizing her full breasts and harmonious figure. She moved with nothing other than feline elegance. Slender but athletic. Rossi would have said, if pressed for adjectives, taut, toned. Rossi noted, too, that her breathing was fully under control. Something of a Houdini. In different circumstances, he might have begun by saying, 'well, Madam, I think you have some explaining to do,' but before he could, Maria Marini had sat down next to her father and, lighting up a cigarette, initiated proceedings.

"If you will hear me out, I will explain everything that happened that day and why."

Was she trying to take control? Carrara, still reeling from the shock, or the chase, or both, had his face in his hands, his eyes flicking from Rossi to Marini and back. Rossi, however, seemed calm despite knowing everything now had been turned on its head.

"Well, perhaps you would like to begin," he offered.

She tapped some ash off her cigarette.

"Let me say first that my life is still in danger, as is that of my father. No one but we four gathered here knows that I am alive. No one else knows that the unfortunate young woman who was murdered, was mistaken for me. She was the tragic victim of an error in, let's say, someone's planning. A series of coincidences and pure chance meant that she was in my car that evening when her assassin believed he would be murdering me."

"What was your relationship with the dead girl?" Rossi enquired. "Perhaps you could begin by giving us at least her name. Does she have a family, that you know of? Why was she there?"

Marini raised a hand at Rossi's questioning.

"I said I would tell you everything, Inspector. But you must first realize that my life had been threatened, and my father, too, had been warned that if he didn't stop his investigations, if certain persons were not allowed to carry out their criminal activities with impunity, free from judicial investigation or observation, then both our lives were to be considered expendable. That is the first backdrop to this story."

"Mafia?" Rossi enquired.

"Ruthless people, Inspector, who answer to no one, and I mean no one."

"And your relationship with the MPD?"

"As you know, I was working for the MPD, Inspector, but as I am sure you also know, I work – worked – for secret service agencies. I had been ordered to infiltrate the ranks of the MPD and to pass on information to intermediaries. Their activities were deemed to be potentially subversive. I had been doing what I believed was the right thing, for the good of the country, for national security. When I was approached to infiltrate the movement, I naturally obeyed. It was my choice but then I found myself being drawn deeper and deeper into areas and missions going beyond the remit of government and state control. What I was being told to do was becoming increasingly more suspect, more sinister. It was no longer clear for whom or for what I was working. I had a crisis of conscience and I confronted my superiors, my handlers, and that is when I realized I was too far in to be able to escape, at least by normal means. I was warned in no uncertain terms that if I didn't continue to furnish information on the MPD and collaborate in certain black ops then I may have ended up, in their words, as 'a casualty'. They warned me that my father, too, was 'a high risk individual' and that if I didn't collaborate it might not have been possible to guarantee his safety any longer."

She stubbed out her half-smoked cigarette before continuing the monologue.

"So, I decided to rebel and for the two or three months preceding the murder I was passing on low-level, useless, or false information as I now believed the MPD was working for Italy and not against it, that the real subversives were my paymasters. I had by then forged a very close, and, yes, intimate relationship with Luca. We had begun to make plans, to think of a better future for us and for the country. It wasn't easy, given the stress that we were all under and so, after a rather torrid time, things came to a head. The separation. His drinking, the threats, though I always knew he was more bark than bite. Luca could never kill. That much I know. For me, what mattered, the only thing that mattered, was that they were wrong and I couldn't go along with it anymore, so I switched sides, if you will.

"I couldn't keep up the pretence indefinitely, however, and they began to question my efficiency, my commitment. I was confronted again, this time in the form of an ultimatum, and I was warned that if I didn't get back onside there would be serious consequences for me and my family and, try as I might, I found myself with no 'exit strategy'."

"You couldn't approach anyone in the police, the judiciary? Was there no one you could trust?" Rossi interjected.

"There are people I trust but they didn't have the means to prevent my being detected. I could have fled but they would have found me, sooner or later, and besides, my father here, would have been completely exposed."

"And the girl?"

Whether it was studied or real, some sign of emotion – regret or melancholy – flashed across her otherwise granitic expression.

"I had befriended a young woman, Kristina, a Ukrainian or a Russian – she was fuzzy about that – but an illegal immigrant. I was working with other NGOs. There, too, I had a surveillance brief, keeping an eye out for subversives, using them as cover for other ops. Initially, she had come looking for help and we got talking. She did some casual work for me, odd jobs, admin and the like, and we became friends. I was helping her to find steady employment with the aim of securing her a *permesso di soggiorno*, a residence permit, which would mean she would be able to stay in the country legally. I had also been teaching her to drive.

"On the night of the murder, I picked her up near her home, which was on my route from work. She asked if she could drive, and I said yes. It was a normal thing we did. I should add, though, that our relationship had begun to change and that she had, perhaps, become slightly obsessed with me. I was beginning to realize she may have even wanted more than friendship. She looked up to me, my success, my confidence. She had even started to dress like me.

"At first I thought nothing of it. I was flattered even but I think she had also been working on and off as an escort as she sometimes had expensive gifts and hard cash. Anyway, she was not particularly stable in that way but she was a good girl, none-theless. That night she was wearing a three-quarter length mac, the same style as my own – everyone in Rome's got them this year – and I had teased her about it. We actually looked remark-ably similar, the same build – she had been sporty, like me – and the same colour hair tied back usually in a ponytail.

"I had to pick up some extra groceries and there was a lot of traffic. I needed to go to a couple of shops and didn't want to double park, so I suggested she drive the car to the garage and that we might meet at my flat. I had just got to the counter to pay when I realized I'd left my purse in the car. The shopkeeper said I could pay the next day, but I said I would prefer to return that same evening. Even so, I left with the shopping and made my way on foot to the car park, just in case Kristina didn't see the purse. I didn't want it to be in sight on the passenger seat as it would have been an easy temptation for a thief.

"When I got to the car park, I went down the ramp to the spot where I usually parked and where I had told Kristina to leave the car. As I turned the corner, I saw a man hurrying past me and away from the scene. He had a heavy-looking holdall in one hand. He hesitated for a moment, looked at me and I saw his face. I also saw a ring flash as he wiped sweat from his brow. It was then that I noticed the blood. I thought he could have hurt himself breaking into a car or that he was an addict or in some sort of trouble. That's why I took some steps towards him, thinking he might need help but I stopped. His expression was not encouraging. I then hurried towards the parking space and that's when I made the awful discovery.

"I am sure I needn't describe the scene other than to say it was sickening. I felt sick physically but I am also ashamed to say that in that moment I saw an opportunity I could not afford to let slip. I had the chance to disappear from the face of the earth and save my life and that of my father. I checked her pulse but there was nothing that could be done. Her skull had been smashed in, her spine crushed by the blows. She had few personal effects, no rings and such like that could identify her, and she had no papers. I dragged the body out of view so that it wouldn't be discovered immediately.

"I took my few personal possessions from the car and planted one or two things on the body – my ID, a bank card, the spare set of keys that were always in the car – then left as soon as I could. I headed straight for my flat to collect some items I couldn't leave there, taking care not to be seen. I even picked up a wig from a Chinese shop. That's the kind of thing we learn in my line of work. From the flat I called my father via an encrypted proxy and we agreed on the plan to have him report me missing and then identify the body. I took some essential belongings but nothing that might be noticed and then went to the Tiber, abandoning my handbag where it would quickly be found."

"And everything seemed to be going so well," said Rossi, "and while you are here enjoying your freedom, Luca Spinelli is in a prison cell awaiting trial for a crime he could never have committed."

"If I come forward, if I were to testify, my life would be over. Do you have an idea who we are dealing with?"

"So, Mr Spinelli must just wait, until the elections are over, before finally being freed when the trial collapses?"

"At least he is alive, Inspector."

Rossi smoothed his face with both hands. He'd been ready for something big but this was one hell of a story. The killer, a killer, was still on the loose but which was which? Was it one and the same person, or some perverse copycat scenario, an opportunist assassin riding the wave of serial killer hysteria?

"Can we presume," a now calmer Carrara interjected, "that Kristina's murder was dressed up as a serial killer murder, in order to camouflage what would have been your assassination by 'them'?"

"Presumably, they decided to kill two birds with one stone. By taking me out, they would have dispensed with a troublesome rogue agent getting way out of control while implicating Luca and making the political capital they needed. It fitted in perfectly with the strategy I had been implementing on a more subtle, long-term basis. Once the media machine got going, the MPD would be in deep, deep water and without Luca working on the campaign they would be seriously short-handed."

She had it all worked out, thought Rossi, studying her cool delivery, like a slick barrister cruising through a pliant courtroom.

"The only error they made was that they didn't get their hands on my computer. They must be really sore about that. I'm surprised they didn't turn the flat upside down."

"I'm sure someone had a look," said Rossi. "Don't think that I know half of what the crime squad is up to. They were in your flat but it was clean."

"And here," said Carrara, "how come they haven't come snooping around here?"

"Well, I'm dead for one thing. My father arranged a no-questions-asked safe house for me. The guards don't know me and I never came here when I was undercover, so when I need to get into the building I either pretend to be someone's maid or use some other ruse. My father has put me on a list of approved persons with my new ID. She opened a cupboard door and took out a carrier bag. Here's one of my outfits," she said. It contained what Rossi could see were overalls and a blonde wig.

"Besides, my father's bodyguard is still reliable. Our enemies would have to neutralize them all if they wanted to get in here and that would bring too much out into the light; it would be hard to manage the reaction."

"But if that ever were to happen," said the judge, joining the proceedings, "there are certain documents in the hands of a very few trusted people that could subsequently come into the public domain. I wouldn't be around to see the consequences but the revelations would create some considerable problems for not a few people in high places. That is the only life insurance policy I possess at the moment."

"And how do you know that this place isn't bugged?" said Rossi.

"It's been swept," the judge replied. "I believe that is the term. In my position, certain things can still be guaranteed, procured. I have access to certain privileges, certain channels of communication which mere mortals, shall we say, can only dream of. Even so, in my situation I am always vulnerable. We live on a knife-edge, Inspector. A very interesting knife-edge, at the best of times, but devilishly sharp, nonetheless."

"And when the time is right, my father can see to it that I have a new identity. I could start again and eventually see my son."

"Presuming, of course," said Rossi, "that I don't just put the cuffs on you both, now, and bring you in."

Maria reached for another cigarette.

"And what would there be to gain by doing that, Inspector?"

"Justice, Spinelli's freedom, the truth?"

She lit the cigarette.

"Don't you want to catch the real killer, Inspector? Or do you want my father to be next? If they want to kill him, they will. They can put a bomb under his car. If they want to kill me, they will. That was made very clear to me. Do you want that on your conscience?"

"You can feel it, Inspector," said the judge, "when the state begins to abandon you. You are old enough to remember Falcone and Borsellino. The heroes of the anti-mafia slowly, inexorably, and fatally left to face their enemies alone, once they had over-reached, once they had come too close to the wrong people at the wrong time. Once they had become too good at their jobs. It can happen to the best of people, Inspector, the most well-intentioned servants of the law. In fact, being the best can mean signing your own death warrant. The mediocre types trouble few people. I rather think you would fall into the former category, Inspector."

Rossi weighed up whether it was a compliment, a threat, or both. He began pacing the room then stopped.

"So I must compromise? That is what you are saying? So that we are all then involved. I too become de facto an accessory to the fact? All are implicated so no one has to take sole responsibility? A strange kind of solidarity, don't you think? Or is that just 'what everybody does'? *Così fan tutti?* I thought that was the sort of thing we were against. All this cosy, corrupt, complicity."

"We are appealing to your better nature, Inspector, to your higher principles," said Maria, "not to your knowledge of procedure, and besides, there may be more ways than one in which I can help you."

"You can help me?" said Rossi. "Go on. Really. Now I'm intrigued!"

"Well, I am an agent, Inspector, whether I've gone AWOL or not the fact remains. And as a secret services agent, I am answerable to no judicial police authority, both in factual operative terms and, if you like, in moral terms. Like it or not, agents can investigate as and when they please. And before you say it," she added, raising a hand to silence Carrara now who was bridling at this latest show of arrogance, "before you tell me that it is precisely this kind of chasing shadows, when we get involved, which causes you all your problems, you will remember I told you I saw the face of the killer. What I didn't tell you is that I had seen that face before."

Thirty-Nine

Jibril and Cristian had given Iannelli a lot to think about: the overcrowding, the lack of privacy, the damp, the inadequate bedding, and monotonous diet. He wanted to know if these privations were the fruit of cost-cutting and creaming-off of funds? And funded it was, to the tune of many millions of government euros. But he didn't see much of that trickling down to the exhausted and traumatized occupants but rather more to the NGOs and cooperatives delivering the services. Cristian and other volunteers were doing good work as were many of the islanders, but he had also seen secret films that had made the Centre for Identification and Expulsion or CIE look more like a prison camp. It showed functionaries ordering men and women to strip naked, outdoors, as doctors carried out inspections or others tossed out packs of replacement clothing and bathing materials. Were they criminals? Had they committed some unspeakable crime that might explain but never excuse such humiliation? No.

Many of the men were desperate to pick up with their lives and reach loved ones and family members in that ever more abstract realm called the outside world. Here, in Sicily, in the sunshine, as the mocking winter breezes wafted dust and sand along the palm-lined promenade, the sudden and absurd stasis and frustration reminded Iannelli of Camus's *The Plague*. It was a severe test of character, a war of sorts.

He knew that in this unfortunate set of circumstances there was at least an element of design. There was human nature to consider and human refusal of nature too. But opportunism surfaced when opportunities presented themselves and unscrupulous opportunism organized to maximize the possible return was, in this context, only one thing. Mafia. Mafia of the simplest and most sublime kind. The straightforward purchasing of any privilege, position, power, access to favours, concessions, impunity, and wealth-making situations which a human individual represented. The only question was how far *la piovra* – the Sicilian for octopus and by extension Cosa Nostra itself – could reach, or had already reached with its ever-probing tentacles.

He was sitting on the quay. The fishermen below were busy fixing nets and scrubbing decks and equipment. He took out his notebook and phone. On the first page he'd written the number of the contact from Iovine and the words "Lampedusa possible"; he hadn't yet entered alphabetically in his contacts. He punched in the digits and waited for it to ring. No answer, again. Iovine had given him the low-down. The story went that it was an ex-police officer with a dossier of information about an array of figures caught up in all manner of illicit activities. His identity remained unknown. It could just as well have been a blind alley, Iannelli thought to himself, slipping the phone into his pocket and sitting back again to enjoy the sun.

No sooner had he done so than it was buzzing. There was no call ID. He answered it anyway.

"Iannelli?"

"Yes, who is it?"

Then just silence as the caller hung up. He got to his feet. Time for lunch. Just behind the quay there was a bar and restaurant recommended by the guesthouse owner. He had his eye on the pasta with sea-urchin's eggs, a local speciality. It had to be fresh but he'd been reassured by seeing the local kids braving the cold water that very morning to pluck the molluscs from the rocks where they anchored. He settled into a corner outside where there was no wind to enjoy the warmth of a suntrap.

At a nearby table sat a sole occupant, a striking redhead. She had been leafing through a book but had also been shooting him not infrequent glances. He called the waiter. It was time for an *aperitivo* and as he ordered he instructed him to ask the lone reader what he might offer her. In her mid-twenties, perhaps, she was dressed in a white roll-neck sweater and a well-worn, brown leather jacket, matching boots, and tight grey jeans. The waiter duly deposited a tall glass of what appeared to be something non-alcoholic and when Iannelli raised his glass she acknowledged, her eyes shielded with large, very dark glasses.

"May I join you?" Iannelli enquired. In Sicilian terms, he had now earned himself the right, but it was imperative that he not overstep the mark or be seen to be in any way presumptuous.

"*Prego*," she replied, indicating the vacant chair waiting at her table.

"Dario Iannelli," said the journalist, reaching out and taking her hand and bowing.

"Rita," she replied.

"Studying?" he enquired, indicating the book now face down on the table.

"Pleasure," she replied. "And you, I believe are working, as a journalist."

"How did you know?"

"Word travels fast here, *Dottore*. And I also believe you would like to speak to my father."

*

They had nearly finished their drinks but the next move hung in the balance as Rita weighed Iannelli by his words and the impression he was beginning to give her.

"I can't guarantee that he will speak with you, but I will try. I don't think I need tell you he is very disillusioned, with everyone, with everything. But if he does see you, you will get the full story, don't worry about that. It is I who answer his phone now when he is out or on the boat. He doesn't need all those interruptions, all the hassle. It's the number you rang, by the way. I heard you were here, and I wanted to have a look at you first. We like to know who we are dealing with here in Sicily, especially when they come from *il continente*."

"And you knew I would come here, to this restaurant?"

"Sooner or later," she answered, "our paths would have to cross."

Il continente. The mainland. Sicily was a world apart, physically, geographically, culturally, politically. At least that was how the story went. Of course, it was Italy, but better to say that Italy in many ways was Sicily, for Sicily and its emigrants had given to the world so many of Italy's identifying characteristics. The passion, the heat, the culture, and hunger for knowledge, the love of food and wine and family, family, family. And vendetta. Cruelty. Conspiracy. Loyalty. It was a land of rich contrasts and exotic meetings, largely due to its having been conquered and re-conquered so many times. The Greeks, the Romans, the Arabs, the Normans, right up to the English and the Americans.

Rita was a lawyer, working mainly for the unions and labour rights groups but also held an active interest in journalism and had written for various local publications. It was clear to Iannelli what side she was on and as he gave her a rundown of his background, it seemed that he was beginning to gain something of her trust. But he wanted to ascertain what her father knew and why everything was so wrapped in secrecy. Could he meet her father now? She shook her head. Not yet, not here. Did he not know that at this very moment they were being watched? She opened her book as if to bring to his attention some amusing passage and, as she did so, she provided an illustrative voiceover.

"Everything is coming to a head and what my father knows, what he discovered, well it's only a question of time before the facts emerge. The question is who will be first to expose who? Who can engineer things in such a way as to get out while the going is still good and let the others take the rap. It's a system, pure and simple and my father uncovered it. With careful and stubborn determination and against all the odds. It's a system within a system, the one that we know exists, but with a new twist, shall we say, and with Rome at its centre. But it will come out because a system built on theft and corruption and dishonesty and immorality can only remain hidden for so long."

She removed her glasses. Her eyes were a dazzling Sicilian blue. *Must be the Norman blood*, thought Iannelli.

"My father went through all the legitimate channels but met only with deception and obstruction. As a police officer he had no other choice. They made his life hell anyway once they knew. He didn't break any law but they managed to find something. They can always find something. So he couldn't go to the press or take the law into his own hands as it would all have led straight back to him, his job and us, his family. So he gave up. For us. But it broke his spirit. He was transferred God knows how many times and harassed and intimidated. When his health really began to suffer, he managed to get out with some integrity intact and at least a part of his pension. That's when he returned here and went back to his father's job. He became a fisherman again."

She turned to another page in the book as if finding some other passage with which she wanted to illustrate her point. By now the acting was natural and fluid on both their parts. She leaned closer to Iannelli and he picked up an even stronger scent of her femininity. It had been a while for him – he'd been so absorbed in his work that he rarely found time to pursue a single man's pleasures. Even just being in the company of and passing time with beautiful women, intelligent women, forgetting about work and the world for a few hours.

"This is my number and my address. Memorize them now," she said, making a note in the margin. "Come tonight at eight and my father will be there. He won't stay long and he may not answer all your questions but he will tell you what you need to know. I'll be doing the cooking, by the way, so I hope you'll be hungry."

She closed the book and leant back. A Sicilian redhead. An Aphrodite. She called for the bill.

"I'll get this," she said despite Iannelli's vain protestations. "You bring the wine tonight."

"Won't you stop for lunch?"

"Can't. Things to do."

As she left, he followed her with his eyes. Did he have a date? Or what? Still, as he tucked into his *spaghetti con ricci di mare*, he felt five or maybe even ten years younger. Then as he walked out into the afternoon, the better for a couple of glasses of Glicine, and an exquisite ricotta-filled cannoli, he felt a foot taller and ready for anything they could throw at him. It didn't occur to him how little he knew of this wondrous place or how costly it could be to try getting anywhere near anything resembling the truth.

Forty

"Perhaps I will take up that offer of a drink," said Rossi, getting up from the table. He shot a concerned glance to a perplexed-looking Carrara.

"Could I offer you some Scotch?" the judge replied, moving towards a well-stocked but probably rarely opened drinks cabinet.

"That would be fine," Rossi lied. Try as he might, he could see no Jameson or Bushmills lurking, but it would do for now.

"Inspector Carrara?" the judge enquired.

"No, thank you," said Carrara, shaking his head. "Driving. Fast, usually."

"So," said Rossi, turning back to Maria, seated and smoking as before, "where exactly did you see this face?" He took another sip of the single malt. It was good enough but not quite what he needed. "I'm guessing it wasn't at the bridge club."

"Not my thing, bridge, I'm afraid."

"Mine neither," said Rossi. "But if you could perhaps enlighten us."

"In my line of work, Inspector, there are what might be called courses, training, retreats, any number of organized encounters in which I and other colleagues meet without knowing whom we are meeting. We work on the basis of pseudonyms, code names, that sort of thing."

"Double 0 something?"

"Not exactly, but you get the idea. Anyway, we were working on interrogation techniques and surveillance and during one session we were watching some guys through a two-way mirror. We had no idea who they were but we had to study their movements and body language and reactions to questioning and, what I can say, with fair certainty, is that the man I saw leaving the car park had been in one of these groups. I really don't forget a face, Inspector. And there was what looked like a small prison-style tattoo on his neck."

"So wouldn't he have recognized you? Especially if he'd been going there to kill you."

"As I said, I saw him. He would have had my description and, yes, seeing me, he may have hesitated but I expect he believed he had already done the job required of him. He was hardly likely to kill twice and, besides, he had lost the benefit of surprise. He was making his escape. Even if he had realized his error he would have aborted the mission. It was too late. What's more, it was raining, I'd put on a rain hat and I had on thick-rimmed glasses for night driving. I'd only just started to wear them that very week and the lights were behind me illuminating him."

"But you can give us a pretty good description, an artist's impression?"

"Yes, of course and it's possible but risky that I might even be able to get access to some classified files, despite the situation I am in now. I may still be able to use some contacts, some limited access to data and channels of communication."

"You get on to that, Gigi, the identikit stuff," Rossi said, turning to Carrara who made a note on his phone. But Maria had not finished.

"So, I think we agree, Inspector, that the killer who was sent to murder me must be the same killer you are hunting for all the murders, this 'Carpenter' the press are going so wild about. And are we also of the same opinion that the idea is to strike fear into the populace while any busy bodies that happen to get in the way get taken out?"

"Don't see why not," said Rossi, "there've been more outlandish theories that proved to have just as much substance."

"And you would discount any idea that it could be someone else simply copying The Carpenter's methods, as cover to get at you and muddy up the trail?"

"Bit coincidental, don't you think?" said Rossi. "There just happens to be a killer on the loose on the eve of major elections and a political murder-scandal erupts. It's all looking rather like Jeremy Thorpe and the liberals."

"I'm not sure I follow."

"Oh, Britain, the 1970s," continued Rossi, "there really are some parallels. The old Liberal Party, considered a spent force, are resurgent again on a wave of public disillusionment with the two big parties. Then it just so happens that their leader is implicated in a plot to kill his gay lover who's been blackmailing him. He got off, or was innocent, depending how you look at it, but the party took a pounding. Never recovered. Less liberal times, you might say, and mud sticks. And a sure-fire method for scuppering a third force in politics, wouldn't you say? How little times change."

"So we agree then?"

"Well," said Rossi, tossing back the rest of his whisky, and wishing he hadn't bothered, "it's a very strong possibility." He reflected again on what Iannelli had said about infiltrating the parties. Well that much had some basis in fact, if Marini was to be believed.

"But if that is the case," he went on, "then we aren't going to be looking for a normal kind of serial killer. If it is political, who's to say he wouldn't be substituted with the next paid assassin? Still, if we got our hands on him all hell would break loose."

"In your experience, Inspector Rossi, does catching criminals stop crime? Crime is an opportunity and there's always someone ready to step in. As for killers, it's we who produce them. Society. The rat race. We, the so-called normal, law-abiding, tax-paying, socially responsible citizens. We are all to blame. They are our bastard-children, Inspector. We have to change society, not just put people behind bars. But for now, this is damage limitation. If we can track him down, in time, perhaps we'll save an innocent life. They'll have to rethink their strategy, of course, but it could win us enough time to ensure that the MPD gets a fair crack of the whip. Sure, this is killing of the worst kind, for pure gain, for political capital, but if we can move in the shadows too, like them, maybe we can see them off at the pass and do a bit of good even. At least for Kristina and the others."

There was a pause before Rossi ruptured the silence with a slow, deliberate clapping.

"Brava! The big speech! You should go into politics in your next incarnation. Ten out of ten for the theory. But the practice?"

Despite or because of the provocation, Maria's gaze was now fixed on him. He in turn was scrutinizing her to see whether there was some fury now behind the well-disciplined, icy exterior. It was not an easy call.

He looked round first to Carrara and then to the judge.

"Do you mind if we pop outside for a moment?" he asked, indicating the balcony overlooking the street. "I think we need some air."

Marini senior insisted on showing them out. Judging by the state of its few plants, the miniature terrace had seen far better days.

"As you know, this is not my habitual residence," the judge proffered by way of explanation, "and I have never been green-fingered."

"Me neither," said Rossi, though Carrara was already moving about and prodding soil and lifting leaves. Rossi took the judge lightly by the arm.

"If you will excuse us, for a moment."

He closed the door and turned to Carrara.

"So? Any ideas?"

"Well, first off, after all that, I would say some lunch was in order. And then you've got some serious explaining to do."

They were in a self-service on the Via Tiburtina and the shuffling queue of tray-bearers was at least short. Rossi had agreed to meet again with the Marinis after he and Carrara had had time to reflect on the courses of action left open to them.

"So," began Carrara, "would you finally mind explaining how you reached your startling conclusion, Mr Holmes? While you two were exchanging conspiracy theories I was feeling distinctly out of the picture."

Rossi smiled. It was nearly closing time and the choice was limited. He surveyed the offerings without enthusiasm before plumping for a *parmigiana di melanzane* with salad and chips.

"Hungry?" said Carrara indicating the bible-sized wedge of fried layered aubergines, mozzarella, and tomato sauce.

"Comfort food," replied Rossi.

The bread basket by the till was empty. He signalled to the smiling, almost elderly man clanking pots and trays, who duly refilled it with an assortment of rolls and pre-packaged slices. Rossi picked up a rosetta roll.

"Today's or yesterday's leftovers?"

"Fresh as a little rose, sir," came the quick-spirited reply. "Rose. Rosetta. Get it?"

Rossi gave a generous smile.

"Besides, go hard as a rock these in a day. Could use 'em as cannonballs."

Rossi turned to Carrara.

"See Gigi? Exhibit number one. The bread."

"The bread?"

"Cast your mind back. You may remember in Marini's flat there were bread rolls. Like these. Remember? And they were fresh."

"The bread was fresh?"

Rossi's face had become more animated now with renewed vigour and wide-eyed enthusiasm. He placed a hand on his colleague's shoulder.

"Somebody bought the bread with the rest of the shopping on the day of the murder and brought it back to the flat. Somebody was in that flat during the day, probably the evening. Ms Marini didn't have a maid. Her father says he had no key. Perhaps it was somebody nobody has mentioned, or even thought to mention or lie about, but call me mad if you like but that's when I thought we might have to turn this case on its head. That's when I began thinking that Marini might not be dead. There was no shopping left in the car and she was hardly likely to have dropped it off and then gone back to the car before being "killed". There was an all-night parking ticket too, so she was home for the night. So, she must have gone back to the flat herself. And that's why we took our little drive over to the judge's place."

They took a table near the door and away from obvious eaves-droppers.

"And then there was the book," said Rossi. "The judge bought a book for his daughter who had been murdered the previous evening."

"Maybe he forgot. Force of habit, shock."

"Well, yes, it could have been but I made a little visit to his local book vendor to see when he bought it. I wanted to push the possibilities as far as they could go, to see if they would stand up to the test. And, as you can see, my instinct was proved right."

"But I thought he was grieving for real. That's the impression you gave."

"Recently divorced. A daughter in who knows what sort of trouble. His own life in danger. I don't think you need to have studied the Stanislavsky method to come across as convincing with all that baggage."

"And too many coincidences?"

"Too many things that didn't fit or allowed room for another possibility, bizarre though it might have seemed. What's more, when we were talking, I thought he might have used the present tense to refer to her. It was ambiguous, fleeting but I felt he noticed it himself then covered it up. It can happen with the recently bereaved. He may even have done it on purpose. He's a subtle operator. He knows how and where to leave clues. At the time I didn't give it so much thought. But put it all together and it makes three. Three pretty significant coincidences."

"So why did she arrange the secret meeting with us? Why not just send a note? Why come and then escape dressed as a nun?"

"I think she wanted to be found. I think they wanted to be found. Or maybe it was to put some distance between us and them in case we were being trailed, which we were, as I'm guessing she probably knew. The chances are that someone's tapping my phone and tracking my e-mails. And she'd know what they are capable of."

"So the judge was in on it all along?"

"Yes, pretty much. Once she involved him he had no choice; what would a father do? He identified her, and he was on the scene that evening, albeit as soon as he had let a decent interval elapse. But he would have known the body was clean, unidentifiable, and left far enough from her car for anyone to make a connection. Then they waited for the dust to settle. There was the cremation. Slightly unusual that, too, for Italy. Certainly ruled out any exhumation."

"So what now?" said Carrara.

"Let's go back and ask them. We've done the hard work and maybe I might be getting a few ideas of my own too."

Forty-One

"So," said Rossi, "let me get this clear. What you are saying is that you want to join Inspector Carrara and myself, on our case?"

"I can help you find the killer but we can't come out into the open. If you bring us in, it's finished for us. My cover will be blown. It's the one big advantage we have. We can't bring Kristina back. It was either her or me, don't you see? Somebody would have been killed anyway."

"And I'm supposed to keep all this to myself? To operate in this highly irregular manner. Do you realize what could happen to me?"

"I know," replied Maria, pacing back and forth now, a panther in a cage, "I know."

"So, tell me why I shouldn't follow the rules and bring you both in and go home and get a good night's sleep?"

"Because you are a good man," she said, stopping and confronting Rossi, her hands gripping the edge of the table between them, "one of the few. And one of the best. Everyone knows that. And besides, we have the upper hand now. They think I am dead. They have Spinelli in custody. They think you're chasing shadows and they're probably sitting back and congratulating themselves and waiting for the next murder. The next move will be to pin it on the foreigners, you wait and see. It's a numbers game. They sit down and plan it all out. It's a plot. I am sure of it. The guy who tried to kill me is one of us, for God's sake! I know the way things work."

Rossi had turned towards the window. He wheeled round to face Maria and her father.

"We'd better get to work on that description then," he said, knowing once again he was being drawn into the labyrinth. Another labyrinth. And what beast lurked at the centre of this one? "And see if it matches with what Marta from the health club has to say about the weirdo. But tracking him down is going to be needle in a haystack stuff, with or without a face. We can't operate in the open or he'll know we're on to him. I can't let my superiors know any of this either. And if he twigs, he'll discover there's been a tip-off and they'll all close ranks. He'll vanish. Then they just bring in a clean skin to do the job and we're back to square one. So, everybody, it looks like we're well and truly on our own on this one."

He turned to Carrara.

"Did we get any decent forensics from any of the murders?"

"Fibres. On Yana's coat. Some hair, possibly. No prints."

"Well, if we do bring him in and we can match them up, we've got a chance. Or if we can get our hands on the murder weapon, all the better. But we have to find him first. Where do you propose we start looking?"

"I thought you might have an idea about that," said Carrara.

"Well," said Rossi, "judging by what we've got – a description, and the notes—"

"The notes?" interrupted Maria.

"Ah, yes," said Rossi, "our killer likes to leave a paper trail, in English. I suggest we go all out on them, for now."

Forty-Two

"So, what the hell were you two doing at San Giovanni! Don't you know it's extra-territorial?"

Rossi was in Maroni's office. Again.

"Keeping tabs on me, then?"

"I like to know what my people are up to, Rossi, especially when they're going about things in a somewhat irregular fashion. So, what was going on?"

"I was at a funeral."

"The truth, Rossi, not games!"

"Confession. I was confessing my sins."

Look Rossi, I told you I don't have time to mess around here. Carrying your weapon inside a papal basilica. And then that ridiculous car chase routine. Do you want to get someone killed? Haven't we got enough trouble as it is?"

"Well, if I wasn't being tailed …" Rossi began.

Maroni appeared to soften for a moment.

"Look, Rossi, I didn't put anyone on your tail, if that's what you're saying, but word gets back to me. Everything, pretty much, gets back to me, and I have to come up with answers. That's the way it is. Do you follow or do I need to translate it into your foreign language of choice?"

Chance would be a fine thing, Rossi thought to himself.

"They're in a huff because I left without offering lunch, is that it?"

"Well you certainly pissed somebody off," said Maroni, "that's why they're coming down on me like the proverbial with this story about Starsky and bloody Hutch in the middle of tourist Rome. Good bit of driving though it was, by all accounts."

"Carrara," said Rossi. "Missed his vocation if you ask me."

Maroni was drumming his fingers on the desk.

"All right," said Rossi, "some information came our way. I thought it was probably nothing but in the absence of anything else, we went along with it."

"A tip-off? Of what nature?"

"Somebody with an identikit on the killer, the killer who is still out there and not that unfortunate sap Spinelli in the cells."

Maroni seemed to stiffen in his chair at the mention of the detained politician.

"And you didn't think of sharing this big breakthrough with me?"

"Like I said, I didn't really think it would be a breakthrough, just a crank, probably, but as it turns out, maybe we've got something."

"Go on. What? And from who?"

"We have a description. Pretty generic but she, it was a she, claims to have been a witness at the car park but can't come forward in person for the usual reasons – shouldn't have been there, married woman seeing someone she shouldn't have been seeing. At least that's the story."

"And you just let her go?"

"She disappeared."

"Bloody magician now, is she?"

"Didn't they tell you what was going on that day?" said Rossi, with well-disguised feigned incredulity, "Your grasses, I mean."

"They're not grasses, Rossi," Maroni retorted, "and I wasn't told. It was brought to my attention. There's quite a difference, you know. And I don't have direct contact with all branches of the intelligence community and, to be quite honest, I wouldn't want to. But in this case I'd like to know how you could let someone with that kind of information slip through your fingers!" he concluded, jabbing one of his own at Rossi.

"It was very well-planned," said Rossi, "there were only the two of us and the place was crawling with nuns. She slipped into the crowd. I could hardly put them all up against the wall, could I? There would have been a diplomatic incident."

"It probably already is a diplomatic incident," said Maroni with an air of exasperation, "at least as far as us lot are concerned."

"You know," said Rossi, "it would be nice to know who my guardian angel is. I might want to pray to him from time to time."

"We all have guardian angels, Rossi, and sometimes we should be thankful for small mercies. There are times when we all need protection."

Rossi appeared to reflect for a moment on his superior's words.

"Are you saying I should be watching my back?"

Maroni had loosened his tie and was scratching around looking for something in his desk debris, between stacks of dog-eared folders and stray papers.

"Need to take this damned pill," he blurted, opening a drawer and extracting a small bottle, managing as he did so to knock over the one plastic cup among the many on his desk that was full of water. Rossi stood up and filled him another from the machine. Maroni tossed back the pill and grumbled something like thanks before continuing.

"All I am saying is that, despite appearances, sometimes, we are all in this together and yes, there are dangers. You know the dangers, Rossi, you don't need me to hold your hand, do you? What I'm saying is don't go in over your depth, not on your own, not on this one."

"'On this road,'" began Rossi, "'man is threatened by many dangers, both from within and without.'"

Maroni gave a puzzled look.

"Aquinas," said Rossi, "*Summa Theologica*."

"Ah," Maroni replied. "Well, can you just keep me in the loop on all this?"

Rossi shrugged.

"What exactly can I do?"

"Normal police work?"

"'Normal police work'?"

"Like normal bloody *poliziotti*."

"I will promise to do my best," said Rossi, "and to be as normal as the circumstances require."

The two men looked at each other for some time.

"Please go now, Rossi," said a more wearied-looking Maroni, "just go, please."

Rossi wandered out of the Questura. Maroni was torn, he could see that, between helping and hindering him. He wasn't a bad man but he had got to where he was by playing the game and, when necessary, turning blind eyes, maintaining the status quo. He was already old enough to put in for early retirement if he wanted. Why hadn't he then? Even so, there was no way he was going to risk all that going up in smoke. His travel projects, his plans for the boat he kept in the marina at Ostia and which he tended every available weekend, repairing and painting it in the spring ready for the summer season and the fishing trips. At least that was the story he kept hearing. Rossi knew all about that and had to admit he envied him just a little. Maroni had "looked after his own garden", as the saying went. Nobody else was going to do it for him, that was clear. Regardless of what went on in the outside world, his little corner of sanity and decorum and comfort would be well-tended. It wasn't quite the "I'm all right, Jack" mentality but it was something close. He had his family, his daughters about to move on to university; why would he want to risk all that?

He wasn't so badly off himself but if he wanted to go higher in this game he'd have to make compromises and he still wasn't the compromising type. He couldn't get his head down and play by the rules, their rules, day in, day out. He'd been tempted on more than one occasion by offers from the private sector, security firms, consultancies, multinationals. He had friends, ex-colleagues more than friends, lured away to take up dull but lucrative positions and who were now enjoying the fruits of their minimal labours.

But was he ready to jump ship? If everyone did that, where would the force end up? It would become just another tool in the hands of the powerful, a toothless lion, a paper tiger. And they would have won. Not like they weren't winning already anyway, but for as long as he could be a thorn in the side of the criminal establishment, within and without, he would keep going. No. He wasn't going to lie down and roll over. His thoughts turned then to Yana and to his own loneliness, but a twinge of guilt went through him too. Here he was, the lucky one. He owed it to Yana to stick with it. He owed it to his colleagues too, men like Carrara, who had the spirit intact and their vision unclouded by cynicism. He owed it to the people trying to eke out an honest living in the face of the menace and the temptations of organized crime. And he owed it to his own father, to his memory. That was always the bottom line. That was where this conversation always came to a dead end.

He gave out a sigh. He had dug himself into a pretty deep hole, again, hadn't he? Let's see. What was he now? An accessory? No, but as a public official his failure to report a crime was an offence punishable by at least a year inside. More fuel for their fire if it all went pear-shaped. But why did it have to happen on his shift? Why did he have to get the bizarre, mistaken identity, bungled, political murder in the midst of the first serial-killer hunt the city had perhaps ever seen? Why him? Or was it more than a coincidence?

He took out his phone and called Carrara.

"Busy?"

"At home," said Carrara. There were distinct family-type percussive noises and shrieks in the background.

"Can I come round, just for half an hour? Need to pick your brains."

There was silence as Carrara appeared to be dealing with a family-type emergency.

"Sorry, about that," he said. "Ah, look, Mick, I'd promised a bit of the old quality time tonight, you know? Could it wait?"

"I've just been up before Maroni," Rossi countered, upping the ante. "Not the happiest camper."

"Ah."

"It'll be half an hour, I promise. Just to get some ideas on a few things that are bugging me, about the case. Then I'll be off."

"Righto," said Carrara. "I'll prepare the ground."

"I'm sure she'll understand," said Rossi.

"No comment," said a tightish-lipped Carrara.

Forty-Three

With irritation, the cardinal decided to take the call buzzing like an incensed insect on his mobile phone.

"Your Excellency!"

"What do you want now?"

"Dispensing with the niceties, are we? Not like you to forgo formality, is it?"

"I am very busy and I would appreciate it if you didn't continue to call me."

There was laughter on the other end of the line.

"Well, I'll cut to the chase, shall I?"

"You can be brief, I think it's better, and please observe the usual protocol."

"Oh, they're not listening to us. You are above suspicion and I am, let's say, invisible to their radar."

"That's as maybe. I still think it would be better if …"

His interlocutor cut him short.

"Now, listen up, and listen good. We have some very delicate relics that need to be hand-carried into the country and we need you to come up with a reliable porter in Lausanne? A man of the cloth, naturally."

"'Lausanne'?" the cardinal repeated. "*Lausanne*?"

"Lausanne. Correct. A considerable number of relics. We'll need a private jet, preferably with something in the way of papal insignia, just for good measure, for good luck, *buona fortuna* and all that. The relics just happen to be in Lausanne. Pure coincidence mind."

The cardinal was sweating cold now. *Hadn't he done enough? When would this end? Why couldn't they drive their filthy lucre over the border like everyone else?*

"Excellency, are you there?"

"I can't do it."

Silence again. Then laughter.

"Ah, you can't do it."

"I can't, I tell you! It's going too far! Haven't I done enough? In my position," he began again, before once more being unceremoniously put in his place.

"Haven't you enjoyed yourself again today, Excellency, 'in your position'? Haven't you been quite the brazen hypocrite, in front of all those special people hanging on your every word? But you know it all comes at a price. This is business now. Nothing more and nothing less. But of course if you want the pictures to fall into less safe hands. And if anything were to happen to me, my lawyers have instructions, shall we say."

"Pictures? What pictures?"

"Ah! There are always pictures, Excellency. Should anyone ever forget the exact details. Where they were, when and with whom."

The pictures. How had he let himself be photographed? How had he let it all slip out of his control!

"Look," he said beginning now to perspire, "give me time!" he almost screamed into the receiver. "Give me time! You must understand that it will take some considerable time."

"How much time, Excellency? Not an eternity, I trust."

*

From the wall of his Renaissance apartment rooms, his prized portrait of Lucrezia Borgia looked down on him now with tacit disapproval. He'd been lax, foolish. Yes. But could he not assert his power? It was his duty to dictate the terms, not be dictated to. The powerful could tell the hoi polloi what to believe. They were the masters of reality, this reality. Yes. Perhaps he had let things slide, had even sat back on his laurels. Much time had passed, in human terms, it was true. Even the strongest could slacken after such a long race. Saint Paul was right. "Do you not know that in a race all the runners run but only one receives the prize?"

He continued to gaze lovingly at his prize. He had obtained the painting "privately", after a long search, and it was the jewel of his collection, much envied and much desired. As he gazed at it, something jolted him back to his senses. This was his purest pleasure not the addiction he had allowed himself to fall into. And at what cost? Was this all that he was capable of? Being blackmailed? Was he so naive as to have fallen for the oldest trick? He, of all people? Yes, his self-assurance had led to his complacency. The Banquet of Chestnuts, the honeytrap as it was known by lesser mortals, by the vile, uncultured worms now pulling all the strings? His time was limited. He knew that. But a flourish? And there was a way. There was always a way. *Costi quel che costi.* Whatever the cost had to be.

He picked up his phone which weighed now like a neat weapon in his hand and he dialled.

"Excellency!"

"You will get your courier," he replied, feeling something of his stately calm now returning. "I will see that it is done."

And with that he pressed his thumb into the cherry-red symbol to terminate the call, as if pressing his cardinal ring into a wax seal, and began to breathe calmly again.

"And you will get your eternal reward too," he announced to the gold and cream furnishings and the sepulchral silken drapes, "sooner perhaps rather than later."

He then moved the small desk on castors to one side and, bending down with a little difficulty, keyed in the digits to open the wall-safe concealed there. He took out only a folded, letter-sized piece of paper and a sleek mobile phone and following the instructions proceeded to make another call.

The content of the exchange was of a secrecy that few men on earth were privy to. When contact had been firmly established the cardinal continued.

"So, it seems that I shall have to 'disappear' and that we will also be making a new martyr. Respecting my last wishes, I will not be afforded the honour of lying in state, in the spirit of simplicity. A simple casket. Yes. A cardiac arrest. The pressure of work, the outcomes of which could not be left to chance. The concomitant stress. Indeed. The martyr will have a less edifying *obituarias* to leave behind. Organized crime. Money laundering. Illegal arms brokering. Exploitation. In the interests of an anti-mafia policy which will be rigorously executed and to avoid the appropriation and laundering of monies and material goods his estate will be frozen. Yes, something like that. The journalists usually know it makes sense. And see that his lawyers' hands are let's say 'tied securely'. Several years of painstaking sifting through every detail of his little criminal empire will suffice. Ah yes. 'The law's delay'. Indeed. So, should anyone not wish to be reasonable, I will have departed the scene, unable to defend myself in the face of outrageous calumny. Yes. I think they will, as you say, 'play ball'. The devil is in the detail, yes. As always. As always. And no, I think his friends and family will understand, don't you? Once they understand who is at the helm. Who is calling the tune. Oh, and the boys too. Yes, one, I am afraid. As a warning to others. 'The wages of sin are indeed death'. Quite right. *Sic transit gloria mundi*. How fleeting these worldly things are. How fleeting."

Forty-Four

"Have you got any ideas then?" Rossi countered as he sipped on an uncharacteristic Campari soda. Carrara had practically bustled him out of the flat as soon as he had arrived. Barely time to salute the *bella signora*, who really was a *bellissima signora*, though Rossi tried not to let his admiration for the smouldering Neapolitan seem too obvious. But she would go and dress in that way. What could he do? He was only human. And why had he himself then ended up with a blonde? He spun the ice in his drink, forming a violent merry-go-round.

"Ideas about what?" said Carrara, "about who's tailing us?" He was looking rakish in his leather jacket, roll-neck jumper and jeans and seemed to be catching the attention of the waitress crossing and re-crossing near their table.

"About 'why', primarily, I would have said. I mean, are they trying to see what we're up to before we do it or just feeding back reports?"

"Perhaps they want us to lead them to the prize," said Carrara, "and then swipe it from under our noses. Or they want to find someone, maybe Marini. Do you think they've twigged? That she's, you know? Not."

Rossi zipped the ice around in his slim jim now with the

216

twizzle stick. The cubes seemed to pursue each other like a dog chasing its own tail.

"So you're saying it's the services and not just Maroni's masters' minions?"

"Do you see a difference?" Carrara replied. "I mean if they are all in it together, the distinction between rogue secret services and bent cops seems wholly, let's say, superfluous."

"Or redundant, as in unnecessary. Lot of Ms in that weren't there?"

"In what?"

"Maroni's masters' minions."

Carrara furrowed his brow and sneaked a look at his watch. The *aperitivo* was having the intended effect. Rossi knew La Signora didn't take kindly to being kept waiting, and he, too, was beginning to feel the first rumblings of gastric intent. He was still half-holding out for the invite.

"It's just I'd like to know who we're dealing with," Rossi finally concluded, "in operational terms."

Carrara's interest flared up again.

"You don't think we're talking targets, do you?"

Rossi seemed unperturbed yet fatalistic as he leaned back further on the wicker chair and into the warmth of his coat.

"It's not so much what Maroni said that bothers me," Rossi continued, "but how he said it. He was rattled, harried, not like he had things under control, and you know how he likes to have things under control."

"So you think they've put the frighteners on him?"

"I don't think they need to," said Rossi, "I think he's got himself into something bigger than he knows how to get out of."

"Go on," said Carrara.

"Well," continued Rossi, "if you were working for the financial police, wouldn't you be asking some questions about a man like our Maroni?"

"What kind of questions?"

"Questions about his income, his lifestyle, the boat we've never actually seen. Small affair apparently but I ran a few checks and it seems he's being rather modest. Just upgraded to a thirty footer. Not registered in his name, requires a rather large mooring, and he's had it moved to one of the more exclusive marinas. And then his kids, who he's transferred to private schools. Looking to get them into American university next. And I don't think they're going to be getting scholarships."

"Could have had a windfall," proffered Carrara. "An American uncle."

"But why the secrecy?"

"Discretion?"

"Fear. He had a moment of weakness. Then another and before he knew it he was doing somebody else's bidding in return for handouts. It's the old story. So, you know what? I don't think they need to put the frighteners on him. I'd say he's in it right up to his neck. They're keeping him there as long as they need him, and he's got no other choice. He's going to grow old on the job. If they let him grow old that is."

In a grimy call box on the further reaches of the grey and equally grimy Via Prenestina on Rome's eastern fringes, Victor could finally hear the voice of his friend crackling down the line. He wasn't so far away. Sicily, in a Centre for Identification and Expulsion or CIE, but he was planning his escape. The place was a joke his friend told him. "They'll have to move us to the mainland soon. It's at bursting point and then when we get to one of the other camps, they've only got a handful of security guards patrolling the fence. All it will take is a bit of nerve and I'm out of there, brother." Jibril, like Victor, like so many others had first made the perilous sea crossing on a deathtrap of a boat and by hook or by crook had reached Lampedusa and thus Italian, European soil.

"Are you eating? What food are they giving you?" his friend asked.

"Pasta, of course. It's OK, though they sometimes give us pig. I think some of them find it funny, you know."

On Lampedusa, the government had been applying its usual shambolic approach to integration and assimilation, which involved reassuring the often fearful public, watching on their TVs, that the dreaded immigrants were behind bars. The CIEs were as good as prisons, though dressed up as holding houses for these citizens of the world, until the authorities established whether or not they had legitimate grounds for political asylum. Broadcasters filled news bulletins with the appropriate images giving reassurances that the laws in place would ensure any bogus asylum seeker was repatriated without delay. The reality was somewhat different. Security was lax on the mainland, with guards on low pay open to corruption or not motivated to keep the detainees inside.

As a consequence, many of the immigrants seeped out into the surrounding countryside, realizing their destiny was in their own hands. Even if they had been fingerprinted and were then expelled they could physically erase their own fingerprints and return again on another boat with different papers or no papers at all. Many of them would be heading to friends or relatives already well-established in France, Germany, Sweden, and the UK. However, the Calais Jungle and the channel tunnel presented more difficulties than other borders.

"Ring me again tomorrow at the same time at this number," said Victor.

"If I have any money left. I'll have to eat, you know."

"You can steal if you have to, you know? It's not a crime if you're hungry. Or you can go to a church. A priest will give you something. You can give them my name." As if afraid of being heard or feeling himself to be in possession of important, classified information, he lowered his voice and put his lips closer to the receiver. "Listen, I've got to know some important people here," he whispered now. "I have met an important business man who knows a cardinal!"

The voice at the other end laughed out loud.

"It's true!" Victor protested. "And he says he can get me a *permesso di soggiorno* and maybe one for you too."

"You told him about me?"

"He asked if I had friends he could meet."

"In return for what, brother? You know there's always a price, don't you?"

There was a pause.

"Victor. Are you there?"

"Yes."

"What do they want from you for all this?"

There was a longer pause.

"Favours," he whispered.

"What kind of favours?"

"Company, that sort of thing. But it's all true! He promised."

"OK, brother, and I'm friends with a journalist and an aid worker."

"Really?" Victor replied.

"No, of course not. I'm pulling your leg. They're all users, my friend, I can guarantee you. They're only helping themselves. But I believe you, don't worry," the older, more seasoned friend assured him with a laugh. "But, look. You be careful. I have to go now. There are a hundred people need to use this phone tonight. I'll be in touch. Wish me luck."

"God bless you, Jibril."

"The same to you, my brother, the same to you."

220

Forty-Five

Rossi and Carrara were back in the office and were squaring up to what they had got themselves into.

"So, she's going to help us find him. The secret services agent is dusting off her investigative credentials," said Carrara. "Where do we start?"

Rossi was procrastinating by sifting through messages on his desk, many of which were handwritten by their still e-mail-shy secretary. He squinted as he tried to decipher the old-school calligraphy and then either consigned them to the wastepaper basket with backhand flicks or moved them to another pile of 'things to do' that seemed to be putting on fat like a middle-aged carabinieri's waistline.

"Where do you think?" said Rossi, stopping and lingering for a moment longer over a more interesting missive.

"Got something there then, have you?" Carrara enquired, hoping that what had now attracted Rossi's attention might be some clue to opening the deadlock in the case.

"Oh, just an invite to my alma mater, The IAUR. They're giving out prizes and one of my old profs is up for a gong. Great guy, all-rounder really."

Then, as if in the throes of some sudden revelation he reached out for the phone.

"Eleonora, this note about Professor Borrego, do you remember when exactly? And no phone number? Just the e-mail address? He's travelling a lot at the moment. Is he? OK. Very well. *Grazie. Grazie.*"

He turned back to Carrara.

"Luigi, I may have an idea."

Forty-Six

Yes. He would send a quick message to Iovine and then drive straight back to Rome as soon as he could. Expecting to get everything he wanted from his scoop, he was planning for the editorial meeting of his life. They would not name their source, there was no question of that. Rita's father, Tonino, would remain in the shadows, for his own safety, but the information had to come into the public domain. Why had the magistrates blocked it and stopped any prosecutions? He was trying not to get too excited, but it was hard. This story could run and run. It could make him. Rita had spoken, too, of pages going missing from Tonino's report. Where had they ended up? Who had made them disappear? These were all very legitimate questions demanding straight answers. But where were they likely to come from?

"All well here. VERY interesting leads. Hope to be in Rome tomorrow night. Can't say more for now."

He left the guesthouse and made his way along the main road until he reached the name of the street Rita had told him to memorize. He worked out which way the numbers were arranged and headed uphill between its wobbly looking houses. Rita answered quickly when he buzzed, and he pushed the building's heavy oak door inwards and jogged up stone steps to her flat on the first floor. The door was already ajar but out of long-practised politeness, he knocked.

"*Permesso*," he called out.

Pleasing cooking odours emanated from an unseen kitchen.

"Here I am!" said a radiant and more relaxed Rita as she swung open the door. She was stunning in a dark green sequinned mini-dress and high fashion beige stilettos. She greeted him in the warm inimitable Sicilian style leaving Iannelli wanting more of the same.

She took the bottle he was still grasping, gave it an approving glance and led him through to the dining room where a fire was crackling in the grate. In an armchair, sat a relatively energetic-looking man, perhaps in his late-fifties, holding a local newspaper while keeping a sceptical eye on the television news.

"Dario, this is my father, Tonino."

He rose to greet Iannelli with the firm handshake of first acquaintance, looking straight into his eyes. As he did so, Iannelli felt the customary hot knife of suspicion go through him but he was inured to it by now.

"It is a pleasure to meet you in person. I have read many of your articles for the *Roman Post* and now I see you work for *The Facet*."

"That's right," Iannelli replied.

"Keep up the good work, that's all I can say. But tell me about Rome."

"Well," interrupted Rita, "perhaps before we get down to business we should start with a little *aperitivo*."

She click-clacked over to the drinks cabinet for glasses. Iannelli, feeling a father's inevitable presence, tried not to look overly interested but she was magnetic. She was walking back towards the kitchen when the telephone on the small, marble-topped table near the door began to ring. She took a few quick steps and lifted the receiver.

"*Sì?*" There was a pause. "*Chi è? Chi è?*" she repeated before slamming it back down. She paused for a moment and then, with a brisk motion, she reached under the piles of magazines and directories and jerked the lead out from the wall socket.

"Nothing. No one. Again."

Father and daughter looked at one another across the room for a brief instant. Their silent interaction seemed to encapsulate the drama and the fear that Iannelli was now beginning to sense, despite the initial levity and warmth he had hoped would dominate the evening.

"C'mon," she said. "They can go to hell. Let's raise a glass."

She hurried back with a bottle of chilled white and filled their glasses for the first toast.

"Salute!" said Iannelli as he began to raise his glass, but Rita put a hand on his arm.

"No," she said. "Remember, you are in Sicily. You must look into the other person's eyes, like this." And as she lifted her flute and brought it against his, the radiance of the crystal competed valiantly, but in vain, with the bright light burning in her eyes.

Yes, thought Iannelli, in Sicily, *always with the eyes. What a fine and necessary tradition that was.*

The meal was more than excellent. For the starter there were toasts of toasted croutons with mushrooms and a rich caponata sauce followed by deep-fried artichokes. Iannelli was already full when the first course – spaghetti with fried aubergines and tomato sauce topped with salted ricotta – followed, but manners meant he had to keep eating and smiling and complimenting the chef. All was rounded off by a delicate but sumptuous main course made with swordfish caught by Rita's father that very morning. While they ate, Tonino asked most of the questions. Unobtrusively, but with a policeman's perspicaciousness, he was logging details, cross-checking for inconsistencies, corroborating the facts as Iannelli presented them. The prize here for Iannelli was huge and he was treating it like an interview, a business dinner, thinking quickly and always trying to be one step ahead.

A substantial file sat on the coffee table around which they were now sitting while they sipped on after-dinner digestive liqueurs.

"It's all in there," said Tonino. "The full reports before they got butchered by whoever it was didn't want the truth to come out. Nobody else wanted to have anything to do with it. Nobody wanted to say that politicians were in cahoots with organized crime, with the cocaine traffic into the capital, with the money laundering. And everyone was getting their share while we were trying to do our duty, chasing shadows and then when we do finally make the link, what happens? We spell it all out and next thing you know you've been transferred. Have you ever wondered why politicians don't get shot these days? Well, you don't need to shoot someone who's on the payroll, do you?"

Iannelli could see that telling the story was difficult for him. It was an open sore and he was dealing with a wounded lion. But he also knew that in his own line of work at times he had to use pathos, convey it to his readers, win them over with it. But if he felt it himself then it was all too often an inconvenience. He expressed his commensurate dismay, his disgust, as and when required, but he had to be clinical. Let the story make the rules.

"You know they had a doctor diagnose me with God knows how many wild and wonderful diseases. While they were doing further tests, I was to be suspended and then they took my gun away. All complete nonsense but, in the meantime, with the stress, I began to get sick for real. Clever bastards, aren't they?"

He threw an eye then at the slightly dog-eared file.

"So, do you want it?"

This was the big break. It was dynamite and it was sitting there.

"What can you tell me about the immigration crisis?" Iannelli asked, sensing there was more to be found.

"Well, it all starts here, doesn't it? The more who come in, the more can be squeezed from the state and shared out between the interested parties. We've got transcripts in there," he added, "from when we trailed people. They talk about drugs and immigrants being just as good earners for them. The immigrants are better, in fact, because they're legal trade. Once they are in, they're a money-making opportunity, whoever's in power carves up the crisis economy as they see fit. Every immigrant is worth X amount while he's on Italian soil."

He gave a deep laugh of disdain. "Did you see that idiot, Mayor Basso, the other day, marching through Rome trying to drum up support for the elections? He said the immigrants that tried to trash that God-awful detention centre – in shocking conditions, no doubt – should all be sent back, with a kick up the arse. It was his administration that had them put there in the first place! And guess who made money out of that? He probably got a kickback off the opposition too when they decided to throw their hats in the ring and cut their losses. You can bet your life on it. And they're all running scared now, what with the MPD putting a cat among the pigeons." He cast another eye across at his daughter. "I'm not too convinced about that lot either. They all want to get on that white horse, don't they? The power that comes with it and then you see what they're really about. But Rita here's giving them the time of day. And a little bit more than the benefit of the doubt."

Rita was scowling back at her father as only a daughter could. "And if the elections go the wrong way, the wrong way for the establishment that is, they are going to be hard-pressed to keep everything under wraps. I think we are living in very interesting times, Dario. Too interesting maybe."

He finished his glass and got to his feet.

"But now I must leave you. We are taking the boat out tonight to find squid, and put down lobster pots. Somebody has to make some honest money." Tonino didn't disguise his enthusiasm about the venture, but for Iannelli the whole idea was like refuse-collection or undertaking – important work but he was glad someone else had to do it.

"Sounds like fun," he said.

"And then tomorrow we've got some tourists to show around. I can take you if you like."

"That's very kind," said Iannelli, snapping back to reality, "but I am expected in Rome tomorrow, as soon as I can get there. I shall be leaving first thing."

"As you wish. Another time, then."

"Another time, for sure."

There was an awkward pause as the three of them stood there, neither, it seemed, wanting to make a move.

"Well, if you want to take up this matter, it is there. If not, you can leave it here with Rita."

Iannelli reached out and shook the policeman's hand.

"Thank you for your trust."

The policeman held on to Iannelli's hand.

"I don't trust anyone, *Dottore*, beyond my own family. I am giving it to you because I am letting go. It's my decision. Trust left long ago."

Iannelli gave an awkward smile as the grip was finally loosened.

"And I'm not making any promises. That stuff there is not official, as it isn't stamped and signed and countersigned. You know the way it works. I don't need to give you a lesson on bureaucracy, do I? But if you can get it into the public arena, maybe something will start moving. No other journalist I ever met wanted to touch it."

"I will see what I can do. Do you have copies?"

"No. That's it. I'm through with fighting now. I did my bit and failed, I suppose. But I tried. You may say it's selfish of me but there comes a time in your life when you have to stand back and say, can I live now? Is it unreasonable to want to live the rest of my life in relative peace?"

"I understand," said Iannelli. "I think, however, that you have done much more than just your 'bit'. But I was just thinking. About the money."

"What about it?"

"Well, how does it move around? Cash, gold bars? We're talking a lot of dough here."

"The safest way, the shortest most discrete route. The ISW, the Institute of Sacred Works, of course. Set up a cover organization, a foundation, a charity, whatever, and then the money flows in and out, like a heart pumping blood around the body. You'll have to look respectable, of course, but that's not difficult. Then it's plain sailing. No checks, no questions asked. No tax. Everybody's happy. Except the Italian state, or the faithful, if they knew how much lucre's going through their beloved Church and where it's all coming from. And if you're buying from me, or I'm buying from you, it's all the same. We both have accounts and no one's the wiser, no one bats an eyelid."

Iannelli helped Rita clear away the dishes despite her repeated protests that it could wait till the following day.

"If you are looking for the dishwasher, there isn't one," she called from the dining room. But he had stopped to look at a picture. It appeared to be of Rita, her father, the mother she had not yet mentioned and, he supposed, a younger brother. He piled the plates into the sink, gave them a cursory rinse then went back into the dining room where she was rearranging the table.

"And this," she said, picking up the folder. "Nobody wants to touch this. They don't think their job's worth it. They don't think their life's worth it. Do you?"

In the low, after-dinner lighting and the glow from the coals, a seductive if slightly infernal aura now illuminated the scene. Temptation. Pleasure. Ambition. Opportunity. They all vied now in Iannelli's fantasies. Then he reached out and for a moment they both held the file suspended between them, its weight much greater than he had expected, until she loosened her grip and it then became his.

As he walked back along the seafront towards his lodgings, out on the dark water he saw the little lights of fishing boats and could hear their engines chugging away like animal hearts. On the boat nearest the shore the men aboard were shining torches down into the water and creating little pools of yellow light. Leaning over one side, as the boat rocked and bobbed, he could just make out a dark figure poised with something like a spear or possibly even a trident, waiting, waiting for just the right moment to strike.

He had bottled it. They'd had another drink after, a coffee, some more almond biscuits and an *ammazzacaffè*, a final, strong liqueur to "kill" the coffee, thus ensuring a sound sleep. Then she'd sent him packing as was always going to happen. The last kiss on the doorstep had been affectionate and warm but he felt she'd kept her distance, verbally and formally. So it was clear there would be no chance of it wandering towards his lips. Her full breasts, too, had pressed against his chest, and he'd had the urge then to reach an arm around her waist to pull her towards him, but he hadn't. Why? Fear of rejection? No, he didn't fear that. Fear of getting in too deep emotionally? Maybe, yes, and bringing her down with him to wherever it was he was now heading? He was taking a road which could lead him anywhere. But this was what he wanted, wasn't it? The big story, the scoop. And what did his mother always say? Be careful what you wish for, Dario. You might get it one day.

But despite his racing thoughts, and the quaint, engaging tableau before him, Iannelli's attention had now become much more firmly focused on the footsteps he had heard following in time with his own and which, as he paused to survey the harbour, had now stopped.

230

Forty-Seven

"There's no need for you to see my face, Dr Iannelli. In fact, it's probably better for you if you don't."

The voice came from out of the shadows behind him. It was not markedly Sicilian, but the tone was southern.

"I wasn't intending to look," Iannelli replied.

"You are not in danger. I have a proposal for you," he continued and Iannelli heard the footsteps once again until they stopped beside him. They were both now leaning on the parapet, like two old friends with no need to fill the silence with small talk.

"You are a good journalist, one of the best."

Iannelli had just been expecting to hear the eulogy to continue with "and a promising young prospect" when a falling star streaked across the sky before them.

"See!" the voice added. "Your timing is impeccable. The Gods are smiling on you. I trust you made a wish."

"Of course," Iannelli replied, "but it doesn't seem to have come true yet."

The voice gave a dry laugh of knowing acknowledgement.

"Look. When are you going to give up this rabble-rousing commie stuff and come and work for us? I know you don't believe it. You know it too. But it's what makes you who you are, right?

The maverick. The gunslinger. Well, come and write for my employer," he said in an almost avuncular tone. "You don't even have to know who 'he' is. Just name your price," he said. And with that he reached inside his jacket and produced a chequebook and an expensive-looking gold fountain pen.

"We can start right now with a down payment. All you will have to do is to write what certain people would rather the people were reading, or write in a way that keeps everybody more or less happy. We don't need people stirring up unnecessary emotions, especially at this time. The country needs stability, continuity."

Iannelli laughed silently to himself at the choice of verb tense "will have to do". His interlocutor's vision was like that of the salesman who, in his own mind, has already sold his product, so convinced is he of the illusion he's peddling.

The hand holding the pen was poised over the chequebook resting on the parapet. A breeze tried but failed to ruffle the pages. Beyond them both was the wide open sea, the boats still there, engines chugging away and the shadowy men still scrutinizing the depths, working, toiling. Honest men, yes. But for what? A pittance? A tradition? A principle? So that he could sit back and fill his face with seafood when he pleased?

So, this was the alternative and this was how it happened. It was as real as this. Money from an offshore account. You could set one up for yourself, too, in Switzerland or San Marino or, now that things were beginning to get that little bit more difficult in Europe, you'd pack your Bermudas and get on a plane to Santo Domingo, the British Virgin Islands or Costa Rica. They would be more than willing to have your money rolling in, like so much surf, and paid generous interest too. If you were prepared to take the risk.

Or you could take the monthly envelopes, *le bustarelle*, stuffed with notes for you to do with as you pleased. And then you would be on the payroll. There's a TV debate, they need a journo to give some "balance" to proceedings – get up there and do your stuff. This is the line to take and don't let the other guy get a word in. Interrupt him, break his train of thought, don't let him get his message across if you think he's smart. Remember, people respect you. You did the hard work to get where you are. OK, you've changed your mind over the years in a few key areas but you've "matured", right?

"Name your price," he said again.

How had he found him? Who had sent him? But Iannelli didn't have time to process all that. This was Sicily, remember. If he got out of this alive he would thank whatever divinity had befriended him and he could dwell on the rest at his leisure. And regret it at his leisure too. Money. Easy money. Did such a thing exist? The hand was poised, waiting. Waiting.

But he had his own gold mine now. The attaché case he was gripping, full of material of such potential sensitivity and with such far-reaching implications it seemed he was heaving around a bomb ready to explode. If he accepted, perhaps he would then have to hand it over, as part of the deal. As collateral. So this was the second gamble of the night. Cash in your chips or hold out, Dario? The scoop of scoops was within his reach. He only had to get it all back to Rome and then he would be in control. He would be pulling the strings for once and the politicians and their whores could dance a merry tune. They could go fuck themselves. All of them.

"In my experience," Iannelli began, "in this life you either have too little money or too much. I personally find the former the easier of the two burdens to have to bear."

There was a moment of silence. The breeze whipped up again as if sent from out of the obscure depths before them.

"So you are saying no? And if I said you could write the cheque yourself?" he said, proffering the pen sideways to Iannelli, as if handing him over the controls of some craft they were both piloting. This must have been the moment many dreamed of. But they would own him then. He would cease to be himself.

"The answer in this case is no."

The same hands then withdrew the chequebook and pen from Iannelli's rationed field of vision.

"You do realize you are making the biggest mistake of your life? You do know that, don't you?"

The tone was less avuncular than pride-stung, superior.

"Well, if that is so, things can only get better," replied Iannelli, unable to resist the opportunity for irony while knowing full-well that this was a moment, perhaps *the* moment, that would remain etched into his moral conscience. More so than leaving the *Roman Post*, more so than abandoning law and paying his own way to study journalism against his father's wishes, more so than leaving his hometown for good for Rome, yes, the infernal city. But there was another story here that could only add to his reputation.

The emissary gave a sigh. "Well, I shall leave you to ruminate on your decision at your leisure, Dr Iannelli."

"I won't be here long," Iannelli replied.

"Of course. I should imagine you will be setting out bright and early tomorrow, for Rome."

So they knew. Tabs on his phone calls? Or someone passing them information?

"Always like to start the day early," he countered but aware now that he was forcing the joviality in his tone.

"Start the day with a bang! Eh?"

A shudder ran through Iannelli's body that wasn't the chill of the breeze.

"So, *buon viaggio, Dottore. A presto, o addio.*"

Iannelli waited until his footsteps had died away. Cats screeched in an alley then he heard an engine, a motorbike approaching, tearing then along the promenade behind him, revving and revving almost until it became a hysterical scream. He froze. Was this it? Could he jump? Death at the hands of assassins perhaps still in their teens for whom this was a playground game, like pulling the legs off an insect. The bike and its whooping passengers drew closer and was then right behind him before disappearing again into the night with a last almost comic squawk of its jaded horn. He breathed again. Was he becoming paranoid? Had it really all happened? Yes, it had, and as a bitter keepsake the emissary's final words remained with him.

"Have a pleasant trip, *Dottore*. Until next time, or goodbye."

Forty-Eight

Iannelli woke early and without the aid of the alarm on his phone. For a moment, all was a sublime mystery, almost enjoyably so. Then he remembered where he was, and why, and all that had happened the night before. He lay motionless on his back for some time. A little grey light was perhaps perceptible. It must have been seven. He checked his watch 6.55. Close. He ran through what he had to do. Check out. Taxi to the port. Fast catamaran back to the mainland. Then a connecting flight from Catania to Rome. Inform the office of his ETA. Sounded straightforward. Sounded. But this was Italy, southern Italy, and things didn't always go to plan. At least not to his plan.

For want of anything approaching a better solution, he had put the attaché case at the back of the wardrobe. Either that or under the bed. No jewel-safe in the guest house but it had also occurred to him that enquiring about one might only arouse curiosity. And even if there had been, he doubted whether it would have been an obstacle to any determined thief, if they, whoever "they" might now be, were aware of its existence or interested in its contents. He washed, dressed in the previous evening's clothes, recovered it from its hiding place and zipped it into his now slightly bulging suitcase. With a view to making time and relaxing at the airport he checked out, forgoing breakfast to the clear dismay of the corpulent middle-aged proprietor who managed, however, to furnish him with a taxi number. The only one. No chance of shopping around here then.

"How long will it be?"

"Twenty minutes. Half an hour. More or less," came the languid reply down the line. Ever-widening experience told him that the "more or less" meant most likely "more" rather than "less". Perhaps he'd have that breakfast after all. The proprietor said nothing, but his look spoke volumes: "welcome back to the fold, lost sheep and sin no more."

As Iannelli took his cappuccino in the breakfast room, the ubiquitous TV, like a raucous guardian angel, was at least tuned to a news channel. And it was shouting from the lobby and not in the actual breakfast room. There were pictures of stoic country people with blackened faces holding various long-handled gardening tools while the bleached grass surrounding their homes and smallholdings smouldered. Then there were ominous shots of crust-topped oozing orange lava flows and the crater from which orange sparks gushed up against a night sky. Etna. Another eruption. Subtitled news ribbons confirmed Iannelli's very different fears.

Due to the plume of ash, all flights into and out of Catania have been suspended.

Then a shot of diggers advancing and reversing with snowplough-like attachments seeking to clear what must have been several inches of volcanic ash enveloping the runway like silver-grey snow.

What now? The taxi could come when it wanted. He'd just have to go to Palermo even if the backlog would be horrendous. The only other option was to hire a car, perhaps in Catania, then get to Messina and take the ferry to Reggio Calabria. Still, he thought, he'd never seen Palermo and chances were there'd be less demand on cars. If no flight was forthcoming then he'd go for the long drive up the Salerno-Reggio Calabria motorway and finally, at Naples, onto the so-called Autostrada del Sole. It was the road that brought Romans and Northerners, and returning exiles out of their grey, monotonous, but remunerated lives in the big cities and back into the sun-drenched South, the Mezzogiorno.

A problem lay in the Salerno-Reggio Calabria's also being one of the most accident-plagued, ill-planned stretches of motorway in Europe, still unfinished after twenty or thirty years. Iannelli didn't enjoy driving at the best of times. He'd go to Palermo. If he was lucky, he could be back in Rome for the early hours of the next day. If he was lucky. And with a *muntagna* calling the shots there was no guarantee of that. But he had to get moving. He took out his phone and called the office. Lisa, the secretary was there, early as usual.

"Lisa, *buongiorno*. Iannelli here."

"*Dottore*, how can I help?"

"Stuck in Sicily. Etna's gone up."

"Ah. So you'll be needing to fly from Palermo?"

"Any chance?"

"One moment," she replied, and there followed a rapid clatter of computer keys.

"*Dottore*?"

"Yes."

"All lines engaged and the site's down. Probably best to go straight there and see what you can find."

It was not what he had wanted to hear.

He finished his coffee and went to see if the papers had come in.

Only the local ones. Sicily first, then "the continent". That was how it worked here. The owner was leaning across the desk making minimal gestures with his eyes and head up towards the TV screen and the 24-hour news channel spooling out the same images again. "*A muntagna,*" he said. "*E'arrabbiata.*" The mountain. She's angry.

Iannelli sat down and scanned the flimsy unfamiliar sheets until he found something of moderate interest. The police had closed a bridge on the Salerno-Reggio Calabria that had partially collapsed. The authorities were investigating the company involved in its construction for suspected mafia involvement and use of sub-standard materials, believed to have led to a workman's being fatally injured. It wasn't heartening reading but, as he reasoned, after a disaster is generally the safest of times.

"Taxi!"

Early for once. At the door there stood a tanned, middle-aged man in clothes decidedly ten years too young for him. That was one of the benefits of unpredictability. Sometimes the surprise was in your favour. Iannelli raised a hand in acknowledgement then bid farewell to the still slouched proprietor who stirred slowly into action to return the salutation.

"*Arrivederla, Dottore.*"

The formal term of address, of course, for they were in the South and there could be no intimacy in this relationship. The use of the title "doctor" conveying respect, or near humble subalternity, could also shield a multitude of unstated opinions, thus implying disrespect. It masked hidden thoughts or the low regard in which a person was held while allowing one to avoid the direct insult. It could, in short, be a pure front, *una facciata*, supreme hypocrisy.

The proprietor looked back to the TV screen and, concurring with the tight little grouping of men in the corner, whose eyes all seemed to be intent on the scene, he pronounced again,

"*E'arrabbiata sul serio, a muntagna. Sul serio.*"

The mountain is angry. Angry for real. They nodded their

agreement and as the door of the guest house closed behind the journalist, these very same men then began to talk of other, equally serious but very different matters.

Forty-Nine

Mott Borrego logged-off from his computer, put on his hat and made his way out of the main university building. He turned down the narrow cobbled street past the mechanic's and the bakery which led to Viale Trastevere and headed towards the corner bar where he was to meet with an old friend. He had been intrigued to read the e-mail the previous day in his hotel room in Zurich not least because it had been so long since he'd heard from this particular alumnus but also because he was well aware of his general aversion to electronic mail. Why was it called "mail"? He'd have to look that etymology up and he made some educated guesses at the word's probable origins to pass the time as he walked, well, limped now really, if he was honest, towards the bar. He laughed to himself as he remembered the time a pigeon had landed on his head. He'd been walking that slow!

There, at a quiet corner table, Inspector Michael Rossi was waiting. He had matured a little since the last time they had met but still looked ever the younger protégée, the thesis-bearing undergraduate he'd first had the pleasure to meet, when was it? Twenty or so years ago? Mottram had been at the other university at the time, full of American zest and ambition until the realities of Italian academic life had kicked in, that merit did not always ensure career progression. A glance through the staff lists showed an uncanny preponderance of the same family name across departments and faculties, in academic and non-academic posts. So, he had pretty quickly thrown his lot in with the IAUR, The International American University of Rome. There at least you had the impression of getting somewhere and things worked! They even had staff to put paper in the photocopiers and you knew what courses you'd be teaching six months in advance.

His field was social and criminal psychology but he had a side interest in all things Latin and Classical, not to mention words and word play, puzzles, and rebuses. His hobbies and his professional interests really respected no distinct boundaries, a Renaissance man if ever there was one.

"How is she?" he said gripping Rossi's hand. It was heartfelt but with that hint of perennial US optimism detectable nonetheless. "Any change?"

Rossi shook his head.

"Stable. Critical. Or was it critical but stable? Is there a difference, do you think?"

"Ah," growled Borrego, "she'll pull through! I know she will! Just gotta hang in there, Michael! Right?"

Rossi smiled. Mott's enthusiasm was always a bonus.

"In the meantime, let's see what you've got there. These the originals?"

Rossi nodded.

"May I?" he said reaching out for the as yet unopened blue Manila folder on Rossi's side of the table.

The file contained the notes found at the various crime scenes as well as outlines of some of Rossi's own scribbled and crossed-out attempts at finding a possible underlying logic or message behind them. He had forwarded copies of some of the notes to Borrego prior to their meeting to give him a head-start. The professor gave the occasional little nod of what might have been

242

approval or agreement as he pored over the pages through his small round spectacles.

"So, I see you've been going down the Latin road, thus far."

Rossi didn't know if it was a question, or something else.

"Seems to be the natural way to go, doesn't it?" he continued.

"If there is a message in all this and not just a goose chase," said Rossi.

"Oh, there's a message all right," the professor nodded and looked up at his friend. "And I think there are a number of reasons why."

Rossi was warming to the prospect of the professor now delivering an elegant exegesis to make the burden of his multiple worries feel just that little bit lighter. Even if he was wrong, it was always a pleasure to listen to the prof setting out his theories, like in the old days when he'd amble in ten minutes late to a seminar, then keep them all spellbound as he set in motion his great machine of thought.

"I think you've got a killer working to a plan but my inkling is that this plan is not all his, and a he it is for sure. Likely an outsider, could be an intellectual, of sorts, and the notes are his way of expressing a certain autonomy, an aloofness. The way he kills is manual, but he expresses his intellect through the notes. So, as a serial killer – more spree than serial, though – he displays the characteristic well above-average to high intelligence. The fact he doesn't get caught and that his murders are in rapid succession suggests, however, he may be an assassin, meaning he mustn't get caught until he has reached his objective or objectives. So, he may well be working for someone but doesn't like working for anyone. He's a user, an opportunist. And this possible Latin motif – matter, mater – could be interesting. It's dualistic. Latin underpins the Italian language, many European languages for that matter, as well as the legal systems, the law itself. Not to mention the Church of Rome. It could even be something linked with a form of cultural nostalgia. The Roman Empire and so forth."

Rossi was intrigued but he felt the analysis, fascinating though it was, could perhaps be running away with itself.

"OK," he said, "wait a minute, Mott. Isn't this all a bit too intuition based?"

Mott put up a hand.

"Just a minute, I'm getting there. I haven't mentioned the last clue, or the latest clue, I should say, I'm afraid. The one that could clinch it."

Rossi sat back and waited.

"Now, Michael, does the name Erasmus mean anything to you?"

"Erasmus. The best year of my youth, in Spain. Well, apart from a few relationship issues."

"OK. Starter for ten. Who was Erasmus?"

Rossi was on the spot now.

"The Dutch medieval scholar."

"From where?"

"Rotterdam?"

"Rotterdam! Exactly. Ring a bell?" said Borrego pushing the page under Rossi's gaze. Of course! An anagram!

"Damn you rotters. Rotter dam! But what does it all mean?"

"Well," said the pleased-looking prof, "it is said that Erasmus of Rotterdam claimed to be the last person who spoke Latin as his first language."

"And?"

"A gesture of defiance? Superiority?"

"Could be."

"But there's more, as I see it. Where do you live?"

"Via Latina!"

"And an anagram of Erasmus?"

Rossi started scribbling. "With all the letters?"

"That would be an anagram."

"The only one I can see is 'masseur.'"

"And where does Yana work? In a health centre."

"Where she works as a masseuse?"

Rossi dropped the pen and looked at his friend.

"So this is not all coincidence?"

"It's what I see, and I don't think there's anything else. So, it looks as though this might just be personal."

Rossi's thoughts were racing now. Erasmus. Latin. Spain. They were all pointing in the same direction. To the murder of Rosa Garcia, his first love, and to his rival: the psychopathic, criminal-minded, once thought to be long-gone from his world, Giuseppe Bonaventura.

"Are we getting somewhere?"

"Why didn't I see it before!" Rossi exclaimed. "Why didn't I see it before!"

"So you think we've got something?" Mott said, trying to pin down what it was had made his friend so suddenly ecstatic.

"Well," said Rossi, "if it means what I think it does then we have a name to go on and maybe a face to go with it."

He couldn't tell Borrego everything, but he let him in on where his reasoning was now heading. The consonance between Borrego's theory and Rossi's subsequent hypothesis left them both stunned but exultant.

"Well, I'll be damned, Michael!" he said, slamming the table and sending a spoon skittering off a saucer and on to the floor, much to a passing waiter's silent but evident displeasure. "Now, you've really got something to get your teeth into," he continued, growling with delight.

Rossi had thanked Mott Borrego for the depth and detail of his insights and when they had caught up a little with each other's lives, Mott left for an "unavoidable but totally pointless meeting," as he put it, enjoining Rossi not to let so much time pass again before their next encounter.

"Life is short, Michael," he said, "and though life often gets in the way, one must carve out time for one's friends."

Looking back, it was clear now that Giuseppe could have grown to be a killer, so had it all started there, in Spain? And how had he come into contact with the Italian Secret Services? Through some high-level contact? Or just as a convenient assassin. One of many hired hands ready to put a bullet or knife wherever for whoever's paying.

And which branch of the services? He began to go over the lexicon like a dogged ploughman turning over the fallow sod. He'd had to reprise his own understanding before for the benefit of others but now it served as a stimulus for his own reasoning. The legitimate services, then the renegade services or *servizi deviati*, with their parallel agendas, bodies supposedly answering to a secret authority claiming legitimacy within the state itself. Who such operatives pledged their loyalty to was the stuff of Russian Dolls. Money. Power. Those were high on the list. Of course, they always came into it, into everything.

The problem was distinguishing between the two sides when they were both wearing the same strip. Who had put a bomb in Bologna station in 1980? Was it fascists or communists or the services trying to lay the blame at their door? But Rossi didn't want to go there. That wasn't police work, that was politics. *Più pulita la rogna*. The mange was cleaner, as the saying went.

His job was to find a way to get Carrara and himself out of the hole they were in, but the harder he tried, the deeper it got. If he could speak to Spinelli again? Maybe he could shed some more light on things, give him some reassurance. He was still inside, officially, because of the risk he might flee the country or interfere with evidence. Innocent as hell as far as Rossi was concerned but conveniently still inside for some.

So, was it to be believed that Giuseppe Bonaventura was carrying out vile femicides in the name of some twisted ideological conspiracy that sought to unite a personal vendetta with the warped logic of the *servizi deviati*? Rossi had always resisted the temptation to find a unifying script behind the horrors he encountered on a regular basis in his line of work. He had always tried to see beyond that. But. But.

A passing waiter swept a damp cloth across the table. Rossi's eyes were drawn to a ray of sunlight striking the shiny laminated surface. Years of passing clients had left myriad tiny scratches, and in the yellowish light, the fleck-like lines formed into a series of concentric circles, as if the work of some grand designer. He recalled Dorothea in *Middlemarch* seeing a similar such image and having her epiphany. The lines and the scratches, going in all directions, were totally random. However, it was only the effect of the light, a particular perspective or an angle, that gave the impression of an order present therein. The events were as senseless and random as the scratches but the instinct was always to see an order, to privilege the narrative over the casual, to find some comfort through closure.

Should he give credit to the grim narrative forming itself before his very eyes? But who exactly was weaving the plot? Was Giuseppe architect or tool? Or a patsy. The old Lee Harvey Oswald trick. Rope someone in who can fit the bill, ideologically or pathologically, feed them the right kind of information, spin them a believable story in which they are wittingly and unwittingly protagonists. Except that they can be written into or out of the self-same story at the drop of a hat, on the whim of whoever's holding the pen.

The tools of the trade. The Carpenter and his hammer. But hadn't Mott missed something there? The name itself, Giuseppe, the carpenter. Joseph, in English, the biblical Joseph. Were the methods meant to lead him or someone else to draw their own conclusions? Torrini's *Messenger* had come up with the name but surely he couldn't be anymore than the mouthpiece, cajoling and caressing public opinion in the right direction. Femicide, or Islamists, an attack on the very core of Italian society – the mother.

The only other logic to the killer's strike pattern was the modus operandi and the signature. For a face, they could try going down memory lane to dig up the old albums. He could contact schools but they didn't always have organized photographic records for pupils, as far as he could recall. They had the artist's impression coming and Carrara and his IT pals on the ageing process. If Marta's description matched Marini's it would be a result. But that tape going missing piled more wood onto the conspiracy-theory fire now growing in intensity even in Rossi's cynical imagination.

*

Rossi looked up at the office clock. A bit more work then the hospital. He'd pick up some fresh flowers on the way. He had got into the habit now, even if he had always found it difficult not to associate cut flowers with departing this world rather than remaining in it. Not like ambling through a field or a meadow where the flowers were all beauty in his eye. But that clutched thing, the bouquet, was more like a badge of resignation. His father? The funeral? Must have been. Still, they'd said it would brighten up the place, the nurses, and when nurses were involved Rossi did what he was told.

His phone buzzed. It was Maria. *Hadn't he told her not to call him?*

"Yes," said Rossi.

"Inspector. I want to speak to you. Can we meet at San Giovanni?"

The voice was softer. Needy even.

"I'm going to see Yana, in an hour or so. Can it wait?"

"OK. Yes. Look, I can come with you if you like."

"OK," said Rossi. "But remember your costume, right?"

"Of course. Later."

"*Ciao.*"

Some new revelation? Or for his ears only? He opened the drawer and slid his Beretta into his shoulder holster. Better safe than sorry.

Fifty

Only a seasoned cop would have been able to tell that the smoking blonde in dark glasses walking across the piazza was in disguise. She had the knack all right. No self-consciousness. Pure, easy assurance.

"So, Maria, what is it you want to tell me?" said Rossi.

"I want to turn myself in."

"You mean you want to go public?"

"Expose it all. Come clean on everything. Get Luca out. Get you off the hook. Go to the press. Everything. We'll take our chances."

"Just like that?"

"Yes."

"And why the change of mind? Why now?"

"Am I allowed to be less selfish for once? It was wrong, a mistake. I admit it. It was not what I wanted but I was desperate. But now, well. I've been thinking. Thinking a lot."

"Well perhaps you should turn your thoughts to this first," said Rossi, reaching into his coat pocket and handing her Mott Borrego's detailed analysis of the notes. "Looks like we might be onto something."

She scanned the notes and the various theories.

"So there's a name?"

"We think so."

"And a face?"

"We're getting there."

She handed him back the pages.

"If we go public now," Rossi continued, "it will all go up in smoke. This is our chance. Despite what I said before, when you sprang your little surprise, if they want to keep Luca inside, they'll find a way. He wouldn't be the first person to kill the wrong person by mistake. And even if you said you had seen the murderer it would all be circumstantial. It could have been a junky, anyone. They'll say you're protecting Luca, the lover's prerogative."

"So this Giuseppe wants to be found. Is that it?"

"He wants something, that's for sure. Most likely me. Let's walk and talk and I'll tell you the rest."

*

Though they knew little or nothing of where she was, she was suspended somewhere. Waiting, possibly. But the threads that held her? If they were to break, would it spell her release, her return, or her final falling? Rossi stared at her lidded eyes. Then he looked away. The pulse was steady, varying by only one or two beats. Her nails would need to be trimmed again, he noticed. He could do a better job himself. Next time.

Maria was sitting next to him. She didn't say a word as Rossi read then sat closer and gave his usual chit-chat while holding Yana's hand, updating her on events in the outside world. It was odd for him, having Maria there but, despite his initial misgivings, he found he appreciated the company. The female company.

"It could have been me," she said.

"It could have been anybody," Rossi replied.

"So we do it then? We go for it?"

"It's the only thing we can do now. We can't bring anyone back, can we?"

"But it's on equal terms. I'm not going to be the woman taking a back seat, if you follow. It's not my style."

"I'm sure we can work something out," said Rossi. The clock had come round to the appointed hour. "Come on," he said. "Let's go. I need to get to work on finding out more about Bonaventura."

He reached over and kissed Yana's lips. "See you tomorrow." Nothing in heaven or on earth could fill the silence that followed.

Fifty-One

So, drive he did. The catamaran had brought Iannelli back to Porto Empedocle from where he had hired a car. It had seen much better days but was the best they could offer. He had seen little point in arguing, anticipating the disastrous spectacle likely to greet him when he finally arrived at Palermo airport. Catania was closed indefinitely, and the backlog of flights was creating delays of up to forty-eight hours. He'd set off for Palermo across Sicily's barren interior as soon as he'd eaten and, after a tedious four-hour drive, had got there late in the afternoon. Hotels were filling up fast, the airport was running out of food, tempers were fraying. Better to be moving was his philosophy and now that he was on the road again he was almost relishing the freedom.

He'd decided not to rush and had spent a couple of hours stocking up on local products, bottles of wine and far too many books. They were stashed in carrier bags on the passenger seat. He had, however, put the attaché in the boot, just in case Palermo's moped-riding, drive-by merchants did a smash and grab at the traffic lights. His rather uncool mobile sat safe within arm's reach. No one would be nicking that, and better to have a ready line of communication, given the previous evening's events.

He was finding it difficult not to drift back to the bizarre situation he had found himself in the night before. He'd been followed, his movements tracked by someone, or something. But who? Checking in to the guest house, he'd had to fill-out the registration card, as always, and that would, as a matter of course, have been made available to the local police. But they'd also known about his meeting with Rita. Well, she was being trailed too, judging by the anonymous phone calls that had so unsettled both her and her father.

The office, not content with his brief message, had called. He'd kept details to a minimum and given them a ballpark figure regarding his estimated time of arrival. Traffic was minimal, however, and he began to relax as for large stretches of the way he had the road to himself. It was only the winter darkness now and some of his hard-to-shake-off thoughts that troubled him. As far as the dossier was concerned, he'd ended up devouring most of the papers in his possession, so captivating were its contents which, in many ways, confirmed several of his own deepest-held suspicions. He took some photos of what he considered key elements, but the sheer volume of material was such that he couldn't copy them all.

As he flicked around again with the unfamiliar radio, the phone beside him began to vibrate. "Not again!" he said out loud, surprising himself a little to hear his own voice. He cast a glance sideways.

Unknown caller.

Perhaps he'd take it. He flicked it on to hands-free. The battery was running down. Two bars. He'd keep it brief.

"Yes."

"*Dottor* Iannelli?"

"Yes."

This time the voice was Sicilian, perhaps even familiar to him. "*Dottore*, you must listen. There isn't much time."

Iannelli did a double take. Was this some joke or another threat? But the voice, though tense, very tense, seemed benevolent.

"Where are you? Tell me? You are in grave danger."

"Who is this?" demanded Iannelli, more anxious now and deciding that whatever it was, it was no joke.

"You don't need to know. Where are you? On the road? I know you are on the road to Messina but where?!"

Iannelli was in the middle of just about nowhere on a state highway. On each side there were rocky slopes and low mountains with irregular tree cover. Up ahead he was able to make out the road curving away into what must have been a thickly wooded glade or forest.

"The kilometre markers on the side of the road," the voice now urged, "at what point are you?"

The signposts were posted at 100 metre intervals. He remembered he had just passed the 97 kilometre marker. For some reason it had stuck in his head as three short of a hundred. He studied the roadside. There it was. His headlights flashed it up. VIII/97.

"I'm approaching 98, anytime now. 200 metres to go."

"How fast are you going?"

Iannelli checked quickly.

"About 100, but who is this?"

"You have a minute, a minute and a half at most. I know the road like the back of my hand. There is a roadside bomb in a truck. It's huge and will obliterate every trace of you and your car. Listen. And slow down. Is there anyone behind you? They may be following. They'll have traced your hire car or attached a transmitter."

Iannelli checked his rear-view. Clear. The voice continued.

"You have three choices: stop the car and take your chances on foot. Not recommended. They will know you are alive. Go back to Palermo. Suicide. Three: jump from the car while going through the woods. There is a blind spot. They will see you enter the woods and when you emerge they will detonate the bomb. You have less than a minute, forty seconds maybe. Are you approaching the trees? Reduce speed and put a weight on the accelerator and jump! Leave your watch. It's steel. They'll find it. Leave coins, jewellery, rings if you have any. Take cash, you'll need it. Are you in the woods yet? *Dottore*? *Dottore*?!"

As Iannelli listened, his hands, which had been gripping the wheel tighter and tighter began to loosen their hold. He felt his mind becoming clear, very clear. He saw Rita's smiling face, his hometown, his family. Through the sunroof, he saw the black, sinewy canopy of the woods rushing now over his head and at the furthest visible point in the distance he could see an opening, a just discernible arch. A door out of the dark.

"*Dottor* Iannelli! Are you there? Are you there?"

Then the ears belonging to the voice discerned what sounded like a loud, dull thump. Then a crackly, hissing silence followed by the percussion perhaps of a car repeatedly striking the cat's eyes or the chevrons on the side of the road. And then there was nothing as the phone and everything else with it went dead.

PART III

Fifty-Two

They were all talking about it now. The cold spell that had transformed itself into the severest winter experienced in Rome since before many people had been born. The TV weather maps showed a distorted target shape with wavy concentric rings in deepening shades of blue. Its dark heart was inching closer to the peninsula from the east and the whole affair, according to the Air Force weatherman, could plant itself slap bang over the country for weeks. Snow was now also the word on everyone's lips. From the eager skiers to the feeble pensioners to the commuting office workers hoping for a day off work. According to your source, be it the chattier-than-usual colleague at the coffee machine or the know-all in the corner bar, it was either a dead certainty within days, a soap-bubble story hyped up as click-bait for the newspapers' jaded readership, or welcome light relief from the recent horrors. What was certain was that the Romans were having more than a few problems adapting to a northern-style *inverno*.

"Thought it was in the genes," said Rossi.

"What do you mean?"

"You know. The ones who survived guard duty on Hadrian's Wall. Didn't they pass on their superior cold-resistance to successive generations?"

Carrara gave a knowing smile. Most in the city today had their roots in the southern reaches of the peninsula. They were the Calabrians, the Sicilians, the Puglians, who could in turn all have been descendants of the peoples that once constituted the Greater Greek Empire of Magna Grecia, thus attesting to a multiplicity of ethnic origins.

They were sipping boiling hot cappuccino's that were cooling fast. The first rays of early morning sun were having no noticeable effect. Nonetheless, their decision to take an outside table had not been altogether unwise. The cold had also decreed that Rossi's coffee be *corretto* with a shot of something stronger from behind the bar.

"As long as there's no wind. That's what the wife says," Carrara muttered to no one in particular it seemed, so sleepy was his demeanour. They had the air of men with time on their hands, but they had been burning the midnight oil, after having left Maria to follow up what lines of enquiry she could by means of her access to intelligence data. The fresh air was a godsend after hours on end cooped up in storerooms and archives tossing around ideas and strategies, going over and over the case. They had then forced themselves to meet early, like betting-oriented drinking companions taking the rash decision to go hunting or swimming at first light only to find that they can't back out.

They had got their hands on some photo records but, as Rossi had feared, there was no standard archiving procedure. There was one grainy image from a sporting event which a well-intentioned head-teacher had given them the chance to unearth in a jumble of old school memorabilia that had escaped being thrown away by its having been forgotten in a junk room. Junk room. Rossi laughed. It was a condemned classroom with peeling walls and a sagging roof, deemed unfit and too dangerous to be used, one of countless examples in the state school system.

They had matched the year to written records of Bonaventura's school attendance and had then identified him with a reasonable degree of certainty. The image was old and small and even when blown-up and computer-enhanced they could only come to the conclusion that it had scarcely been worth the effort and the copious inhalation of dust, and while Rossi hadn't mentioned it, he had sensed that the graft was getting to Carrara. He had made veiled references to the method's being outdated, that they should have been concentrating their energies on the technological side of things, the databases, taking a fresher approach. Rossi knew Carrara, and knew when his jibes were good humoured. Now he had a sneaking suspicion that there was more. He could have been wrong but his instinct was alerting him to something.

Other attempts had focused on family members but they'd had to tread carefully. Rossi was pretty sure that the family was well-to-do Roman bourgeoisie, in part due to details dropped into conversations and clues picked up from certain aspects of Giuseppe's lifestyle. The military service could be "influenced" by the contacts one held or could draw upon. He'd certainly never been a Conscientious Objector, a CO. Indeed, violence must have been an early feature on his horizon. Along with drugs and sexual deviancy these were his main vices, despite his academic excellence, his one-size-fits-all bonhomie. Rossi remembered something, too, about a parachute regiment with strong fascist associations. Then there was his taste for certain wines, his clothes, a particular way of speaking he had tried to camouflage with a rough-edged, hipper Romanesco but which emerged nonetheless from time to time. Yet, despite this, he had also been reserved, perhaps even to the point of secrecy. Even then Rossi hadn't trusted him. The dark heart had been there somewhere.

"C'mon," said Rossi, "let's go and see how the artist's impressions have come out. There should be some workaholic in the office by the time we get there. And let's see if we can get them to do anything with this," he added, getting up and wafting the photo without any great conviction. He gestured to the waiter to bring the bill as he zipped his coat a little tighter. "Your shout, I believe, Gigi," he said as he began to move away.

"Again?" Carrara replied. Rossi turned around, surprised by the lack of humour in Carrara's response.

"Are you keeping count?" said Rossi.

"No, no," said Carrara. "I just don't remember. Whatever." Without meeting Rossi's eyes, he deposited the notes and coins on the table.

As they walked away, they didn't have any cause to notice the proprietor putting down his cloth to turn up the volume on the sputtering transistor radio. The hourly news bulletin then related an astounding litany of yet more deaths: a cardinal in the Vatican, due to natural causes; in a far less salubrious part of the city, an African in rather less natural causes; and in Sicily, a body vaporized by the roadside detonation of a truck packed with explosives. None of these dead, however, was a woman and an hour or two later, this same TV nation began swallowing and digesting the first reports from the near-apocalyptic scene of the explosion. They'd managed to keep a lid on it for as long as they could, happening as it had, in the dark early evening in the middle of nowhere and also thanks to a thick blanket of silence. Complicit silence? Sicilian *omertà*?

Theory and counter theory and all manner of rumours abounded. Were they sure it was a bomb? Had it not been a collision? It must have been a fuel tanker that had exploded. Who'd been first on the scene? Why had it taken so long to be reported? Subsequently, the press had been informed and then they had been able to get close and set up their arc-lights and their outside broadcast unit. Then the truth had begun to emerge, or had then been allowed to emerge.

Fifty-Three

Rossi made his hand into a fist and in a paroxysm of rage dealt a blow to the table sending an explosion ringing round his empty flat. He had the right to grieve for his friend. He had the duty to drink to his memory and to swear vengeance for his killers. It was personal, and it was another blow against him. He thought of the last time they had spoken. He had perhaps given Iannelli short shrift and now here he was, the survivor, while they would probably never even find Iannelli's remains, vaporized by the intensity of the blast. They were coming at him now from all directions, piling the pressure on, knowing, surely, that there was only so much he could take. Yana suspended between this world and the next, his friend gone, and two more murder victims to add to the list. First a local scumbag's decapitated torso and then an African migrant with his throat cut, trussed-up like an animal and left in a bin bag on the side of the Via Tuscolana, with a pig's head thrown in for good measure.

Rossi tried to massage the accumulated lack of sleep out of his face and then, resigned, held his head in his hands. He had tried to sleep during the day to make up for the all-nighter, but it had been useless. *How could he sleep now?* He put on a CD of the saddest, most plangent songs, the ones his Irish grandfather had sung by the fire and which he had learned by heart, too, as a child. *Some died by the roadside, some died with a stranger. And wise men have said that their cause was a failure.* The whiskey bottle beside him was half empty but he knew he still needed more. What was happening to his country, this city? Iannelli. Dead. It couldn't be. The device on the Palermo-Messina road was so huge it had left a crater 30 metres wide and 5 metres deep. A lethal mix of several hundred pounds of diesel and agricultural fertilizer, it had annihilated all in its path. Rossi, of course, had been among the last to know. Didn't you see the morning news? I was busy dammit! Why did nobody inform me? We thought you knew. Yeah, right.

Grief vied with duty in his embattled psyche. They had had so many great times, great discussions, fallings out even, but always they had been bound by a common sense of doing what was right and exposing evil wherever it might hide. Now he alone had to carry the flame. But Dario would not have wanted him to grieve for long. Dust yourself off, there's work to be done. That was his way.

He grabbed at the papers, the preliminary reports, and swallowed the rest of his drink. The words on the page though were surreal. He couldn't connect but knew he had to. Forensics were still searching for any personal effects that might have survived the intense heat, but it was complicated, too, by the bomb's having been packed into a hijacked meat lorry that had not been emptied of its cargo. An anonymous call had been made to a local newspaper, a hire car was unaccounted for, and no single, male motorist fitting Iannelli's description had been seen boarding any ferry for "the continent" neither that evening, nor the following morning. His mobile phone, of course, was dead too.

As for the local Roman hood, Pietro Marciano, he'd had myriad enemies and the press had "revealed" his involvement with both the n'dranghetta – the Calabrian Mafia – as well as with Cosa Nostra, all of which was news to Rossi. He had been a Mafia unto himself, an unscrupulous street villain who'd worked his way up, even coming to challenge the big boys. But what did it matter to him when he could only stand by and watch as the anti-mafia boys swooped in like Feds all over the dead guy's business affairs, sealing up every possible opportunity of a lead as tight as a body bag?

The African's death was being painted as another settling of scores. Still no identity. Paperless. Seemed West African, possibly Nigerian. Fingerprints erased. So, the working hypothesis was that it was within 'the community' and its murky underworld. They'd appealed for witnesses but weren't holding their breath. No. That internecine narrative got cooked up all too readily sometimes, especially when there was little chance of any public outcry. Who cared about the death of an African living on the fringes?

And then there was the cardinal, one of many of the Italian *porporati*, the purple-clad princes of the Church. On any other day, it would have made something like headline news, but his death had been tucked between the inside pages like a bribe. He'd slipped away in his sleep. Heart attack. Private funeral arrangements would be made in accordance with his wishes and all deep within the walls of the Vatican City, hidden from prying eyes.

But what was also news to Rossi were the suggestions that Iannelli had been close to figures in both the Sicilian and Roman underworlds, that there were dark shadows not so much around the circumstances of his death but behind the reasons for his being in Sicily and which may have led to the hit. But it was lies, all lies and it was so easy now that there was no one to speak up for him. They were falling over themselves to rubbish his character and airbrush him and his discoveries from history. Doubtless some pale facsimile of a journalist would try to step in and appropriate his mantle, that of the voice of the ordinary people against the powers-that-be. All a sham and an insult to his memory. Rossi threw the papers aside.

He closed his eyes and, as he did so, he imagined he heard Dario's voice amidst the melee of confused thoughts in his head. He couldn't just be a spectator here, an ordinary bystander. Mafia killings would be a given until politicians got out of bed with them and started turning the screws. He had known things, things he had referred to. So he was dead, they'd got their man but what else had he known? But Rossi feared those secrets had gone to the grave with Iannelli. A stunned Iovine had been in touch and he was no better informed. They too, at *The Facet*, had been waiting on his return, believing he was onto something of immense proportions. But Dario had been holding back on the details, intending as he was to deliver them in person. Was intending to. Past tense. And now what?

They were all feeling under siege and rumours were circulating again about high-profile figures in the institutions who'd been sabre-rattling. There was talk, too, in some circles of the deepening gravity of the security situation transforming itself into a "potential coup scenario". But Rossi knew it was also time for him to pull out the stops.

He stared into the whirling patterns in the wood on his kitchen table and reached out to pour himself another drink. It was barely numbing him and he was drinking his whiskey undiluted now. Yet it tasted of almost nothing as it slid down his throat like the water he might have mixed with it. As easily as human life itself could slip away.

Fifty-Four

Rossi's organism had finally won the battle with his besieged mind and he had collapsed into a deep whiskey-soaked slumber, waking late the next day when his phone rang and rang again and then rang out. Things were not much clearer but he had observed the ritual of mourning and that, at least, had given him some small solace. He had showered, shaved and, to get his mind back into action, had taken a long walk across the park and far out onto the Appian Way. There the tombs of the Roman patricians and patriarchs still lined the thoroughfare, and he imagined some such similar monument for Iannelli would be as fitting as it was impossible.

He had returned home aching but shriven and plunged himself into a hot bath before welcoming Carrara for an afternoon of brainstorming and planning.

"You know they haven't got a clue, don't you? Maroni's crowd," said Carrara. "They're sending their guys out like headless chickens and here we are with the only leads worth anything and we're having to work as if we were subversives, or some kind of terrorist cell holed-up and eating paranoia from a can for breakfast, lunch and supper."

"I don't see any other way round the problem," Rossi replied without lifting his eyes from one of the many newspapers strewn across the couch. "Do you?"

The previous day and night's drinking and thinking and drinking again had left him fuzzy and indolent but, while realistic about their options, he was not resigned to any predetermined fate. Iannelli was gone and it was time to move on. He had wanted to help in some way but Iannelli's family, his parents, from whom he had been effectively estranged, had made it known that they were dealing with it themselves. They had shut him out.

Carrara was pacing the apartment. A man of action without any action becoming very frustrated indeed. Something had got into him. That was now clear. Irritation, frustration, and some of it, too, was aimed at him. He had tried to commiserate with Rossi as best he could but there was an underlying tension he couldn't disguise, no matter how much he felt for him. It had to be Marini. She had volunteered to work with Carrara on what they both did best, trawling through databases and scouring underworld contacts, thus freeing up Rossi, who had enough on his plate with Yana, to think of other possible approaches. But they had never worked this way and the unnatural distance now being put between Rossi and Carrara was taking its toll on the trust between them and their old reliable equilibrium as Maria began to modify Carrara's outlook with her secret service ideas.

"Want to go back to the old days, Gigi?" said Rossi. "The balaclavas, the stakeouts, the big prize?"

That was the life Carrara had been living when Rossi had met the up-and-coming detective who would become his future partner. Rossi had been on a train to Naples, a slow train, by choice, one Saturday morning, heading down to see to some business with distant family that couldn't be put off any longer. The athletic young guy who had got on at Caserta and sat opposite him in the carriage, had, at a certain point, leaned across and asked if he might see his newspaper.

"Yep," he'd said then, handing it back with satisfaction and pointing to the front page. There was a spread of a long-wanted Camorra boss being bundled into a police car by undercover agents.

"We got him. And that's me. First photo I've seen of it." Rossi had introduced himself and they'd kept in touch. Carrara had married, decided a move to a more liveable city wouldn't hurt, and they'd been on the Rome Serious Crime Squad ever since.

They'd both watched as Rome changed, and often for the worse. The dark side had always been there, the machinations of the criminal establishment, the obscure bidding of the "deep state", but it had begun to spill over more and more into everyday life in a way that was unnerving now in its spasmodic cruelty.

Rossi began to reflect on that first meeting and how things had subsequently evolved. Carrara had been a poster boy of anti-mafia back then and had enjoyed it, had thrived on it. He had been one of the main men, joining the force straight out of school and rocketing up the ranks. But what if he missed it now? Perhaps he didn't want to be playing second fiddle to Rossi anymore.

"I want to do something," said Carrara. "I want to make things happen!"

Carrara was still formidable in terms both of his physical presence and his application and focus, but he wasn't the rock star cop anymore. He was a family man, he was getting older. He was getting like Rossi even and maybe that was bothering him.

The intercom buzzer rang. Rossi looked at his watch.

"Well, she's bang on time."

"That's secret service training?" quipped Carrara. "They'd never have had you, would they?"

Rossi considered a response but resisted.

"And now here's something you can do, Gigi," he said rising with some reluctance from his reading and giving himself a cursory smartening. "Get the coffee on, will you. Big pot and strong."

As soon as the door had closed behind her, Marini gave no sign that she was intending to stay.

"I've had an idea," she said. "Can we take the car?"

"For what?" said Rossi, who had just been getting comfortable.

"I've been going over the case notes," she said. "Gigi let me see them."

Rossi glanced at his colleague. Marini looked at them both in turn.

"I've just got a feeling about something," she continued. "About the Luzi murder and I want to see if you are with me on it. Can we go?"

"C'mon then," said Rossi rising and grabbing his coat off the back of a chair, "the coffee can wait. Where to?"

"To the crime scene. Where else? Back to square one."

"We've been through it with a fine-tooth comb already," said Rossi.

"OK. But have you been there at night?"

＊

"So we just continue to wait?" said Rossi growing colder by the minute.

"Watch and wait," Marini replied.

No sooner had she spoken than a vehicle swung into the car park and took up a position opposite them. A tall, shapely figure in a black polo neck got out of the passenger's side. From the driver's side, a stocky, leather-jacketed male emerged. They began to smoke and throw a few glances around, interested but not interested. They were waiting but not waiting. Then discarding their half-smoked cigarettes, they got back into the car. A few seconds elapsed before the driver flashed his headlights.

"Don't answer," Marini whispered. "They're looking for company."

"Company?" said Rossi.

"Doggers," said Carrara. "You don't get out much, do you? Swingers, if you like."

"Wife-swapping," said Rossi. "Is that what you're saying?"

Marini nodded.

"Look."

Another car came crunching up the gravel slip road.

"More of the same?" Rossi enquired.

"Seems like it."

There was another flash of headlights from the first car but this time the second vehicle responded in kind. Then the former's interior light went on to reveal what appeared to be a semi-naked female figure reclining in the passenger seat while being attended to by her companion. A youngish man in a tracksuit got out of the second car and walked towards the first car.

"Seen enough?" said Marini. "That's what most people come here for after hours. Casual encounters. Car sex. Voyeurism."

"And Luzi?" asked Carrara glancing towards Rossi who was, despite himself, still observing.

"Don't you think you should ask him?" said Marini.

Fifty-Five

Back at the flat she took off her dark-brown, three-quarter length leather coat and with visible relief also removed her blonde wig. She threw them both on to the arm of an empty chair and sat down opposite Rossi from where she then began to undo the various accoutrements keeping her long, glossy hair under wraps until she finally shook it loose. Once she had lit her first cigarette, she began to put forward her own assessment of the situation. *So, she was planning on staying*, thought Rossi. But for now, at least, in line with her declared wishes, he was quite prepared to take a back seat. He'd hear her out.

She had no real opinion on the motives behind the various killings other than to say that the Luzi killing had more to it than met the eye.

"That's your job. Police work," she said, "and not what I'm here for. I'm more of a psychologist. I need to know who I'm dealing with and what he's capable of."

Carrara had brought in the much-needed coffee.

"So tell us: what you do know," said Rossi cutting in with just a hint of irritation at the superior tone she appeared now to be honing. Paying no visible heed to his imprecation, she started by outlining the essence of her thesis.

"We know he likes women, attractive women. We know he kills women. Let's focus on that side of his character. Maybe he stalks vulnerable individuals, couples, or frequents swinger sites, maybe it's his thing. So why couldn't we go down that road?"

"Some sort of a trap, then?" said Rossi adding extra sugar to his double espresso. "A honey trap, if you like?"

She shrugged.

"The guy's a deviant, by your own admission. Highly sexed. He could have met Luzi there, maybe by arrangement. Maybe both of them. Have you checked her phone traffic?"

"Her phone went missing," said Carrara, "but her call records don't reveal anything out of the ordinary. Only calls to her husband."

"Her computer? Her husband's?"

"Nothing to report," said Carrara. "ClearTech came through fast on that and it was negative. And anyway, he, or they, could just as well have been in the wrong place at the wrong time. Like the others. Like Kristina."

"But can't you see that it gives us a possible lead?" continued Marini. "People go there precisely for that. At that time of the night, in percentage terms, it narrows the circle. What was she doing there? And even if she was there by chance, which I doubt, there must be some connection between Bonaventura's predatory sexual profile and the murders. He exploits an aspect of his victims' vulnerability. There's no other matrix. You've exhausted every alternative line of enquiry."

Rossi certainly knew of Bonaventura's predilection for casual sex and prostitutes back in the Erasmus days when they'd all been more libertine than even he may have cared to admit. Giuseppe though had had a predatory and insatiable appetite. His serial infidelity, passed off as mere sport in a country with a very pre-feminist attitude to sex, had not been something he had tried particularly hard to hide while he was with Rosa, but it later became an issue that had helped to drive them apart. Afterwards,

Rossi knew he had revelled in the other opportunities that came his way in Spain at that time – the influx of South Americans, the boom in transexual prostitution, all coupled with the ready availability of cocaine. There too rumours had circulated as to his conduct. Life on the mean backstreets and out in the forlorn hinterlands of the Valenciana had been cheap, especially the lives of foreign street workers. And Giuseppe's bragging comments could be very close to the bone. The kind of girls he mixed with were psychologically fragile, badly damaged goods more often than not, and at least one had disappeared in dubious circumstances.

"So we could start checking out all the usual outlets," said Rossi, trying to reassert a bit of old-fashioned authority. "The 'piazzas', the car parks, the strip joints, escort agencies and so forth. And what about the singles bars?"

"That's a mammoth task, don't you think?" Carrara countered. "And with what manpower? We're doing this on a shoestring, remember? And besides, couldn't it have the opposite effect? Scare him off if the place is crawling with cops? And I mean we can hardly distribute his photo, can we?"

"We could try, but it might just work in our favour too," said Marini, rising now and with fresh confidence striding towards the window.

"Wouldn't open that if I were you," Rossi warned. "Don't you think we might be under surveillance?"

"I wasn't going to," she almost snapped and then, softening, "but if you'll hear me out, Inspector," she said, wheeling round on a well-stacked heel to confront the still-seated Rossi. "What if we were to attempt to nudge our deviant into more niche activities?"

Carrara glanced at Rossi who was still looking at Marini. She had one arm held across her chest while supporting the elbow of her smoking hand and appeared to be revelling in the role she was attempting to carve out for herself. Unless, of course, it was

Rossi's own imagination getting the better of him. His own more primal urges.

"Don't forget," she said, "you know something about him. You knew him for real. I, or we, can profile him; it's part of my training. He needs his kicks. He's a man on the edge and he must have a weakness. He didn't just go into the health club because he planned to get to you through Yana, he did it because he wanted to get sexually close first. It was part of his plan to violate her and you – high risk but that's his Achilles heel. Then, while we're targeting the more obvious vice locations, we get to work in other areas. The area of adult social media. That's where it all happens now, Inspector. We can go to the dark web, too, if needs be. And we get every man we can out on the street, a general security crackdown. No one will be able to move without feeling us breathing down their neck."

She seemed now to have clicked into corporate presentation mode and was hand-gesturing to an unseen audience a few feet in front of her.

"We keep it strictly focused on Rome, narrow the parameters. He's here, somewhere. And what's more, unlike most of the punters, I'll be a real woman who's looking for real and not just selling. I think, gentlemen, you might just find the circle could narrow surprisingly quickly."

"So you are the bait in this trap?" said Rossi realizing the full import of what she was proposing.

"Who else?" she said, stubbing out her cigarette and folding both her arms now across her chest.

"And you don't think this is all just a massive shot in the dark?" said Rossi. "You really think you can find him? One in a million? I mean, why should he break his cover anyway? And for what?"

"Isn't it what police work is all about? You do vehicle checks, road blocks, organize reconstructions to get people to jog their memories. And criminals get sucked back into their routines, slip up, and give themselves away. It's hard graft, sure enough.

It's a numbers game. This is exactly the same thing but in a virtual sphere. And if the perfect opportunity were to present itself, it could be too good for him to refuse. And I can recognize him, regardless of whether he's using whatever pseudonym or proxy server – either from the ring or the tattoo. What do you think, Inspector?" she said turning to Carrara, leaning over then to extract another cigarette from the packet before running her fingers through her long, dark hair.

"If the perfect opportunity were to present itself, what do you think a man would do?"

Carrara looked just a little too long at Marini's erotic posturing for Rossi's liking. He was letting her get under his skin and Rossi could see it now plain as day. And she wanted him to see. Rossi got up, stretched, and rubbed the back of his neck. Far too long in the same position. Far too long without any healing hands. He made as if to take the floor and began to pace the apartment as he spoke.

"So, imagine we do nail him via some Internet video chat link or whatever. He's a suspect, that's all. How do you propose we bring him in?"

"Simple," said Marini. "We set up a meet."

"Just like that?"

"It's what people do. People like that I mean. They meet, Inspector, in their vehicles. You saw it with your own eyes. They check each other out. They put aside any moral qualms, take precautions if they've got their heads screwed on, then they fuck. And then they go home. End of story. Until next time. Until it becomes an addiction. And I can tell you, Inspector, for many it very quickly does."

Rossi raised an eyebrow. Carrara was now giving nods of approval. Had she won him over so easily? With the plan or with the delivery?

"Except in this case he won't be going anywhere. We put the cuffs on him. We can trump up any charge we like and then we get to work on the evidence. I'll have identified him already anyway, you can get some forensic – you do have some traces, fibres or whatever?"

"We have something," said Carrara, "but we don't know for sure if it's his."

"So you get some of his. Work your way back in this story and fill in the gaps. I know it's not going by the book, but you don't need me to tell you that, do you?"

"And you're going to give me a lesson in ethics now, are you?" said Rossi.

"You know what I meant. It's a dirty job, that's all, but it has to be done. Don't tell me you never played dirty, Inspector. Don't tell me you always stick to the rules."

"Well," said Rossi, "seeing as you are in the process of re-writing the book, tell me how I can explain away bumping into the suspected murderer while making routine enquiries? They'll have me picking the lottery numbers next with my luck."

"In a lay-by, on a country road, probably," interjected Carrara. "That's where these things go on, I believe," he added, glancing towards Marini who was perched now, catlike, on an arm of the sofa, legs crossed, the svelte curve of her gluteus maximus a work of art in its own right.

Rossi clapped his hands in an Alleluia gesture.

"So it's all worked out. I am so glad. I didn't think police work could be so easy, really," he laughed.

It was Marini's turn to bristle now at the inspector's sardonic turn of phrase.

"Well, do we do it or not?"

Rossi didn't like it. She was getting way too cocksure. Whose case was this? Who did she think she was with her fancy pants secret service plans? It was as if you could do everything today via a computer link, as if a murderer would just drop into your hands, like buying a book or a CD.

"No," he said, raising his voice. "No, we don't. We stick to the clubs. We stick to the car parks, the strip joints. We do road checks at the same times of day as when the murders happened. We try to jog memories. We build it up patiently and meticulously. And it all takes time and your proposal is a waste of precious time, and impossible, if you ask me. We'll be out there," he added, jabbing a finger towards the exterior, "on the streets not posing behind a screen!"

Marini seemed less taken aback than satisfied to have got a rise out of Rossi, while a look of some incredulity had spread over Carrara's face. He must have been warming to the idea, as he was warming to Marini's charms. She was getting in the way, deliberately, for whatever ego-fuelled reasons she had, but his instinct was telling him "no" on this one, above all because it was slipping out of his control. Still, he was going to wrench it back.

"So, are there any other bright ideas you've been holding on to, Inspector?"

"Well," said Rossi, "now that you mention it, what I was thinking was that we can't even begin to do this without more manpower and the only way I can see us getting that is if we, that is I, can convince Maroni our cryptic clues are worth following up on. He's not exactly an intuitive person and he may well laugh me out of court, if he's in the mood for laughs, but it's the only way I can see it being viable."

Carrara let a sigh escape at the thought of the slogging kind of police work Rossi was now proposing.

"I mean we're most likely being tailed," Rossi went on, not entirely convincing himself, oblivious to the silent Carrara's musing speculations, but asserting what he felt was his authority regardless. "Tailed, trailed and just about shadowed everywhere we go anyway. So, if they think we're swallowing some way out acrostic line of enquiry – I don't have to say I think it's Bonaventura – he may just go along with it. It gives us the leeway we need and if we do have to call out the cavalry, it's more likely in that scenario that it will come. And it will probably keep our mayor happy, too, if the police are 'seen to be policing', given the problems he's been having. Don't you think? It's damage limitation, at least."

"Well, it looks like he's dragging his feet on this snow business too," said Carrara slumped now and drawing some weak solace from scrolling on his phone.

"Snow? Ah, yes," replied Rossi, "well, we've all seen what happens in Rome when it rains – chaos – so imagine if we got a white-out!"

"A 50–50 chance apparently, of 'significant coverage' towards the end of the week, whatever that means."

"Have we got any snow chains at the Questura? Little job for you there, Gigi. Don't want to be caught with our trousers down, do we?"

"Can't you just call someone about that?" said Carrara. There followed an uncharacteristic pause.

"No, Gigi, I want you to do it," said Rossi, again modulating his tone accordingly. "Can't I trust you to do it?"

Rossi's patience had cracked. Silence settled on the flat. The initial enthusiasm, albeit shared more by Carrara and Marini, had all but evaporated and they seemed like members of a lost expedition approaching defeat, or actors playing out an ill-rehearsed three-hander. And simmering below the surface each couldn't help but harbour and nurture their own opinion as to who was now *il terzo incomodo*, the gooseberry, who had made the cosy set-up into an awkward crowd.

Fifty-Six

They were still there. They'd been there for hours now. There must have been detailed business to discuss. Just three of them, from what he could gather, so hardly a social gathering; one with a shapely silhouette but otherwise only their vague forms visible through the pale curtains. He would wait. Of late, his movements had been so surreptitious and clandestine that he felt he shared more DNA with the shadows he sheltered in than with any human being. And what a curious feeling it was. No. It was better to be sure. He'd come this far, and he'd decided which was to be his next port of call. He would wait until the lights were out and he was sure the others had left before making any move. But he could arouse suspicions in his present location. Too many apartment blocks. Too many eyes and ears.

He picked up his heavy holdall and, keeping his eye on the fourth floor window, he moved away. Then he turned left along Via Latina towards the great opening of the Caffarella Valley Park. In the distance he could make out the silhouettes of the pines and cypresses lining the Appian Way. The only sound apart from some distant, sporadic traffic noise was the constant chortle of a water fountain, the local *nasone* or big nose.

He took up a seated position on the wall from where he could see straight down the road to Rossi's building. In Rome, in winter, there was precious little nocturnal activity, especially so in these family oriented suburbs. It was work, home, dinner, TV, bed. If anyone did pass they would take him for one of the park's down-and-outs, even though the current cold meant only the toughest could be found circulating these days. Recently, however, inactivity had morphed into a virtual curfew, for reasons known to all. So, as soon as someone left a building, he would hear it. The lock clicking would be like a branch snapping in a forest and would be his signal to make a move. It was unlikely the girl would be alone, if she had any sense. That would leave only Rossi. Then he would check the coast was clear before making himself known again.

Fifty-Seven

Rossi needed to be in control, but he felt his grip was slipping on this one. Marini had left if not in a huff then certainly under a cloud. They had agreed to disagree but he had made it clear that he was in charge. Meanwhile, he had sketched out his own plan for targeting red-light zones, strip joints and sex clubs – legal and not – calculating what leverage might be available in terms of promises and favours owed, blind eyes to be turned, and frighteners to be applied. Zero tolerance on this one. They couldn't afford it to become an open secret. A tight modus operandi would be key to the success of the plan – that and their accumulated knowledge of the vice scene.

"That scumbag Marciano could have come in useful, couldn't he?" Rossi reflected as he held the door for Carrara. "He knew the vice world inside out. We could have pressured him for info. What was he doing getting himself carved up like that?"

Carrara shrugged.

"Got in too deep, I suppose. Occupational hazard in his line of work. We could get on to his family," he suggested.

"Why not," said Rossi, musing now as was his wont at the late and sometimes fecund hour. "Put it on your list. Not our case but there might be more than meets the eye there too," he said, forcing a smile for the first time in a while. "And while you're at it, have a sniff round the Muslim community. There's a mosque down there by the kebab place. That lad in the bin bag. And the pig's head. Who do you think that message was for? Too many killings at the same time, don't you think? They don't look connected but it has to arouse some suspicion, even if it does mean throwing the net much wider than we'd planned."

Carrara, glanced at his watch. "Anything else, sir?"

"No," said Rossi. "Get back to your family while you can," he added, feeling a sudden wave of tiredness and taken aback by the perceived lack of goodwill in his colleague's irony. "Unless there's something you should be sharing with me."

"I think you know how I feel about it."

"You think I'm barking up the wrong tree?"

"Something like that. Maybe. Look, I'm tired. We're both tired. Let's talk tomorrow. I'd better get some sleep."

"OK," said Rossi, giving him the benefit of the doubt. "I'll just sit here and think out a few things, then hit the sack. Will you be all right on your own?"

"I'll run all the way," Carrara answered with a half-hearted laugh. Rossi gave his protégée a warm squeeze on the shoulder.

"Look, Gigi," he said, "I'm just not wholly convinced, about her. I have a hunch, that's all."

"It's OK," Carrara replied, softening and turning towards Rossi. "But I just don't feel we're getting anywhere. A new approach, some new blood could be what we need and I think she's giving us a shot in the arm. She knows her stuff. She's good."

"And is she good at anything else?" said Rossi looking Carrara straight in the eye.

"Do you think I'd be that stupid?"

"You don't think it's obvious then? C'mon, Gigi! Is it payment on delivery or is it coming in instalments?"

"You don't need to worry, Mick. Everything is under control."

"If you say so."

"It is."

"Well you trust me on this one and give me some time."

"Do you think we've got time?" he said nodding towards the window and the city beyond. "He's out there. Somewhere."

The drinks cabinet was running low across all departments. It seemed no time since he'd restocked and though he tended to be selective in his recollections, it hadn't been long either since the time before that. Settle for a beer. Lesser evil. But he'd have to draw a line somewhere. Sometime. Tomorrow. He filled a glass. Always a glass.

He went out onto the balcony. The wind was cutting but it felt good on his skin and for a few moments he savoured its sting. To his right he saw the lights flickering in the Castelli Hills. What he wouldn't give to be walking in the wide open air now. Away from everything – the apartment, the open prison of this balcony, the confinement of the case. He had an overpowering urge to be out. Out. He had, after all, been sitting around the whole day and now feeling his energy levels topped up again he wanted to move. Somewhere. Anywhere. He grabbed his coat and keys and tucked his Beretta into his belt.

*

Not a soul. Not a sound. The city was on lockdown now every night. He turned right away from the old city and walked with steady, quick strides along Via Latina towards the hills in the distance, holding them in his gaze as an unlikely but possible, theoretical, eventual destination. Far away between him and the small, sleeping hill towns, the lights of a jumbo slowly lifted and swerved away from Ciampino, its signature a ragged far-off rumble. He wanted to be on it. The only other sound was the familiar steady trickle and gurgle of the fountain. He had passed it and was leaving it behind when from the shadows there was a scraping of shoes and a metallic clunk, as if of an iron bar or a hammer, as a figure emerged, stopped and called out.

"Michael!"

Rossi wheeled around, his wiry frame and limbs tensing in preparation for fight or flight. In a split second, his hand had reached for his Beretta.

"Michael," the all too familiar voice repeated. "It's me."

Fifty-Eight

The two men stood facing each other at a distance of only some six or seven yards. Rossi's hand was on his weapon, but he had not drawn it. Did he know who this man was? He was wearing a baseball cap with the peak pulled tight over his eyes and what looked like a football shirt under a rugged padded canvas jacket. He had heavy work shoes and on the ground beside him sagged a large holdall, like a sleeping, beige mongrel. It was half empty but contained for sure some weighty object or tools, weapons, a hammer even.

But instead of reaching for the bag, he raised a hand and indicated a point in the distance across the parkland and fields where the neat silhouettes of the treetops on the Appian Way could be seen against the pale moonlit sky.

"*Domine, quo vadis* is just about ... there, but I thought I'd meet you here."

Then something clicked in Rossi. That level of refined wit could be the work of only one man he knew but how could it be? *Iannelli*? The two men approached each other, released by the tacit understanding that there was nothing now to fear. The stranger removed his cap and gave his face a cursory wipe. It was him all right.

"But how on God's earth?" said Rossi before reaching out and grabbing him by both shoulders. For a minute he just stared then threw his arms around his friend. "And in reference to your little joke," he then began again, "despite appearances to the contrary, I am not Peter fleeing the city."

Rossi felt a sudden landslide of emotion sweep through him. He had been on the verge of giving up hope, what with Carrara's wavering and his own doubts about Marini and Yana, but now this.

"And I'm not intending to be crucified for a second time," Iannelli countered, "as it were. You will forgive me the blasphemy this once, won't you? After all, I have been through the mill." He looked down at himself and his unlikely apparel. "But it's not actually all as bad as it seems."

"Given the circumstances, you look fine," said Rossi.

"And you will remember that story is apocryphal, as have been reports of my death."

"Greatly exaggerated then."

"But not without some justification."

Rossi was still trying to square the Iannelli he knew with the clown-like figure before him.

"My disguise," said Iannelli, indicating again the heavy proletarian garb hanging on his light, scholarly frame.

"You had me fooled," laughed Rossi.

"Well, I couldn't take any risks. Can't wait to get out of it though."

Rossi was now piecing together the scenario which must have really unfolded both in Sicily and after and wondering why an incognito Iannelli was now standing before him, a Christ-like figure as good as risen from the dead. He put his head in his hands as if to confirm for himself that he was not dreaming. He rubbed his face up and down. There was a God; there was some justice in the world. Iannelli had cheated death, somehow.

"Allow me to carry your bag, *Signore*," he said, grabbing the well-travelled holdall. "What have you got in here?" he added, giving it a shake feeling now as if he too had been reborn.

"Bricks, and old pipes. If I was going to be a workman, I had to be a convincing one."

"Workman?" said Rossi. "The plot thickens."

"Don't worry," Iannelli laughed, "once you get me a drink and get that fire of yours stoked up I'll give you the full gen. But only you, mind, for now. You do know that I am a somewhat wanted man, don't you? Or I will be, once they realize there aren't any of my pulverized bones on the Palermo-Messina."

"Well, they'll have their work cut out trying to sift through that crime scene," commented Rossi. "I'd say you could sit easy for quite some time, possibly forever, if you were so inclined."

"I would kind of like to have my identity back," said a more concerned-looking Iannelli now as the initial euphoria began to subside and something of the strain started to show through. "And a bite to eat. I've been lying low since I got back to Rome."

"And your folks?"

"I bit the bullet, made a call. They're sworn to secrecy and hey, we might even start talking again. Who knows."

"Come on," said Rossi, "I'll smuggle you in. If anyone sees you I can say I've got a burst water main. But where were you exactly?" he continued as he shepherded Iannelli back towards the safety of the flat. "Are you going to keep it a secret? Was there someone else in your car …? Did you …?"

Fifty-Nine

In another part of the city, another tired but determined wanderer had been having rather less luck in tracking down his missing friend. For two nights he'd received no communication. Up to then, they had always managed to keep their appointments in one way or another. Calling the public telephone was a tried and trusted channel. Even if it was busy they would manage to find a window when they could talk. He had tried for an hour one night, two hours the next, but nothing.

And as time passed he began to worry for his friend's safety as well as his own, for he was alone in a city he knew only from a crumpled tourist map and the hearsay advice and anecdotes of fellow migrants and asylum seekers. "Refugees", as they used to say. But where was the refuge? Or "displaced" people. But that made him feel like a piece of furniture or a chess piece moved from one square to the next often by an unseen and sometimes sadistic hand.

He had surprised himself with the rapidity of his journey but knew he'd got lucky. While the guards had been watching football, he and a bunch of assorted fugitives had slipped out of the Detention Centre through the fence which had already been cut but never properly repaired. Then they'd wandered towards the motorway and on to the service stations. Learning on the fly, they had identified a HGV with a Roman registration and had tried their luck. It was a simple (simple!) case of getting behind the vehicle when it slowed down, or stopped, opening the doors and swinging up inside it. But not a refrigerator truck, if you wanted to get out alive. Closing the door behind you, you sat tight or hid, praying the oxygen would last. Those already inside made the rules and decided how many was the safe limit. Not like those godforsaken creatures packed by traffickers into trucks out of Serbia, forgotten or abandoned and left to asphyxiate in an unimaginable final circle of hell.

It was never easy having to turn others away. They had pleaded with him, some of them even carrying children in their arms. He'd had to use violence, too, when stubbornness got the better of one or two. As such, he had distinguished himself among the little brigade they then constituted – like Greeks in the belly of the horse before Troy. He had displayed the necessary qualities of leadership: decision, ruthlessness, and charisma. On the anxious journey it was he who kept their spirits up and he who managed to convince them to hold their nerve whenever doubts crept in.

To their astonishment, the truck had taken the Messina-Calabria ferry and then set off on another long road journey. By listening to the sounds outside and decoding their significance they had managed to work out that it was all consistent with a sea crossing and when the driver left the vehicle they allowed themselves to relax for a while. The door had been left on the latch, as it were, and had not been one of those to be checked. God was smiling on them, for sure, on this day at least.

When the vehicle came to an abrupt and decisive halt and its contents were about to be unloaded, they'd had to make their decision. Make a run for it? Go quietly? Bribe the first person they could? Jibril had cautioned them to hold onto their precious savings, to hide their jewellery or currency, if they had any left, and to first evaluate the situation. His language skills would be their first gambit. They would pretend first that they had no real knowledge of Italian. He could then ascertain what, if any, were the intentions of their hosts by way of his faked ignorance. If there were a crisis, he would use English.

It had all been much easier than they had envisaged. After some initial consternation on the part of the two sleepy young-sters that had opened the doors, the warehouse they had ended up in had become their gateway to the Italian capital. Most of the staff that had gathered round to savour the welcome break in their routine had seemed not unsympathetic to their plight and, despite some protestation by one decidedly fascist-looking forklift driver, they had concluded that turning a blind eye would be safer for all involved. Less paperwork, less hassle for everyone. "Vai! Vai via!" They had repeated, as Jibril and the others, following their strategy of near total non-comprehension to the letter, had dithered and gesticulated. "On yer way! Go! Go!"

They had found themselves on the outskirts, somewhere to the south-east, and in the absence of viable public transport had begun to walk. As they neared the city proper, each had taken his own road, some with plans to head towards the north and Milan or Bologna, others to France, Switzerland, Sweden or even England. Finally, Jibril was left alone with only the telephone number and address of his friend.

By the map it seemed he was not so far away, but the reality was different. He walked and walked, his constant motion at least tempering the worst effects of the biting cold. Apart from a change of underclothes, he was wearing everything he owned. But he needed more precise directions as he risked wasting time and energy in the city's bamboozling design.

Getting the attention of local people was not so easy. He had washed as well as he could but knew that the voyage had taken its toll on his appearance and thus his demeanour. Being also physi-cally big, he understood that he must have appeared threatening, so he tried to work out who would be less frightened by his periodic requests for information, even stooping slightly, as if supplicant.

Sometimes they thought he needed money and either averted their eyes or, in some cases, gave him small sums despite his attempts to convey embarrassment. Where to get a bus ticket, which bus went where? How to find this street or that street in Rome's often nonsensical urban tableau. All required information and orientation until, late in the evening, he found the area with its landmarks as his friend had described them – the elevated stretch of motorway in the distance, the small, forlorn park with its insignificant ruin of a crumbling Roman watchtower, the square, the street, the building, and the name on the intercom, an Italian name, the name of the owner of the property where Victor lived.

When he had once again given his friend's name and again explained in English to a rapid selection of interlocutors speaking variously broken or more or less coherent English, he was allowed to enter the building. The flat was on the ground floor, the most dangerous and crime-susceptible, yet he noted there were no bars on the windows.

A plump, late middle-aged man wearing bright traditional clothes showed him in. He imagined he might be from Cameroon, judging by his French cadences. Jibril brought out letters to show him, letters which proved that their friendship was real, going back many years. His host didn't appear overly interested in checking his credentials but rather more in public relations concerning what he grandly called "the residence".

"We have been asking the landlord – I am only his agent, shall we say – for heaven knows how long, to make the residence secure. But each time he fobs us off, or promises, and nothing happens. Four times we have been broken into now," he added, shaking his head, "four times."

"These are my quarters," he appeared to joke, indicating a

small but well-appointed box room with the most solid door in the house. The next slightly larger room was an improvised dormitory. There was a mattress in the corner, a bed by the wall, a wardrobe fashioned out of a clothes rail and a curtain.

"We are all nationalities here," he said, "but we get along very well."

Jibril explained how he had not heard from his friend for nearly three days. The self-styled agent listened and nodded, fiddling with a button on one of his long sleeves.

"Do you know anything?" Jibril asked, urging him for a shred of news.

The man looked away as if in search of something. Another, younger occupant was returning. He was strong, probably once athletic but now with the beginnings of a middle-aged man's pot belly stretching his work-soiled T-shirt. Jibril imagined he was a construction worker, a labourer, probably Eastern European.

"No," he replied. "I do not. But there have been rumours."

"Rumours?" Jibril enquired, turning back to the agent. "Rumours of what?"

The labourer had begun undressing, removing his T-shirt to reveal a tattooed upper torso, then continuing as if uninvolved but listening nonetheless.

"Must I tell him," he said, shooting a glance at the agent, his senior by at least ten years.

"Well, there have been stories," the agent said. "About a murder. A terrible, terrible murder."

"A body was found," the younger man broke in, "after Victor disappeared. An African. His throat cut and dumped in a plastic bag."

He turned to the agent.

"He has the right to know. Maybe then he will be able to identify him if we are all too cowardly to."

Jibril felt his knees giving way and the blood leaving his head.

A chill went through his body but he managed to summon the strength to ask again.

"And the rumours?" he urged. "What are these rumours?"

It was clear to Jibril now that if he were to discover something it could only be through this straight-talking if coarse man and not the seemingly gentile sibyl who had welcomed him.

"That he might have been involved, caught up in something bigger than he realized. With the Vatican. You know he went there? Had friends?"

"And did anyone contact these friends?" asked Jibril, clutching now at any shreds of hope. "Is there a number, anything, a diary he left?"

"I made a call," said the younger man, "useless though I knew it would be, but they said they had never heard of Victor. They knew no one of that name. Then they asked questions, too many questions for my liking."

He walked to the corner where there was a small bookshelf and a collection of personal items above a neatly made mattress bed.

"Here," he said, "have a look for yourself, if you think there's anything that might help. Here are all his possessions, just as he left them. And if you are wondering, I didn't stick my nose into his personal affairs."

With that he slung a towel over his shoulder, slipped into his flip-flops and walked out of the room.

"I will leave you now," said the agent, at which point it occurred to Jibril that no one had actually introduced himself and neither had he. Why? For fear? Fear that names might mean trouble. "I'm very sorry I couldn't be more helpful. But if by the end of this month he does not return, we will have to give his place to newcomers. We have a rent to pay, you know. Unless you want to rent it. We can discuss the price."

"I will not be staying," Jibril replied. He picked up what looked like a diary and a notebook and stuffed them into his bag.

"If these help me find him, I will take them."

"You can take them. Take what you want, really," he said extending his hand in a gesture of implied largesse. "But there is, I am afraid, no money."

Sixty

"Right," said Rossi, "so you jumped from a moving car seconds before a roadside bomb detonated and you survived to tell the tale?"

"Look," said Iannelli, jerking up one leg of the baggy corduroys he was wearing courtesy of Rossi's limited wardrobe, "where do you think I got a bruise like that from? Five-a-side football?"

"I believe you," said Rossi. "How else would you be here? But I didn't think it was actually that dramatic. I didn't think you had it in you that's all. It is all rather James Bond, isn't it?"

Iannelli tossed back the remaining wine in his glass.

"I had thirty seconds to make a choice. I was in Sicily. I had just been propositioned by a figure from God knows what part of the underworld or 'deep state' and I'd had the temerity to turn him down. Then I get a phone call telling me I'm about to become the next Giovanni Falcone or Paolo Borsellino. Given the circumstances, it didn't feel like a practical joke. I'm afraid it felt all too real. So I did it. I made a decision and I jumped."

"And lost all those books and wine."

"Had to put something on the accelerator."

"Jesus," said Rossi. "You've only gone and set the bar just about as high as it can go, haven't you?"

"I could have done without the hassle, actually."

"And then you walked all the way or what?"

Iannelli reached out with a slight grimace to pour himself some more wine.

"I had no choice. I wasn't really so 'with it', as you might imagine. I felt the power of the fireball where I was, even in all those trees. My ears were ringing from the shockwave and I'd taken a nasty blow on the head. I was conscious but just about. I had to get moving. It was nearly dark anyway, which gave me cover, and to cut a longish story short I ended up at a bus stop in the middle of nowhere and decided to throw caution to the wind. I was that exhausted I couldn't think straight. I got lucky, I suppose, and I told these Romanian guys I was on the run from the Mafia, that they were going to kill me and I needed help."

"Just like that?"

"Must have been the bump on the head. But it worked."

"And they gave you the outfit? Right?"

"Yep. Turned out they'd had run-ins with the gangmasters on a farm and didn't hold the local Cosa Nostra in very high esteem. They were only working there to get enough money so they could move on up the country and they just happened to be heading back to Romania for a wedding. A thirty-six hour coach journey. So, I became one of them and slipped through unnoticed, if anyone was looking for me or might have recognized me. I had enough cash to get us a hire car at Reggio and we made good time in the end."

"And then you casually made your way over to my place?"

"Where else could I go? I didn't know who or what or how many were after me. I was pretty sure that you weren't though."

"I appreciate the trust."

"Think nothing of it. Well, as long as they think I'm spattered across the Palermo-Messina, I can sit tight, I suppose."

"And then?"

"You tell me. It's uncharted territory. I mean this isn't my style."

"Well," said Rossi, exhaling and leaning back in his chair, "it looks like you'll be getting yourself an escort, 24/7."

"A virtual prison sentence then? Means they've won, doesn't it?"

"It's either that or a new identity."

"Not much of a choice, is it?"

"No," said Rossi. "But, you're alive. More wine?"

A more despondent looking Iannelli shook his head.

"Now," said Rossi, filling his own glass, "let's see what I can knock up in the line of food. Then we can start thinking about the next move. Hungry?"

"I could eat a horse's head."

"And then do you think you might share with me something of what you were sniffing out down in Sicily?"

"Perhaps," said the journalist. "But only if you tell me something about what you and Carrara are up to. And who's the blonde by the way?"

"Asked you first," said Rossi.

Sixty-One

"We'll be fine!" Each word was accompanied by a nervous nod in the direction of the three most concerned-looking public officials before him. "It will be just like in '85 – a dusting of snow, the kids'll be able to scrape together a few snowballs before it all melts and then it'll be over again, for another twenty years. What do you expect to happen? This is Rome, not Turin!"

The committee of public officials, civil protection officers, and party functionaries gathered before him for the breakfast briefing did not appear to share all of his certainty.

"If I may, Sindaco," began the skirt-suited manager responsible for coordinating the hypothetical gritting of the city's roads, referring to the notes on her clipboard: "latest reports mention 'possible significant coverage' – we are still waiting on the exact figures for precipitation and the night-time minimum temperatures, but despite what you say, it does seem to be going in that direction."

Basso was getting agitated. He was behind with his appointments – official and non – and the meeting had been dragging on well beyond the allotted time frame.

"*Dottoressa*," restraining his natural urge to bawl her out of it, "I have seen those reports and, as I said before, my team and I are monitoring the situation. We keep a contingency plan running anyway, but on a skeleton basis, as the plant and overtime costs are, as you might imagine, rather high."

"Are you saying that the funds are not adequate?" she replied. "I believe," she added, referring again to her papers, "there are ringfenced resources for this eventuality."

"Yes, but we don't need to go overboard with manpower and hiring and getting specialist machinery into position – snow-ploughs and the like – not to mention fuel and maintenance expenditure. Besides, you'll see, it will all blow over and we'll be able to give ourselves a slap on the back for not having wasted public money unnecessarily," he concluded, with forced jocularity, scanning the room with rodent eyes for signs of reciprocity, signs that were not, however, forthcoming. "So, we keep a close watch on the forecasts and we take it from there."

"And are you in a position to give assurances that you have the personnel in place who can interpret the data fully?" asked a not entirely convinced-looking senior member of the Civil Protection Division. "You will remember that it is, after all, down to the council to implement the necessary action and not us. We can only intervene in the event of a state of emergency or natural calamity being declared."

"Of course," the mayor replied.

"So you have the necessary means and logistics?"

"I can go on record, here and now, and assure you that all departments know what is expected of them and have been fully briefed and prepared. And I repeat, *Dottore*, that while we are talking about two or three centimetres of snow, the matter can be managed with the minimum of interference and without causing undue alarm or inconvenience to the citizens of Rome. Citizens who already have quite enough on their plate, as I'm sure you'd agree. And now, *signore e signori*, if there is nothing else, may we perhaps adjourn?"

Driving across the city towards the hospital to drop off some fresh flowers and have a quick look in on Yana, Rossi was feeling newly energized and rather satisfied with himself despite having had to deal with an increasingly embattled Maroni. He'd left Iannelli in the flat again in lieu of a better idea emerging and had managed to pin "the boss" down in his office before "high level meetings" and "engagements" had whisked him away from the world of mere mortals. Something was brewing though. A glance at the wastepaper basket's compacted contents told him Maroni had been shredding a lot more documentation than might have been deemed natural wastage. From the look on his face he had been able to see storm clouds were gathering there too.

While Iannelli had slept, he had stayed up late the night before working on his plan to target the clubs and red-light spots. In the meantime, his own renewed positivity and general demeanour seemed to have blunted all his previous negativity. If Iannelli could cheat death, well, maybe? He wasn't one for miracles but the more luck there was going around the better. Carrara was still nursing something approaching rancour but had, nonetheless, gone through the motions with Rossi's strategy.

Then he'd had to get away again – there was a mountain of work to get through – and Iannelli was still holding out on his next move. It was like juggling career and family, Rossi thought to himself. Dario was still in shock, he was sure of that. But he would, if he could, persuade him today to do the only possible thing, which was to give himself up, as it were, innocent though he was of any crime.

He reprised the morning's conversation with Maroni.

"You can have your bloody manpower," his hassled superior had conceded when he'd managed to detach himself from the phone. "Take them off whatever job can wait but just don't go breaking anyone's balls whose balls you shouldn't be breaking. Got it? We'll need every friend we can get before too long, Rossi. Mark my words."

Then he'd stared at him for some seconds before asking: "Have you got any idea what's going on?"

Rossi had shaken his head. So Maroni was chasing shadows too? Or bluffing?

"Just trying to get my hands on this psycho," Rossi had replied.

Maroni hadn't even seemed overly perturbed by the far-fetched, at least by his standards, theory regarding their potential quarry's cryptic missives.

"Well, they have to mean something, don't they, Rossi? So you may as well put that stunning intellect of yours to the test and follow it up as you see fit! After all, you're the professor. And the philosopher. And God knows what else."

For Rossi, from the moment he had walked in the door that morning, the pervasive atmosphere of nervousness had echoed something of the way it had on the eve of Tangentopoli, the mega bribes scandal of twenty years previously. That had seen the whole political establishment rocked to the foundations and a large chunk of its leaders, ringleaders more like, either doing time or put out of the game for good. Yet, it was at moments like this that Rossi could enjoy a little of the interest accrued on his own account. Sure, he might have bent the rules, at times, to get at the bad guys, but he'd never taken even a penny to let one villain off the hook. Schadenfreude, was it? Delighting in the misfortunes of others? Well, what if it was? So be it.

His thoughts shifted back to his lodger. Regardless of the choice Iannelli made, sooner or later the story would have to break. And after having heard some of the details of his Sicilian escapade, Rossi felt sure Maroni's allusions to "something very big" was likely close in shape, substance, and being to what Dario had half-unearthed on his travels. And it was probably going to hit the proverbial fan whether Dario went public on it or not. The time was ripe. The storm clouds were full, the atmosphere charged, and the attempt on Dario's life had opened another Pandora's box. Hitting a journalist, and a journalist of Iannelli's standing, meant the gloves were off. Yes, Rossi, too, felt that the wheels were turning, that the lumbering machine of change and imminent turmoil was moving. He now also suspected that much, if not all, of the bizarre violence convulsing the city may very well have constituted bloody cogs in its complex, interconnected, and infernal mechanism.

But his immediate objectives were Giuseppe Bonaventura and Yana. Iannelli's incredible return had given him not only new hope but also a new pure anger. And even if it was personal, well so be that too. He'd been doing his duty for years and now he wanted his payback time. This morning he felt alive and hungry again, spurred on, pushing now to get his man and, yes, to get his revenge. If it was him, he wanted him. He wanted to stand before his nemesis and look him in the eye and then? A traffic light flicked from amber to red. He stopped abruptly to the annoyance of the stream of traffic behind him.

As he continued to savour the fantasy, he passed the imposing mass of the thirteenth century Torre delle Milizie tower and his mind wandered from the present inferno to things medieval: to dungeons, to darkness, to other Gothic horrors from collective and personal pasts. He remembered then a picture in a school textbook, of the oubliette, where prisoners were thrown and, as the name suggested, forgotten. As he pondered that most base form of incarceration, the message about "the black hole" again came to mind.

It seemed an age ago now though it had been only some ten days. A black hole of missing money? Iannelli's discovery of a network of large-scale corruption and establishment complicity? The fascist legacy waiting to be reclaimed? Were the pieces of some huge, dark, puzzle coming together? Or was it a Jungian reference, one perhaps for him: the hole in your life? The so-called "dark web"? Was that where he was hiding? Was that where perhaps he wanted to be found? Maybe his first hunch at the beginning of the case hadn't been so far off after all. But his reverie was broken by the buzz of an incoming call. He checked his phone. He'd missed the call the first time but it had been only moments before and now he took it with something approaching alacrity.

Like a jagged knife tearing through flesh, Rossi had pulled the car over, slicing the pavement and the road and even butting into one of the roadside wheelie bins, jam-packed, overflowing and un-emptied as usual. A teetering bottle fell from its precarious lodging and shattered. A female dog walker collecting her dog's ejections in a plastic bag afforded him and his parking efforts a disgusted sideways glance, but Rossi couldn't have been more oblivious. He had his head in his hands now. Then, in a paroxysm of rage that sent his erstwhile observer and four-legged companion both skittering along the street for fear, he pounded the steering wheel until only the near exquisite pain in his fists and wrists made him stop.

There had been another. A carbon copy. Not a witness, not a clue. Another defenceless mother bludgeoned to death on another Roman street but this time in the centre, near the old Roman gate of Porta Pia. Name: Daniela Ferrante. Age: 42. Morning again. Dead for maybe two or three hours and missed first at work. On a side street, the body had been dumped over railings into a basement. Carrara was already there and had given him the lowdown. Prior to getting the call he had been "throwing ideas around" with Marini and she was with him now, under the most convincing of covers, as a journalist, Carrara assured the incandescent Rossi. Complete with blonde wig, no doubt. Was Carrara losing it? Was the stress getting to him too? He slewed the car around and reached out to hammer the siren on. Then he cut through the slovenly traffic like a man possessed.

He was to blame. No one was saying it to his face, of course, because only he knew. If they had gone to work on Marini's surveillance plan, did they think they might have seen this murder off at the pass? Of course not. In the space of two days they couldn't have hoped to get a breakthrough. But he should have known all along. He should have seen it! That was what he was good at, wasn't it? Now here they were quizzing this poor unfortunate who had just joined the widowers' club. Not particularly nice, Rossi reflected. They often weren't. Looked like the kind who never lifted a finger and maybe let his missus out once a year. Not a murderer though. That was clear enough but he played the field, if he still could. No, judging by his waistline and taste in clothes, he probably paid for it now and then when funds permitted.

They'd left the crime scene in the hands of forensics, and after managing to persuade a stubborn Marini to get back into hiding, they'd headed straight to the family home. Carrara, to his credit, had picked up on Rossi's dark demeanour and he had already run through the best part of the question gamut as they sat opposite their interviewee in the lounge.

"Social media?"

"What?"

"Facebook, Twitter and the like. Did she use them?"

"Didn't even have a computer. Said she'd had enough of looking at a screen all day at work. Didn't want to know about having one at home. That's mine over there," he said, sheepishly enough to have awoken the curiosity of a vice cop with time on his hands. But he wasn't a suspect. Rossi was going through the motions as far as he was concerned but wanted to know more about his now deceased wife.

He got up from his chair, depositing the coffee cup he'd been nursing for the last twenty minutes or so on the dining table covered in plastic sheeting. They did it to protect the surface, didn't they? Like people who kept their car seats enveloped in squeaky cellophane long after they'd left the showroom. As if it were ready for murder.

Rossi excused himself and by means of a few well-understood gestures enjoined Carrara to continue with the few remaining formalities. He took a look around the kitchen. All in order.

Nothing very personal about the decor. Brand names in the cupboards. A TV family. Not a book in the living room. Not a book in the house. He nodded to the uniforms manning the entrance to the flat and went down the stairs into the apartment block's vestibule which he also gave a quick once-over. A decent building, well kept. Not too much graffiti. He checked his phone. Nothing of note. There were footsteps on the stairs behind him.

"As random as random can be, eh?" said Carrara joining him.

"Seems that way," Rossi replied. "A quiet street near her workplace. Do you think she was watched though? Followed from her house? If this is matricide our killer must be keeping some tabs on them."

"Stands to reason," said Carrara.

"I mean," said Rossi, "you can spot a woman and you can guess she's a mom, but you don't actually know, do you?"

Carrara gave something like an adolescent's shrug. He seemed to be harbouring some residual bad feeling or suffering withdrawal symptoms without Marini around and Rossi sensed it. Whether or not she'd entrapped him emotionally or erotically, she'd made him feel more valued and that was in part Rossi's own fault. He had been taking Carrara a little too much for granted and the pressure on all of them, like some emotional hothouse, was blowing every minor grievance out of proportion. Thus, the situation called for cool heads or, in counselling or anger management parlance, a cooling-off period. The only problem was that it would take time and that was a commodity they didn't have on their side.

"Gigi," said Rossi, with a change of tone, "look, I've been thinking. About the other night and our difference of opinion. I want you to go ahead with the plan. I've been a bit short-sighted on this one. It was arrogant of me to shoot it down and I should have heard you out or proposed a compromise but in the cold light of day, and now after this, well I think it's at least worth giving it a try."

306

"Well we're not picking up much through the standard channels, are we?" said Carrara his face like a storm cloud now visibly brightening at the edges at the prospect of getting his chance. Rossi shook his head and his thoughts turned to the office covered with the victim's photos, Post-it notes, maps, conjectured rebuses, street names, and red lines and wild hypothetical links. Now they had this new entry to add. They had got the number crunchers and the uniforms to plough through the gamut of standard procedures – searching and scanning for the connections, their children's schools and friends, old school mates, bars they frequented, figures in common, driving instructors, doctors, shops they usually went to but no pattern that might lead them to their man had yet emerged.

"Get yourself what you need," said Rossi. "Manpower, equipment requests and such like and get to work on it. The other side of the coin is this though: I'll need forty-eight hours or so to think through some stuff on my own. There's something else I'm working on and it could just complement Maria's approach. For which I need you to put your trust in me. As for the rest, I'm handing you full control."

"Is it going to be another of your surprises?" said Carrara smarting a little now from the sting in the tail of Rossi's proposal.

"Let's call it a hunch."

"But I remain in the dark?"

"I'm asking you to trust me, Gigi," said Rossi, gauging now just how much the invisible bond that had united them so well for so long had been loosened.

Carrara hesitated for a moment as Rossi looked him straight in the eye. Maybe it would work for them both. Either way it would be the acid test. If Marini was rocking the boat for her own egotistical reasons and Carrara wanted to go along with her, so be it. Maybe he too wanted to strike out on his own, knowing a victory in this case would be the launchpad for great things. But only time would tell on that. If they got a result all the better for the city and the force but Rossi was firm now and had decided exactly how he was going to formulate his own strategy. He had stunned Carrara but that was how it had to be. He only hoped he would thank him before too long.

"I want you with me on this," said Rossi. "Even if I can't let you in on it yet, I want you to know that you were right. That I wasn't thinking outside of the box, that Yana and the whole Spanish connection had thrown me off course. It had all been getting to me, and I've been drinking too much. It's my fault not yours. But I just need some time. Maybe we both need some time."

Carrara was weighing it up. The relationship was on the line but it was down to them both to salvage it, and if he too was honest with himself he would have to say he found it hard to see how things had come to this. But somehow they had.

"Whatever you say, boss," he replied, his tone restored to something like that of the old Carrara. Rossi felt a powerful wave of relief wash over him and gave his partner a good-natured slap on the back.

"I'm counting on you, Gigi, and you know where to find me," he said, making then for the main door.

"Oh, and you might want to be getting back to Luzi," he called back over his shoulder. "You know, about his nocturnal habits, and maybe what he does mornings too. Maybe we're missing something big there."

So, the king was still giving orders even when he had abdicated. And then pushing open the street door he went out, back into the cold.

308

Sixty-Two

Rossi parked as near to his house as possible but decided to stretch his legs anyway. He passed the familiar shops. The hairdresser's, the *tavola calda* takeaway serving pizza-by-the-slice and sit-down lunches for workmen, and whose proprietor spent the spare moments of his day eyeing young girls.

He passed the computer shop in which he had set foot perhaps two or three times before, always with written instructions and dizzied by his inability to choose anything. Then he stopped. The window was full of innumerable gadgets – black or silver boxes, cubes, tablets, drives, and pads of every description. Did you actually need all these to be up-to-date? But his eyes were fixed more on the human element now as he crossed Emporium IT's threshold.

At the till, the usual part-timer was there and rolling a cigarette that didn't look like standard issue.

"Are you going to smoke that?" Rossi enquired.

"Not now," came the reply with a gesture towards the clock on the wall. The sacred lunch hour fast approached.

"Do you know I'm a police officer?" said Rossi.

The youth shrugged.

"Don't give a fuck," he said. As if out of solidarity, his oversized black T-shirt proclaimed "Anarchy".

That's the spirit, thought Rossi, beginning to feel his idea now hatching.

"Listen, do you know what a splitter is?"

"Over there," he muttered holding the filter for his joint-in-progress between pursed lips and giving another sideways jerk of the head, "digital and analogue."

"And a firewall, a worm, a Trojan horse?"

"Can't buy them," he said, with a slight chuckle of derision, "You make them, like viruses. You have heard of viruses?"

"Yes," said Rossi, nodding. "And hacking? What do you know about that?" he continued. "In practical terms."

He looked up now from his handiwork.

"What do you wanna know?"

"I'd like to know if you know anyone who'd care to make themselves some extra money, that's all."

A flicker of interest animated his previously uninterested movements.

"Look," said Rossi, "what do you say if I buy you lunch?"

*

There was a note on the kitchen table when Rossi returned to the flat.

"Gone to do the decent thing. Cheers. M."

"So, I'll be seeing you on the eight o'clock news," Rossi muttered to himself, as he made tea and pottered around the empty flat, trying not to associate the new-found space with new-found loneliness.

He sat down to mull over more pressing matters. The young shop assistant, Gabriele, Gab, had proven to be a veritable gold-mine of ideas and information and, once he had understood the nature of the arrangement, had also proven to be a most able teacher. Rossi had pretty soon scratched through his anarchic veneer to uncover an acute intelligence which, coupled with a devil-may-care attitude to risk-taking, had convinced him he could rely on and trust this neophyte with helping him to execute the rest of his plan. Yes, he was just a little mad, he reflected. But he was mad and feeling ever so slightly alive and maybe even enjoying the job again, despite everything else.

The plan was for Rossi to drop by the shop just before closing, and Gab would then set about explaining to him the various strategies available to them – strategies which would allow Rossi to make a much closer examination of the lives, the virtual lives, of some, if not all, of the victims so far. Then, if necessary, they might have to do what Gab had termed some "entering" and potentially some "breaking and entering" to sites and possibly property "if the need arose".

"You get me into the buildings and I'll get you into the networks. OK?" Gab had said, leaning back after his very satisfactory lunch of pizza, fried stuffed rice balls – arancini – and Coke. "Then we can talk about a fee."

"A hundred up front," Rossi had countered, still pondering the ease with which he was contemplating what were highly illegal acts, "and guaranteed immunity. Then we'll see about results-based bonuses." It wasn't much, but Rossi knew for a kid of his age it was enough to matter.

"For tonight?"

Rossi had nodded.

Gab had chewed it over, but not for long, before giving his assent.

"*Va be'*. OK. It's a deal."

Rossi felt as clear-minded and forward looking as a traveller who, after wandering in dark woods, has realized that the road out is within sight. He knew now that he had to focus on the victims again and not just on their presumed killer. These women had all had very normal public lives, and unremarkable private ones, as their enquiries and the testimony of husbands and family had borne out.

But something was growing in Rossi, a doubt, a suspicion that they – he, Carrara, and now Marini – had made a gross under-estimation with regard to these women. They had jumped on the serial-spree killer solution, concluding that they were not being killed by people they knew. Then they had conjectured a motive and following the trail presented to them had arrived within what seemed like touching distance of their quarry. At least in theory.

But they had ignored or overlooked another vital element which he now theorized was both the "how" and the "why" in this case. He laughed to himself. Oscar Wilde would have loved it. In each of the cases, apart from any public life and private life, they had failed to take into account the possible existence of a secret life. And from what Gab had told him about how to unearth such things, he now also had reason to believe that not only had they failed to look in the right places but that someone had been putting obstacles in their way.

Sixty-Three

On the same day, in two different parts of the city, two very different men, both without papers, had turned up on police and state premises. Jibril stood before the City Morgue and Hospital of Legal Medicine. He had spent the previous evening a fugitive from the bitter cold by riding first the trams and then the night buses before getting some sleep on a park bench once the sun had come up to give some semblance of warmth. For his lunch, he had bought bread rolls and tinned tuna and had then walked the city for hours on end as he turned over his options.

He waited. In the early darkness, the building had the same sobering effect it had on all who would subsequently have to cross its threshold, not only because of its barracks-like security but also for the air of grim detachment its soiled, grey concrete exuded, not to mention evident questions of basic cleanliness and organization.

"I have come to identify my friend. I think he may have been murdered," said Jibril when an answer finally came from the intercom. "His name is Victor … I believe a body was found."

The gate opened and when he was inside he found himself before another barrier.

"*Documento*," said the sour-faced, unshaven official.

313

Jibril shook his head.

"No ID?" the man asked looking up now.

"No."

"Wait," he said indicating a room with a few stiff wooden chairs.

There ensued a conversation first by telephone which Jibril tried in vain to follow through the small glass window behind which the wizened functionary was seated. The latter then hauled himself out of his chair, disappeared into an adjacent room and came back with another younger uniformed employee who with a hand gesture bid Jibril come to the desk.

"What exactly is it you want to do?"

Jibril explained his predicament again in as calm and polite a way as he could. The younger employee grimaced as he appeared to strain to understand Jibril's accented but otherwise clear Italian.

"You want to identify your friend? Is that what you're saying?"

"Yes."

"And you've got no documents, no ID, nothing?"

"No."

"Nothing we can do. Without ID, I can't let anyone in."

"But I only want to know if he is alive or dead."

A bright female member of staff in her mid-forties carrying files and papers had entered the small front office.

"What seems to be the problem?" she enquired. The second official gave an enigmatic backwards jerk of the head.

"Says he wants to identify a body."

"And nobody told me?"

"Thought you were out," the squat first official mumbled somewhere into his own chest.

She looked at Jibril for a moment then summoned him to a side entrance and into another room where she closed the door. She indicated a seat and sat down opposite him. He began to wonder if he would now need money. He knew exactly how much he had in his pocket. It was enough for a week, maybe two.

"What's your name, please?"

He gave his name and a surname.

"And the relationship, with your friend?" she asked. She was firm but kind too, Jibril noted.

"He's my best friend. We grew up together, in Nigeria. He came here to Rome before me and now he has disappeared. I must know if he is alive or if he is dead."

"Was your friend in any trouble?"

Jibril shook his head.

"He is missing. That's all I know."

She looked up now at the tall, slim African seated before her. In his eyes she thought she could see the glassy beginnings of defiant tears or maybe it was just fatigue.

"Do you have anyone who can vouch for you, Jibril? An embassy official, a doctor, for example."

"I know a journalist," he said, scenting suddenly an opening, and he reached for his wallet from which he produced Iannelli's business card. He passed it across the desk, and after studying it she slid it back accompanied by what seemed to be a gentle sigh.

"Follow me," she said rising from her chair and gesturing with an open hand. "This way, please."

Dario Iannelli strolled past the group of plain-clothes officers chatting at the entrance to the Commissariato Appio Nuovo, just a short walk from Rossi's house. He had borrowed some of the inspector's clothes and cut a much more respectable, if not distinguished, figure. For once, more or less at a loss for words, he wasn't sure quite how he was going to describe his current situation.

"*Buongiorno.* I was wondering if you could help me."

"Yes."

"My name is Dario Iannelli and, well, despite what you may have heard, I am not actually dead."

The young female officer who had been hunched over her papers did something of a double take.

"Sorry, but could you repeat that, please?"

"I am Dario Iannelli. The journalist. I'm not dead."

The officer scrutinized the serious and civilized face in front of her for a moment before turning rather pale. She recognized him now from the TV, even without the make-up.

"Oh, *Dio!*" she exclaimed almost scrabbling then for the telephone. "Er, one moment, please," she said gesturing to him with her free hand to come round to the inner sanctum behind the glass screen while banging out an extension number with the other.

"Come quick. Got a slight emergency situation. You wouldn't believe it if I told you. No."

She put down the phone and took a breath to regain her composure.

"Do you have some ID?"

Iannelli opened wide his hands, like a mime from some wordless Beckett play.

"Nothing?"

"All gone up in smoke I'm afraid, on the Palermo-Messina."

For a moment, in the female officer's mind, it seemed that cold logic had now sown some small seeds of doubt regarding the veracity of this apparent miracle.

"But I do have someone who can vouch for me," said Iannelli sensing the slight change. "Inspector Michael Rossi. He lives just round the corner."

He glanced down at himself.

"These are actually his clothes. Would you like his number?"

Jibril walked out into the bracing cold of the winter evening. Many in his situation might have been thanking the lucky stars above their heads. After all, he was, at least nominally, a free man, grateful not to have been detained as an illegal immigrant.

316

A criminal. Whether it had simply been easier for them to turn a blind eye or that there had been genuine kindness behind their showing him the door, he could not be sure. He cared little. His actions now were automatic, mechanical. He wound his scarf around his neck as many times as it would go and tucked the end inside his jacket, his rather too-thin jacket. He walked on, and he kept walking, first alongside the tramlines and then under the railway bridge and further on towards Porta Maggiore – like a miniature l'Arc de Triomphe, as far as he could see, but actually another of Rome's ancient gateways. A door between one world and another. The capital, the polis, and the empire beyond. It was here, too, outside the city walls that the graves began.

Entering the old city proper he found himself, although he didn't yet know it, on the Esquiline, one of Rome's seven hills and its highest. The almost icy wind was being channelled hard now between the handsome if somewhat neglected ranks of grandiose Renaissance-style palazzi flanking both sides of the once-majestic Via Principe Eugenio up to the square of Piazza Vittorio. But most of this, too, was lost on Jibril.

Was this the right road for the mosque? He'd been told there was one near here. He asked an elderly North African who pointed a bony finger in the vague direction of the other end of the square, indicating a point beyond the obscure shadows of the railing-encircled gardens. He kept walking. A huge white "M" on a red background told him that here was a Metro station. As he passed, crowds surged up and out from below the ground to climb the broad stone steps. He might have taken some comfort from so many of them not being natives here but various shades of brown and yellow and darker brown and black. Their languages also were a hotchpotch of almost anything but Italian. He might have been encouraged, too, by their tired but determined and often smiling faces, by their chatter and by their apparent sense of purpose and vigour, but he wasn't. In fact, he hardly noticed them at all. The only thing that Jibril could feel now was the nothingness. As if the house he had lived in all his life had been burned to the ground and he was the only survivor. That and the bitter, biting cold.

Sixty-Four

"Well, you might not believe it," Carrara continued, "but I think we may actually be getting somewhere with this strategy. Maybe even a contact."

For two days, they had felt as if they had been in a blind alley and he had wished on more than a few occasions that Rossi might have been there to give something like direction. As luck would have it, Maria had now come through with what she was sure was a positive lead. She had been hammering at her nail day and night and had finally hit on something.

"Really?" said Rossi at the other end of the line.

"We've had the lads out every night on all the usual street locations, been hassling the clubs and the brothels, and we've doubled the road blocks and random checks and it seems like it may just be working in our favour."

"So, there's a contact? With Bonaventura?"

"Possibly a contact."

"Ah."

Carrara's enthusiasm, however, did not seem in any way diminished.

"Well, it's funny but since we started cracking down – it's been dressed up as a mayoral anti-crime initiative – it seems that there's

319

been a surge in the online side of the business. It's like the men, husbands mainly, are afraid of getting a spot fine sent to their home address, so they're staying off the streets and looking around on the sites instead."

"How interesting," said Rossi reaching for a newspaper and trying not to knock over the glass perched on a cushion.

"And Maria thinks she has a contact with a profile that ticks all the right boxes. She's got a load of them but now she says she's really starting to narrow them down."

"Has she actually seen him?"

"No. Not yet. She's trying to build up trust but the signs are quite good."

"Time frame?"

"Don't know."

"And what have you seen?"

"A few of the messages, the exchanges. Pretty hardcore some of it, by the way."

"I can imagine."

There was a pause.

"You don't sound too impressed."

"No," said Rossi, "no, it's not that. It's just, well. It all seems so, I don't know."

"So not like police work?"

"Well, yes. In a way."

"Not our way of doing things, right?"

Rossi was now twirling around the finger or so of Martell remaining in his glass while scanning the newspaper propped against another cushion.

"It's certainly not the weather for street work either, is it?"

"Doesn't usually seem to stop 'em. After all, work is work, isn't it?"

"Suppose it is," Rossi half sighed. "And look, now that you mention it, I'm going to be coming back on board. Sorry it took a bit longer than I'd thought."

A slight pause ensued.

"Had a brainwave?" Carrara enquired.

"Well, I've certainly had enough of sitting around. Fancy a bit of action myself now and seeing as you two are going places, it looks like you might need an experienced head, once it all kicks off. What do you say?"

"Sounds great to me, Mick. Glad you're up for it."

"Actually, never been better."

"What happened then? Have you been on a retreat or something? Given up the booze?"

"Well, let's say that after a period of quiet reflection I have been getting in touch with my inner child, or inner teenager, again."

"Meaning?"

"Meaning that's for you to work out, Gigi, don't you think? But I'm certainly ready to 'hack it' again, as they say. And what do you say to tomorrow morning, at the office? Or will I be disturbing you … two?"

"Nothing to worry about there. Maria's been working from her own place and liaising via a secure link. Says she works better alone."

"She'll be asking for a salary next. Does she know how bad the pay is?"

Carrara's laughter was real. Rossi smiled and sensed that Carrara knew it too.

"If we were in it for the money …" Carrara began.

"We'd be the villains instead," Rossi finished. "Or in politics."

"I have to say I'm looking forward to something like intelligent conversation again."

"The lads not stretching your cognitive capacities then?"

"Not overly, no."

"Tomorrow it is then."

"Tomorrow it is then," replied Carrara.

"OK," said Rossi, then as if remembering something: "Oh, did you get on to Luzi again?"

"He's been out of the country for business, but he's coming back today. I left a message with his secretary. I said I thought it could wait, that it was purely routine."

"Get on to him," said Rossi, "and why don't you ratchet it up a bit. Say you need to see him asap. Oh, and send me a report through of what you've been up to while I've been away."

"OK," Carrara replied, "will do."

It was later that afternoon after the Metro had brought him back to Castro Pretorio station and thence to his well-furnished and welcoming executive office at Piazza della Croce Rossa that Luzi finally cracked. He'd taken a shower in the en suite bathroom and then a glance at the papers had told him of the latest victim. The killer still at large. Police looking for one man in connection with all the murders. Then there had been the phone call, the polite and business-like tone of the officer who had interviewed him the first time. But it was serious now. It was too much. There had been too many. He would have to tell. He couldn't go on lying. Could he come by, later, for another little chat? A few loose ends to tie up. Some new lines of enquiry. Yes, it would have to be today. He did know there had been another murder, didn't he? They required his full cooperation. Was he a suspect? Not over the phone, Mr Luzi. Not over the phone. But he had told them everything! Everything. No. Not everything.

The days spent in Ljubljana absorbed in official business had been a false oasis of banality and innocence. He had tried to shut out that other, illicit, world he had made for himself and had thought that he could put it all behind him. But now as he stared at the familiar four walls, as he thought about returning later to the empty house, as he thought about what he had done that night, his cowardice, his folly, he knew he had no escape. How many times had he played out the scene – their prearranged meeting, his pretending to stumble on her with another man, then making himself the third in a sordid triangle. To put life

322

back into their marriage. Life on a razor's edge and, yes, the fire of their dangerous fantasies had energized them like nothing else had. Until that night. He held his head in his hands. The image would never leave him. Her stockinged leg on the dashboard, his approach, his anticipation, and then the discovery. At the sight of the blood frenzy he had frozen, a million voices racing through his head before he began to run. Then he had stopped. She was dead. Murdered. He could not tell the truth. He had to live on, but he couldn't live with the shame of his double life and the shame of having left her at the mercy of a beast, all to satisfy his fantasies.

So, he had gone back, the calculating coward that he had so swiftly become, to remove any sign of his own involvement, moving first the body into a less provocative position and removing from her handbag any incriminating erotic paraphernalia before finally subtracting her phone from the scene. He had never been there. They never met there. They did not lead a sordid double life. It was all a mystery he could not explain.

He took a sheet of the headed paper before him and began to write. Why? For who? Who cared! There was no one now. He stood up and raised the sash window. A chill early-evening gust greeted him and for some reason he first removed his jacket and then his tie. He placed them on the back of his chair, as if he were going to take a restorative, executive power nap. The court-yard below was empty except for cigarette butts, the odd plastic cup rolling around. He pressed the buzzer on his intercom.

"Silvia, could you come to my office please, as soon as you have finished what you are doing. I think something here is not quite right."

Sixty-Five

Rossi glanced across the room to his joyously disordered dining table-cum-desk. Rarely used for dining, it was strewn with fragments of Roman amphorae he'd unearthed here and there, growing towers of books as well as the fruits of his cyber adventure with Gab. His phone wires and modem and splitter were in seeming spaghetti-like disorder, but he would see to putting them right shortly, now that he knew how it all worked.

That had been quite an education. There was nothing like taking a refresher course, or a beginner's course. He took another sip on the cognac now warmed almost to perfection. Perhaps they would be all right, after all, the old team. Carrara was just impatient sometimes, that was all. Still, he would keep to himself what he had found until the moment was right. Until the moment was ripe. He had left himself no other choice. But at least he had something approaching an ace up his sleeve. It was as if he'd sneaked in extra training for some big race. Wait and work on the remainder of the plan. He took another sip and then spun the golden liquid around again watching it and the light playing until a vortex formed then as quickly vanished. Yes. Almost to perfection. Almost.

He woke with a start. His phone was buzzing on the table next to his keys and making an infernal racket. He staggered over.

"Yes, who is it?"

"Me, Mick. Gigi. Bad news, I'm afraid."

"How bad?"

"It's Luzi. He's dead."

"How?"

"Suicide."

"When?"

"This afternoon."

"Any note?"

"Yep. 'Sorry. I didn't do it. Sorry.'"

Sixty-Six

"ID, please," the officer asked once the car window had been fully wound down. They couldn't stop them all, so they worked on the principle of gut-feeling or probability. Some sort of numbers game. And this vehicle fitted the bill, primarily because of its ordinariness. Because of its anonymity, the kind of anonymity, according to the logic, that could so often slip through the net. At least that's what he thought.

It was an unremarkable but sturdy Fiat. A bit rough around the edges. A bit like the occupant. He was probably in his 40s but fit, slightly unshaven, even if a little agitated, perhaps, for the inconvenience. With the window down, on a night as cold as this, the secure little cell he'd been cocooned in was now flooded with icy air and had become decidedly inhospitable. Or perhaps it was because of where he had been stopped and why. For this was Tor Sapienza, on Rome's pretty much forgotten north-eastern outskirts, with its crumbling tree-root distorted footpaths and litter-strewn waste ground and hinterlands. He could only be doing one thing here, at that speed, in a red-light area: cruising, kerb-crawling, on the lookout for prostitutes.

"ID, please," said the officer despite the driving licence's appearing to be in order. Instinct here, too, was telling him to cross-check. All seemed to be fine, as he shone his torch on the particulars which matched with those on the licence. Almost all. He rubbed his thumb across the passport-sized photo's borders. Was there an edge there? A razor cut possibly? Or was it just a crease, wear and tear? He looked more closely. One of the entries seemed to be in an unfamiliar font. The light wasn't great. He remembered his training. Easiest European document to forge. This though would be his first. Better to check.

"One moment, please," he said. The driver seemed resigned but unperturbed. Perhaps relieved that his motives for being there were not as yet on the officer's agenda. Just more waiting in a day of waiting his fixed stare seemed to say; the driver's bane, in Rome.

The ID wasn't stolen but his colleagues had confirmed the anomaly with the font. There was the outside risk that it could be a cloned ID. They would have to bring him in. As the officer returned, a little rush of adrenaline was coursing through his veins; with minimal movements he undid the flap on his holster. That too would be a first if he had to draw his weapon. A state policeman. Not a carabinieri. Those guys got plenty of action. Too much action. Sent them to Iraq. Nasiriya. Car bombs. And when they returned. He'd seen them. Jumpy. Paranoid. Unpredictable. Better off here. But in the police you could also have your moments. That's what they had said, and it was partly why he had joined.

His colleague followed just five or six steps behind grumbling to himself. Stefano would insist on doing his job properly, wouldn't he? Bringing him back to the station would mean an even longer night. But it had to be done. Duty calls. Still, at least they'd be out of this place for a while. This *maledetto*, God-forbidden, blasted heath of a no-place and its seedy car parks and filth-strewn lay-bys. Something nice and hot. That's what he wanted. Something nice and hot inside him. But in that instant, as the flash flared and the rapid crack crack crack sent the silhouette of his friend's body crumpling into the ground, the few yards separating them and which he now tried to bridge were like every second he had ever lived and each second like just so many miles.

Sixty-Seven

"… the journalist who arrived at a police station three days ago to the great surprise of the duty officers is now under twenty-four hour police protection and will then move to a secure location with a round-the-clock team of bodyguards to guarantee his safety following the attempt on his life.

"Security has been stepped up across Rome following the fatal shooting last night of a police officer in the Tor Sapienza area of the city. The officer was gunned down while making routine vehicle checks. Another officer also received minor gunshot wounds but is not in a critical condition. The gunman was able to evade police after a brief pursuit through the east of the city. The Home Secretary made the following statement:

"'The government has approved plans, with immediate effect, to station armed military personnel in key points across the city in response to the killing and the ongoing security crisis. Soldiers and armoured vehicles will be posted across the city in tourist areas and other key locations. They will also have increased stop and search powers. We aim to protect business and tourism but above all our citizens from the wave of criminality that has seen parts of the city become no-go areas, especially for our women. We don't know who is behind these vile murders and the upsurge in crime-related killing but the safety of our citizens is paramount in the face of threats from whatever quarter, be they politically motivated or not.'

"In response to accusations from sections of the opposition and particularly from the MPD that the move was symptomatic of a continuing drift towards authoritarianism, the minister replied that the people 'wanted firm government at a difficult moment. This is a time for experienced hands rather than idealists and dilettantes and not for a leap into the unknown'.

"And opinion polls released this morning by IGM and Telital show a significant falling off in support for the MPD, while the New Alliance has seen an increase in its support. A spokesperson for the MPD declined to comment, in line with the movement's declared policy of non-cooperation with the media. A post on the movement's blog, however, questioned the impartiality of the polling organizations.

"Controversy surrounding the Imam Mu'ammar Al Mughrabi and his planned visit to Rome has heightened … The Imam who has previously declared his support for an Islamic State within a state and the freedom to apply Sharia law in Muslim communities is expected to arrive in Italy from France later this week. Groups from across the political spectrum, including a broad coalition of women's organizations, have voiced their opposition to the visit.

"Torchlit processions will take place tonight in the capital and in cities across the country to commemorate the women murdered recently in the city. In Rome, traffic will be diverted between the hours of 8 p.m. to 10 p.m. and the procession will conclude with prayers at the Basilica of San Giovanni in Laterano led by Cardinal Arsenio Caramaschi."

"There," said a bedraggled Rossi flicking off the radio, tossing aside his newspaper and beginning to pace the office. "They said it. And can anything else happen to make things a bit more complicated?"

"What?" asked Carrara taking a quick sip from his takeaway cappuccino before going back to his laptop.

"Well, they're saying there might be a political motive behind the murders."

"By which they mean Islamic, right?"

"Well, they sandwiched it pretty well with the story about the Imam. The *Roman Post*'s been hinting at it in their 'have your say' column. All made up, of course. Gets a nice little fear ball rolling though. Get everyone in the bars talking about it. And now the Church is sticking its oar in."

"Sowing the seed?"

"Just a bit. Little by little. And a hell of a dangerous game, upping the ante like that just because they can."

"Yeah?"

"Well, if they can see that it's generating headlines then some crank might want to get on the bandwagon for real, while they're making capital out of it for their own ends, as usual."

"You really think it's that planned out?"

"I'm afraid I'm beginning to think so," said Rossi. "And it's not like our lot are going out on a limb in the media to shoot the whole thing down, is it? They should be calming the waters, not stirring them up. They should be admitting how bloody hard it is to catch a killer, especially when he's this good at what he does."

"When he's got secret service training you mean?"

Rossi slumped back into his chair. So, they were being led back to Marini's theory, even if the latest lead heralded as the big breakthrough had got them nowhere. Now Luzi's suicide had given them a new headache, robbing them of a suspect and a possible witness. It had also bolstered Marini's and Carrara's more outlandish theories about where to take the investigation.

"You don't believe he did it, do you?" Rossi asked.

"I don't know," said Carrara. "But I do think he may have been there, seen something."

"In what capacity?"

"For kicks. Maybe watching the wife with other guys."

"Any proof of that?"

"Middle-aged couple, no kids. Looking to spice things up? It takes all sorts. Did you see that documentary the other night? You'd think they're all at it."

"So, what happens?" said Rossi. "He goes too far with the welcome and sees his wife get killed, by a psychopath? Our psychopath? Or some game spirals out of control?"

"He panics, runs."

"And the phone?"

"May have had second thoughts, returned to the scene, survival instinct kicks in and he removes the incriminating evidence. He could have been there and back fast."

"And now, racked by shame and guilt, rather than spill the beans he takes his own life?"

"And the shame for someone in his position, at the head of an important Catholic charity. He was a major player. A friend to the purple princes of the Church."

"So he takes his secrets with him. And we're still in the dark," said Rossi.

"Either that or he couldn't go on without her. But he says 'sorry. I didn't do it'."

"He says sorry twice. To her and to us?"

"And that's as far as he's willing to go. Doesn't leave us much."

"But d'you think it all strengthens the case for the hook-up theory? It's not as if Luzi could have been behind the other killings, is it? You did check his alibis?"

Carrara nodded then gave a characteristic shrug.

"No, not a chance. They're cast-iron. So, what other theory is there? Whoever our killer is, he's not leaving any game-changing clues. He could go on like this for as long as he wants. It's all we've got. The city's in a virtual lockdown. What else do we do? Bring in a curfew?"

Sixty-Eight

At least he hadn't had to bring the bad news to the widow. Would much rather do this, or visit a crime scene. Rossi was waiting, sitting beside another hospital bed except here the signs were more encouraging. The injured officer was being given the once-over by the consultant who seemed happy enough with the repair work executed by his colleagues.

Rossi's thoughts had moved on yet again to confront the architect of the violence. So, had this been his work too? Another front in the war? A change of tack? From what Rossi could gather it had been a planned hit. This was no petty criminal or drug renegade. The car and the licence were registered to the ID card, albeit false, which took considerable knowhow. If he'd been some dealer, he'd have hightailed it out of there the moment he got cold feet – the cops weren't heavily armed, after all – or he wouldn't even have stopped in the first place. No. He'd been primed and ready for them and the phoney ID had been the trap and maybe a message. Another message. Here I am, keep guessing, keep looking. Oh, and by the way, I'm upping the stakes and slaughtering cops now. Inching closer. To you?

But it still also hinged on whether Marini's assailant, who'd been meant to take her out of the game, was the same guy racking up the general body count. Or had it just been a one-off political assassination attempt? And even if by some absurd stroke of luck they did manage to lure him into their honey trap – as a seasoned detective, the idea made him laugh – then they'd have the chance to discover the truth. But if, and only if. Maybe this survivor could give him something, reveal a chink in the armour.

"How long have I got?" Rossi enquired.

"Keep it brief. He's had a lot of sedation and he needs rest."

"He's the only witness we've got."

"Ten minutes, max, and don't push him too hard."

Rossi nodded his assent and waited till the white coat was out of earshot.

"Did he get a look at him?"

"Seems not," Rossi replied. "All happened too fast."

"But we can put the name out now, can't we? I mean our face from the descriptions, from the artist's impression, matches the one on the ID closely enough."

"I suppose we could try," said Rossi. "But it could be any of a hundred thousand dark-skinned southern males."

Carrara looked crestfallen and resigned.

"And it could drive him further underground? Is that what you're thinking? Or if he's got handlers and he's doing their bidding, they just call him off?"

But Rossi's eyes had brightened. He had something. Carrara could sense it.

"If," said Rossi, "and it's a big if, he really is still doing their bidding."

"And you don't think he is?"

"Well," said Rossi, letting Carrara glimpse the same small opening he now wanted to see, "I've been thinking that this doesn't fit with the profile. I'm thinking he might have gone AWOL, a loose cannon. I don't see this in the script, if script there is. Look, let's say it's all as Marini makes out and Iannelli wants to believe. And they may be right. But where does the cop killing fit in? It's high risk. Too high risk. Sooner or later he's either going to get caught or plugged. He's a lone wolf. That's what happens. And that's why it doesn't look right. I say he could have gone freelance. And what about the Porta Pia murder? Isn't it just a bit too symbolic? I mean, it's where and when the Church's temporal political power finally collapsed, the final iconic assault on Rome and the Pope's sovereignty. Isn't it saying: 'look out! The enemy is at the gates again'?"

Rossi wanted to believe his own theory but even though he had turned it over repeatedly he kept finding himself back at the beginning. When the politicos smelled blood in the water and saw even the slightest chance for swivelling the whole narrative around to favour their own agendas then they went for it, of course.

"And it's not like what we do is viewed in isolation," Rossi went on. "Crime pays, doesn't it? Politically, it's a tool for them to lever themselves to where it is they want to get to. And we're always in the middle."

But he knew there were still too many dangling questions, too many searches for reassurance, for some shred of confirmation.

"Is it enough?" asked Carrara.

"I don't know. I don't know. Is nothing fresh coming in on the road checks? The new call for witnesses? Anything?"

"Nothing to report," said Carrara. "But have you seen this," he continued showing Rossi an article tucked away in the inside pages of his newspaper.

Priest Linked to Cardinal is Arrested.

"Seems this guy was flying millions out of Lausanne into the country on a private jet with papal insignia on behalf of a naval contractor. And there's a slew of Italian and ISW bank accounts also regularly filled with 'charitable donations'. Dummy accounts.

Numerous banker's drafts. Money laundering, pure and simple."

"Interesting," said Rossi, taking the paper and scanning for details. "Says he used to be an accountant in the ISW itself and they reckon he was paying off a secret service agent to get safe passage. The cardinal's not around to defend himself though."

"And his people are denying all knowledge of it. The old bad apple excuse."

"Probably the tip of the iceberg, too," said Rossi.

Back in the office, Rossi was swinging in wide arcs in his chair, his mind firmly on Bonaventura. The remnants of a hurried takeaway lunch were abandoned on the desk. He was underground. Deep underground. Yet he could come out and do this and disappear without a trace. They had to be dealing with a battle-hardened pro.

"Hang on a minute," said Carrara, "message here from Maria. I'd missed it."

"Go on," said Rossi. "I'm all ears."

"Says she wants to see us. Says it's 'potentially big.'"

"'Big' like what?" said Rossi, his residual patience now paper thin.

"Wait. Says she's working on fixing up a meet, online, possibly for tonight. Still in the early stages but she thinks it really could be him."

"Like the ones you mentioned in the report?" Rossi replied. "They were all dead ends, wind-ups."

"No. Says she's got an identifier. Remember the tattoo?"

"The tattoo!" Rossi exclaimed. "Who'd be stupid enough to let a tattoo give him away?"

"That's exactly the point. She says it's a tattoo that's been covered over and it's on his neck in the same position as the tattoo she saw on the guy leaving the car park."

Carrara looked up at Rossi who had put on his best poker face. Did he detect in Carrara's voice a note? Something? A certain tone? Then Carrara's head shot down as he started tapping the keys again.

"Couldn't he just have cut himself shaving?" Rossi proffered. "And stuck a plaster on it."

"Well, unless she did actually get something through her famous 'channels of communication'. Remember?"

Rossi raised an eyebrow while still scrutinizing his colleague for any small sign. Any hint that his unease and recent distance could become a problem. But Carrara was absorbed again.

"S'pose she'd better come and show us what she's got then," said Rossi, stretching and yawning. "What do you say?"

"I'll set it up. What time?"

Carrara was in his element now with the renewed promise of action. As long as it wasn't clouding his judgement, thought Rossi glancing at his watch.

"I'm going to the hospital in the afternoon. Then I've got a few things to see to and after that I'm beginning to think it's time to go and rustle up some specialist hardware. If this is a night op and we're going alone we need to be prepared. Sometime after five, maybe six. My place?"

"Sounds good," said Carrara rattling out the reply on the keyboard. "But, er, what hardware's that exactly?" he said, snapping the laptop shut.

"*Ferri*," said Rossi bending back the thumb on his right hand, straightening his index finger and swinging his arm around until he was pointing at Carrara. Plural noun, from Latin *ferrum*, meaning iron. Or, to lesser mortals, pieces, shooters, or just plain old guns.

Rossi pushed the buzzer on the door and a familiar face peered out from the room at the back of the shop. The door clicked open. A waft of wood, varnish, and engineering oil filled his nostrils.

"Michael. It's been some time. Thinking of taking up shooting again?"

"I need a favour, Gennaro."

There was no reply as the owner made his way towards the counter and began to fiddle with some small mechanism laid out on a leather cloth.

"It will be a long time before I ask you for another," said Rossi, handing him then a piece of paper with his order. Gennaro stopped what he was doing and stroked his short, white beard.

"Can you do it, today?" Rossi asked.

"Identical," he said, reading the note. "New."

"Apart from the serial numbers."

"And life or death I imagine."

Rossi nodded.

"And I can give you my word that nothing will come back to you. Whatever happens."

"Your word, Michael?"

"Yes," Rossi said. "My word."

Sixty-Nine

"It is an inexact science. What we know about the human brain and its ability to repair itself or even to 'farm out' its functions is so minimal. People often won't accept that we can only give answers based on the statistics before us, the empirical data. Other than that, we are feeling around in the dark. However, on a psychological level, you can at least draw some comfort from the positive signs. In that sense, hope is a legitimate option."

Rossi felt he'd already had the conversation a hundred times. The doctors were not always the same. To the best of their ability, they would pick up where someone else had left off, often adding a personal insight or even seeming to hold a radically different opinion of how things were or might pan out. That was the nature of the modern health service. Discontinuous, often at breaking point, underfunded, but trying – and often managing – to provide excellence. Just like the police, he thought. Just like him.

The white coats came and went and then they were left alone. Hand in hand. More his hand than hers. He read to her again and put on music as he had been advised to do. Then when the appointed hour came round, he prepared to leave. Only this time he lingered longer, as he would have done before setting out on any mission, knowing that tonight could be the night when, well, anything might happen.

He walked across the car park, opened the car door and tossed the shoulder bag containing the weapons onto the passenger seat. Three Berettas with laser-guide aim. Accuracy at 20 yards: extremely good. Stopping power: moderate, and the weapon had its critics due to dissatisfaction with the intermediate calibre but that was the least of his concerns. Rossi disliked guns with a passion, having seen what they could do, but he knew now he had no choice and the only plan he could envisage, risky though it was, meant he had to put his trust in weaponry. But it had to be on his terms and it was a chance he would have to take. The sky had turned an ominous seal-grey. Were those a few drops of icy rain on the windscreen? He checked in to get the forecast via the service radio. Rain moving towards sleet as the evening progressed. It was a British forecast. Possible snow showers. Nothing dramatic but it was grimly cold again.

There was a steady stream of traffic along the Via Appia Nuova in and out of the centre. It had been lighter in the afternoon, probably as a result of the dithering mayor's last-minute decision to allow the schools to close. He'd left it up to the principals themselves, so, something like chaos had ensued as parents with kids in different institutions had had to juggle work and childcare arrangements. And when the weather deteriorated in Rome, there was also a sort of hardwired self-preservation tendency among the citizenry to resort to their cars, so as to guarantee their complete autonomy, all of which put even greater strain on the city's already stretched road network.

Rossi veered off the now increasingly congested carriageway of the Appia and onto Via Cerveteri hoping to at least keep moving. As he passed the carabinieri barracks he looked up at the sleet slanting across the sodium yellow searchlights above its fortress walls. Was it thickening to snow already? It seemed to come and go, changing state and changing back again, uncertain as to which way to go. He knew the feeling.

He parked as close as he could to his own building and ducked into the entrance. He took the lift to the fourth floor and then, turning both keys twice in their respective locks, he was home. They would be here soon. He dropped the holdall in the lounge and headed for the kitchen where he began opening cupboards. First the weighing scales he had got from the supermarket with his loyalty card but used only once. Nice though. Digital. Then a bag of flour. That would do the trick. Didn't actually have to make a cake. Just look like he was going to.

He took out the weapons. Identical. Semi-automatics they all knew inside out. These would do the trick all right. He laid out a cloth on the coffee table and with deft, practised movements began stripping them down. They were working a treat. No complaints there. He reassembled them and left a loaded magazine next to each weapon then covered everything with another cloth. He proceeded to switch on the computer at his work station and get the electronic side of things up and running. Carrara would be delighted to see how well he was coming along. A fully-functioning splitter was in place and the option of creating a local network too, all thanks to his very efficient new IT assistant. Time for a drink. Tea, of course. There would be no messing around with alcohol for the foreseeable future, whatever that might be. He had to be fully on his game. Had to be one hundred per cent focused on this one.

Mid-sip, the intercom buzzed. He took a quick look down to the street from the balcony. They had come together. Very cosy. There were a few sporadic snowflakes falling now for sure, but it still couldn't decide whether to snow properly or just fizzle out. And the wind. "Cut you like a bloody knife that would," he said out loud. He wanted more certainty on the forecast though. It could throw everything up in the air.

Without ceremony, Carrara and Marini assumed their positions at their respective computers.

"I won't dwell on the details," said Rossi, hovering around like a trapped fly as his associates set-to with their hi-tech preparations.

"We're waiting for a message to come in," said Carrara, by way of explanation and sensing Rossi's agitation. "It's a waiting game now."

"And you believe it?"

"We can't do worse than we're doing at the moment," Carrara countered. "Do I need to update you on the body count?"

Rossi rubbed his chin with a look of distant, silent scepticism. But cultivated scepticism this time.

"Well, before you get too busy, come and get your toys," he said, unveiling the hardware taking pride of place now at the centre of his living room. "Even if I don't think you're going to get a dickie bird from this guy now. Not this way. He's too busy shooting cops to get his rocks off."

"He's a gamer," Marini began with seeming assurance, as they sat around like the unlikely remnants of the knights of some minor round table. "Can't you see he's pushing all the rules to the limit? It's a part of what gets him his kicks."

"Well, I don't game," said Rossi without lifting his head. "One for you," he added with apparent indifference, placing a weapon in front of each of them in turn, "and a full magazine."

They took hold of their firearms, weighing them and turning them over.

"Remember to have them cocked and in position one," said Rossi, "when we're there and on the way. We don't know how this could go. Expect the unexpected. So, don't go dropping them. Trigger's easy and there's a laser guide," he pointed to his own weapon, "here. But I'm sure I don't need to tell you I don't want them to be used, if it's at all possible," he cautioned, looking at them both in turn.

Marini got to her feet and reaching behind her back lifted her sweater enough to be able to slide the Beretta into the waistband of her stretch black jeans.

"Out of sight but not out of mind," she said, adding then in what might have been mock schoolgirl tones, "may I please go to the bathroom, Inspector? A little bit of pre-match nerves I expect."

Rossi nodded his assent, indicating the direction with a jerk of his head. She sauntered past him as if supremely certain of herself. But this was his operation now and the message seemed to have been clearly, even if not openly received.

"Tea, Gigi?" said Rossi clasping a conciliatory hand on his colleague's shoulder while accompanying him towards the kitchen.

"Maria seems very confident she's going to get a game, as it were, don't you think?" he said as he filled the kettle.

"Ready and up for it, I'd say. And you've been doing some therapeutic homebaking, I see," said Carrara.

"Had the best of intentions," Rossi replied, "before life got in the way, again." He reached into the cupboard for cups and a crumpled box of teabags. "Only got Earl Grey, I'm afraid."

The bathroom door opened and closed.

"Going to join us?" Rossi asked as the newly refreshed Maria took up a position at the entrance to the now-cramped kitchen. Rossi and Carrara took their steaming brews back to the lounge and sipped in silence. Rossi picked up his Beretta from where he had left it on the table and slid it into his holster.

"A bit more milk, I think," he said rising to return to the kitchen where he clunked around before re-emerging with a muted but satisfied smile.

"I suppose we'd better outline the plan then," he began. "It's us three, right."

"With the option of calling in backup, of course," added Carrara.

"Maroni's had response units on alert for all eventualities since the Tor Sapienza debacle and a radio channel's open for that," Rossi replied. "Chopper's on standby too, even if, the way this weather's going I think there'll be zero chance of getting anything up."

"So, ground it is," confirmed Carrara.

Rossi nodded and opened out a map on the table. "If and when, of course. If he goes for the centre, we can converge on his position. He knows that, I'm sure. Might even want it, for all we know, but if he continues to operate on the fringes, in the peripheral areas, we're more limited in terms of rapid response."

Rossi was expecting Maria to pass comment, and she didn't disappoint him.

"So what you're saying is that we haven't got a clue and we have to hope for the best, unless he goes for something spectacular in St Peter's Square or Piazza San Giovanni?"

Rossi could only shrug.

"He took everyone by surprise out in Tor Sapienza," he said, "because we were doing spot-checks without having the necessary precautions in place. From now on, every spot check will be military style with readiness to give covering fire from at least one officer and with all occupants out and splayed on the bonnet. If it means us going back to how it was done in the '70s, well that's how it has to be. That officer was shot walking back to the car. It was as naive on his part as it was tragic, I fear. But hindsight doesn't help anyone, does it?"

Carrara looked into his tea. As every cop knew, it could have been him. Or the next bullet could have his name on it.

"Oh and tonight," Rossi asked, "how long exactly do you want to wait? I mean if you don't get any comeback on this 'meet'? Because I actually think I'd like to be on the ground. If there's going to be another hit I want to be out there!" he added gesturing towards the window. "Not stuck behind a screen chasing nobodies."

"We're not chasing nobodies," shot back a suddenly rattled Carrara, "we're trying to find a shortcut!"

Rossi fumbled for a moment in a folder on the table.

"We should be saturating the city with this picture, every one of us," Rossi said almost shouting now and holding up a copy of the artwork, an age-advanced school photo blended with the artist's impression they'd got from Marta. "We can flush him out, get him on the run. Somebody's bound to have seen him somewhere. He's got to be someone's neighbour; he must get his cappuccinos in someone's bar!"

"How does half an hour from now grab you, on the GRA?" said Maria from behind her screen in a soft but certain tone.

"What?"

"Just got a message," she said with barely-concealed pride.

Rossi leapt to his feet.

"Let me see."

"He's not going to show himself, if that's what you think. It's just a yes to the meet. Wait a minute. This shit happens all the time you know. Doesn't mean he'll show. Could be a hoaxer, get cold feet, but that's how it works."

"What is it?" said Carrara now joining Rossi hunched over Marini's shoulder as she flicked between windows and dialogue boxes.

"He wants proof."

"What do you mean?" said Rossi.

"That I'm female."

She stood up, shoved back the chair and without a moment's hesitation began peeling off her close-fitting cashmere sweater.

"I thought that would have been clear enough to most," said Rossi whose eyes were, despite himself, drawn now to the spectacle unfolding beside him in his own living room.

"He – if it is him – thinks I could be a CD."

"A what?"

"A CD. A cross-dresser. Now, if you'll excuse me gentlemen, I'm going to have to remove this, momentarily," she said indicating the expensive-looking and enticing black lace bra framing the even more enticing architecture beneath it.

"And he's watching you now?" said Rossi as he studied the bookshelves and the wall and flicked a glance at Carrara who was suppressing a half-smile. "I trust he's not hearing any of this, even if we are off camera."

"If it's him," she added again, "and the microphone's deactivated, don't worry. You can turn around. That's all he's getting, for now. And forever. It could all be bullshit and maybe that's all he was after but we've got to try something."

As she reached for the cashmere, it was Rossi now who had to make further demands on her. He reached under the table and pulled out a hitherto unmentioned box of tricks.

"You can leave the sweater for a minute. You and we will be needing one of these," he said holding up what looked like a miniature battery pack from which some slender cables protruded.

"You want me to wear a wire?"

"You have to wear a wire," said Rossi, "if we want to get anywhere on this. We'll be permanently in contact. Here's the switch. It's ready to go. A bit of duct tape and we're away. Oh, and I would suggest you exploit your natural contours to conceal the mike. If you know what I mean. If it is Bonaventura, he won't miss a trick."

"You could always put it in position yourself, Inspector, with your experience."

"I'll leave that to my partner," said Rossi. "If it's experience that counts, he's the man for the job. Aren't you, Gigi? How many years in anti-maf?"

Carrara then exercised a surgeon's rapidity and dexterity and in a matter of thirty seconds Marini had returned to her former more subdued splendour.

"Can't we run something on his IP address?" Rossi asked.

Carrara shook his head.

"He'll be on some proxy, or TOR, or a series of untraceable servers. Like you said, he's no fool."

Maria had gone back to her PC.

346

"He's given me a turnoff, on the ring road," she cut in, "we can get there in what, twenty or so, with this traffic?"

"Tell him to wait," said Rossi beginning to sense that time now was their biggest enemy. Time and the weather.

"He's already said he won't wait more than ten. After that, all bets are off."

"He's not risking then," Carrara chipped in.

"Gigi, do you know the spot?" said Rossi now shucking on his heaviest winter coat.

Carrara was zipping around on his virtual maps.

"Yep," he said. "More or less. It's remote enough, big lay-by, just zooming in now, then a disused warehouse or something with waste ground."

"Is it a meeting place for you know who?"

"For doggers? Is that what you mean, Inspector," said Maria who was trying to slip on her own coat with one arm while tapping away at the PC with her free hand.

"Looks like it is," said Carrara, "but I rather think it'll just be us tonight."

Rossi had sat down and, deep in thought, appeared to have forgotten all sense of urgency.

"What do we do then? Go for it," he said. "It's now or never, I suppose, time's ticking. And we've got to get across this damned city."

He got up and strode over to the window. The rain had turned to sleet and was now morphing, almost cosmically, oscillating between fast-falling wet grey globs and slower and more buoyant flecks of white.

"Get a weather report, Gigi, quick, and make sure it's up-to-date."

Carrara whipped out his phone.

"C'mon," said Rossi, "let's go, we've got to go, now! He won't wait!"

He snatched up the box with the rest of the hardware.

They ran down the stairs and Rossi bundled the stuff into the

347

back of the car. Maria was already making towards her own vehicle parked further down the road.

"Where are you going?" Rossi called out.

"I'll follow you," she said, turning as she walked, "then when we're there you hang back and leave it to me."

"Well take one of these for Christ's sake," said Rossi, holding out a walkie-talkie, "so we can coordinate our movements until he shows. Then we use the wire."

She came back and took the radio as Rossi gave the radio a final once-over.

"We can talk and plan as we drive. We can't just go storming in. And let's test the wire while we're at it."

He opened the glove compartment, pulling out an earpiece and receiver from a tangle of assorted electrical junk.

"Move away and say something quietly," he said, fixing it onto his ear.

"Let's nail the bastard," said Marini.

"OK. We've got contact," Rossi replied, "but if we nail him we take him in, remember?"

She stalked off towards her vehicle. Rossi looked after her as she got into the silver SUV complete with bull bars.

"Well, I suppose she's taking the biggest risk here," said Carrara but sensing something of Rossi's annoyance. "And two cars are probably better than one, if anything were to go wrong, don't you think?"

"I think," said Rossi, "that everything is probably already going wrong. We're going dogging in a snowstorm with a secret services renegade triple agent – at the last count – with a death wish, who's officially been cremated. But what's worse is that we don't appear to have much choice. C'mon," he said, "we're running late, for a date. What's the story on that forecast?"

It was not looking good. In his office in the Campidoglio Palace on the Capitoline Hill, Basso was under siege. Reports were coming in thick and fast, faxes and calls he had been trying to field through his many not-so-efficient secretaries but upon which he had now placed a total embargo. "I'm too busy to take any calls unless it's the President, the Prime Minister, or the Holy bleeding Father." In the north of the city, the snow that had been forecast had begun to fall. But it had not gone away. And it was getting heavier, more intense by the minute, and he wanted answers. Why hadn't he been told? Why hadn't he been briefed?

The effect on the blasé and largely unprepared public was also spiralling out of control, with confusion being stoked by the mixed messages going around. It was only 2.5 centimetres and it was all going to blow off. It was going to be 25 centimetres and it would get worse as night fell and temperatures plummeted. The roads hadn't been gritted. They couldn't get to the snowploughs. There weren't enough snowploughs. They didn't have the right diesel. They didn't have the mechanics who could attach the snowploughs to the tractors. Those snowploughs that were working were all out of position. It was better to make a dash for it. It was better to stay put.

And it was Friday evening. Everyone was trying to get home! There were jams at every major junction in the northern part of the city and the knock-on effect was spreading to the main roads into and out of Rome, the Via Salaria – the salt road! And onto the GRA – the ring road. Vehicles had overturned, lorries had jack-knifed, motorists were getting stranded, some were abandoning their cars and walking without weighing up the consequences, the very real risks. And A&Es were being stretched to breaking point with fractured arms, wrists, and hips. Then there was the litigation and there was already talk of a class action. The outlook was grim.

"Get me Grassi, Civil Protection."

"Tried already, Sindaco."

"Well try again!"

He slammed the phone down. From his window he could see the proud head of Marcus Aurelius sitting astride his horse at the centre of the deserted piazza. The snow was forming a papal-looking skull cap on his usually uncovered curls. The philosopher-emperor. The mayor without a clue.

His desk phone buzzed.

"Sindaco, *Dottor* Grassi for you."

Basso snatched up the receiver like a spoilt child going for the last biscuit.

"Grassi?"

"Sindaco."

"What's happening? What's going to happen in the next twenty-four hours? It's beginning to look like chaos out there. I need to know."

"It's snowing, Sindaco."

"I know it's bloody snowing! But how much? They said 2.5 centimetres, 3 at the most."

"Precipitation, Sindaco."

"What?"

"Precipitation of 2.5–3.0 centimetres."

"And just what the hell is that supposed to bloody mean?"

"It means, Sindaco, that the volume of liquid that could fall as a result of the front now crossing Lazio and most of the central peninsula could be in that region. If, however, it were to fall as snow, that volume would translate to something in the range of 25 to 30 centimetres or more."

There was a pause as Basso scrabbled to collect his ragged, disparate and desperate thoughts.

"You mean to say there could be over a foot of snow, in Rome?"

"And much more where it drifts and on the higher ground in the outlying areas. It's really quite anomalous."

"And why didn't you tell me?" Basso almost whined.

"You may remember that it was brought to your attention and you, Sindaco, gave assurances that you had the personnel in place to follow up on the data from the Air Force and the Met Office. It's the very same data that we use, Sindaco."

Basso had his forehead buried in the papers strewn across the dark, lustrous surface of his mayoral desk. With both hands he swept its entire contents floor-wards.

"*Pezzo di merda*!"

"Sindaco, is everything all right?"

"'*Pezzo di merda*'! You fucking piece of shit! You set me up! You set me up! *Bastardo*!" he screamed into the phone.

"Sindaco, I think if anyone 'set you up', it was your own doing. We did warn you."

A sound of car horns and sirens was now audible from outside his mayoral sanctuary. He would have to face the people sooner or later. But he was finished. This was the last straw, after all the other fiascos. After the crime wave, the incompetence, the favours for friends. The city was heading for bedlam, and he was the architect.

"And just what do I do know? Eh?"

There was a pause before his seraphic interlocutor picked up the conversation again.

"Once the cabinet sits to discuss a state of emergency, we can begin to move. We have plans in place but not the necessary means. That was your responsibility, Sindaco. We shall have to muddle through, I suppose. Perhaps you could at least begin the process of closing the stable door, now that the horse has well and truly bolted. Oh, and just for your information, I have been recording this conversation. Should you have any problems at some future point remembering what exactly was said today, I can always jog your memory. Will that be all, Sindaco?"

There was no answer.

"Sindaco? Sindaco?"

Seventy

Rossi and Carrara were trying to make time. The slathery rain and sleet were making visibility a problem, and despite Carrara's having taken all the back roads he knew to avoid the more predictable bottlenecks, he was losing some of his usual composure behind the wheel. Rossi glanced behind again. Maria was displaying at least some of the skills of a seasoned pursuit driver. She didn't take any nonsense and had a big enough vehicle to pull it off at the intersections and bully her way into an advantage during lane changes, leaving plenty of blaring horns in her wake. Carrara worked on sheer speed and acceleration coupled with lightning fast decision-making to gain his edge, but still they looked again and again at the clock ticking down with mocking indifference. *Was this the only chance they were going to get?* There would be no rain check to pick up here, Rossi feared.

"What was the forecast then. Did you get it?"

Carrara finessed his way through another seemingly impossible gap.

"Sleet turning to snow and spreading from the north increasing in intensity."

"But how much?"

"Said 2–3 centimetres."

"That can't be right: 2–3?" said Rossi noting the fast-disappearing crop-stubble in the roadside fields. He glanced at the temperature gauge. It was hovering around 2.5 degrees Celsius.

"You do realize that it's not melting, don't you?" He turned up the radio.

"Better see what's going on."

… on the Via Salaria … snow is making driving conditions treacherous and there has been major disruption following an accident at the turn off for …

The unusual atmospheric conditions meant the signal was coming and going.

… Police are advising that motorists only travel if absolutely necessary and to carry snow chains … the mayor, Achille Basso, has also warned of unprecedented difficulties and a potentially critical situation towards evening and into the early hours. Responding to criticism from the city prefect and opposition parties that the city has been left unprepared, he has stated that the situation is without precedent and was "unforeseeable". The head of the civil protection … has also entered the debate saying the mayor …

"You get the message," said Rossi switching it off. "How are we doing?"

"Next right, I think, and we're on the GRA."

"She still there?"

Carrara shot a glance in the rear-view. She was.

"Well, we've come this far," said Rossi. "We may as well go all the way."

Carrara slowed down to take the predetermined turn off, leaving behind the ring road and climbing up the slip road towards the first car park. Car park was a grand term, for it was a patchily tarmacked handkerchief of waste ground, once the site of a factory whose remaining buildings formed a shattered and crumbling hulk barely visible now against the steely dark sky. There was no illumination beyond the last street lamp which shed a little pool of yellow onto the straggly bushes and weeds growing out of the fissures and after that it was complete darkness. Below them they could see the GRA stretching away and curving around the city in a gentle arc, the headlights and tail lights streaming out like a continuous ribbon of Rome's own team colours.

"Park there," said Rossi, indicating the furthest corner to the right and next to one of the still-standing factory walls.

"We're in position. Get over on the opposite side," he said calmly into the radio, "facing the entrance, and turn this thing straight off when you see anyone approaching."

"OK," came the answer. Rossi and Carrara watched as the SUV then entered the car park and manoeuvred into the agreed position.

"Turn everything off now," he said to Carrara. "We're here, in the dark. He'll see us eventually – and we could be anyone – but we lie low first."

The radio crackled again.

"In position."

"OK," said Rossi. "What's the signal?"

"He flashes his headlights. I flash back and turn on the inside light. Then, if he wants to, he approaches."

"And then what?"

"I check him out. We chat. Then I open the passenger door, and as he comes round, I get out, draw my weapon and all hell breaks loose, right?"

"No. We keep it calm!" said Rossi. "Draw your weapon and get out of the vehicle. Take a step back. Arrest him. Hands on the bonnet. Don't disarm him even if you feel you can. We'll have put on the lights and we'll be moving in on foot to give cover while you then back away. We frisk him, we cuff him, we bring him in. That's all you need to do. Then we get out of here before we have to build an igloo."

"If it's him," cut in Carrara.

"Obviously," said Rossi. "And there'll be no heroics, no revenge, no beatings. Nothing."

"And if he runs for it?" said Carrara. "Do we take him down?"

"No," said Rossi. "We pursue him. What time is it?"

"He's late. Unless he was early."

"Oh, he'll keep us waiting," said Rossi. "He could be watching us right now."

A shiver ran up his spine. In the confusion they hadn't even considered night-vision capability. In a millisecond, there could be a round drilled through each of their heads and they wouldn't have had an inkling. Too late now. He glanced behind. Only blackness. He checked his laser aim under the dashboard. That was something at least. He could just make out a reflection on Maria's vehicle and the snow that had already begun to accumulate on its roof.

"And now we wait."

He pulled his collar tighter around his neck as the residual heat in the car dissipated. He hoped it wouldn't be long, whatever happened. The waiting was the worst part. It brought back memories.

Then out of nowhere came the sound of tyres crunching the rough tarmac and an engine revving as some twenty or so yards to their left another vehicle, a large white jeep of sorts, swept into the car park. It slewed around and stopped at a similar distance away to their right so that the three vehicles formed points on a triangle. It sat there for some moments, ticking over as if it were a large beast breathing after its exertions. Then its headlights were turned off. Then the engine. Then they all held their breath in the cold and the dark and waited.

Seventy-One

"Did you ever think it would come to this?" Rossi whispered.

Maria's wire was registering the occasional shuffle and scratch. He could hear what seemed like her breathing. The jeep flashed its lights on and off, twice. Rossi nudged Carrara, as if he hadn't seen it. There followed a seemingly endless wait until Marini returned fire with a flash of her own headlights and then there was another interminable pause before her inside light came on. It had all, however, been only a matter of some fifteen seconds. So far, it was going to plan.

Rossi put a hand on the weapon cradled now in his shoulder holster. The jeep's inside light flicked on as the driver's door opened then slammed shut with weighty decision. Rossi could just make out a shadowy figure becoming more and more solid as it approached the light spilling from Marini's SUV, until finally blocking out most of the illumination as it reached the vehicle. Had she lowered the window yet? But there was nothing coming through on the wire. He tapped his earpiece. Not even the background noise.

"Bloody wire's gone," he hissed to Carrara. "We'll have to wing it."

Their suspect then moved around the car as planned, and Marini's vague form on the driver's side became visible again.

"Open your door, quietly," whispered Rossi, disabling the inside light, as he squeezed the handle on his side. "Let me get close before you switch on the headlights. Then follow but come round wide from the other side."

There was a loud cry from Maria.

"Police! Hands on the car!"

Rossi took it as his cue to leap out onto the now inches-thick carpet of snow. Keeping low and heading straight for Marini, he slipped his weapon from the holster and barked his orders as the headlights then illuminated the whole scene.

"Don't move! Police!" he barked.

Carrara was now moving, describing a wide arc to Rossi's right as he too, keeping low to the ground, homed-in on the vehicle. As Rossi approached, he could see a dark-coated figure splayed across the opposite side of the bonnet of Marini's SUV. She was standing just a couple of feet behind him now in a firm, authoritative stance and was angling her weapon with both hands at the nape of his neck.

"Everything under control?" Rossi enquired.

"All according to plan," came the response.

"Positive ID?"

"Take a look for yourself."

The car's inside light shed enough light across the bonnet for Rossi to give confirmation. Older, some hints of grey at the temples, slightly heavier, but him all right.

"Well, let's get the cuffs on him, shall we?" said Rossi, tucking his Beretta back into its holster and giving Carrara the signal to approach. "We can talk in the car. Good work."

"Just a minute," said Marini taking a step back then to raise her weapon in Rossi's direction. "How about you just throw that on the ground."

"Do what?" said Rossi.

"Throw the gun on the ground, there," she said indicating the shadows out of the headlights' reach. "And slowly."

Rossi glanced across at Carrara, who had snapped into a kneeling firing stance, but did as asked.

"Don't move, Gigi," said Marini tracking him from the corner of her eye. "I don't know about you but I was top of the class at marksman's school. I might not get you both, but one of you's going down. So keep it very, very calm."

"Just leave it, Gigi," said Rossi. "Drop the gun."

"I've got her if you want," said Carrara. He was cast-iron steady, the laser an unwavering dot on Marini's temple. Marini's aim, meanwhile, was boring a red hole between Rossi's eyes.

"Put it down," Rossi said again. "No one is getting hurt."

Carrara remained firm, then lowering his aim, he flicked on the safety and tossed the weapon away. The flakes had thickened and were rushing across the headlights' beams now.

Marini, her weapon still trained on Rossi, also released herself from the firing stance.

"Well," she said. "So, here we all are."

She walked forward and jammed the muzzle of the gun hard into the back of Bonaventura's skull, her finger tightening on the trigger as she revelled in her own performance.

"Maria," said Rossi, "it's not for you to take the law into your own hands."

She looked up.

"Revenge, you mean? It's not my job to mete out revenge? For what he did to Kristina? You're smart, I'll give you that, Rossi but I think you've gone and got the wrong end of the stick on this one. None of this is about revenge. Well, at least not for me it isn't."

She cleared away some of the snow from the bonnet with a swipe of her hand then laid her gun next to Giuseppe Bonaventura's still immobile hand.

"You'll be needing this, I suppose," she said stepping back. "It will really confuse the ballistics when they find this is the murder weapon. Non-police issue and against all the regulations. But I'm getting ahead of myself. You two must have so much to say to each other."

Carrara seemed to be gathering himself to make a lunge for his weapon.

"No!" cried Rossi halting his colleague with a firm hand gesture.

From his prostrate position, Bonaventura took hold of the gun and raised himself up off the bonnet. It was him all right. No mistake. He weighed the weapon with apparent satisfaction.

"Michael," he said, "it's been so long."

Rossi gave no answer.

"And what a night for a reunion," he said gesturing to the sky and the candid tableau in which they now found themselves. Rossi gave a grim laugh.

"I thought you might have preferred to smash my skull in with a hammer. Or is that method reserved for defenceless women? How many is it?"

It was now his adversary's turn to acknowledge the dark irony with a dry attempt at laughter.

"Michael, Michael, I was following orders. Nothing more and nothing less. In our line of work, someone has to do the dirty deeds. Killing has become my second nature. It's how I pay my way in this vale of tears. And if a few innocents have to fall by the wayside so that the status quo can be maintained, so be it. It's the grand design, Michael. The powerful must rule and with an iron fist. It's bigger than me, than you, than all of us. But we all play our part. But this, now. This here is personal. And you know why."

"Do I?"

Memories seemed to have visited Giuseppe's face as before Rossi's eyes it began to transform itself into a mask of evil intent.

"You mean you don't remember what you did to me?"

"You deserved everything you got," Rossi replied, without hesitation.

"You stole my woman. You set me up. I did time because of

you, Michael. And then I had to drag myself back to where I am now. I had to take the hard way. I'm not bitter but I do believe in vengeance, and what goes around comes around. You of all people should know that."

"It was nothing less than you had coming but I'm surprised it's taken you so long to crawl out from beneath that stone you've been hiding under."

"I bided my time, Michael. A dish best served cold and all that. Oh," he said, changing the subject with theatrical over emphasis, "and by the way, how is Yana? That is what she calls herself now, isn't it?"

"What the hell do you know or care about her?"

"Oh, just wondering if she might have had some nostalgia. You know, for the old days. The good old days. Back then I was doing the rounds in the underworld. Let's say my efficiency did not go unnoticed or unrewarded. There was a lot of merchandise to shift in and out of those places, a lot to dispose of too. You know the kind of things – overdoses, clients getting carried away with the rough stuff, the snuff trade. Who knows, our paths may even have crossed. She might have been one of the madams there holding a clipboard and ticking it all off."

Rossi felt his muscles stiffen at the provocation. His fingers first reached for the weapon that was not within his reach and then began to shape themselves into a futile fist.

"Do you honestly think I would believe a single word you're saying?"

"Oh, but you should," he said, nodding and pointing his gun at Rossi as if it were an admonishing finger. "Because I'm in control now, not you. You will let me know when she's back on her feet, won't you?"

"You won't get anywhere near her," Rossi growled, knowing that the provocation was meant to destabilize him, as well as hurt him where it could hurt most. He had tried to kill Yana, but had failed and she would outlive him whatever he had to do to guarantee it.

"Well, I guess you won't be around to know that. Maybe I'll look her up myself," he said and raised the weapon, aiming it at his old adversary. "Perhaps you'd like to run, Michael, it could make it more fun, for me, of course. I've been taking out too many soft targets recently. It gets a little boring, you know."

"So you're not going to use your hammer on me?" said Rossi. "I thought you liked to get close to your victims."

"Oh, I do, Michael, when they smell nice. All that perfume and sexuality. But I'm afraid my hammer's in the Tiber now along with my other tools. Never to be found. So, this will just have to do."

It was then, with the sound of something approaching a frenzied battle-cry, that Carrara dived to make a desperate lunge for his stranded weapon. In an instant, Giuseppe had swung round and, taking swift aim, squeezed the trigger. But as Carrara went tumbling across the snow the gun gave only a dull click.

"Don't shoot, Gigi!" Rossi shouted. "It's a trap."

As Giuseppe cursed, re-racked the slide on the Beretta and positioned himself to take aim again, Maria, from inside her coat, had already drawn a snub-nose revolver to deliver the one and only decisive shot – into the back of Giuseppe Bonaventura's skull.

She stood there, the diminutive weapon at ease in her hand. Carrara had grasped his gun and, rolling away, had swivelled to lock on to his target. A thick black slick was spreading from where Giuseppe lay on the virgin snow. Keeping Maria in his sights, Carrara got to his knees. He'd managed to gash his head and lip in the attempt and looked dazed but still he held his ground.

"Don't move, Michael," she said. "Just stay where you are. I think we have a few things to straighten out."

"Really?" said Rossi. "I think it's you who've got the serious explaining to do."

She walked around from behind the car pointing the snub-nose at Rossi with rock steady assurance even as she reached down to pick up the inspector's weapon.

"Here," she said, checking it had been de-cocked before tossing it onto the snow at his feet. "No bad feelings, I hope."

"I should be dead," said Carrara still holding her in his sights.

"Me too," said Rossi.

"Giving me a gun with no firing pin was very clever, Inspector," said Marini. "You were really trying to look after us."

"You seem to have been looking after yourself with that," he countered, indicating the revolver aimed at him now from her hip. "So, that's what you wanted so much, is it?" he said, indicating the cooling pool of blood issuing from the dead man's skull. "Well, you got it. And just how far were you intending him to go with that little mise en scène you decided to cook up? Are you telling me you would have let it go down to the wire? He could have killed me without so much as a by your leave."

"I'd taken the pin out, Inspector. It didn't jam. Give me that much credit, at least. I just wanted to see what you were capable of, under pressure. And you were good. Very good. And I could hardly take him out in cold blood, could I? It would have been something of an anti-climax."

"Well," said Rossi, "at least I knew you were up to something when you swapped your gun for mine back at the flat. I guessed you'd want to have it your way. You like things your way. That's why you went to the bathroom, isn't it? You couldn't believe I'd actually give you a weapon, so you checked it out."

"Very smart," she replied. "Cleverer than I would have thought."

"So," said Rossi, with a pragmatic air, "you got your revenge, against our wishes, and got some kick out of putting our lives on the line too. Giuseppe's dead. What do you want now? Or do I have the feeling there is yet more to this than meets the eye?"

"Now, I just disappear. It's all that simple. I wanted to make it more interesting, shall we say. Giving him that final illusion of power was cruel but wonderful, erotic almost. Then bam! But you'll never see me again. Job done. You've got your corpse. He admitted everything. You can sleep tonight with a clear conscience that justice has been served."

Behind them the car radio had crackled into life.

"They're looking for me," said Rossi putting on hold the marginal gloss he would have made on Marini's disturbing psychological admission. "Perhaps I should let them know we are, shall we say, 'busy'?"

"Well let's go and see," said Marini with near jocular levity and giving Carrara clearance. He lowered his aim with visible reluctance, strode back to the car and reached in to take it, but it had gone dead again.

"I will admit," said Maria, as the three of them stood there in the snow, "it did get a bit too complicated, but I suppose that's just the way I am. And at least that's one chapter closed. So, I can go back to rebuilding a life; you've got your killer."

"Who's been very conveniently denied the right to a fair trial," said Carrara.

"He was guilty as hell – he admitted as much," replied Marini.

"And we'll never know who sent him," Rossi added, "or why he did it. They'll slip back into the shadows as always, right? But doesn't it just seem like he'd done his job? Wasn't it all as if his time had come? Like he'd become expendable? Or am I reading a little too much into our clever or fortuitous stumbling upon him like we did?"

"I think you should take from this what you can, Inspector. Count your blessings. You'll need them."

The radio sputtered into life again with a squawk. Marini gave Carrara a sign of assent with her gun.

"Put the pistol on the bonnet then answer it but no clever shit, OK?"

She was calling the shots now and she looked like she'd slipped into the role like a natural. Carrara did as ordered and reached in again for the radio.

"Yes," said Carrara into the handset and straining then to hear through clouds of static. He turned back to Rossi. "It's Bianco. The channel's bad but I think he's at the hospital. Says they want to talk to you."

Ignoring Marini, Rossi bound towards Carrara and tore the handset away from him.

"Yes!" said Rossi.

"Inspector?"

"Yes!" said Rossi again.

"They tried calling you but most of the mobile networks are down, with the snow and all, but there's something important."

"What?" said Rossi with growing impatience.

"It's Yana."

"What?" demanded Rossi. "What about her?"

"She's spoken."

"She's done what?" he shouted. "You'll have to speak up!"

"I said she's spoken. Yana. Today. We've been trying to reach you. We think it might be important, for the case."

The signal was crackling and wavering again, but Rossi could still just make it out.

"What did she say? What?"

There was a pause. A few perfect flakes settled on the shiny black handset while he waited for the response.

"She said this," he said, "only this," and then enunciating with great care, "she said 'it was a woman'."

But Marini, arms outstretched, was already behind them and pointing her weapon.

"Out of the fucking way!" she ordered before exploding a round through the open car window and tearing the radio apparatus apart.

"I've got four left, so don't even think of being heroes," she warned as Carrara, unsteady now as more blood trickled down his face, made a reflex lurch for his own weapon.

"You did it! You tried to kill Yana!" he shouted, abandoning his effort.

364

"And I'll kill you at the drop of a hat, *bello*," she replied.

"And you murdered Kristina," said Rossi. "Had she rumbled you, or what? Was it blackmail? Or just another easy target?"

Marini was holding Rossi in her sights now.

"Let's say I was planning on being out of here before it came to this but if you really want to know, I don't see why I shouldn't let you in on the secret. It wasn't in the script but it'll be like pillow talk, won't it? After all the fun we've had."

She reached under her sweater, yanked off the wire and, dropping it onto the ground, crushed it under her heel for good measure.

"Giuseppe was working for us. For the services. For our branch of the services. So, what he said to you before he departed this mortal coil was true. But I'm afraid he'd gone way beyond his brief. He was getting out of control. That cop getting shot in Tor Sapienza – that was all his work. So, we had to rein him in. And that's how I got him here, under the pretence that he was going to have you, Michael, at long last. That was what he had so wanted and for which he'd been playing ball, up to a point. That was why he was working for the … well let's just say 'for us.'"

"So he was surplus to requirements."

"He was a dangerous killer, Michael."

"Don't give me that shit. He was your killer and you knew all along."

Marini gave a sigh which, while theatrically affected and self-consciously condescending, in pathological terms appeared all too real.

"It's a war, Michael. A long, dirty war. Unpleasant things have to happen so as to maintain the status quo. We have never gone away and the strong must rule."

"And women must die for that? You make me sick."

"It's what we believe in. And it is, I admit, a heavy responsibility."

"So you're a fascist then," said Carrara with disgust and spitting more blood onto the snow.

"Yes," she said nodding, "if that's what you want to call me. A fascist, yes. Undiluted. Black-hearted, through and through. A guardian of the patria, the real state. Not this illegitimate farce they call a democracy. Government by the people! Government by those strong enough to seize it! We govern the real state of affairs from within, unseen. Custodians of the flame, sentinels at the gates, holding back the hordes, the infidels. I would prefer that but yes, fascist will suffice."

"You're insane!" said Carrara leaning against the car clutching his head and steadying himself.

"Well it all just fitted together so well," she said. "It was quite beautiful. We had Spinelli inside and his party of populist fools in fibrillation, we had the city running scared, the crime squad's best men in the palm of our hand. You did well though, Rossi, I'll give you that. You picked up on everything, all the clues. So, when Kristina's moment came, I had that little note worked out and I thought I'd just muddy things up by leaving it where you'd find it further down the line. And sooner or later you might have got him, with the risks he was taking.

"But, like you say, his time had come anyway. And it was already the moment to change tack – perhaps time to put a bomb somewhere, or bring an airplane down – and then when we realized how much he was getting into the role and getting out of control we had to reel him in fast. One cop killing, while unfortunate, was acceptable, to help create a certain tension; but two, three? That would look careless, don't you think? And if he'd been caught, if he'd talked, tried to drive a bargain? Where would that have left us? With a major headache. And you can't always count on somebody letting him fall down the stairs, can you?

"So, that's where you came in. You were the bait. Before that, he was on the payroll, doing what he did best. We had plenty on him, while that actually mattered to him. The drug ops, the prostitutes, the trafficking. So, he was cooperative, up to a point and let's say we intimated you could be obtainable. He was a dog that's got used to fresh meat. He wouldn't settle for tinned stuff. Then this rumour goes around that he's tested positive for HIV – we have a line of communication with all that side of things, every little helps – and that he was going on a spree, going to take down as many as he could. Cops above all. He was out of our hands, he'd gone off the fucking grid.

"And yes, it was me who tried to kill Yana. Let's say I had to demonstrate my loyalty. Volunteer to do some of the dirty work. And Giuseppe was proving to be so erratic. We'd lost all contact with him for a time, so I stepped up at short notice, as it were. But she was good – very strong, and attractive too, for a Slav. I could have got to appreciate a girl like that. But she'd seen me, so we couldn't afford to take any risks. Really, it was nothing personal. And by the way, it wasn't Giuseppe who showed up at the Wellness. That was just a little trick on our part. A red herring, as they say. Confused you, didn't it?"

"How many Hail Marys do you want for your confession?" Rossi sneered. "But before you do finish, there's just one thing missing in all this. You haven't mentioned the money yet, and I've been following it."

"Oh, really?" replied Marini. "So what have you discovered? That money talks? That it makes the world go round? That it doesn't grow on trees? Go on. Do enlighten me, professor."

"That it's all you and your lot care about. Fuck your ideology and bullshit about the patria. You're screwing this city and the country for money full stop. And you'll do anything to hang on to it and make more and yet more of it for you and your friends in high places, in the Church, and the government and you're prepared to stoop to anything because it's the drug you're hooked on and you can't get enough of it."

Marini made a gesture towards the ring road and the city behind her.

"This Rome of yours, Rossi, you know what it is? I'll tell you. It's a kind of old, dirty, ignorant but actually very fuckable whore.

It's like Switzerland without the cuckoo clocks and the efficiency and with dog shit and double parking on every street. But in my experience, everything that goes through this place comes out looking pretty damn good. Money, guns, drugs, people, you name it. If you can get over your hang ups, put aside your principles, you come out smiling. It's Babylon, Rossi, whether you like it or not."

"Rome's mine too, and it's frauds and cowards like you who've been whoring this country for too long. You've squeezed every cent out of it and you still can't stop. That's why you got scared when the MPD decided to call time on the party, isn't it? But all your cosy little arrangements with the cardinals and the ISW could just be coming to an end, so you hatched your little project. Your murder project. Your strategy of tension 2.0 for the twenty-first century."

Marini gave an empty laugh.

"You don't have a shred of proof of any of that. You can't even get near us, Rossi. And you know it. But if it makes you feel better to think you know it all, by all means have your little fantasy. Dream your fucking dream."

"And your child? That son of yours?" said Carrara. "What about him?"

"Oh, he'll survive. He won't be the unluckiest kid in the world. It happens all the time. We have to fall in love for this, you know. Or at least appear to fall in love. That's how we get inside their lives, maybe your life. My father doesn't know. He never understood what I wanted to do. I tried telling him what made me tick, how I felt about the world and where it was going, the filth, these sub-humans who think they can sit at the same table as us. The Jews, the Muslims, the fucking queers. So, I hid it all. He'd defend me to his last breath but he knows nothing of what I do. I'll move on. Change name. Change city. Maybe country. Begin again. Another project. And you know, gentlemen, I have to say that, thinking about it all, and what's in store, I really can't wait.

And now, if you'll both kindly turn around and kneel down. We have talked long enough. I think that it is time."

*

Rossi had always thought he might have seen his whole life pass before him while awaiting execution, but it wasn't to be that way. Instead, as he watched the flakes gliding in front of his eyes he thought only of Yana, his mother and father already gone from him, and was otherwise at peace with his thoughts and with the world. He'd done his duty, he'd done his best. He hadn't left an heir. That could be one regret. Too late now.

Carrara beside him had his head bowed, his eyes closed and was, Rossi supposed, praying to his God. The suffering would be worse for him – family man that he was. Rossi saw his God all around him. He loved snow. Always had, ever since he had first seen it as a child, in England, waking up to that quiet, perfect world without compare. If the world had a soul, this was it.

There was a click. The pistol cocking? Then the unmistakeable sound of a car door opening and slamming followed by the engine jumping into life. Rossi was first to turn and see Marini steering the SUV out and across the car park to where a broken wire fence gave onto the snowy fields stretching away behind them. Snow tyres, of course. She'd come prepared. Carrara, too, had now come to his senses. They both got to their feet.

"I can take a shot," said Carrara training his gun on the vehicle.

"Not much point," said Rossi. "There's no pin in yours either."

Seventy-Two

Below them, in the middle distance on the GRA, the headlights and tail lights were now scarcely moving at all. Everything had come to a grinding halt as the snow continued to wreak its impish chaos. And there was no sign of it stopping. Carrara and Rossi looked at each other.

"Did you bring those chains in the end?" Rossi enquired.

"Would I let you down?"

"And would I?" said Rossi reaching through the car window to produce a half bottle of Jameson from the glove compartment.

"We let her get away, didn't we?" said Carrara.

Rossi shrugged and took a generous swig before passing him the bottle.

"Sometimes you have to accept there's only so deep you can go, if you want to see another day."

"Did you know all along? That she was behind it all? Did you know she killed Kristina? Whoever she really was."

"I knew she wasn't white as the driven snow," Rossi replied. "But other than that, I was taking a gamble. Her switching the guns told me she was planning something but I still wasn't sure if she was only looking to take out Giuseppe."

"But how did you know?"

"I weighed it, in the kitchen, on the digital scales. I'd put one less round in mine. You'd never notice the difference. As for Yana, I hadn't twigged that it was Marini. But during my sabbatical, I got myself a consultant and guess what we found? All the women had been on dating sites but from their work computers. And ClearTech, the company we've farmed all the IT forensics out to, had overlooked key aspects of all the victims' behaviour. So someone along the line must have suppressed or muddied the data trails leading to the same social sites used by all the women involved, apart from Yana."

"How did you get in?"

"Through the central computer system and then the ministry where Paola Gentili worked and with a bit of bluster and a bit of breaking and entering we hacked their network. Some clever bastard, of course, had booby-trapped everything so that when we found a trail it triggered a data self-destruction bug. Like when a bank's been fiddling the books and they smash up all their hard drives and shred their documents. But they could blame it on hackers, anyone they like. But what I'd seen was enough; that they'd had online presences with unknown potential suspects right up to the day before they were killed."

"So we were being deliberately misled?"

"Highly probable but difficult to prove. By whom we'll never know, but I wouldn't rule out Silvestre's having had a hand in it. He's had it in for me since I blew away his protection racket scam, even if he did get away scot free. Anyway, we were always going to be chasing shadows. And even if we went public they could just put it down to glitches in the system or teething problems with outsourcing. But there were the money trails too. Iannelli came up with a few names and we were able to hack into some accounts of business figures with links to the ISW and it all started to fit together. The trafficking, the money laundering, the Lateran Treaty connections, and Spinelli's plan to cut off the Church's financial oxygen. Then there was the cardinal's timely or untimely death, depending how you want to look at it and his links with the Lausanne money-laundering bust."

"I should have guessed it," said Carrara. "It was staring us in the face."

"I suppose you'll say it's my fault, my technical Achilles heel."

"Well, you do tend to want to do it your way, don't you?"

Rossi ignored the comment.

"Then again," said Rossi, "thinking about it, would you suspect a false report from the forensics lab? You wouldn't because we know them. Even if samples do disappear."

Carrara shrugged as if from long experience.

"They can always put a spanner in the works if they want to. If the money's right."

"Well," Rossi continued, "he still must have been pretty smart, using multiple identities and cross-checking responses. Some of the women could have even entered into face-to-face hook-ups. Too trusting, naive, maybe searching for attention and falling for easy flattery. He was able to track them down and study their movements, creatures of habit that they were, and that way, he could go in with minimal risk, and get out fast having studied his escape routes and checked for CCTV. He got women who didn't change their routines, either because they were foolhardy or because they had never considered the risks. And that was how he was able to commit one perfect murder on the heels of another. But he had changed the rules of engagement by the time Marini decided to make us think that we could trap him. That was risk-taking. But he was only ever going to be there if it was low-key, just us three. Like she said, I was the bait, and she must have promised me in return for his showing up and probably an extra wedge of hard cash to persuade him to put a stop to his death fetish fantasy."

"But it was all hypothetical. You didn't know for sure, did you, about all this? And then what about Kristina?"

"Kristina's killing was different because Marini didn't keep regular hours. Like her father said, she was notoriously unpredictable in her movements, so she would have been difficult for an assassin to pin down. If it was meant to be a hit it didn't seem so plausible and she was hardly the kind of woman to let herself get trailed, was she? Even if it was a hit or precisely because it was meant to look like one, I had my suspicions that it couldn't have been him. But there was no proof to the contrary. Until we made our discoveries in the flat – the groceries, then the judge, and then she came out of hiding anyway with that fantastic tale of intrigue which, despite its unlikelihood, we couldn't *not* believe. Still, whatever way it could have gone, it wouldn't have brought us any nearer to stopping the killing as it was all being directed by her, by 'them.'"

"And what about him?" said Carrara gesturing first to the corpse cooling in its thickening blanket of snow before reaching out to take another swig. "How are we going to explain away that?"

"Leave him. He's not going anywhere. It will have to be another 'settling of scores'. Rather a lot of those, aren't there? Ever wondered why? Very convenient for us. He'll have some false ID for sure."

"Is there a murder weapon there by chance?" Carrara enquired. "Better take a look."

The boot was empty save for the standard spare tyre, jack, and some oily rags. A stolen car, of course. Rossi went back to his own vehicle and opened the boot.

"You'll need one of these then," he said, holding out a sturdy and well-used lump hammer. "Found it years ago. Never used it. Should fit the bill. Chuck it under the seat. It will speed things along when the lucky patrol car finds him in a few days' time. I suppose we could get Marta to identify him. That would be something."

"They'll get the glory, when they do."

"Well, I told them Bonaventura was our man. So the glory, if glory there is, will be mine too. And yours, of course."

"At least there'll be less paperwork."

"Oh, by the way, there was just one more thing. We did actually get a little bonus out of this."

"Really?"

"Gab boosted my wi-fi so he could pick it up in the bar across the road. I wonder how much he managed to lift from Marini's PC while she was at my place. Could make for interesting reading."

"You crafty son of a bitch!"

"C'mon," said Rossi, "get those chains out, or we'll both be stiffs."

Epilogue

It had been the capital's heaviest snowfall in living memory. The body of Giuseppe Bonaventura was eventually picked up following an anonymous call, and Rossi's theories matched with the forensics to link him to the first two murders and the final killing but in the absence of DNA not to the 'Marini' case. The Colosseum and Tor Sapienza shootings remained unsolved as did the attack on Yana – no reliable witnesses, no DNA, and then the rumours began to circulate that at the Colosseum plain-clothes officers had been seen in the crowd with guns drawn straight after the shooting. All of course strenuously denied and labelled as sheer paranoia.

Yana had no recollection of her own assault. When she had first spoken, the doctors had concluded that it must have been a moment of mysterious clarity only to have subsequently been filed away again in the depths of her sub-conscious. Spinelli finally went free despite admitting to having concocted the drugging story in a moment of panic. The potentially incriminating e-mails had been his own work during moments of alcohol-fuelled instability. Some mud, however, had stuck and the elections saw caution and suspicion get the better of the Italians as a broad coalition took over the reins of power in the interests of the country and to maintain the status quo, thus changing everything so that nothing might change at all. Achille Basso, however, would not be so lucky in his attempts to retain office.

Iannelli's discoveries and subsequent articles became the catalyst for a maxi police swoop on the capital and beyond, netting myriad bent public officials, politicians, and assorted pseudo-do-gooders caught with their hands in the cookie jar in a systematic network of corruption, bribes and fraudulent practices linked to the management of the immigration crisis, public works tenders, and cocaine provision to the city's needy. Maroni, however, was not among those led away to the cells. His previous agitation had been due to his wife's new-found lust for life following his coming into a large inheritance from an Argentinian rather than an American uncle. Gab, meanwhile, had promised to devote part of his life's work to cracking the few impenetrably encrypted files he had managed to capture from Marini's computer as he embarked on setting up his own business.

It was summer when Rossi was called to a smallholding outside the GRA where an SUV flagged up as of high importance on the RSCS database had been discovered in a ravine. The body of the long-haired, female, sole occupant in an advanced state of decomposition but without any identification, gun, or personal computer remained "unidentified" and filed, stored, kept – what was the word? – in the city morgue before being buried in a grave marked "unknown". A fitting end? Rossi's initial disquietude had been allayed by a subsequent phone call from the judge, who had long since assumed legal guardianship of Marini's son.

"She left me a note," he said, "saying she had to 'disappear', perhaps for a long time, and that's the last I have heard from her."

Have heard. Verb tenses again? Rossi couldn't but wonder.

As for Rosa Garcia, a Colombian cocaine ring had been smashed and among the many crimes attributed to them was her murder. Rossi had at least laid to rest one of his ghosts while knowing, as his father used to say, that the ghosts were as numerous as the blades of grass.

He was in excellent spirits as he parked the car on Via Merulana then stepped out into the mild night air.

"Shame Dario can't be here," he said, "but with the bodyguards, it would be a bit too much of a squeeze."

"So, it's just us, for once," said Yana, "think you can manage that, Inspector?"

Rossi smiled and kept his distance as she swung herself out and then, with her crutches, set off at a cracking pace as they left Shwarma Station's enticing offerings behind them and crossed Via Merulana. Tonight was to be an Italian meal in an Italian trattoria. With Italian antipasti, primo, secondo, vino and dolce followed by caffé and grappa and nothing else. A traditional night. Yana had insisted on it and Rossi had put only one condition: that, tonight, she explain the story of her daughter.

It was Friday and with summer and the tourist season well and truly underway there came a considerable buzz as an international array of sightseers milled around this edge of the historic centre, moving from one church to another, to ancient ruins and between ice-cream parlours and restaurants and bars dotted around the piazzas and the side streets.

Rossi and Yana, however, moved away from that busy human hub behind them into the quieter alleys, first passing the modest baroque facade of The Church of Maria of Perpetual Succour on the corner of Via San Vito and then the Church of the Holy Saviour, and continued towards the northern end of Piazza Vittorio. They stood for a moment to admire the stolid if modestly proportioned Roman Arch of Gallieno and the precarious, ready to crush you, appearance of its interdependent stones. It had been like that since an earthquake in the fifteenth century but it was still there, like an upside-down smile with one crooked tooth. They then took their table in their favourite trattoria that dwelt in its shadow.

At the local mosque across the street, as usual, a small crowd had gathered and remained following Friday prayers. To think that this same site had only a few years previously been a private members' club where strippers and adult performers catered to Rome's more libertine clientele. Outside, opposite its wholly unassuming entrance and the assorted tidily arranged footwear, there were a number of sub-groups in little knots whose members were chatting and exchanging pleasantries. There were men in traditional robes, North Africans, Sub-Saharan Africans, Bangladeshis, Indonesians. Others on the further edges of these groups had gathered there less for devotional reasons and more out of established habit. Some were sitting on the steps or on the stone bollards to chat and nibble on sunflower seeds and cashew nuts while sharing bottles of Peroni drunk from plastic cups.

The members of one of the groups began to amble their way back along Via San Vito towards the large opening of the Piazza of the Basilica Santa Maria Maggiore from where Rossi and Yana had just come. Of the group, all wore beards though one had only more recently begun to grow his. All were quiet and serious as they listened to the elder. All but one were dressed in casual, western clothes. The other in his white robes, the elder, had the air of a preacher or an Imam. Whether he was or not, they treated him with the respect due to a figure of comparable standing.

"Look," he said, like some kind of tourist guide himself now, indicating the Basilica's splendid triple-arched facade, the gold leaf and intricate mosaics of *Christ Triumphing in Glory* with the saints and the angels. "Look."

Below, diminutive almost as mice on the church steps, a few hopeless drunks and homeless were sprawled on cardboard, ignored by gaudily dressed *signore* on a night out, perhaps to the nearby opera. Before this great Christian temple on the steps of Maderno's seventeenth-century fountain, the carefree young of the city and travellers alike had gathered to pass the time, play guitars, and intermittently pummel drums, smoke, roll joints, and swig beer and wine from the bottles being passed around.

An earnest-looking priest, meanwhile, and some other higher-ranking cleric cut a diagonal line across the piazza, head-to-head, locked in conversation about who knew what business of the soul or the world. A gaggle of middle-aged American sightseers stopped to take pictures, some of the tipsier-looking females striking sexy poses, pouting, and revealing extra flesh for the lens. Lost-looking stragglers from a pub crawl had managed to negotiate the traffic zipping round the piazza and they weaved from side to side in identical black, bedraggled T-shirts coined and emblazoned for the occasion. A traveller's dog howled and there was a scream, a shattering of glass, then a litany of foul language from a member of one of the tribes occupying the lower tiers of the fountain's steps. The T-shirted transgressors raised their hands in slow surrender and staggered away in whatever direction they could.

"Look, Jibril," the white-robed figure said again now taking the newest member of his company by the arm, "behold, my brother – these infidels, these fornicators and drunks, this destitution. All these are signs." He began then to quote, from memory:

"'When much wine is drunk, when giving charity becomes a burden for a man, when women are dressed, yet they appear naked. All these are signs, as when nation shall call upon nation to destroy Islam, and people shall copulate like donkeys in public. These too are signs. Signs of the end times – times, my brother, that very soon will be upon us.'"

Read on for an exclusive extract from the new DI Michael
Rossi thriller:
A COLD FLAME

Publishing June 2018

One

The few flowers left in the vase had withered to dry brown stalks in the August sun. "You're still sure this falls within our brief?" said Carrara as they stared at the cold, charred remains of the ground floor flat. All the bodies had now been removed but their presence lingered. "It's a fire, isn't it?" said Rossi. "Probably arson. Why not?"

They were standing in the welcome shade of the elevated section of the *tangenziale* flyover, on a side street off the busy, grimy Via Prenestina. It was hot, cripplingly hot.

"Even if there's a file open on it already?" said Carrara. "A file that's as good as closed." Rossi shook his head and continued to gaze into the blackened ruins.

"It's August. You can get away with murder in August. Who was on it?"

Carrara leafed through the case notes.

"No-one I know. A guy called Lallana. Racial homicides. Seconded to us in June and then transferred out again, on his own request, now buzzing all over the place with Europol. I got hold of him on the phone but he wasn't keen on talking. Says it's all in the reports and he's got nothing more to add. He had it down as a hate crime – seems the victims were all foreigners – but not a single, solid lead. No witnesses, just the one guy who survived it."

"A survivor?" said Rossi.

"Was. Dead now. Had 90% burns. Should have been long gone but hung on for nearly a week somehow."

"And all while I was on holiday," said Rossi.

"You can't be everywhere, Mick," said Carrara glancing up from the notes. "I mean a break was merited, after Marini."

But Rossi was still struggling to comprehend the present horror. Shooting, strangling,

stabbing – that was one thing – but *burning* to death. They must have been locked inside when the fire started. Some might have woken but had been unable to get to a door or a window, the security grilles put there to keep them safe from intruders thus consigning them to their fates.

"But why wasn't anyone able to get out?" said Rossi. "Because they locked their room doors every night?"

"Correct," said Carrara. "Normal practice in bedsits, but no keys for the security grilles were found, not even after a fingertip search."

"What about the front door?" said Rossi. "Couldn't they have got out with their own keys? They all had one, right?"

Carrara took out a blown-up scene of crime photo.

"The lock. Tampered with, the barrel and mechanism all mangled up and debris left inside. It could have been someone trying to force it – an attempted break in, or sabotage. The occupants might have been able to open it from the inside to get out, if they had got as far as the door, but the bolts were still in place and nobody could get in. By the time the fire guys got there it was too late."

"And their forensics?" said Rossi.

"Well," said Carrara, "significant traces of ethanol – one story goes that there was a moonshine vodka operation – and they did find the remains of a timer switch next to the burnt-out fridge.

Lallala maintained it could have been foul play or just some home-brew set up that got out of hand. He didn't exactly go all out for the former theory. In the absence of a clear motive and witnesses the coroner delivered an open verdict. Have a look for yourself."

Carrara handed Rossi the relevant report.

"Open?" said Rossi noting with contempt the irony. "Someone locked those poor bastards inside."

"Like I said," continued Carrara, "no keys for the window bars were found but no-one lived long enough to tell any tale."

Amongst the scorched masonry and fallen timbers, one of the grilles lay across the small desert of debris, like the rib-cage of a once living and breathing being.

"Any names?" said Rossi.

"Just the one," said Carrara. "The tough nut. Ivan Yovoshenko. He was found in the communal bathroom and had dog tags from his conscription days. But for them he would have been a zero like the rest."

"And nothing on the others?"

"Nothing," said Carrara.

"Well, they can forget checking dental records," said Rossi. "These guys could probably just about afford toothpaste."

Carrara fished out another sheet.

"There's a list here of presumed missing in Rome and Lazio for the last six months, but no matches with this address. The word on the street is that they were five or six single men. probably illegals, but anymore than that…"

"Sounds familiar," said Rossi. "But no friends, no work mates?"

Carrara gestured to the desiccated blooms and a brown, dog-eared farewell note or two.

"Paid their respects then made themselves scarce, I suppose," said Carrara. "If it's a hate killing. If it's racial. You know, probably thought 'who's next?'"

"But a landlord?" said Rossi, sensing an opening. "Tell me we have an owner's name." But Carrara was already quashing his hopes with another printout from the case folder.

"Flat sold to a consortium two months ago as part of a portfolio of properties, a sort of going concern with cash-in-hand rents through an established 'agent' who hasn't been seen since the fire."

"That's convenient," quipped Rossi.

"Says here they always sent an office bod to pick up the cash in a bar and the go-between got his room cheap as well as his cut. No contracts. No paper trail. No nothing."

"And no name for the agent?"

"Mohammed. Maybe."

"That narrows it down. And the bar? Anyone remember him'?"
"*Nada.*"

"A description?"

"North African. About 50."

"Great," said Rossi. "Well, it looks like the late Ivan's our only man, doesn't it? See what the hospital can give us."

"And then a trip to the morgue?"

"You know, Gigi, I was almost beginning to miss going there."

Acknowledgements

I wish to thank my family for being book lovers all and especially Denis, Liam and Noel for reading an earlier version of *A Known Evil*. Thanks also to Chris Modafferi and my colleague Daniel Roy Connelly for helping to get the publishing ball rolling, and to Conor Fitzgerald for his generous insights into the genre. Finally, I would like to thank Ger Nichol, my agent, in Ireland, and Finn Cotton, my editor, in England, for their sterling work.

KILLER
READS

DISCOVER THE BEST
IN CRIME AND THRILLER

Follow us on social media to get to know the team behind the books, enter exclusive giveaways, learn about the latest competitions, hear from our authors, and lots more:

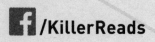/KillerReads   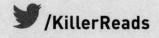/KillerReads